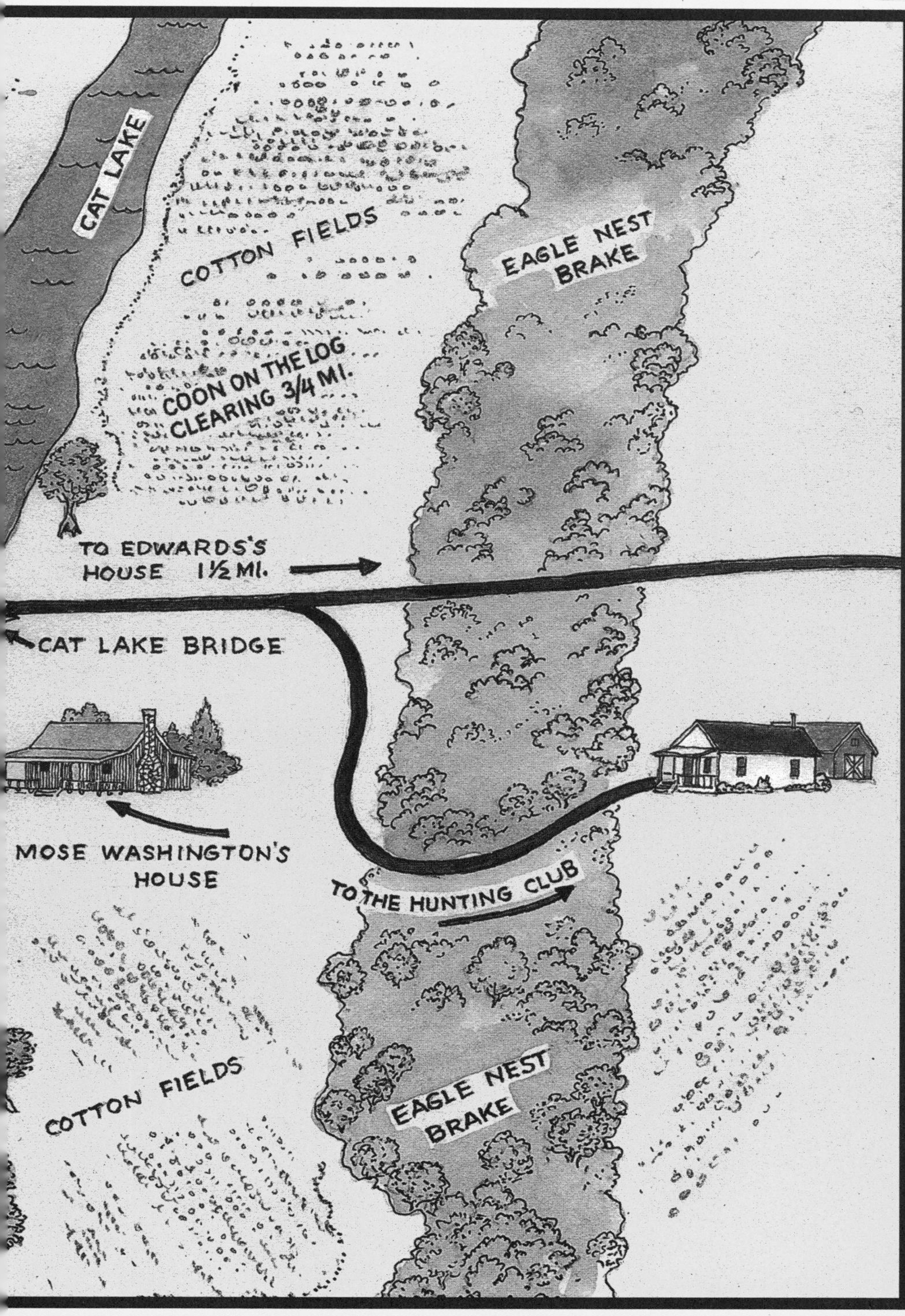

CAT LAKE

COTTON FIELDS

EAGLE NEST BRAKE

COON ON THE LOG CLEARING 3/4 MI.

TO EDWARDS'S HOUSE 1½ MI.

CAT LAKE BRIDGE

MOSE WASHINGTON'S HOUSE

TO THE HUNTING CLUB

COTTON FIELDS

EAGLE NEST BRAKE

WEDGEWOOD GREY

WEDGEWOOD GREY

A Novel

JOHN AUBREY ANDERSON

THE BLACK OR WHITE CHRONICLES:
BOOK TWO

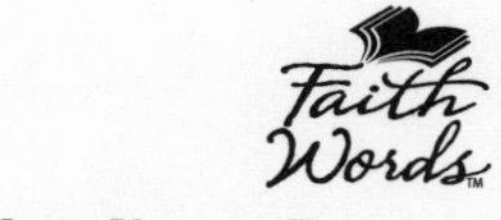

NEW YORK BOSTON NASHVILLE

This book is a work of fiction. Names, characters, places, and incidents are the product of the author's imagination or are used fictitiously. Any resemblance to actual events, locales, or persons, living or dead, is coincidental.

FaithWords
Hachette Book Group USA
1271 Avenue of the Americas
New York, NY 10020

Visit our Web site at www.faithwords.com.

Printed in the United States of America

First Edition: February 2007
10 9 8 7 6 5 4 3 2 1

Library of Congress Cataloging-in-Publication Data
Anderson, John Aubrey, 1940–
Wedgewood grey / John Aubrey Anderson. — 1st ed.
p. cm. — (The black or white chronicles ; bk. 2)
Summary: "The demonic assaults that plagued a young woman in 1930s Mississippi follow her to the 1960s, where she battles to assist the victim of a racially motivated attack"—Provided by the publisher.
ISBN-13: 978-0-446-57950-6
ISBN-10: 0-446-57950-5
1. Race relations—Fiction. 2. Mississippi—Fiction. 3. Spiritual warfare—Fiction. I. Title.
PS3601.N544W43 2006
813'.6—dc22 2006007620

For Nan

WEDGEWOOD GREY

CHAPTER ONE

It wasn't the first night he'd spent in the loft of the old barn.

A broken deck of scud was left over from four days of mid-April rain. The low-hanging clouds took slow turns with bright stars and a rising moon, competing to determine how much of the night's influence would be dispelled. The closest man-made light was more than a mile to the west—a single dim bulb dangling from a cord outside the Parkers' old toolshed.

The barn where he slept was on the east side of the Parkers' plantation; it and a small shotgun house were on semi-permanent loan to the Central Delta Hunting Club for their deer-hunting headquarters. Each spring the club members would keep the deer fed by planting several acres of corn along the strip between the cotton field and the edge of Eagle Nest Brake. Every fall the same men would come out and plant the strip in winter wheat.

In the evenings, just after dusk, wedgewood-grey shadows would materialize at the edge of the wooded brake. They'd graze along the boundary of the field then, as full night descended, the shadows that could turn themselves into deer would move farther from the protection of the trees. On those nights when there was enough moonlight, he'd fix himself a comfortable place where he could see the fields through the loft opening, and he'd spend the night in the sweet-smelling hay, enjoying the peace offered by his surroundings. On darker nights, if there was a breeze moving through the woods to mask his sounds, he'd leave the warmth of the hay and slip into the trees of the brake. He'd stay downwind of the animals, creeping along like a wraith, sometimes crawling close enough to hear them munching the grain. More often than not, they'd sense his presence before he could get close and transform themselves back into silent shadows.

On moonlit nights like this one, when the temperature was mild and the wind was gentle, he'd make himself comfortable in the barn's loft and watch the shadows become deer while he thanked the good Lord for the years he'd had with his Pip—his own God-given, graceful doe. On this night, well before midnight, when the substance of his prayers became shadowlike, sleep came to him there in the soft, warm hay.

Beyond the woods and across the lake, the light over the door of the toolshed moved back and forth in a shallow arc—a patient pendulum, measuring the waning seconds of the night's peace.

The crunching noise of tires on gravel came to the loft, waking him in time to see the opening of the drama.

As soon as he heard the sounds he rolled over and crawled away from the loft opening. He pulled off his hat and pressed his face to a place where a narrow strip had been broken off the barn's siding, getting positioned in time to watch the car pass in front of the empty shotgun house and move the last few yards toward the barn. Below him, at the base of the ladder where the stalls were, the dog murmured that he was awake. The man whispered for him to stay quiet.

While he slept, eddies of fog had felt their way through the woods and pooled at the edges of the field. As the car approached, the quiet mist dissolved the deer and pulled them into its stationary swirl, turning them back into soft pieces of the darkness.

Most of the local white men didn't care one way or another if Mose wanted to sleep in the unused barn, but this was late Friday night—he checked the position of the nearly full moon—after midnight. It wouldn't do to be caught in here by some shined-up young white boy who might think it would be fun to try to scare a grey-headed old colored man.

The car came to rest in front of the barn's only door, its lights pointing at the edge of the muddy field where the road ended.

Mose stayed still. He couldn't see into the car, but he could feel its driver staring at the bleak field. Scattered skeletons of last year's cotton stalks stared back.

After a long moment, the car backed and turned, starting back the way it came.

A half mile to the west, in the direction of Mose's cabin, the brush and trees of the brake wove a wicker-basket filter for four sets of headlights playing follow the leader on the road through the brake.

Below him the car's brake lights came on, and the car stopped. The driver of the car saw the approaching lights.

Over in the woods, the second set of headlights pulled up alongside the first; the flickering lights showed two pickups moving side by side. They rolled another fifty yards and stopped midway through the woods. The following lights moved up behind them and went out. The damp air carried the sound of slamming truck doors.

The only path to the world of reasonable men was blocked.

On the west side of the lake, inside the Young Parkers' house, Susan Parker's eyes opened. She looked at her alarm clock; it was past midnight and she was wide awake. Susan normally slept the night through; on those rare occasions when she didn't, she spent her time praying. As she closed her eyes to pray, one of her hands explored her husband's side of the bed—it was empty. She sat up and saw him standing by the bedroom's bay window. Blue-tinted moonlight spilled onto the floor around his feet.

"Bobby Lee?"

"I'm right here."

"What're you looking at?"

"I was prayin'."

"You're praying?"

"Mmm."

"About what?"

Bobby Lee Parker stared at the moonlit night. "Well . . . I don't know if I'm sure."

Waking up to pray wasn't unusual for Bobby Lee, having him not know what he was praying for was something new.

"Are you okay?" she asked.

"Mmm. I woke up a few minutes ago an' prayed for a while in the bed. I finally got up an' moved over here."

"And you don't know what you're praying about?" There was plenty to pray about. Their son was out at that air base in Nevada. Missy was newly married and living in Texas. In the spring, ten sections of wet cotton land needed all the prayer they could muster.

"That doesn't sound right, does it?" He tried to organize his thoughts. "I started off with the usual stuff . . . the kids, you, me, the farm . . . but I keep comin' back to Mose . . ." his voice trailed off.

"Mose?" she prompted.

"Mmm, just Mose." A cloud moved in front of the moon, darkening the room. "Is that strange?"

Susan swung her legs over the side of the bed and felt for her slippers with her toes. "It would be if I hadn't just waked up feeling like I ought to be praying for him myself. I'll make us some coffee."

Bobby hadn't moved. "Should I go check on him?"

She abandoned the slipper hunt. "On Mose?"

"Mmm."

She thought about his question for a moment. Pip Washington, Mose's late wife, had been instrumental in Susan Parker's becoming a Christian and had guided her growth in understanding how to live the Christian life. Pip had been dead for more than two years now, but Susan could parrot what Pip would say. "I guess you better decide that for yourself."

"I'll be seein' him first thing in the mornin'. You reckon he'll be all right till then?"

Pip would also say, "That's in God's hands, baby. C'mon."

The moon reasserted itself, and Bobby Lee turned his back on the window. "You can stay in bed if you want to." She could hear his smile. "I can pray for Mose while you get yo' beauty sleep."

"Not hardly," his smile had spread to her face and voice. Susan Parker did not have what it took to miss an opportunity to pray for Moses Lincoln Washington, and Bobby Lee was smiling because he knew it.

To most folks, Mose was a quiet old black man who owned forty acres and a little cabin on the east side of Cat Lake. To those same people he was the man who'd spent five years in Parchman for what happened to Blue Biggers.

To Susan and the rest of the Parkers, Mose Washington was first, foremost, and forever the father of Mose Junior Washington. As an eleven-year-old boy, Junior almost single-handedly built a bridge between the two families. During the past fifteen or so years—because of what one young boy did—the Washingtons and Parkers had all but breached any assumed color barrier. The special friendship between the two families at the lake—one black, one white—was something that most people in the Delta's segregated society watched with wonder.

Bobby Lee left his slippers and followed his wife to the kitchen, his long bare feet slapping against the brick floor.

Outside the house and beyond the lake, the clouds were overpowering the moon again, winning the war for darkness. It would be five hours before the Parkers knew why they had been awakened to pray for their friend.

Mose had been living back out at the lake for more than a year, and, other than Mr. Bobby Lee, he didn't get many visitors. He and Mr. Bobby Lee met on one side of the lake or the other several days a week to drink coffee and visit.

Years earlier there had been a large community of folks living out at the lake—back during the Second World War.

In those days, Mose's family, his job at the gin, and his little bit of land had done what was needed to fill his life. Then, on a bright summer day in June of '45, Mose Junior had sacrificed his life to save his best friend. In the fall of that same year the two Parker families—Bobby Lee's and Old Mr. Parker's—out of appreciation to God and the Washington family, had "tithed" a full section of land to Mose and his family for as long as any of the Washingtons lived. Mose was probably the richest black farmer in Mississippi, but money was a poor substitute for a family. Pip had been gone for two years, his boy for fifteen, and his daughter was busy with her own life. Mose was content to rent the tithed land back to the Parkers and spend quiet days with his God and his dog and his white friend.

Of the Parkers, only the three oldest lived out at the lake now; everybody else had just seemed to leave all at once. Bobby Lee's wife, Young Mrs. Parker, stayed busy doing things busy women do. Old Mr. Parker had died while Mose was in prison. Old Mrs. Parker was getting up in years, but she still puttered around in her yard and baked things. Missy, the only Parker girl, had been married and gone for more than a year now. Bobby, the Parkers' boy, had joined the Air Force nine years back. Bobby Lee said the boy made a name for himself when he shot down some Communist airplanes over there in Korea.

Bobby Lee Parker and Mose had run the Parker gin together for years, but when Bobby Lee hired Scooter Hall's son to run the gin office, Mose surrendered the oversight of the mechanical side to Roosevelt Edwards. Bobby Lee still owned three sections of good cotton land running along either side of the brake and another seven on the west side of the lake, but he didn't do much farming. He hired two men as managers and left the farming and ginning to other folks. When he and Susan weren't traveling around the country, he spent the biggest part of his time with Mose.

The men were two fifty-something-year-old close friends with nothing demanding their attention but the beauty of sunsets and sunrises. They spent a good part of their time on the porch of one house or the other, or out under the trees—talking, or reading their Bibles, or praying. As many days as not, they'd take some sandwiches and a thermos full of coffee and ride around in a truck and look at the crops and talk. Mostly, Bobby Lee would do the talking; Mose would enjoy his coffee and nod and add an occasional affirming murmur. They'd talk about the things old men talk about—the crops, the weather, their children, politics. And they'd talk about God and Heaven and the demons that had visited them on Cat Lake.

Some of the whites and coloreds of Moores Point made mean-spirited comments about the friendship between the wealthy white man and the great-grandson of a slave. Mostly, though, the events of the past drew reasonable folks to total acceptance of whatever suited Mose and Bobby Lee—they were the fathers of Mose Junior Washington and Missy Parker, the two special children who had stood in the maelstrom of The War At Cat Lake.

And maybe once a month—on a nice Sunday afternoon—Pearl would come.

His daughter didn't come to the cabin as often as she had at first; she was practice-teaching at that school down in Jackson now. When she did come, she and Mose would sit on the front porch of the cabin for an hour or so and visit—except in the winter. She came even less in the winter; the little cabin by the lake didn't suit her anymore. There never had been any paint on the old place, inside or out; the cypress boards, shaped at a long-ago sawmill and nailed in place by slaves, still turned wind and water but had long since weathered to a medium grey. In winter, the fireplace could keep the house warm, but Pearl said the smoke smell got on her clothes.

The child always parked in the sun, never in the shade of the cabin's big pecan trees—Pearl remembered the exact spot where the blood had been. There were still nights, right when sleep came, she'd hear her daddy talking, then the drawn-out musical chord of the screen door's spring as her momma stepped onto the porch. The sound of her momma's calm voice came next . . . then Pearl's almost-sleep would be shattered by the roar of the shotgun and the scream of the man. The white men came that same day and took her daddy to Parchman Prison. They'd kept him there five years.

Pearl was barely fourteen when Pip bought a fine little white house in town, just up the street from the church. Mose was in prison and Pip couldn't farm their land by herself, so she rented it back to the Parkers and started teaching at the colored school.

The women in town had accepted Pip because they didn't have to worry about their men bothering around with her. Pip was a fine-looking woman, but none of the colored men in

Jones Addition messed with her. They spoke, and they tipped their hats, but that was all—the black folks knew who had pulled that shotgun's trigger when Blue Biggers showed up at the cabin on Cat Lake.

Nowadays, when Pearl came to the cabin, she and Mose would sit on the wooden porch in the same old cane-bottom rockers, surrounded by a varying population of sleepy cats. The mockingbirds out in the pecan trees would fuss at the squirrels and each other and at the cats, the redbirds would mind their own business, and Pearl would fidget and fret. It didn't sound like fretting, because most of the time she used her classroom voice-of-reason tone. "Daddy, this is no place for you to stay."

Mose would rock and respond gently to Pearl's complaints. Pearl never rocked.

Mose didn't waste his time trying to make her understand. The big pecan trees in the yard shaded him in the summer. The soft breeze from the lake, cooled from traveling across the waters and up through the shade of the trees, would curl its way through the screen door of the house and go right on out the back, taking the heat with it. In the winter, the trees held off the wind, and the fireplace kept him warm.

Pearl might give the tall trees a cursory glance. Folks around the lake claimed that demons had been involved in the shooting of Blue Biggers. There was a second shooting back in the spring of '58. Folks at the lake said demons tried to use a white college boy to kill Missy, and Mose stepped in to stop them. When the shooting was over, two more men were dead.

Pearl never particularly cared for Missy Parker; she didn't like being where there had been so much killing, and she thought people who believed in demons were superstitious.

"Daddy, you've got no business roaming around out here all by yourself. You need to come home with me. You need to be around people. What if something happened to you out in those woods?"

"Pip's been dead for more'n two years now, child, an' walkin' these woods with this here dog is 'bout all I'm good for." For him, his next four words said it all: "An' it's quiet here."

"But I could help take care of you if something happened."

His voice had a deep gentleness to it. He'd sweep his arm in the direction of the lake. "Honey, this here is home. An' what could happen to me?" Then he'd point at the dog. "Didn't I just tell you I got this here dog; he's smart as most town folk." The hound would open one eye, acknowledge the moment of small praise by banging the wood floor a couple of times with his tail, and go back to his nap. Pearl and the mockingbirds would fret.

The conversation would go on like it did every time Pearl came. She'd worry out loud; he'd smile sometimes, frown others, rock, and rub the dog's long ears. The cats would stretch and stroll across the dirt in front of the house just to antagonize the mockingbirds. Pearl would squirm around in her rocker and talk about her work at the school and maybe the cotton crop and the folks she knew in town, but the subject always came back to her worries about him.

"I've still got the house in town, Daddy," she'd say. He had signed it over to her when he moved back out to Cat Lake. "You could move in there."

"For what? So them women in that church can bother theyselves in my business? Humph . . . I don't reckon." He never got mad, but she could tell by his tone and the further descent of the corners of his mouth when the subject was closed for the month. Like clockwork, after they had visited for about an hour, he'd almost frown and say, "I don't need to be in no town, Baby. I ain't got no job to do, an' I don't want none. I got the good Lord an' His Book . . . I got this here dog, an' a gun, an' plenty to eat . . . I reckon that'll do me 'til He comes an' gits me."

Right before leaving, she'd always say that if he got a telephone she could call and check on him more often. He always told her he'd give it some thought, but that's about as far as it ever got. Then she'd tell him to call her if he needed anything. He'd say he would, but he wasn't going to spend his money to talk on a telephone.

Pearl always parked out in the sun, but she never managed to make it to her car without glancing at the spot where the man had died. It had happened when she was still in grade school; the memory was as fresh as last week.

The barn and cabin had been the headquarters for the Central Delta Hunting Club for thirty years. The "fixed up" shotgun house had become a camp house the club members used during deer season. They would play poker and shoot dice and drink and tell lies every night, and the ones who weren't too hungover would go out and hunt deer in the mornings. The gravel-and-dirt road that led to the club was a curved tunnel through a stretch of thick brush and tall hardwoods the locals called Eagle Nest Brake. The north-south line of woods separated the fields around the hunting club from a full section of cotton land behind Mose's house.

Mose hadn't told Pearl about sleeping in the barn at the hunting club. Nor had he told her about crawling up close to the deer on the cool nights . . . about the soft, nervous sounds the bucks made . . . the restless snorts because the deer knew something was wrong, but they didn't know what it was. He didn't waste his breath trying to tell her what real contentment was; she was too young; she wouldn't understand. He'd smile to himself every time she left to drive back to Jackson. *Bless her heart, Lord, the child is smart . . . Pip done good by her . . . but she don't know a dadgum thing about nothin'.*

Mose looked down from the hayloft in time to see the car's interior light come on and the passenger door open. A small form wearing a white shirt clambered out and ran around to the driver's side of the car. An arm came out of the driver's window and handed something to the figure that stood there. The moon took its turn just in time to show a young colored boy, moving hurriedly, shrugging into a dark shirt or jacket of some sort. The boy was talking to the person in the car—leaning forward, speaking earnestly. Mose couldn't make out the words.

The voice that came out of the car was a woman's. A hand pointed toward the south end of the brake and then west toward the county road.

The boy clutched the hand in both of his. Sounds of an intense plea came to the loft.

Another hand came from the car. Whatever it held was dark with white marks. The boy took the offered object and stuck it beneath his shirt. One of the hands from the car rested on the boy's shoulder while the woman in the car spoke warm assurance. When she paused, the boy shook his head and spoke words of increasing desperation.

The soft voice coming from the car took a firm tone; it reminded Mose of Pip. He couldn't make out the words, but he could hear the urgency.

Mose could see the boy's thin shoulders sag under the weight of the woman's words. The child leaned forward into the car for a moment then stepped away. Holding one hand at his waist, he started across the field, moving west toward the woods and lake. He looked back at the car more than once.

A shrill barking sound, like a crazy person laughing, wrenched Mose's attention away from the boy to the place where the trucks were waiting for the car. The black man mumbled something to himself while he crawled across the floor of the loft and started down the ladder to where the dog was.

While the man groped his way down the ladder the boy was running crouched over through the muddy field, moving in the direction of the brake. The small form was halfway to the woods when the car began to move down the road to the waiting trucks.

CHAPTER TWO

On the floor of the barn Mose knelt by the dog; he leaned close to his friend and rubbed his ears. "I wants you to go on to the house, now," he whispered. The Redbone hound moaned as if he understood and pushed his head against the man's chest. "Go through them woods an' stay quiet. Don't be messin' along now. You go git under the house an' stay till I comes." He watched the taillights creeping along the muddy gravel road for a long minute, then said, "I reckon I'll be along directly."

The dark red hound reached out with his front paws, arched his back, then stretched his back legs one at a time and yawned. He padded out the door and across the field, his white-tipped tail cutting wide arcs against the darkness.

The man picked up the gun propped by the ladder. Bright metal showed through the blue finish around the action and on the end of the barrel, picking up the dim light from outside. Out of habit he blew on the action then brushed at it absently with his hand. He walked to the door of the barn and stood watching the boy and the dog, like the sleek deer, become part of the night. Out in the cotton field, rainwater stood in the row middles . . . parallel mirrors, colored silver-blue by the moonlight.

A slick snap violated the silence when Mose pulled back the pump-slide to open the gun's action. He couldn't see well enough to tell, so he felt with his fingertips for the shell that should be where he wanted it. It was. He eased the action shut, checked the hammer position with his thumb, and stood in the door of barn for the briefest time, his lips pursed in thought. With a sigh of resignation he shrugged his shoulders and moved out of the barn, heading to the right of the direction the boy had taken. The path Mose took would bring him to the edge of the brake just north of the trucks.

Over by the trucks, the reflection of the car's brake lights bounced off the water standing in the fields.

The old man picked up his pace as much as he could.

He was almost to the woods when the damp night air carried the sounds of the woman's voice to him; she was speaking quiet words of reason to a man who sounded angry. It seemed strange to Mose, because the man who was using the angry words kept laughing at something that the soft-spoken lady was trying to say. The man followed everything he said with that crazy-sounding laugh—that animal sound. The woman would try to be heard again, and the angry man would drown her out.

He reached the cover of the brake and was moving south toward the trucks when another man added his anger to the crazy man's. The woman stayed calm. He couldn't make out her words, but the voice inflections told him she was a colored lady.

He quickened his pace intent on getting to where he needed to be. Until now, moving quietly through the woods had always been a thing of peace . . . but deer usually didn't kill you if you tried to sneak up on them. He was getting close enough to make out the woman's words as she tried to reason with the men. He could hear the words they yelled at her—the kind of words dangerous men speak. Sounds of a struggle came through the night and approaching panic highlighted the edges of the woman's voice.

Over in the woods, south of the road, the young boy heard the beginnings of fear in his mother's voice. She had been insistent, in the face of his urgent protests, that he should get back to the main road and try to find help. Hoping that she would not be angry with him for his disobedience, the boy turned north and started jogging. He would beat Mose to the scene by a handful of crucial seconds.

Someone over on the road screamed. The crazy man quit laughing.

Less than two hours earlier Tripper Sherman had been a high school freshman winding down his Friday night with some friends. Now he was trapped in the cold and wet of a muddy road, bleeding from a deep cut on his face and surrounded by madness. Out in the brightness from the headlights two men were doing a grotesque dance with a panic-stricken black woman, jerking her back and forth, laughing and cursing. Tripper lowered his head and prayed that the darkness surrounding the scene was his sleep. He shut out the reality of the blood on his face and the sour taste of vomit in his mouth while he begged God to let him wake up and find out that he was in a nightmare. *It has to be a nightmare, God. I can't be out here on this road with people who are fixin' to hurt a helpless woman. I can't be here. Please, Lord . . . please let me wake up.*

* * *

Identifying the exact beginning of a nightmare might normally be a hard thing, but Tripper could come close. It began somewhere around the time Stan Dailey said, "We're gonna have some fun!"

In the Mississippi Delta, dating was for those boys who had a driver's license, and Tripper was four months short of fifteen. He and Whit Jackson—because Whit's daddy let him drive outside town without a license—had hung around the Dairy Freeze over in Indianola until ten thirty. Saturday mornings came early at the Jackson house, so when they decided to call it a night, Tripper had Whit drop him at Dennison's Store. Whit went on home, and Tripper walked into the store to catch up on the latest batch of what he called "The Wild Tales of the West."

Tripper's Friday and Saturday evenings frequently came to a close at Dennison's combination service station and grocery store that sat north of Moores Point, out on Highway 49. Dennison's was open twenty-four hours a day, and Tex Leland was the all-night cashier. Around midnight, about the time Tex was midway through his third beer, the stories would start.

Highway 49 West branched off from Highway 61 up in Clarksdale and ran south to the Mississippi Gulf Coast. The first one-hundred-mile stretch ran through the Delta to Yazoo City; from there it was another hour to Jackson. After midnight, Dennison's was the only business open on the one-hundred-mile stretch between Clarksdale and Yazoo City, fifty miles to the south. The store provided the only opportunity for nighttime travelers to get gas, information, or anything else.

It had been a wet spring, and the highway—which was suffering through its fifteenth month of a one-year repair job—was no more than a wide, muddy track, complicated by poorly marked detours. Several times a night, motorists unfamiliar with the desolate two-lane thoroughfare would pull into the lone oasis and buy five gallons of gas so they could ask how bad the road was in one direction or the other. It was good that the travelers asked, because Tex—or maybe Doc Perriman, if the folks were colored—was skilled at making some sense of the confusion and disorder brought on by the Yankees who had come across the Mason-Dixon Line for no better reason than to inflict damage on something that belonged to the people of the South.

Some time around midnight, Tripper was sitting on the counter listening to Tex when two pickups pulled up out front. Five of the local boys, all of whom had driver's licenses, parked in the gravel between the gas pumps and the Yankee-ravaged highway.

Doctor E. G. Perriman, T. S. (Tire Surgeon), looked up from the inner tube he was patching and made an assessment of the arrivals. He spoke to all five of the boys, preceding each name with "Mister." An older black gentleman standing next to Doc removed his hat and bestowed a genuine smile on the young men; he mixed nods and several dignified bows for his greeting.

Four of the boys walking across the gravel completed the exchange by waving or speaking to Doc and the old man; the fifth white boy was intent on trying to make it to the store without falling down or colliding with one of the blue-and-orange gas pumps.

On weekends, the late-night activities at Dennison's bordered on being ritualistic. Those who were present would rotate positions in the store, alternately joining the ones listening to Tex at the counter or taking turns at abusing the pinball machine. The ones who listened to Tex's tales would stay mostly silent; the ones who were occupied at the pinball machine used the constant clacking, pinging, and chinging as a backdrop for visiting on whatever subject presented itself. The pinball conversations centered themselves mostly on cars, sex, sports, and arguments about pinball rules. The boys who weren't going steady with someone would tell blatant lies about their most recent triumph with a girl. The ones who were going steady kept silent about their relationships and lied about how fast their cars or pickups would go. Every one of the boys knew the lies for what they were, but every boy in the crowd usually managed to become envious in one department or the other.

On this night, the boy who'd had trouble navigating around the gas pumps surrendered his place at the machine early and stretched out on some nearby stacks of Purina Dog Chow. He was the lucky one.

The population of the consolidated high school down in Moores Point was less than two hundred, so the kids all knew each other. Unlike the local girls, the male students didn't bother to classify themselves according to age, so the fact that the boys who entered the store were scattered across the age spectrum from sixteen to twenty did not preclude them from including Tripper in their company. The two twenty-year-olds, Frank McClellan and Jerry Nations, were both in college at State but still adhered to the local rules.

There was an underlying reason for the college guys to be friendly—they were both frat rats. The fraternities at Mississippi State, like those at every other university in the nation, were always on the lookout for prospective pledges. Guys who could mix well and keep up academically were especially sought after, and Tripper fit the profile. He was clean-cut, well liked, on his way to being a good athlete, and he made good grades.

Frank McClellan took the opportunity to "rush" the prime prospect. He bent over and searched through the drink box by the pinball machine, held up two cans of beer, and looked a question at Tripper.

Tripper wasn't a veteran beer drinker, but he nodded and held up one finger.

Two more trucks pulled up outside and three young men, the shortest of whom was wearing cowboy boots, swaggered into the store without acknowledging the presence of Doc or the old man.

Tex glanced up at the newcomers and kept talking.

McClellan brought the two cans over to the counter and handed some money to Tex. While Tex made change, McClellan picked up the church key and popped open the beers. He pushed one of the cans across to Tripper and boosted himself onto the other end of the counter to listen to Tex.

Tripper raised the can, said, "Thanks," and took a short swallow of the free beer.

Tex finished with the register and digressed enough to catch Frank up on the first part of his story, then picked up where he left off. Two of the group over by the pinball machine argued heatedly about whether or not one of them had violated some ever-changing rule. The fellow on the dog food sacks was no longer participating in the evening's social activities. The three latecomers stood inside the front door, laughing at something the one in the cowboy boots was saying. They were rolling their own cigarettes.

Tex interrupted his story in midsentence and frowned while he studied the three by the door. The storyteller ended up offering a negligent shrug and turned back to Frank and Tripper to continue the spellbinding account of one of his unforgettable conquests in Arizona, or maybe it was New Mexico.

It didn't surprise any of the boys in the store that the smokers had chosen to stand apart; they were different.

Oliver Wendell Bainbridge, the one in the boots, was the middle son of a U.S. congressman from one of the states over north of Georgia. Ollie was a local celebrity because his younger brother and his cousin had murdered each other a year earlier. The killings had taken place in the Parkers' woods, down south of Moores Point. The roster of people in the Delta who didn't care for Ollie's family was a long one; the list of those who didn't like Ollie was longer. The tallest man in the threesome, Farrell Whitacher, was Ollie's roommate at Mississippi State. Farrell was a known troublemaker but more of a follower than a leader. Stan Dailey was the weakest point of the triangle—a toady who wanted a reputation as a tough man and thought he could acquire it by hanging out with tough people.

When Tex started having to raise his voice to be heard over the racket made by Ollie and his buddies, he said, "You boys take that stuff outside."

Ollie growled some cuss words, and Stan Dailey added a louder chorus while the three smokers stepped outside. They regrouped under the light over the gas pumps in time to watch a southbound car pull off the highway and stop in front of them. The car's interior light came on, and a black woman unfolded a road map and stared at it.

Doc Perriman and the old man were nowhere in sight when the woman got out of the car and looked around. She walked toward the three men near the gas pumps, carrying her map. Bainbridge nudged one of his companions and stepped out to meet her.

The boys inside who took time to notice saw the white man's arms move as he talked to the woman and gave directions. When he finished, the attractive young woman smiled, said something, and returned to her car. After the woman's car got back on the highway, the three white men started laughing.

The three huddled for a moment, then one of them broke from the group and jogged to the door. None of them paid any attention to a dark car sitting in the shadows at the edge of the gravel.

Stan Dailey stuck his head in the door of the store and yelled, "Hey, y'all! Hey!"

Everybody in the store, except the dog food boy, looked at him.

"Y'all come on! Hurry up! We're gonna have some fun!"

McClellan bounced off the counter and grinned at Tripper. "C'mon." He yelled at Tex over his shoulder. "I'm taking a six pack. Put it on Daddy's ticket."

McClellan got to the front door and turned around; Tripper was still perched on the counter. The college man hooked his head at the kid without a driver's license. "Hurry up, man. This'll be a real hoot."

Tripper would remember for a long time that he could've chosen to stay where he was.

The four trucks left the service station in a convoy. Bainbridge and Whitacher led off; Dailey followed. The Newsome brothers, Doug and Buster, took Nations in their pickup; McClellan and Tripper brought up the rear. Tripper was feeling pretty cool because he was riding in the pickup with McClellan. They each had another beer while they followed the others, winding their way south past Moores Point till they got to the bridge over Cat Lake. The lead truck stopped and everybody got out and gathered on the bridge. The car that had been sitting away from the lights at Dennison's Store stopped well short of the bridge. No one noticed it.

Bainbridge was already laying out his plan when Tripper and McClellan joined the group gathered by the lead truck.

"That high-and-mighty nigger woman asked how to get to Jackson, and I gave her very precise directions to the hunting club. Right now she's finding out that she's in the middle of nowhere." He looked around at the darkness as if expecting someone to sneak up on them. "We'll go into the brake, and when she comes back this way, we'll trap her in the woods and scare her all the way back to Detroit or Chicago or wherever she came from."

Murmurs of dissent came from some in the group. Tripper Sherman didn't know Bainbridge, but he knew his reputation. He said, "Not me. You boys can do whatever you want. I'm headin' for the—"

Bainbridge's fist came hard and fast, totally unexpected. Tripper staggered but managed to stay on his feet.

Bainbridge grabbed the smaller boy's shirt. "What's your name, sonny boy?"

"That's Tripper Sherman," said Dailey. "He oughta be home with his momma."

"Probably named after that gutless Yankee." Bainbridge stuck his finger under Tripper's nose. "Nobody's leaving here, you little snot; those that try will answer to me. You back off and keep your yap shut." He shoved the smaller boy away from him.

Tripper looked at McClellan, but the boy from State was looking at the ground. Stan Dailey was snickering.

Tripper and McClellan rode in silence as the four trucks drove into the brake and blocked the woman's exit. When they stepped out of the truck, McClellan said, "It'll be okay, Tripper. They'll scare her a little, an' I'll get us outta here."

Tripper nodded and dabbed at the blood on his cheek.

When the woman's car got to the trucks, Bainbridge and Dailey walked to her car and started yelling at her. Tripper watched, praying that no one, especially the woman, would get hurt. When Bainbridge and Dailey pulled her from the car, she started to scream. Bainbridge hit her in the face and knocked her down. The beer and revulsion collided inside Tripper, and he leaned against one of the trucks and threw up.

Bainbridge dragged the woman to the center of the road between the car and trucks. She said something to him and he bent over her and tore her blouse. The woman was struggling to get up when Bainbridge and Dailey started kicking her. Whitacher stood a few steps away with a beer in one hand and a cigarette in the other.

After a few minutes the kicking lost intensity. The woman lying in the road moaned some, but she had quit pleading with her attackers. The three who stood over her took a beer break.

Ollie Bainbridge went to the bed of his truck and reached into it. When he turned, he held an ax handle loosely in his right hand. He grinned at those who stood close to the trucks. "I can tell that none of y'all were ever in the Boy Scouts because none of y'all are prepared." He walked back to where the woman lay in the mud, tapping the end of the handle in the palm of his left hand. "My mother gave me these boots for Christmas, and I'm not planning on wearing them home with blood on them."

The group's first known adversary pushed his way through the brush at the edge of the road. He advanced on Bainbridge. "You stay away from my mom."

Bainbridge, taken totally by surprise, whirled and stared at the boy. It took him one instant to decide that the boy was no threat and another to see that he was alone.

"Well, well, well. Looks like Mommy's got herself a big hero." While Tripper and the others stood transfixed, unable to react, Bainbridge stepped forward and swung the club in an horizontal arc at the boy's head. The boy took the brunt of the blow on an upraised arm and went to his knees in the road.

The crowd watched as Bainbridge loomed over the boy. "Well, Little Black Sambo, how about it? You here to rescue your mommy?"

The woman was struggling to her feet while the mob watched Bainbridge and the boy.

The slender club came back at the victim on a level with the man's belt, striking the defenseless boy just over his ear. The child landed on his back between the truck and the ditch and lay motionless; blood covered the side of his head. The woman made it to her feet in time to see the assault—the sound she made was more like an animal's growl than a woman's scream. Stan Dailey turned to grab her and she launched a kick at him. The combination of his trying to dodge and the power of the kick between his legs combined to lift him off the ground. The ax handle did its work a third time and the woman collapsed into the mud.

In the woods just yards to the north, Mose could not yet see the scene in the road. He heard Dailey's shrill scream and attributed it to the woman. He tried to move faster.

The child in the ditch woke up. The ground was cold and wet. The sound of voices drew him toward full consciousness. He couldn't remember the exact chronology of the events that caused him to be there, but he could feel that his arm wasn't working right, and he wasn't sure why. He straightened his legs and started to roll onto his side. When he tried to use his arm, the men standing near the trucks heard him gasp in pain and turned in time to watch him sag back into unconsciousness. The smallest one walked to where he was and knelt over him.

"Get away from him, punk, or get ready for the same medicine he got."

Tripper, who had remained silent because he didn't want to be beaten again, decided that he was more afraid of being a coward than of taking a beating. He straightened and drew close to Bainbridge; he wanted to look into the eyes of the leader. "I don't know about these boys here, Bainbridge, but I ain't puttin' up wi—"

His speech was interrupted by another blow from the hard fist of Ollie Bainbridge. The force of the punch landed Tripper on his back in the muddy gravel by the nearest truck's bumper.

No one said anything to protest the cruelty of the act; McClellan and Nations stooped to help Tripper up.

Bainbridge stopped them. "Leave him in the mud, or I'll put you down there with him."

"You can't whip everybody out here, Ollie." McClellan spoke as he might to a person he'd watched step across the boundary to insanity.

Ollie's fist punctuated the fraternity man's sentence and drove him backward, where he collapsed on top of his friend. "I don't have to whip everybody, buddy boy, just the ones that give me their lip."

Dailey and Whitacher stood beside Bainbridge—Tripper and McClellan were in the mud. Nations and the Newsome brothers watched Tripper roll out from under McClellan and drag himself close to the nearest truck. The second blow from Ollie's fist had deepened the cut on his cheek, and his eye was beginning to swell shut. He pushed himself up with his hands, then got his knees under him and paused to gather the energy he would need to stand.

The little boy in the ditch regained his senses as the smallest white man in the group propped his hand on a truck bumper to pull himself out of the mud. The truck's headlights illumined thick red hair and a young but resolute face. The boy was on his knees, bleeding from a deep cut on his cheek. He locked eyes with the kid lying in the ditch, then looked up at the one with the club and said, "You can't kill everybody, Bainbridge, but you're sure gonna have to kill me before you do any more to—"

The groggy black youngster started getting his hopes up when the white boy intervened for him. The child was trying to fight off the closing blackness when the one with the club stepped in close and kicked the redheaded boy in the stomach.

Despair and darkness draped themselves over the young boy when his only defender went down.

He could feel and hear, but his sight was failing him. The mud in the road was getting colder; pain radiated up his arm and seemed to gather around his ears; large beads of sweat felt cold on his face. He called on his eyes to open, but they refused. When he heard the whisper, he didn't know if it was real or a delusion. "Son?"

The boy screwed his eyes more tightly shut and tried to pull his knees close to his chest.

The voice came out of the darkness again. "Son?"

It was a white man's voice, but he hadn't seen any of them come near him. He slowly processed what he knew and decided that it was his imagination, or a ghost . . . or an angel. He forced his eyes open long enough to look into the dark. There was nothing there. He let his eyelids drift closed again and used his good hand to block the glare from the headlights. He felt hot . . . and cold . . . and like he was going to throw up.

I'm more than ten years old; I don't believe in ghosts, do I? I am ten years old, aren't I?

The question worked its way through his mind for a moment, then his thoughts drifted again. Maybe he was dead and the voice was an angel. Probably not, because every angel he had ever imagined was black. He traced his thoughts back, trying to remember why there was no such thing as a ghost.

Someone told me there were no ghosts, didn't they? What was it that Gram told me? It was something about God didn't do something about ghosts. What was the something God didn't do? Do I know what God doesn't do?

More words came to him from the darkness, interrupting his discordant thoughts. "Stay real still." A ghost that gave orders. He almost giggled at the thought and then remembered that there was some reason why he shouldn't make noise.

"Uncover your eyes." The voice was low and smooth . . .

each word spaced and spoken deliberately. The angel talked like a drunk teacher.

The ghost chided him gently when he moved his hand from his eyes. "Move slowly. Men don't see well in the dark." The voice went back to its soft cadence. "Things that don't move are almost invisible. You move real slowly now. And don't talk."

That must be it. It was the ghost of that old Miss What's-her-name . . . she taught me in third grade . . . what was her name? She was the one who used to show up for afternoon classes with droopy eyes and slurred speech. He'd overheard two teachers joking about the "coffee thermos full of martinis." Now that she's a ghost, she talks like a man.

This time he smiled in the direction of the ghost. He wanted to see what a ghost looked like up close. He moved his head slightly to peer into the dark then remembered that ghosts were invisible and let his head sink back to the muddy road.

The voice was quiet for a second, then it spoke again. "You can't see me, son, because I'm not moving. First, you slide over here, and then I'll go help that lady."

The boy remembered the attack on his mother. The ghost was here to help. He had decided to risk going to the apparition just as he felt something move near his good arm. Something tightened on his sleeve.

"Ghost?"

The tension on his sleeve was gone instantly and his ears picked up the barest sound of something sliding across the wet leaves. The pitch of the low voices near him changed because the men by the truck lights had turned toward him.

The men by the trucks heard my voice.

Fear made his mouth taste like it had something bitter in it. His memory told him he should have stayed quiet. He didn't want the man to hit him again, but somebody had to do something, and the ghost had told him he would help his mom.

He squinted at the group by the trucks without moving his head. His eyes were not working right, and their images drifted from side to side in front of him. Several of the men in the swaying picture were looking in his direction. He had to close his eyes tightly every few seconds because the motion made the nauseated feeling worse. These men were going to kill his mom . . . and then him. After a long time the men turned away.

He was trembling and near throwing up and frightened of the men who stood by the trucks; they hadn't given him a long beating yet, but they would be coming back. He decided he would take his chances and go to the ghost. He moved an inch at a time, staying on his back and using his good elbow, pushing with his heels, scooting himself headfirst toward the woods. The mud in the ditch was colder than the road; he worked himself through it and across a layer of wet leaves nearer to where the ghost's voice waited. He knew the brush was just inches away, but he couldn't make his eyes focus on it.

He heard wet sounds near his head; the voice came again to his ear. "No talk."

A cold hand slid past his head to his neck, tightened itself around the thin material of his jacket collar, and started dragging him away from the men. He held his injured arm close and tucked his chin to his chest while his body was drawn across the cold, wet leaves and mud in smooth, steady moves. Fire worked its way up his arm and across his face, bringing him closer to reality, and he stifled a moan . . . he thought he could feel the bone in his arm pressing against the skin and forced down the bile that rose in his throat. The hand dragged him again, nearer to the protection of the woods. He peered hard into the brush, searching the darkness for the origin of the voice. Just inches away the thick brush seemed to form into a solid shape, but he couldn't quite make it become real.

The shape moved close; warm air with a coffee smell came with it. "Okay, kid," the ghost from the darkness had a plan. "If these guys get the upper hand on me, you crawl as far away into these trees as you can and wait. There's an old house back down this road about a mile. When daylight comes you find some colored people and tell them to get you away from here. You tell them your mom is in trouble."

A finger, sticky with the cold mud, came out of the darkness and touched his forehead, resting there. "Nod your head if you understand."

Only the feeblest light was allowed to work its way to the boy's position. The rest of the arm that was attached to the hand near his head disappeared into the dark void around him.

Where was the body that went with the hand?

He shook his head slowly from side to side.

The whisper came back, more insistent. "Partner, if they kill me, you'll be next."

Partner?

The boy carefully released his grip on his injured arm and reached into the night. His small trembling hand explored the dark and found the sleeve of his rescuer; slender fingers crawled up the sleeve like a tenacious spider until they grasped the ghost's collar. He tugged gently until an ear was touching his lips. His voice trembled in time with his hand. "My mom is . . ."—ragged breath swept across the ear—"back there. I . . . go."

"I'll take care of it. I promise," said the ghost. "Hide here. Stay quiet."

The ten-year-old body moved slightly from side to side when the child shook his head for the second time. He pulled more insistently on the collar and whispered two words back to the ghost. "I . . . kill."

The ear next to his lips stayed motionless for several seconds, then the ghost spoke again. The warm air that smelled of coffee, unlike what would come from the mouth of a ghost, came to his ear . . . the soft voice had acquired hard edges. "I'll go get her. We'll be back." After the darkness said this, the boy's blurred vision told him that something to his right moved and he was alone. The dark woods drew closer and enveloped him.

The dynamics of what was taking place on the road were about to change.

CHAPTER THREE

Tripper Sherman regained consciousness. He looked up at the edges of the darkness around him and prayed, *Please, God, this can't be happening to me. Please let it be a dream.*

In the wet brush near the north edge of the road, the old black man eased across the wet leaves, crawling on his belly, praying every inch of the way.

Have mercy, Lord. What am I doin' out here? I'm messin' with these wild white folks, an' I'm gonna git myself in a pickle fo' sho 'nuff.

The air was motionless. The old man could hear the sounds of small animals around him.

As he drew near the edge of the roadside ditch, he paused. Six feet from his left hand stood a figure that was little more than a rearrangement of the dark shadows. The dark figure watched the old man and smiled without moving any muscles on its mud-covered face. The boy's ghost welcomed the old man; even if he didn't help, he might create a diversion.

Mose prayed. *Lord, I reckon I'm the only person on God's earth who can save that woman out there. You, an' Me, an' this here shot-*

gun. An' I reckon they ain't no way I can come up on these here men in the quiet . . . I needs some breeze to stir these here trees around some so can't nobody hear me.

A second figure stood on the opposite side of the old man. He was clothed in resplendent white light, and no living man had ever seen him. He watched the scene unfold with eyes that missed nothing; the humans and their choices would always interest him. His role was to watch and guard—to approve was not within his purview—but he smiled. Even as the old man thought the prayer, the tall figure received his orders and moved his hand. Overhead the clouds gathered momentum and a gentle wind off the lake caught the tall trees in its invisible current.

Mose smiled at the answered prayer and thanked the One who created the wind. He started to rise to his knees, but something tugged at his senses. Making no more sound than the clouds, the darkness on his left seemed to change shape. The old man swiveled his head slowly and stared hard into the nearby night. He moved his eyes back and forth, straining to pick out something definite in the woods; nothing but shades of black and grey came back. A cold drop of water left an overhead limb and doused his ear. He stayed unmoving.

There ain't nothin' out there, Mose, 'cept the wet. Best be gettin' on with this here rat killin'.

He argued silently that he couldn't help the lady if he got killed trying.

Killin' rats is right. An' I best be alive to get it done.

Nothing moved in the woods, and he turned back to his calling.

The mud-covered figure on his left—the boy's ghost—had been gone for almost a minute.

The breeze cooled his legs through his trousers; the sweat on his cheeks mixed with the leftover raindrops from the surrounding brush and tickled his face on its way to his jawline. He didn't feel the coolness.

It was time to move.

He knee-walked the last inches to the edge of the ditch. Light from the trucks barely leaked into the brush. He stopped at the edge of the protective cover and closed his eyes.

Lord, I don't want nothin' in my sorry life but to die knowin' I done Yo' work. Don't never let me get to thinkin' 'bout myself. This here woman needs me . . . an' we all needs You. Bless me an' what I figure to do . . . an' make me brave. Amen.

The bright figure on Mose's right stepped in close to his shoulder. In its right hand it held a double-edged sword. The angel leaned down and rested his left hand on the stiff, salt-and-pepper hair on Moses Washington's head; when it straightened, a shield the size of a small platter appeared on its left arm, and its surrounding brilliance intensified.

Mose eased the gun forward until the tip of the barrel just cleared the brush, pulled the stock near his cheek, and rested his thumb on the hammer. He could hear his own heartbeat. Less than ten feet away the white men were silhouetted against the lights from the trucks.

He could see two men moving near the woman. Another man stood a step or so from the first two, watching and taking drinks from a bottle.

Farther back, near the pickup headlights, a small group clustered together and tried to ignore what was going on fifteen feet away. The ones in this group had watched the attack start but wanted no part of it. The Newsome brothers alternated between watching the three in the road and staring at the ground; McClellan and Nations had turned their backs; Tripper was lying in the road.

Mose moved the gun's barrel up and down on the bushes so that the branches snapped against each other. The five over by the trucks didn't hear anything, but Bainbridge and his two henchmen pulled away from the sound.

Ollie Bainbridge's eyes swept along the roadside and came to rest on the spot where the shotgun poked through the bushes. "I can see your eyes shining through those bushes, so you can forget about hiding. Step out here, and let's take a look at you."

The white spots that Ollie saw disappeared for an instant when the eyes in the bushes blinked, then reappeared.

None of the others could see anyone. The road was empty; no one had walked up; silence surrounded them. They weren't sure who Bainbridge was talking to, and those by the trucks were convinced that lunacy had completely overtaken him. In the next instant all eight of the white men heard the words that came from the quiet woods.

"I 'spect if you can see my eyes, you can look down and see the barrel of this here shotgun."

One of the boys by the trucks cursed in frustration, or maybe it was relief.

Bainbridge glanced nonchalantly at the gun's barrel and looked back into the eyes in the brush. He swayed as he turned to the people behind him and said, "Okay, boys, better be careful now . . . we been surrounded by Uncle Remus."

He turned back and took a step in the direction of the brush to see better into the eyes behind the gun. When he spoke next, it was with the confidence of a man who knew where all the chess pieces were going to be at the end of the game. "I see the gun, nigger," he sneered, "and you and I both know what can happen to you just for pointing it at me."

"What'll happen to me's piddlin' enough, mister; you're the one what's on the wrong end of this here gun." It was the tone of the words, or the even cadence, or maybe both that carried the sound of conviction to the men in the road.

That the old man in the woods didn't sound scared threw Bainbridge off his stride. He caught up quickly and decided to see what he was up against. "I figure you'll get one shot out of that old single-barrel. After that, me an—"

Mose was praying; he already knew that unless God stepped in, he was going to have to kill the white fool who was doing all the talking. He figured he might avoid additional bloodshed if he told the other men what they were facing.

Tempered reason spoke again from the brush. "Wouldn't you jes' know it . . . that high she'ff taken away my old single 'cause I kilt a man with it. What I got here now is a Winchester pump, carryin' heavy-load shells. After the first shot the rest of these here mens'll be makin' they own choices; you'll be a gut-shot dead man." The men in Eagle Nest Brake would all carry different memories of that night's horrors to their graves. The single memory they would all share was the doomsday sound that came from the darkness when the black man cocked the shotgun.

For a black man to challenge a white man from over the barrel of a shotgun wasn't done in most parts of the nation; in Mississippi, it invited sure death for the offending negro. That the old man was ready to die—whether he killed anyone or not—spelled something foreign and forbidding for everyone but Bainbridge.

Bainbridge pulled a half-pint bottle from his back pocket and held it up in a toast to the man on the other side of the ditch. "I'll see you in hell, old man."

Mose never raised his voice; he never changed the pace of the soft words. "I ain't much to talk 'bout religion to foolish white folks, but I can tell you this—bein' in hell is the only thing what'd be worse'n what this here shotgun'd do to yo' middle. An' if'n you don't light a shuck right soon, you gonna git a chance to find out what I'm talkin' 'bout—you hear me now." The old man's voice betrayed nothing but firm purpose.

Bainbridge took another step closer to the man in the bushes. "Old man," he wanted to lower his voice, but something inside him turned it into a hoarse screech, "you don't know who my father is . . . and you've got no idea what'll happen to you if you hurt one of us. Now, back off in those bushes and go on about your business."

The group by the trucks was beginning to murmur leaving sounds. They heard what Bainbridge said to the black man; when the old man responded, his words were soaked in resolve.

"Boy." It was the first time any person present had heard a black man call an adult white male *boy*. "Whether or not somethin' happens to me ain't important. God put me here to look out for that woman there. If you set yo'self on hurtin' her again, then you done set yo'self on dealin' with this here load o' shot. Them that stands between me an' her's gonna die. It's simple as that."

The men at the trucks were certain that Bainbridge's mind was gone—he was crazy enough to get them all killed. They multiplied their protests—working against his madness, trying to convince him to withdraw.

The thoughts of the madman had been drowning out the escalating protests of those around him. When their voices finally penetrated his consciousness, he realized they were trying to get him to leave with them. "C'mon, Ollie, let's go get a beer. We can—"

"We've got beer!" Bainbridge screamed. He lent authenticity to their fears regarding his madness by spinning around and throwing the whiskey bottle at them. The bottle shattered the windshield of his own truck, and he screamed louder. "Leave?" He started waving the ax handle; tears mixed with the sweat on his face; his voice went up an octave. "Leave?" He took a step toward them, dropped his voice to a whisper and hissed, "Nobody is going anywhere till we've finished what we came here to do. We're going to build us a fire, and we're gonna have a sacrifice." He grinned. "We're . . . going . . . to . . . burn . . . them . . . alive!"

* * *

Confused thoughts of escaping to safety with a ghost circled in the mind of the youngster as he approached consciousness. He opened his eyes as the headlights of the nearest pickup went out, then came back up to full bright. Bainbridge and the others turned and faced the truck. From the silence behind the lights came a rapid clash of metal that is familiar to every man who has ever hunted—someone had just jacked a shell into the chamber of a pump shotgun. The small group in front of the trucks looked at each other; they were surrounded by one madman and two unseen people holding shotguns.

The boy near the ditch heard a familiar voice speak from behind the lights. "Gentlemen," the voice spoke in a conversational tone, just barely above the whisper he was used to, "it's over." The words were so soft that the listeners weren't sure they needed to feel threatened.

Ollie Bainbridge recovered first. When the voice quieted, he relaxed. He smiled while lowering the ax handle, and stared toward the headlights, waiting. The two men standing near the woman were easing over to be closer to Bainbridge. Tripper Sherman was on his hands and knees, watching blood drip off the end of his nose.

Bainbridge laughed. "Step out here, old buddy, so we can get a look at you before we stack you up with our sacrificial offerings and have us a barbecue."

"What everybody out here is going to find out tonight is that you don't have any buddies."

Dailey and Whitacher were aware that the man behind the light was between them and their firearms that hung on gun racks in the pickups. They thought the same thought at the same time: *If this guy behind the lights gets away there could be trouble. He'd let folks know what happened out here.* Without a word or look they each slid a tentative foot sideways in the direction of the darkness offered by the brush.

The voice spoke again without changing its tone or volume. "I'll kill the next man that moves toward the woods."

The two who considered the flanking movement had, in their formative years, been told that they didn't need to have anybody tell them what a rattlesnake sounded like. Like all boys, they were told they would recognize the sound instinctively when they heard it. Neither of them had heard a rattlesnake yet, but they heard promised-death in the voice of the man behind the lights. They froze where they were.

Ollie Bainbridge wasn't as impressed as his followers. "You talk big for a man outnumbered eight to one."

A voice, harsh with emotion, butted into the conversation to correct Bainbridge. "Uh-uh. Not now, not ever again." Forest Aaron Sherman III leaned on the nearest bumper to help himself stand. He decided that if he was going to live past this moment, he was going to do it in a way that he wouldn't be ashamed to look back on. "I guess I'm goin' to end up dead anyway . . . or beat up . . . but I'm out of it." A pause. The boy jerked his thumb at the headlights. "I'm with him."

Tripper turned and spoke at the headlights. "I'm against what's happenin' here. It's seven to two, mister. I'll fight alongside you or by myself; you just tell me what you want done."

"Show me your hands. Slowly." It was as if the truck spoke to him.

The boy eased his hands up slowly, while Bainbridge said, "You better hope he kills you, you little creep."

Tripper knew in that moment that untold people would suffer if Bainbridge lived. He interrupted his surrender long enough to turn and speak to his enemy. "One of us sure better hope he does, Bainbridge."

The truck gave instructions to Tripper. Each time he followed a prompt, the voice gave him a new one; the other white men stayed quiet and watched. "Show me your palms . . . interlace your fingers, and put your hands on your head . . . keep them there . . . turn away from me and sit on the ground facing the woods . . . not there, closer to the ditch . . . close your eyes and keep your mouth shut." There was no hurry. The man used a tone he would use to order breakfast. The men watched in silence until Sherman was seated in the mud with his back to them.

"Buddy," Bainbridge began, "I figure you got maybe five rounds in that pump, an' there's still seven of us—"

But before Ollie finished his threat, one of the group standing near Tripper stepped toward the trucks.

McClellan moved to put his hands in front of him, showing his palms to the truck. The others in the road watched in silence while he put the empty hands on his head and sat down in the mud. Tripper muttered something to him, and the other boy squirmed around until he was facing the darkness of the woods. Both had their shoulders hunched as if expecting to receive a blow.

The truck spoke to its two captives. "Spread out and keep your mouths shut."

The boys wiggled in the mud until they were separated.

Bainbridge laughed. "Well, well, well. Looks like we're separating the men from the girls."

The voice lectured, "The average man, if he kills someone, does it because he's scared." The tone changed from lecture to reason. "If I have to kill someone here tonight it'll be—"

"Bubba, you're in way over your head."

"It'll be," the voice picked up as if Bainbridge had not spoken, "because the ones who died didn't believe what I just told you. If you give me reason to think you can hurt me, I'll need to kill you."

The men who were still standing digested the words. No one moved.

Bainbridge snatched Whitacher's bottle from him and took time for a long drink. All he wanted was to see the woman dead—her and her kid and everyone who opposed his midnight madness.

Dailey and Whitacher swiveled their heads back and forth between Bainbridge and the trucks; they wanted out. The Newsome brothers stood by the trucks; they thought they should surrender but kept their gazes fixed on the ground. *What would people think?*

The sixth holdout was Jerry Nations. He had spent every moment since Bainbridge attacked Tripper on the Cat Lake bridge looking for a chance to sneak away into the night. Every remaining day of his lost life would be soaked in what might have been, and he would die of acute alcoholism before he reached midlife, still trying to escape the effects of a single bad choice. *Maybe if I had sided with that kid . . . that Tripper Sherman. How could he have known?*

The man in the dark saw the trepidation.

"Those of you who want out are still free to step aside . . . now." He paused. "You know the drill. Move slowly . . . show me your hands . . . put them away and turn your backs."

Nations made his only good decision of the night by joining the two in the mud.

The man with the pump shotgun spoke to the five who were still standing. "Boys, you're letting one fool decide whether or not you get to see tomorrow. From now on, every word he speaks will be to get you to screw up your courage. I can't let that happen because if you start getting brave, you could hurt me. Give it up."

Dailey stayed where he was because of a misplaced sense of bravery. Whitacher didn't want to be implicated in what happened to the captives and was putting his hopes in Bainbridge to keep him out of trouble.

Bainbridge wanted protection. If he could get to the woman he could use her as a shield. Whitacher was already between him and the voice at the trucks. He whispered at Dailey to move back and shield him from the old man in the bushes.

The voice behind the trucks saw the problem developing. He cursed silently, hoping that the old man had a clear shot. His cursing and hoping didn't work; Mose could no longer see Bainbridge because Dailey had moved to screen him.

Bainbridge said, "Well, it looks like I'm the big dog again."

The man behind the trucks said, "You need to know that I won't let you live if you harm that woman again."

Bainbridge cackled. "You can't stop me from killing her."

"But you won't survive."

A mixture of growls and curses came from Bainbridge and rained on the night. He needed to insure that both the black woman and the boy died. That meant he needed to stay alive long enough to do his evil. He stayed where he was, held hostage by a meddling old black man and a white stranger.

Mose no longer had any reason to pray silently. "Lord, You seen fit to bring me an' this other fella here to protect these helpless folks, and You done showed us we can't do it by ourselves."

The growls from Bainbridge's chest became hoarse whines. Dailey and Whitacher made gasping sounds; the cool night air couldn't stem the tide of sweat on their faces. Bainbridge hissed at Mose, "Old man, you're meddling in something that's going to cost you your life. Pull out now and I may allow you to live."

If Mose heard Bainbridge, he didn't show it. He continued his prayer as if he were alone in the world. "Father in Heaven, the evil one who stands against Yo' cause is usin' the life of this man. I ask now, Lord, that it would please You to show Yo'self strong on the side of those of us who is weak. Amen."

Across the road from Mose, the answer to his prayer—weeping quiet tears of frustration and fear, pain and exertion—was dragging himself away from the protection offered by the woods. He stopped outside the reach of the headlights and went to work trying to push himself into a sitting position. The woman in the road was his responsibility—his dad had made that clear.

The smallest actor in the drama was preparing himself to follow through on his promise to take care of his mom.

CHAPTER FOUR

The ten-year-old was in shock and didn't know it. The cold mud of the road felt warmer now. He moved carefully, getting his legs in front of him while he looked for his mom. Tears and sweat mixed with the blood on his face and stung his eyes; he wiped them slowly with the sleeve of his good arm. The headlights mixed with the shadows around him and made things seem dreamlike . . . a man was talking, but his words weren't clear . . . his head throbbed and the images around him were blurred. A smear of white in the road caught his attention . . . his mom was on her back out in the road . . . she wasn't moving . . . the man who had hit him was inching closer to her. The child looked at the darkness behind the truck lights.

The ghost was back there, wasn't he? That was his voice giving the orders, wasn't it?

The man who had hit him and his mom was quiet, moving closer to his mom, planning evil.

Working slowly with his good hand the boy reached beneath his jacket, taking his time, getting a grip on the thing his mother had handed him from the car. When it came out, its black and white surfaces reflected the glow from the lights—it was an Army Colt .45 automatic with mother-of-pearl grips—

his dad had carried the gun in the wars in Europe and Korea; it was here now . . . in his war.

He had given up trying to make his left arm work right, and his good hand was slick with blood. He settled the gun carefully in his lap, wiped some of the blood on his jacket, then struggled to get the grips securely in his hand. It was heavier than he remembered, and he'd never tried to shoot it with one hand. He stayed seated and finally managed to keep the gun out in front of him by bending his legs and propping his arm on his knees—the tip of the barrel moved in a circle that took in everyone on the road. Sweat stung his eyes, but he didn't have a free hand to wipe them; more frustration brought on wetter tears. He probably wouldn't have been able to cock the gun, even if he had remembered to.

Bainbridge edged into position next to the woman. He knew that the two men with the shotguns couldn't get a clear shot, and he was readying himself to retake control of the situation on the road. Whether or not he eventually got killed mattered less to him than getting to kill the woman and the kid. He was already smiling.

A bright being appeared at the boy's side, a near-twin of the one standing at Mose's shoulder. The angel saluted his ally across the road, leaned close to the boy, and touched the tip of his sword to the gun's rear sight. Making no more sound than a stationary drop of oil, the gun's hammer eased back and cocked; the barrel tilted slightly and became stock-still. The boy's eyelids drooped, and he sagged forward slightly, instinctively tightening his grasp on the pearl grips. The messenger from Heaven put an arm around the child and held him up; the gun remained unmoving, firmly fixed in space, while the boy held on.

* * *

Farrell Whitacher turned his back to Ollie and froze—something wasn't right. A trumpet sound could not have heralded the retribution he expected any more clearly than the cold sweat he could feel seeping out of his pores. He didn't know what form the reprisal would take, but the feeling that he was too near the destined target seemed to stop his heart. He didn't consciously hear Bainbridge take in the breath to speak, but he expected words to come forth—and they did.

"Well, boys, I'm—"

When the self-appointed leader started to speak, Whitacher hunched his shoulders; the impending judgment was rushing toward them and there was no doubt that he was too close to where it would be executed. He shaded his eyes against the glare of the lights and looked into the darkness on his right.

The next sound in the woods was not a crescendo—a crescendo builds slowly.

What Whitacher would remember, but have little opportunity to reflect on, was that the muzzle flash came from the wrong place. His eyes were directed at the place where the old man was when the woods around him became bright white, then pale rose, then reddish orange. Whitacher saw that; his brain processed it, then he heard the blast of the gun. He was immediately and acutely conscious of a sticky, wet spray that covered him.

Someone screamed—Whitacher thought it might've been him. *That was too close,* he thought. *Some crazy fool shot close enough to spray mud all over us . . . he could've hit somebody.*

He turned around to find that Ollie Bainbridge had shown his true colors by being so scared that he had leaped backward and landed in the road. Whitacher was afraid to laugh but thought, *Yeah, he's a big, brave man . . . till the gun goes off.*

He was feeling of the sticky mess in his hair while he waited for Bainbridge to get up. There were sharp pieces of something in the gooey stuff, probably gravel. Without really thinking, he held his hands so that the truck lights could illumine them. Dozens of white splinters, covered with blood and scraps of Oliver Wendell Bainbridge's brain, were sticking to the places where his fingers had touched his head. An unbidden thought came to Whitacher when he saw the fragments of Bainbridge's brain: *Well, he wasn't usin' it anyway.*

Dailey hadn't seen where the bullet came from. He pointed his finger at the lights. "You poor fool, you—"

The second blast from the gun seemed doubly loud, and young Dailey landed in the mud with one arm flung across his hero.

This time more than one man screamed, and real terror visited the men on the muddy little road that ran through Eagle Nest Brake.

The being bathed in bright light leaned forward and let the black child fold into the ditch. Mose and the man behind the trucks saw the boy go down. They were equally astonished by the turn of events and both of them moved closer to the group, readying themselves for whatever might come next.

Whitacher and the Newsome brothers froze with their backs to the trucks. The screaming had stopped. Someone was sobbing. The ones who were still alive didn't need to examine Bainbridge and Dailey to know they were dead. There was a killer in the darkness behind them, but they were afraid to turn around. The breeze chilled them. The question that occurred to each of them was answered while they were asking it.

"We'll kill as many as we have to." The timbre of the voice might have been the same if the man behind the lights had been speculating on the possibility of rain. "You choose."

Unbelief washed through Whitacher like heated water; he couldn't believe he had survived the executions. If he could stay alive, he would see to it that the old black man and his helper paid for meddling where they shouldn't. He interlaced his fingers and put them on his head and was turning his back when the man barked, "Stop!"

Whitacher froze; the short-lived relief fled. He could feel himself sweating again.

The voice moderated. "You in the back."

Tears came to Whitacher's eyes, and his voice betrayed him by wavering. "Muh . . . eee?"

"Yes."

Whitacher, in his haste to give up, had moved his hands straight to his head. The voice said, "Show me your hands." A pause. "Palms out."

Whitacher showed his hands.

"Smart. You know the rest of the drill. Do it."

When Whitacher sat down, two men remained standing in the road. They stood with their hands in the air but made no move to sit. The shorter of the two leaned toward his companion and whispered earnestly.

"Talk to *me*," said the darkness.

The two in the road were Doug and Buster Newsome; they stayed silent.

"Boys, I don't know if you know what a stalemate is, but this isn't one. You're under the gun, and you are going to give up, or I am going to kill you graveyard dead. What's it going to be?"

The short one hung his head and barely whispered, "He's my brother . . . m-my big brother."

"And?"

"An' he says we can't give up."

"Is that right, brother? You're planning to sacrifice your little brother on the altar of stupidity?"

The older brother spoke like a pouting child. "If we give up, everybody's gonna know what happened out here. My momma's a good lady—what's she gonna do if we go to prison?"

"That's it? You've decided to worry about your mother?" The first hint of emotion came from behind the lights. "I've got an idea that you've been living on the edge of 'no good' all your life. If your mother is any kind of woman at all, she'll be so ashamed of you, she'll kill you herself and drape your sorry carcass on the nearest barbed wire fence. You've got a chance to keep your kid brother alive for her by quitting, and you're willing to break her heart."

More pouting. "You don't understand."

"Well, one of us doesn't; that's for sure." The voice paused then came back. Colder. "Your kid brother's out of it."

The younger brother looked first at the darkness, then at his brother, then back at the darkness. "Out of it? What's that mean?"

The voice in the darkness returned to neutral. "Your big brother's too stupid to make a good decision—I may have to kill him. After he's dead, you can still choose."

Tripper Sherman listened as the willing executioner reasoned for the lives of the two holdouts.

"Whether you die or not, this time next week everyone in the nation is going to know what happened on this road; if you have any brains, you'll all make a run for it as soon as you get loose. I don't want to kill you two—especially a kid who doesn't know where to put his loyalty—but I'm backed into a corner here, and it isn't my choice; it's yours. I have to make sure we have enough time to get away, and I can't do it unless you two are tied up. So choose—right now."

Tripper Sherman could not remember ever doing anything brave, but he spoke because he'd had enough death to last him till he experienced his own. He raised his head and spoke out loud to the taller of the two boys.

"Doug," he waited a second for the shot that didn't come, "you two might can get past this if you're alive . . . at least you'll have a chance." Still no gunshot. "I'm leavin' tonight. I've got some money at home, an' I'm goin' west. I'll take you both with me."

"You ain't even fifteen yet, Tripper, how in the—"

"Age ain't got a dadgum thing to do with it, Doug. I've had some time to think. We were wrong. We should of done whatever it took to stop him." He paused. "We can't be right if we put up with somethin' that's wrong."

The shooter stayed silent.

"I made up my mind not to stay around here before this man showed up. I was goin' to turn Ollie in before I left—he was a cur dog." His voice became softer, matter-of-fact, like the voice in the dark. "You an' Buster can come . . . or you can stay. Like the man says . . . you choose."

When Tripper finished his speech, Buster sank to the road, putting his hands on his head. He made an awkward turn on his knees and worked his way to a cross-legged position. He tilted his head up to his brother. "We didn't do nothin', Doug, an' we should've. Don't die for not doin' nothin'. We can go out west with Tripper. Okay? Please?"

An hour after they left Dennison's Store, two of the original eight were crying and two were dead. Retribution and Farrell Whitacher had not yet met.

The man used the last of the rope from the hunting club's barn and tied Tripper securely to a tree. Tripper said, "I want to thank you for not shootin' me."

"You've got a lot of years ahead of you, kid. Use them better than this."

"I'll try."

The man stood in the darkness and looked at Tripper. This was the one who had come closest to stopping the wild man; maybe he'd understand. "Kid?"

"Sir?"

"The bad guys held the high cards too long tonight. That's not all your fault, but you were here. You need to think about whether or not you're going to let it happen the next time, and you've got to outthink the ones you can't outfight."

"I think I've already decided that."

"I think you have too." The man stepped closer. A strong hand squeezed Tripper's shoulder; the smell of cigarettes and coffee came on the night air. "Good luck."

"Thanks anyway, but I reckon I've ruined my life."

The dark figure had already turned away—he came back and put his mud-covered face close to Tripper's. "Listen to me, son," he growled. "If you forget everything else that happened here tonight, you need to remember this . . . this isn't a crossroads, it's a threshold."

Tripper looked at the mud-covered face and nodded soberly. "Yes, sir. I'll remember."

The man went to see how Mose was doing with the woman.

The boy had crawled out onto the road to be by his mother and passed out again. Mose was kneeling over the pitiful little pair.

The white man made eye contact with Mose. "This isn't good."

"We needs to move 'em, an' she's bad hurt."

"I'll get one of those trucks, and we'll take them both to a hospital."

Mose shook his head, "We can't git nowhere near them

trucks, boss; people 'round here knows who they belongs to. If a muddy white man come in town in one of them trucks, haulin' a ol' black man an' these two, we'd be in Parchman 'fore the dew dries."

"What do you suggest?"

Mose had been thinking. "Move them trucks outta the road. We'll put these two in her car an' take 'em to my house. We can decide from there." Mose didn't want the men tied out in the woods to hear his plans.

They stopped in front of the cabin. The boy was breathing normally but was asleep or unconscious. The two men eased the lady out of the car. The dog came out from under the house to watch while they carried her toward Mose's truck.

The woman's eyelids fluttered and she said, "Put me over there on that porch."

"If we do, we'll have to move you again to get you into the truck."

"Put me on the porch, gentlemen."

They knelt with her. She winced when they lowered her to the bare wood.

She took a breath then looked at the men. "Where's my son?"

Mose said, "He's in the car, miss. He ain't beat up too bad, but he took a good lick on the head an' I'm right sure his arm is broke."

"Where are the men who beat me?"

The white man leaned closer; flecks of drying mud fell from his face and clothes. "Ma'am, your son killed the two that beat you. The others are tied up."

"Bill shot those men?"

He thought he needed to defend the boy's actions. "Yes, ma'am. If he hadn't, they'd've killed you both."

The lady showed what remained of a beautiful smile. "He's his father's son."

"That's all over now, ma'am, and we need to get you to a doctor."

The woman ignored the man with the muddy face. "Are you gentlemen Christians?"

When the white man recoiled slightly, Mose stepped closer and bent over her. "I'm a Christian, ma'am."

"I'm dying." She looked at the two of them then out at the car. "My son doesn't have anyone but me, and I'm dying."

The white man spoke again. "We're wasting valuable time, ma'am. You need a doctor."

The lady shook her head slowly. She looked at Mose, the man who would understand. "I'm dying, and there are things that need doing. You get busy doing them while I'm still here."

Mose knew what to do. He straightened and spoke to the white man. "Mistah, this here's Miss'ippi. Me an' you, an' that boy an' her, was in on the killin' of two white folks. If we gits caught, we won't even make it to the courthouse."

The man didn't understand completely, but he knew when to listen to the resident expert. "What do you want me to do?"

"Look in her car. Git those things that have their names on 'em. Git her purse. Look an' see is there anything valuable, stuff like that. Hurry up now."

The woman whispered, "Get my suitcase; there's money in my purse. Everything else will just slow you down."

"Yassum."

The white man retrieved the purse and suitcase and put them near her on the porch.

"His father's watch is in that suitcase; there's a note." She coughed and a pink mist covered the front of her blouse. "Make sure my boy gets them."

The white man hesitated. "What about you?"

She rested an understanding hand on his arm and coughed again while she shook her head. She smiled the smile again.

"This gentleman can tell you about me." She turned to Mose. "Will you . . . take care of my son? He has no one else."

Mose's own son had been just about this boy's age when he died. "Yassum. I'll raise him jes' like he was my very own."

"What about—" she stopped to cough. "What about Jesus?"

Mose held her hand and told her what he knew. "He's right here."

"And what about you?"

"God's all I've got now, ma'am . . . an' He's all I'll ever need."

Her eyes closed. "And you're all my boy's got—he doesn't know Jesus yet, and he's been blaming God for his father's death. I have to leave it to you to help him understand." She closed her eyes and frowned for the first time. "He's your son now."

Mose said, "Yes, ma'am."

"Tell him his father and I are waiting for him in Heaven. You tell him that."

Mose said, "I'll tell him, ma'am."

The lady could no longer hear him.

Mose slipped his arms under the lady's body and picked her up. "Open up that door there."

The white man opened the door and stood back. "What're you going to do?"

"I'm gonna lay her out properlike."

"Lay her out?"

"Get her ready to be buried. We her only loved ones now. It's proper."

The white man was worried about the old man's sense of reason. "Mister, we're short on time here. Every minute counts."

"Time enough, son, time enough. Hand me two sheets outta that chiffarobe then bring me in that suitcase."

When the man came back with the suitcase Mose said,

"Now, git the boy and lay him on the kitchen table. We got to fix something on his arm 'fore he can travel."

The ghost said, "I can handle that while you do this."

The white man finished first and came back into the bedroom. "What now?"

Mose was finishing his job. "Is the boy awake?"

"No, sir."

"Well, it can't be helped. Bring him in here."

The man carried the boy in his arms, and Mose directed him to the side of the bed. When they were in position, the white man held the boy, and Mose bowed his head and said, "Lord, we forever in Yo' care. Our sister is with You even while we prayin'. I ask, Lord, that You would give me what it takes to tell this young boy 'bout You. We got to go from this place soon, askin' for nothin' but the protection what You give us an' for the salvation of this fine white man an' this here young boy. Forgive us for our haste. Amen."

"Bring him closer." Mose motioned, "Now, lean down."

The man leaned over the woman with the boy. Mose took the child's hand in his; he touched the small, limp fingers to the boy's lips then to the woman's.

"That'll have to do," Mose said. "He'll need to know 'bout that one day."

The white man straightened. "What now?"

"You got a car?"

"Yes, sir."

"Macon Lake is less'n a mile back down this road." Mose pointed to the east. "You take the lady's car an' drive it off in there—you'll see the open place over on the far side of the lake, right south of the bridge. After you cover up the tracks, you get in yo' car an' git gone. I'll take care of what needs doin' here."

The ghost started to turn away.

"Just a minute." Mose put one hand on the man's shoulder and bowed his head. "Lord, this here is a brave man, an' I pray that You would pour deep an' abidin' blessin's on him an' his. An' I pray even more that You would see fit to draw him to Yo'self. Amen."

When Mose looked up, the man was watching him, a half smile on his face. "Should I go now?"

Mose didn't smile. He tapped the man's chest with a black finger. "Go in fear, son. I figure you to be a man what's treadin' a dangerous road in a dark world. Go in fear."

The two took time to shake hands, and the man disappeared.

Dawn was two hours away when Mose pulled into the Parkers' driveway. Bobby Lee and Susan met him at the back door; the dog stayed with the truck.

"Mornin', Mose. We just been prayin' for you."

"You was prayin' for me?"

"Yep. Come on in for a cup of coffee."

"Best not." Mose stayed on the back porch so he could keep an eye on his pickup. "We got to get on down the road."

Bobby Lee stepped through the door and peered through the darkness at the truck. "Who's *we*?"

Mose took several precious minutes to tell the Parkers what had happened out at the brake. They listened without comment until Mose finished, then Bobby Lee said, "Where's the white man that helped you?"

"I reckon he can take care of hisself. I tol' him to drive the lady's car off in Macon an' git gone."

Bobby Lee was disgusted with himself. "I should've come over there."

Susan was the practical one. "There's nothing we can do about that now, and we need to get Mose on the road. And he can't go in that truck."

Bobby Lee put the past behind him. “She’s right, Mose. The boy needs to lay down, an’ the law’ll be lookin’ for yo’ truck.”

Susan said, “You better take my car.”

Mose and Bobby Lee were both shaking their heads. Bobby Lee spoke their thoughts. “Too new. The police would be suspicious of a black man in a car like that’n.”

The silence was only seconds long when the answer came to Bobby Lee. “Daddy’s old car’s over in the gin shop. We’ll put your truck in there, an’ you can take his car. It’s good enough to last you a few years an’ old enough not to attract any attention.”

Mose knew he was right but had some misgivings. “What will the police say about you helpin’ me?”

“It ain’t like we helpin’ you. Anything we got is already yours for the takin’.”

“What’ll you tell them?”

“We won’t be here. We’re leavin’ on vacation as soon as you git outta sight.” Bobby Lee, taking his cue from Susan, was beginning to plan ahead. “An’ you’re gonna need some travelin’ money.”

Mose hooked his thumb at the truck. “I got a tow sack full in the truck. Had it buried under the house.”

This made perfect sense to Bobby Lee; he nodded and went inside to get a flashlight.

The two men took the pickup to the gin to make the swap, while Susan waited at the house. The boy moaned without opening his eyes when they moved him to the car’s backseat; the dog curled up on the floor by the child’s head.

Bobby Lee bent over to touch the child’s face. “Who put the splint on his arm?”

“That white man. Looked like he knowed what he was doin’ too.”

Bobby Lee looked at the expert work and nodded.

When they came back from hiding Mose’s truck in the

shop Susan put a paper sack containing a thermos of coffee and some sandwiches on the front seat of the car. She handed Mose a piece of paper and explained it to him. "Today's Saturday. Call that number at noon on Saturday, two weeks from today, person-to-person for Bobby Lee; he'll be standing near the phone. We can make more plans then."

"Yes, ma'am." He opened the car door and took off his hat. "Me an' this here boy 'preciate what y'all done for us, an' there ain't no way we can ever make it right. I don't reckon I'll be comin' back, so I needs to tell you ain't nobody ever had no finer friends than this here family has been to me an' mine."

Bobby Lee had backed away a step; Susan drew close to the old man and put her hand on his arm. "Oh, Mose," tears glistened in her eyes, "everything we hold precious today is in our lives because of what your Junior did. Missy and Bobby are alive, and we're all Christians because of what you and your family did for ours . . . what we owe to you will never be repaid this side of Heaven." She hugged her staid black friend for the first and last time, then stepped back to stand by her husband.

The two white people held each other and watched the car's taillights fade into the darkness. Bobby Lee shook his head at the unfairness of it all, already missing his friend. "C'mon. I guess we better pack an' git outta here."

"Where will we go?"

"Somewhere where nobody can find us."

Susan was watching the empty road. "Where will they go?"

"He wouldn't say. Said if we didn't know, we wouldn't have to lie."

"They'll go to Mound Bayou, won't they?"

"Yep, sure will."

CHAPTER FIVE

Mound Bayou, Mississippi.

Sometimes the old ways die hard, so men don't have to.

Scattered fragments of the ancient Underground Railroad were still in existence in the spring of 1960; the network of folks who helped runaway slaves "follow the drinkin' gourd" to the "free states" had passed along their calling from one generation to the next for more than a century. Mound Bayou, situated in the middle of Mississippi cotton country, seventy-five miles south of Memphis, served as a latter-day waypoint on the twentieth century's version of the fragmented pathway. The small community was the most prosperous of the three all-black towns in the state and had been a haven for black people running from trouble since its founding in 1887.

Five years out of medical school in Michigan and four and a half years into the boredom of nine-to-five pill-pushing, the man moved south to the all-black town, thinking himself a missionary. The journal on the desk in front of him was what he'd once thought would be the seed of a book chronicling his achievements; instead, it had become the daily documentation of an abiding friendship. He sat at his desk, adjusted his reading glasses, and took up his pen. *Lord, this coming summer will mark my twentieth year here, and I see nothing that I've done to draw any of these people nearer to You. I only ask, Father, that You would choose to use me in Your cause.*

He paused and looked out the open window. This was his favorite time of day, and his mind smiled at a memory from the early days of his marriage. He woke his wife on their honeymoon and said, "Look outside, baby. It's a beautiful morning."

His new bride had come out from under the sheets long enough to survey the star-spangled sky, pulled the covers back over her head, and announced, "Where I come from, we call that *night*."

They were married ten years and eleven months, and for the first five years she enjoyed sleeping late on any morning she didn't have to get up. That all changed when the baby came.

The mother and daughter were inseparable. They were up early every morning to eat breakfast with him. They entertained him and his patients with impromptu plays or concerts. The two lived luminescent lives, brightening every heart that crossed their paths. The interlude lasted six years, until his ladies—as they called themselves—were killed in a car wreck down by Cleveland.

The man sat in the cool of the near darkness and wrote while the neighborhood's roosters competed in foretelling the day's soon coming. He ended his writings with a not uncommon plea: *Lord, I ask only that You use my life . . . not that I would have myself to be known or famous, not even that I would know myself to be effective . . . only that I would come to Your presence to find that I seized every opportunity You offered me to be Your man.*

The being who rested his hand on the man's shoulder was robed in light brighter than the foretold day. He read the entry in the man's journal, comparing the written prayers with the day's preordained events, and smiled.

It was early Saturday morning and the sun wasn't fully up, but the air was getting close, and the overweight black man mowing the dew-laden grass had already sweated through his undershirt. When the car turned down his street, the only sound in the neighborhood was the pulsing *shing* of the reel mower blades against the cutting bar. In the middle of each pass across the tiny yard, the man would step into the shade offered by the porch and juggle a cup of hot coffee and a fat cigar; during his breaks he kept a breeze flowing over his face with a funeral parlor fan. Most doctors would've told him he needed to quit smoking and lose thirty or forty pounds.

The car stopped right in front of his house as he was taking one of his coffee breaks. A man stepped out and stretched while he looked up and down the row of neat homes. He had timed his arrival so that folks who were going to the fields or fishing were already at their appointed places; store clerks and such were still in the bed.

When the driver determined that the street was, indeed, empty, he looked at the perspiring man and said, "Mornin'."

The man by the mower kept the fan moving and nodded. "An' already hot."

The traveler opened the back door of the car and let a good-looking Redbone hound out; the dog trotted across the street to a light pole to do his business. The man by the car pretended to watch the dog while he gave the nearby houses a more thorough going-over. By the time the dog came back to be let into the car, the man had made his decision. He opened the car door for the dog then stepped through the little wooden gate and passed by the sign that said Doctor's Office; he'd never seen a black man drinking coffee out of a cup with a matching saucer. "You the doctor?"

The doctor wrote his journal in words he had acquired in the world of academia, but he spoke his grandmother's dialect. "Only 'cause I wouldn't live through a full mornin' of doin' yard work. Name's Carlson."

The two measured each other without either offering to shake hands. "I hear you can keep quiet 'bout things."

"Oh?" The doctor took a long pull on the cigar and blew a series of smoke rings before he asked, "What kind of things?"

"I got a young boy out in the car needs yo' help."

The funeral parlor fan continued to generate its breeze. The doctor ignored the car and studied the man; he wasn't a field hand. "Is the boy injured, or sick?"

"Injured," said the newcomer.

"Is he bleedin'?"

"Not anymore."

The yardman took a deliberate sip of the coffee before he asked, "You the one that hurt him?"

It was a question the visitor would've asked. He shook his head. "White mens."

The black people in Mississippi had taught the doctor that the proper use of the English language was not a prerequisite for natural dignity. He took another pull on the cigar while he considered his visitor, then said, "You don't talk much, do you?"

"This ain't somethin' that needs talk."

"Mmm . . . we'll see. Bring him inside, an' we'll take a look."

"I can't have nobody see him here, an' I needs to hide the car."

"An' why would you need to do that?"

"The two white mens what beat him did the same to his momma. She died."

The doctor waited a moment then asked, "And?"

"That child out in the car, he killed them two white mens."

"Well then," the fan never stopped moving, "since I haven't heard about any killin's till now, I suppose it happened last night."

"It did."

The keeper of the journal put down the cup and pointed

the cigar. "Bring the car up the driveway. I'll meet you in the back an' show you where to park."

The man checked the backseat when he got to his car. The dog was in his place on the floor; the boy was still breathing, but he hadn't moved.

The two men put the car out of sight and carried the boy into the house through the kitchen. When the doctor had him situated on the table under the X-ray machine, he walked back to the kitchen and called through the screen door, "Spring!"

Within seconds the kitchen window of the house that backed up to the doctor's sang back, "She be there directly!"

Spring appeared within a minute; she was fifteen or twenty years younger than her boss and half his size. The nurse-housekeeper-office-manager-midwife-cook came across the backyard tying her apron. When she got to the room where the boy was, she stopped, put one fist on her hip, and pointed at the dog. "Git that hound outta my house!"

The dog was standing by the examining table focusing his sad, hound dog expression on the boy. When the woman spoke, he looked at her without changing his expression or location, and the boy's human guardian made his longest speech of the morning. "The boy's in bad shape, an' the dog knows it. The dog stays with the boy."

Spring was used to having her way with the easygoing medicine man, and she had the bluff on most of his patients; the man in the starched khakis gave no indication that he was one to back up. She sidestepped. "Is he the boy's dog?"

"I reckon he ain't decided that yet."

Spring went for the middle ground. "Humph. Well, keep him out from under my feet."

And the man gave it to her. "Sit against the wall, Dawg."

The dog's toenails clicked across the linoleum and he sat.

* * *

An hour later, the doctor—who by now had heard what happened, but not where—was washing a residue of white plaster off his hands and talking over his shoulder. "The arm couldn't've been broken in a better spot; it'll heal clean in about six weeks. He's got a concussion, but I think he'll be pretty much over it in a day or so. Keep him quiet. Keep water in him. An' stay close to him for a couple of days."

The man, more relaxed now that he'd heard the boy would be okay, said, "I'm obliged to you for takin' us in."

Carlson faced him while he dried his hands. "The doctorin' part was easy. You two got to disappear." He looked at the dog. "You three."

"I been thinkin' on that. It won't take 'em long to come lookin' here."

"Where'll they be comin' from?"

"Down to Moores Point."

The doctor's skin tingled, and something cool trickled down his back. The hand-drying slowed. "Cat Lake's right there south of Moores Point."

The old man moved closer to the table, resting his hand on the boy's good arm. "That's right."

Spring heard their words and stepped in from the kitchen. "You from down by Cat Lake?"

"I was."

The young woman looked at the man first, then let her gaze linger on the dog; the dog gazed back. Spring's eyes started to glisten; her lower lip trembled; she was already shaking her head in dismay. "They say Mr. Mose Washington down there don't go nowhere without no dog."

The man confirmed their suspicions without taking his eyes off the boy. "I guess they right, miss, 'cause I sho' don't."

Spring sagged against the doorjamb, and the tears came. "I can't believe this. An' look at how I been talkin' to you. My momma told me a thousand times my mouth was gonna embarrass us both, an' now look at what I done. She gonna kill me."

Every black person in the Mississippi Delta knew what Mose Washington's son had done at Cat Lake. In the years following the incident, most of the white folks who picked up the story secondhand wrote the events off to chance, and the eyewitness accounts were attributed to folklore. The black folks in the Delta, and the white folks who had witnessed what they called The War at Cat Lake, had no doubts about what had happened. They all knew that the boy had faced a demonic attack, and he would forever be a hero in the eyes of the people who knew the truth. Mose, because he was the boy's father—and because of a succession of extraordinary milestones in his own life—received his own measure of unsought adulation.

When the young woman started to weep, the dog left the boy in Mose's care; he came close to Spring and leaned against her knee. Mose smiled for the first time in several hours and shook his head at her plight.

The doctor, who rarely, if ever, got the upper hand on the lady he paid to boss him around, took the opportunity to assert himself. "I been tellin' you the same thing, an' you don't listen to me either. Why don't you fix us somethin' to eat, an' maybe we'll forgive you."

Spring recovered enough to straighten up and wipe her eyes with her apron. Her hand strayed to the dog's ears. "It ain't right for you to have to run from the law."

Mose's smile became more gentle. "Well, miss, the good Lord sometimes sees fit to let what seems right come up short against what is."

The men had eggs, sausage, grits, and "the best biscuits in Bolivar County" for breakfast. The dog wouldn't leave the boy, so Spring took his plate to him and came back to the table to fiddle with her coffee cup. She said, "What're you gonna do now, Mr. Washington?"

"We best be gettin' on down the road right soon. We needs to find a place to hide for a few days then head on out." He looked her straight in the eye. "An' my friends calls me Mose."

"Yes'r . . . Mose. Do you know where you gonna hide at?"

"No. I figure God will give us the answer."

She looked at the doctor, and the doctor nodded; God had already given Carlson the answer. "It just so happens I've got a little shotgun house set back in some woods near the Sunflower that would be just right for a man an' a boy an' a dog."

Spring was making circles on the table with her cup. "Mose?"

"Yes, ma'am."

"Could you take a minute an' go over an' see my momma?"

"I suppose so. We ain't in no bad rush."

"I 'preciate it, an' she'll be much obliged." She offered a half smile and confessed her motive, "An' maybe she won't kill me."

He stood on the back steps of the house and tapped on the door facing.

A small, slender lady came to stand behind the screen door and shade her eyes at him. She was about his age or older: light-skinned, blue-eyed, and beautiful. "Can I help you?"

"Well, I don't rightly know. I come over here 'cause yo' daughter say she'd like for me to meet you."

The lady looked over his shoulder at the doctor's house. "Did she now? Well, step in here, then, an' let's get acquainted."

Mose took off his hat and stepped into a small kitchen that spilled into a sitting area. The lady held out her hand. "I'm Belle Hodges."

Mose took the small hand. “Pleased to meet you. I’m Mose Washington.”

Mrs. Hodges glanced out her kitchen window at the doctor’s house then back to Mose. “From down at Cat Lake?”

“Yes, ma’am.”

Without releasing his hand she let her eyes close and lowered her head for a long moment; when she looked up, she had tears in her eyes. “It’s right fine of you to take time to come over here, Mr. Washington. I meet few enough people today who’re taking a stand for The Cause, an’ I reckon you’d fit in the class with those that do. An’ I reckon I owe that girl-child a three-layer cake.”

Mose was rarely embarrassed, but the woman’s words touched him. “Why, I just come ’cause she asked me to. She’s a fine young woman.”

The lady smiled. “That child’s a trial an’ a caution, an’ she’ll be the death o’ me soon enough. If I know her, she got herself in a pickle, an’ havin’ you come over here is supposed to get her off the hook.”

He had to smile with her.

“Well, now. Tell me what brings you to Mound Bayou.”

The telling took only a few minutes. When he finished, Belle Hodges said, “Well then, they’ll be comin’ here soon, so you’ll need to be on yo’ way. Before you go, though, let’s have a moment of prayer.” She took his hand again and led him to the sitting area. They knelt on a rug by the sofa.

She prayed first, and he followed. When he finished she said, “Lord God in Heaven, we have few enough who stand strong for Yo’ cause. Give this man wisdom, long life, an’ strength, an’ pass it to that boy in his care. Let that young man hear this man’s strong heart an’ Yo’s. Give us that he would become one who knows You an’ makes You known. We ask, Lord, that You charge Yo’ angels with the strong care of these men. Amen.”

Two bright beings stood over the praying couple. When the woman closed her prayer, they echoed her last word.

Mose and the boy and the dog left town thirty minutes later with enough food to last a wagonload of men three or four days. The doctor said he'd come out and check on them the next day.

The sun was in the middle of the sky, and Mrs. Sherman was in the back bedroom of a small house in Moores Point. It was not uncommon for the young boys around Moores Point to stay out all night camping, or hunting coons or frogs, or doing whatever boys do—but Tripper Sherman's staying gone all night without first calling his parents had never happened. Tripper's mother—her head and heart bowed—knelt by her bed and prayed for the protection and well-being of her only son. The God who heard Mrs. Hodges' prayer heard Mrs. Sherman's.

It was Saturday noon before the six young men in the woods of Eagle Nest Brake slipped their bonds. The white man who tied them up was long gone, along with the three black people; Ollie Bainbridge and Stan Dailey lay where they had fallen. The survivors set out for town on foot because someone had taken the distributor wires out of the trucks.

A large demon and a cluster of his lieutenants watched the boys approach the bridge. The smallest of the evil group asked, "Will we kill them, master?"

Fifteen years earlier the larger demon had orchestrated the actions of the evil angels in The War at Cat Lake. He had been stymied in his efforts to kill the Parker girl but had since taken part in the destruction of eight other humans near the lake. The quiet black man and his wife, assisted by the Host of Heaven, had stood in his way more than once, but they were gone. The events of the night had not gone his way, but he wasn't through yet. He snarled at his minions, "Watch and learn."

Tripper was moving slower than the others, in small part because his chest and midriff were stiff and tender, but mostly because of the weighted dread that threatened to drive him to his knees—he was going to have to tell his parents what happened. Frank McClellan walked beside him at the rear of the group. "I'm sorry about this, Tripper. I never should've hooked us up with Bainbridge."

Tripper took his time speaking because it hurt to breathe deeply, and words wouldn't fix what he had done. "I made my own choices. They were bad ones."

"What're you gonna do when we get home?"

"What needs doin'. I'm gonna tell the sheriff what happened. An' I'm gonna take whatever they dish out."

"It could get tough."

Tripper didn't have to search for words. "Not as tough . . . as what we let happen to that lady an' her son."

"We didn't hit her, Tripper."

"Yeah." Tripper spit into the gravel in an effort to get the taste out of his mouth. "An' we didn't stop it."

"You did all you could."

For a boy who was short of fifteen, Tripper had some definite beliefs about the responsibilities and privileges associated with being a man. He had to spit again. "Not if I ain't dead, I didn't."

The others in the group had spoken no more than a couple of words.

They were near the middle of the Cat Lake bridge when Farrell Whitacher slowed his pace. He came to a stop by an old ladder and turned on the group, "We need to get our story straight before we go farther."

Tripper kept walking. "I've got my story straight, Farrell. I stood by an' watched while a couple of no-good men beat an innocent woman an' her boy near to death. She an' that little kid are probably dead."

Whitacher's voice was raspy. "What happened here last night may have been unjust, Tripper, but that does not mean we deserve to go to prison."

Whitacher seemed aloof; the words coming out of his mouth were strained, and every boy in the group noted that the Delta farmboy's choice of words sounded too much like an English teacher's.

Tripper stopped and faced Bainbridge's sidekick. A cool breeze off the lake didn't slow the sweat creeping from Whitacher's hairline.

"Are you okay, Farrell?"

Whitacher's voice dropped half an octave; his voice was hoarse now. "Do not change the subject, Sherman. I said we need to get our story straight, because I do not intend to receive a prison sentence for something that idiot Bainbridge did."

Four boys stood confused; trying to figure out why a kid they had known all their lives didn't sound like himself. They looked first at Whitacher, then at each other, then all eyes turned on Tripper.

Tripper's face was bruised and cut; one eye was swollen shut. He stepped closer to Whitacher and squinted at him through his good eye; the expression on the older boy's face reminded Tripper of what he had seen in Bainbridge.

Tripper nodded as if he understood something. He winced when he took a deep breath and drew closer still—planning and praying. For the first time since they had gotten in the trucks to follow Bainbridge, it all made sense. *Lord, after what happened last night I got no right to ask, but would You look out for me while I try to handle this?* He was within a step of Whitacher; the other boys were quiet, watching without comprehending.

When Tripper got his feet set, he gave Whitacher the test: "I think my Lord Jesus Christ would have me tell the truth."

The older boy's body seemed to swell as he drew in a long breath. A string of unintelligible words—a garbled, guttural language that was ancient before the Noahic flood—erupted from a distorted caricature of Whitacher's face. Everyone but Tripper scrambled to the far side of the bridge.

Tripper had made himself vulnerable by standing too close to the newest monster, and the evil sounds were still on the bridge when Whitacher made a clawing grab for his throat. Tripper made his move. He let his knees break—managing to duck inside the attempt to seize him—and got his arms around Whitacher's legs. When he came out of his squat, he brought Whitacher up with him and dumped him over the bridge railing. There was a muffled thump, but no splash.

Buster Newsome came near and looked over the railing. "Good gosh, y'all! Farrell went crazy right there in front of us."

Whitacher was lying on an old wooden float at the bottom of the ladder; one of his legs was twisted under him. Tripper—his chest heaving and his knees trembling—joined the younger Newsome at the rail. "He's got a demon in 'im . . . like Bainbridge did. Hearin' the name of Jesus set 'im off."

"A demon?" Newsome watched the thing on the float trying to twist onto its stomach. "Are you kiddin'?"

Whitacher got his hands under him and snarled at the air around him while he tried to push himself up.

Newsome saw it first. "Omigosh, that's blood comin' out of his eyes."

Tripper nodded. "That's one of those things like what killed Mose Junior Washington—an' at least one of 'em got into Bainbridge."

"What're we gonna do now?"

"Nothin' we can do, 'cept run for it."

"Can't we fight it or somethin'?" Newsome didn't sound like he really wanted to try.

"They're spirits, Buster. Can't anything hold out against 'em 'cept for prayer an' the Holy Spirit, or maybe angels."

"Aren't you a Christian? Can't you pray or somethin'?"

"Daddy says they used to be angels, an' they're powerful. I think I'm gonna wait till I've got a little more prayer time under my belt." Tripper made himself turn away from the railing. "I don't know about you boys, but I'm leavin' 'fore that thing gets back up here."

Buster didn't have all the convincing he needed. "You reckon he can climb that ladder? His leg looks bad broke."

Tripper, already steps away and moving, spoke over his shoulder. "I ain't stayin' to speculate, hoss. I ain't the fastest man in the county, but I'm hopin' I can outrun a feller with a broke leg." He'd said enough. "An' I can practice prayin' while I'm gettin' a head start."

When Tripper started jogging, McClellan was at his elbow.

Buster Newsome took another look over the railing. The thing on the float was no longer Farrell Whitacher, and whatever the boy had become was dragging itself to the ladder. Buster left the railing and caught up with the two who were making the smart move. He yelled at his brother, "C'mon, Doug. We need to get some distance on that thing."

The folks in the Delta weren't known for talking fast, but they didn't think slow. Both of the remaining boys took a quick look at the clawlike hands that pulled Whitacher's body across the boards of the old float. It dragged itself to the foot of the ladder and fastened its hands around the lower rungs. Doug Newsome and Jerry Nations looked around and found themselves alone on the bridge. They left the railing and sprinted to catch up with the leaders.

They looked back at the bridge when they got past the Parker gin. Nothing.

* * *

A bright being stood alone at a distance and watched the activities of the demons. He said, "Come."

A taller angel appeared at his side, his sword in his hand. "My Leader."

The first angel pointed his sword at the float. "Go there and stand against these evil ones. The Father would have the world know that He has sent us on behalf of those who have embraced the freedom offered by His Son's name."

The second angel acknowledged the order. "For Him who sits on the throne, and for the Lamb."

The boys rounded the curve at Gilmer's Grove, jogging north toward Moores Point and watching over their shoulders. They were minutes into their journey and feeling better about their escape when they heard the first sound—*foomp!* A hollow resonance, partially muffled by the cypress trees around the lake, came from the direction of the float. The startled joggers looked back, but they were alone on the road. *Foomp!* The first faint concussion was followed by a slightly softer copy. *Foomp!* Eerie and earnest. *Foomp!* They were coming at evenly spaced intervals, as if from a slack-sided bass drum.

Buster Newsome took another look over his shoulder and said, "Uh, Tripper . . . will your prayers still work if you do 'em out loud?"

Foomp! The concussions continued, growing gentler, continuing to fade as the boys jogged toward town.

The frightened group pulled in close to their new leader and picked up the pace. Tripper Sherman prayed the way his momma and daddy prayed, asking in the strong name of Jesus Christ for God's protection. His prayers were accompanied by the receding sounds of a lone percussionist playing his own rendition of a funeral dirge.

* * *

An hour or so later, two Allen County deputy sheriff cars, one from the Mississippi Highway Patrol, the county coroner's station wagon, and an ambulance were evenly scattered between Eagle Nest Brake and the Cat Lake bridge. The policeman from Inverness and the one from Moores Point made the mistake of coming out to help contribute more sightseers. Ghastly is not a strong enough word to describe the scene that confronted the small crowd.

CHAPTER SIX

Sheriff William Wallace Hollinsworth languished in the chair behind his desk. The humidity was overwhelming the worn-out window unit in his office, and his only hope for survival rested in the arms of an antique ceiling fan. During his ten-year tenure as sheriff, Hollinsworth had gained an average of four pounds a year; he was overweight, overworked, and over-stressed. A shooting on Friday evening had robbed him of Friday night, and he had just multiplied his need for sleep by wolfing down one-too-many chiliburgers at the Dairy Freeze. His walrus mustache was weeping sweat and his eyelids were drooping when he leaned forward to put out his cigarette and heard footsteps in the hallway. A grey uniform was making its way toward his office. He didn't want to be bothered, but the door to his office was wide open and the uniform filled it. It was five after two on Saturday afternoon.

Corporal Kenneth Dixon, Mississippi Highway Safety Patrol, said, "Afternoon, Dubby."

"I'm busy," said the sheriff.

Hollinsworth started in law enforcement as a state trooper, and he and Dixon once worked the Indianola district out of the highway patrol's Greenwood office. Hollinsworth left the state job back in '50 to pursue the more lucrative role of Allen County sheriff; Dixon was content where he was. The two lawmen were well acquainted, but they weren't friends.

"I think you've got some bad news coming."

"I don't want any news—good or bad—till I've had a nap." The sheriff took off his reading glasses, propped his feet on his desk, and tilted his chair back to show that he didn't want any company either.

Dixon was trying to do Hollinsworth a favor. "It's about the killings out at Cat Lake."

Hollinsworth already knew that a handful of local white boys had staggered into Moores Point an hour earlier, claiming that some folks had been killed out south of the town. He didn't have the details yet, but apparently the boys were spreading the story that some kind of evil spirit did the killing. He growled at the trooper without bothering to open his eyes. "I was up most of the night 'cause of a shootin' scrape out at Heathman. Havin' to listen to some Halloween story about a devil runnin' loose out in the Parkers' woods comes second to me gettin' some sleep."

Dixon carried a lot less weight than the sheriff, and on a longer frame; he didn't move. "I came by the Parker place on the way over here."

The sheriff gave up. He sighed audibly, tilted his chair upright, and rubbed his eyes. "Yeah? You see any goblins?"

The taller man propped himself against the door frame. "That was three white boys that ended up dead out there at Cat Lake. The five who walked into Moores Point are pretty shook up."

"That right?" Hollinsworth processed the information and was unimpressed with what he'd heard so far. The sheriff was only mildly interested in the dead folks' skin color; when it came right down to it, a dead person's race rarely contributed anything of significance to the goings-on in Mississippi. The people who got themselves murdered in the Delta counties were mostly black folks or pieces of "po' white trash." More often than not, the well-to-do folks who occasionally killed each other turned out to be black or white trash wearing expensive clothes. Whatever the perceived class of the dead folks, the deceased were invariably trying to do the same deed to whoever sent them to their eternal reward.

"Yep. And a black woman. A fisherman found a late model car in Macon Lake this morning—it's probably tied in. We'll run the plates after we bring it up." Dixon knew Hollinsworth had a history with Congressman Halbert Bainbridge. "One of the dead boys is a college kid from out of state."

"A black woman and an out-of-state kid? Well, that's news." The sheriff pulled out his cigarettes and looked up to hear what else Dixon had to say.

"Seems like the out-of-state boy was from over in the Smokies . . . last name of Bainbridge."

"Aw, shoot." It didn't take a meteorologist to see the signs of approaching bad weather. Hollinsworth threw the cigarette pack at his telephone and motioned with his lighter. "Step in here an' shut the door."

Dixon pushed himself off the door frame and closed the door.

Some memory about Dixon nagged at the sheriff; something that used to get under his skin when they were both working for the state. "Sit."

Dixon backed into a chair.

The man behind the desk got his cigarette going while his visitor settled in the chair. "Don't tell me the dead college boy is kin to that congressman."

Dixon didn't smile. "Okay. I won't tell you he's the good congressman's middle boy."

The sheriff of Allen County had been raised by Bible-believing parents and held to a fairly firm standard regarding profanity; he said it created more problems than it solved. On those rare occasions when his men cursed in his presence, he would remind them, without getting preachy, of his stance. When the highway patrolman told Hollinsworth who the boy was, the high sheriff created more problems than he solved for thirty seconds without repeating himself. When he recovered he asked, "You told Thompson yet?" Frank Thompson was the lieutenant in charge of the highway patrol substation over in Greenwood.

Dixon nodded. "He was getting primed for us to take jurisdiction at first . . . wanted to use that new evidence kit we got." He had to smile. "When he found out who the boy was, he decided we didn't want to be messin' in the business of the county mounties."

"Mmm. He was due to make a good decision."

"Could be."

Hollinsworth pulled a bottle of antacid tablets out of his desk and shook three or four into his palm. "What about the FBI?" He popped the tablets into his mouth and chased them with a gulp of day-old coffee.

"Nothing yet. But it won't be long. I expect that old man in Washington will have them snooping around here before supper."

Hollinsworth nodded and mumbled a couple of half-hearted problem-causers. FBI men all talked like they came from some place up north, and as far as he was concerned, the federal government's unwelcome meddling in Mississippi's business had started a century back and hadn't let up.

Dixon stayed quiet while Hollinsworth thought through his options. It was obvious that the FBI would be the heavyweight in any clash over jurisdiction, but Hollinsworth wasn't known for giving in to agencies or people just because they were more powerful than he was. In fact, it seemed as if he stepped up his resistance in direct proportion to the size of the intervening entities.

While he weighed the implications of having another son of Halbert Bainbridge's killed in his county it passed through

Hollinsworth's mind that he might be having a nightmare; he hoped so. Just over a year earlier, the congressman's youngest son had been murdered over east of Cat Lake. On that occasion, Hollinsworth made a courtesy telephone call to Congressman Bainbridge to break the news to him that his boy and the boy's cousin had apparently killed each other out on the Parkers' place. Halbert Bainbridge immediately launched a wide-ranging tirade of profanity against the Parkers, the sheriff, and the whole state of Mississippi. In the weeks following the killings, the sheriff—who originally assumed that his gesture of sympathy might pay off in political capital—got a thousand and one angry phone calls from various politicians.

"What are the odds of a U.S. congressman losin' two sons in homicides?" he mused.

"Pretty good if they're as worthless as their old man."

"And both on the Parker place?"

"That lengthens the odds a tad," said Dixon.

"You got an opinion?"

"Yep, but you won't like it."

"Well?"

"Like the kids said, there're demons involved."

In that moment the sheriff remembered why he and Dixon never quite hit it off—Dixon was one of those Bible thumpers. He exhaled smoke from his last drag off the cigarette, spit a shred of tobacco off his tongue, and leaned forward to crush the cigarette out in his ashtray. When he finished stabbing the ashtray, he splayed his fingers and pushed them through his hair and down to massage the back of his neck, getting his emotions harnessed. When he finished rubbing his neck, he hoisted himself out of his chair and walked over to stand in front of the window unit. "Demons," he sighed.

Dixon waited. The trooper had rehearsed this exchange on the ride from Cat Lake to Indianola; so far the sheriff had spoken his part according to the script. The ridicule would start shortly.

Hollinsworth turned to face him. "How come you went into police work, Dixon?"

The patrolman didn't have to react; he'd had this conversation with one person or another every month for the last ten years. "Go ahead and make your point, Dubby."

"Why would a Christian want to be a lawman?"

"You've caught my act, Dubby. Did I ever let the law down?"

Hollinsworth turned back to the airconditioner without answering; knowing that Dixon was one of the best lawmen he had ever worked with made the room hotter. He finally said, "I'm gonna ride out to the Parker place; you comin'?"

"I'll be right behind you. I'm going by the Dairy Freeze to pick up a couple of hamburgers." Dixon was glad he had postponed his dinner break till after he made his first stop at Cat Lake. "Dubby."

"What?"

"I've never seen anything in a car wreck as bad as what's out at that bridge."

"Right." Hollinsworth was ten years older than Dixon and a veteran of the war in Europe; he'd seen it all.

When Dixon got back out to Cat Lake, the air was hot, humid, and dead still. He parked by an empty ambulance and walked to where the sheriff and the county coroner were waiting in the center of the bridge. Hollinsworth was leaning on the bridge railing, his back to the float; his hat was off, and he was mopping the band with a sweaty handkerchief. The coroner, a fifty-year-old physician from Indianola, stood next to the sheriff, his hands deep in his pockets, staring down at the float; smoke curled into the air from the latest in a long line of cheap cigars. The men weren't bothering to talk. A single crow and the thin buzz generated by a swarm of flies below the bridge provided the only sounds.

When Dixon got closer, the doctor took out the cigar and nodded at him. " 'Lo, Kenny."

Dixon's nose told him that in his absence the sun had started to speed the decomposition of what was on the float. "Afternoon, Doc."

The doctor said he smoked the two-for-a-nickel brand because their smell was stronger than some of his customers. He stuck the cigar back in its place and peered through the smoke at Dixon. "Dubby says you've already been out here."

Dixon stood so that his eyes couldn't stray below the edge of the bridge; he'd seen all he needed to see of what was down there. "Uh-huh. I left here about an hour ago."

The doctor went back to his long-distance study of the thing on the float. He was rocking back and forth on the balls of his feet, oblivious to the putrid smoke cloud that was making him squint at the body. "Whaddayah think happened?"

"He did it to himself."

The sheriff's body suffered a small convulsion.

Eleven men had seen the body down on the float; the three standing on the bridge were the only ones who hadn't thrown up—yet. The other eight men were making themselves busy somewhere else.

The doctor continued to stare at the carnage on the float; smoke trailed the tip of the cigar as he rocked and nodded his head. "Yep, that is *precisely* what he did."

The doctor kept his attention on what was left of Farrell Whitacher. Dixon had to wait less than ten seconds for the question. "Either one of y'all wanta speculate on how a man could do that to himself?"

When Hollinsworth gave no indication that he heard the question, Dixon nodded. "The boy was possessed by a demonic being; the body was too broken up to make it up the ladder, so the demon used what he had available to destroy it." He paused then added, "The demon wanted us to know what happened."

Hollinsworth heard the words and couldn't block the pictures his mind painted of what the boy had done to himself; he pushed away from the railing and walked toward the east end of the bridge. He almost made it to the gravel road before he threw up.

The doctor took little notice of Hollinsworth's actions; he'd had occasion to do the same thing himself, and his mind was otherwise occupied. He stood with his hands steepled in front of his face, fingertips repeatedly touching against each other, offering silent applause for his thoughts. He kept coming back to the fact that he was an open-minded man; his job required it. Now, barring the presence of some powerful drug, he was being forced to go outside conventional precepts and agree with Dixon. The story about the War at Cat Lake was familiar to him and had been told to him by trustworthy men. If what he was looking at was the work of some kind of spirit being, his thinking needed some realignment, and he needed to talk to someone who knew about demons.

The sheriff spit into the lake two or three times before he walked back to his post near Dixon.

"Well," the doctor said, "we may as well bring up what's left. I'll find Spunk and get 'im started."

Hollinsworth was lighting a cigarette, shaking his head. "Not yet. I'm gonna let the FBI handle it."

The doctor was startled. "Just like that?"

"Just like that." Hollinsworth looked at Dixon. "You can get 'em up here faster than I can."

Dixon lifted a hand in acknowledgment and walked to his car. He was back in less than five minutes. "Thompson's already called them. They'll be here in about an hour."

Highway 49 headed straight north out of Jackson and split at Yazoo City. One branch, 49 West, turned left to wander up through Yazoo City, Belzoni, Indianola, and twenty smaller towns; 49 East continued straight through Greenwood, then angled west to rejoin its twin. The two became one again when they met south of Clarksdale.

On their ride up 49, Fuller drove and lectured. The agents turned left at the split, and were immediately in Yazoo City. They passed through the east side of town, along the full length of Broadway Hill, passing stately, turn-of-the-century homes, postured on broad, lush lawns.

For years the enforcement of federal laws for the northern half of Mississippi fell under the purview of the Memphis field office of the Federal Bureau of Investigation. However, so that the citizens of Mississippi wouldn't feel neglected, the FBI converted its satellite operation in Jackson into a two-agent field office; the responsibility for supervising that vast operation rested precariously on the narrow shoulders of Special-Agent-in-Charge Bertrand B. Fuller Jr. Special Agent Jeff Wagner, one month out of the Academy and already questioning the worth of an organization that would employ Fuller, tried to stay awake.

"The Mississippi Delta starts at the bottom of this hill, Wagner. It's the most abrupt and extreme sociological change you'll ever encounter—a hundred thousand rednecks scattered around a floor-flat cotton field a hundred and fifty miles long and sixty miles wide, and they all know each other. They're suspicious of anyone who was born outside the Delta; they openly, and forever, distrust anyone from the North; and those of us who work for the federal government come in one notch above registered Communists."

"So, how do we get anything done?"

"We probably won't. We'll be up here on and off for a week, and I doubt that we'll get anyone to give us directions to the men's room."

"Then we're wasting our time?"

"Uncle Sam's time, Wagner, Uncle Sam's time." Fuller was trying to cultivate a senatorial tone and repeating himself helped him practice. "And besides, the best cooks in the world live here . . . if you like fried food, that is."

"I like fried food."

"Good, because the only thing they don't fry is dinner rolls and watermelon."

The red light in the middle of town caught them, and Wagner let his gaze linger on a cluster of black men gathered by a telephone pole on the corner. An old man in the group made eye contact and Wagner nodded. The man took his hat off and nodded back. The light changed.

"What about the black people?" Wagner asked.

"What about them?"

"Well, you said there were a whole bunch of rednecks that all know each other. What about the black people?"

"The Delta black people fall into two categories, Wagner. Field hands and cooks."

"That's pretty narrow."

"Always keep it simple, Wagner, always keep it simple. Most of the black people will yield to any white person that comes near them—it's the field-hand mentality. The cooks don't always yield."

"The cooks? Black cooks?" Sometimes Fuller didn't make sense.

"Uh-huh. Male *and* female—some assumed responsibility because they work in the house—or maybe some elevation in class. Maybe because they have access to sharp knives. Who knows."

"Strange." *And who cares?*

"Plus, the women cooks are the ones who think they own any children in the house. You'd be better off trying to take a cub away from a grizzly than to cross a black cook that's been given the responsibility of caring for white children."

Wagner laughed at the warning. "That's why I brought my gun."

"Humph." Younger agents possessed little understanding of the need for proper decorum.

They crossed the railroad tracks at the bottom of the hill and drove past a car-cluttered service station. On the west side of town, Broadway Street became a straight, flat corridor enclosed by unpainted shotgun houses crowding up to the roadside ditches. Half-naked black children stood on the porches and watched the car pass. They were in the Mississippi Delta.

Wagner's first observation was that West Texas was not flat.

Fuller said, "Get ready to experience what the South was like when the Civil War ended." He didn't smile.

Fuller was the FBI's youngest SAIC, and he didn't always try to hide that he intended to go all the way to the top. He gave no discount to the fact that two hundred other agents gladly passed on the role of SAIC in Jackson because they had no desire to office out of a broom closet in a state where they were barely tolerated.

Fuller talked and Wagner watched water-filled ditches go by. Per Thompson's directions, they left the highway at Inverness and took a shortcut through the back roads to Cat Lake.

Hollinsworth and Dixon spent the intervening hour walking over to recheck the area in Eagle Nest Brake where the bodies of Bainbridge and Dailey were still lying on the road. They got back to the bridge in time to watch a nondescript sedan park by the highway patrol car. The driver got out and put on a suit coat that matched the car; the passenger was comfortable in shirtsleeves with the cuffs turned up.

Hollinsworth propped his ample rump on the bridge railing and waited for the government men to come to him; Dixon met them halfway. The older man—the driver—held out the flip wallet with his badge and ID. "I'm Bert Fuller, SAIC for Jackson. This is Agent Jeff Wagner." The guy behind Fuller was brand new and looked it.

"Kenneth Dixon." Dixon shook hands with Fuller and pointed at his companions. "That's Sheriff Hollinsworth there, and that's Doctor Watson."

Fuller approached the sheriff, and Hollinsworth took the agent's extended hand. "Pleased to meet you, Fuller. Where you from?"

Fuller was from the north side of Baltimore. "Born and raised in the South, Sheriff. This is Agent Wagner."

"Howdy, Sheriff." Wagner's height was about average for a former offensive end at Texas A&M.

During the past four years the sheriff had gained his allotted sixteen pounds. During Wagner's three years of law school, six months of walking around Europe, and four months at the FBI Academy the former football player had shed twenty-five. Wagner was as amiable as a favorite uncle and hard as a horse's hoof. He wrapped his hand around the Mississippi sheriff's and drawled, "New York City." Dixon overheard him and smiled.

Fuller hadn't missed a Saturday afternoon of golf and driven a hundred miles into the previous century to make friends. "Well, Thompson said you had four bodies. Are they close by?"

The float wasn't visible from where the FBI men stood; Hollinsworth and Dixon stayed where they were and let the FBI boys follow the beckoning of Watson's cigar. When Fuller and Wagner saw what was on the float, Fuller recoiled and turned pale.

Wagner held his tie against his chest and leaned over the railing for a closer look. "Son!" he exclaimed.

The veteran officers stood silent while the younger agent studied the stationary raft for a full minute—making sure. Wagner looked at Watson, then back at the body. "That guy did that to himself."

Watson exhaled. "I b'lieve you're right."

Fuller stepped farther away; Wagner was still leaning over the railing. "Has anybody come up with a good 'Why'?"

Watson played with his cigar and hedged, "Not yet. You got any ideas?"

Wagner straightened and looked at his boss. Fuller had his handkerchief over his mouth; he waved it at Wagner to answer. "There're some powerful drugs showing up on the West Coast and in New York, but I can't imagine having them surface in this part of the country yet. But how . . ." His voice trailed off and he turned away from the float. "What have you guys come up with?"

The doctor said, "Well, of what's been speculated so far, I think I like the drugs answer the best."

Fuller had been away from the spotlight too long; he risked trying to talk without throwing up. "How long will it take to do toxicology?"

"That'll be up to the boys in Jackson," Watson answered. "If I had to guess, I'd say they'll have most of what we need by late tomorrow morning. I'll go down there an' watch over their shoulders, an' I'll have 'em send samples of everything to your lab."

"Fine." Fuller backed another step. "If there's no more we can do here, why don't we go look at the other bodies."

Dixon led off. "Follow me."

Fuller took two steps and froze. "Are they like this?"

"Nope," Dixon kept walking. "Just plain dead people."

The agents were taken first to look at the woman's body then to the road to see Bainbridge and Dailey. The black woman apparently died from being beaten. The two white men were shot between the eyes at close range with a large-caliber weapon, probably the handgun found by the road. Both FBI men got to hear about the way the boys were tied up: the bindings were put in place by a man who wanted to keep the kids securely bound without having one of them lose a hand to poor circulation. Dixon had captured the whole picture in four words; there was nothing out of the ordinary about the other three bodies.

Wagner thumbed through his notes on what the five surviving boys had told the local investigators and asked, "Who moved the bodies?"

Hollinsworth, whose deputies were responsible for protecting the crime scene, bristled. "Nobody's moved anything."

"The witnesses said Dailey landed on top of Bainbridge." He pointed. "Their bodies are six feet apart."

The sheriff shrugged. "A million possibilities. It was dark . . . the kids were scared . . . Mose or the white man moved 'em . . . you name it."

Fuller wasn't interested in how the bodies were positioned. He satisfied himself that one of them was definitely Oliver Wendell Bainbridge, while Hollinsworth gave him some insight on dealing with the boy's father. The senior agent made a mental note to let someone at FBI headquarters be responsible for contacting Congressman Bainbridge.

Whitier Priest was U.S. Congressman Halbert D. Bainbridge's chief of staff only because his father was one of Bainbridge's major contributors. By the time he had been on the job a week, Priest knew that Bainbridge was the most uncouth, unscrupulous, and irreverent man with whom he'd ever been associated. That a man of Bainbridge's ilk could rise to such a position of prominence didn't upset the younger man; it encouraged him. Late on Saturday afternoon, the chief of staff strode through the door of Bainbridge's private office without knocking and started to pace and frown while Bainbridge attempted to carry on a phone conversation.

Bainbridge, who spent his waking hours cycling through varied levels of anger, watched Priest pretend to be authoritative and let his mood darken; he hated Priest *and* his pompous father. He covered up the phone's mouthpiece, called Priest a foul name, and snarled, "Sit down, or get out."

Priest did neither. "I need to talk."

Bainbridge told the phone, "I'll see you tonight, sweetie," and hung up. "This better be important."

"Sir, Ollie's dead." Getting to tell Bainbridge that one of his good-for-nothing sons was dead was good; telling him how the fool died was going to be far better.

Bainbridge didn't change expression. "My son Ollie?"

Priest was saving part of his news. "Yes, sir."

"What happened?"

"He was murdered in Mississippi, Congressman." Priest hesitated then lowered his voice to convey the best part of his news. "Apparently by a black man."

Bainbridge was out of his chair and bearing down on Priest before the man could react. "A what? My son was killed by a ni—?"

Bainbridge regained control of himself before he said the word that could cost him votes; he never knew what kind of fool might be listening in his outer office. He stopped for an instant to stare into space then turned and grabbed a handful of Priest's tie; there was a follow-on issue that was more important than whether or not his son had been killed or who had killed him. "Is his killer dead?"

"They haven't caught them yet, sir. The—"

"Them? Them who? What happened?" Flecks of Bainbridge's spittle sprinkled Priest's face.

Priest had hoped for a strong reaction to his message; now he was trying to anticipate how much anger the congressman might inflict on the messenger. He kept his voice even and inched away from his boss as he related the sketchy details he'd been given. When he mentioned that Ollie was killed on the Parker place, a thoroughly enraged Bainbridge grabbed a leaded-crystal ashtray off his desk and hurled it at him. Priest sidestepped, and the missile went through the glass front of a two-hundred-year-old bookcase. Bainbridge looked at the wreckage and screamed—he couldn't decide who he hated more, the Parkers or his chief of staff, so he launched a cursing tirade against both. He was almost out of breath, his face purple, when a thought came to him that overrode his anger. "Does my wife know?"

"Not yet, sir. I came straight to you." Priest retreated to a point where he could use the office door for a shield if the old fool got totally out of control.

"Get out."

"Yes, sir." Priest managed to get out of the room without laughing in his boss's face.

A recovering Bainbridge sat down at his desk and pulled the phone close. Another one of their imbecilic sons had managed to get himself killed, and Bainbridge was going to get to break the news to the person he despised more than anyone else in the world. He closed his eyes while he formulated the words he would use. Estelle Bainbridge was the only person in the world who hated the black race more than he did; the anticipation of how she would respond to his news was coursing through him like the effects of a strong narcotic. Before picking up the phone, he took the time he needed to fully savor her expected reaction.

The FBI wasn't officially on the case yet, and Fuller wanted to sleep in his own bed. At five o'clock, the SAIC said, "Well, gentlemen, I guess that does it for today. We'll be back up here tomorrow afternoon. Can we meet at the county courthouse?"

Hollinsworth was resigned to having the Feds under his feet for at least a week, including Sundays. "Sure. How about two o'clock?"

Fuller looked at the other men; everyone nodded.

"Excellent. See you then."

* * *

When the sun disappeared, the FBI was on its way back to Jackson; the bodies and Watson were a half hour behind them—on their way to the state medical examiner. The local lawmen had scattered.

"Hi, honey."

Mabel Hollinsworth's silent husband passed her puckered lips on his way to the hall closet to put up his pistol rig. While he was there he got out the bottle.

She met him on his way back to the kitchen and managed to kiss an unresponsive cheek. "Are you all right?"

Hollinsworth walked past her, filled a water glass level-full out of the bottle, and walked into the den without flipping on the lights; she followed. He plopped down in front of the television set and put his glass on the table at his elbow, using his dead mother's Bible for a coaster.

His wife watched him and his whiskey while she thought her own thoughts. The man didn't really like to drink. He stayed drunk for a week when he lost his brother in Korea; otherwise, he took a teaspoon-size sip at every New Year's party to show people he wasn't stuffy. He kept the whiskey on hand for visitors.

"Sugar, you want me to turn on the TV?"

Hollinsworth replied by reaching down and pulling off his boots.

She perched on the edge of her chair long enough to say, "I'm fixin' to go over to Momma's for a while, baby. She's wasn't feelin' too good this afternoon."

He didn't move.

She walked to the kitchen, considered the back of his head, and thought, *This might take a little longer than usual.* She faked a lilt in her voice and spoke to his back. "If I'm not home for supper, there's chicken salad in the refrigerator, or you can eat down at the Freeze. Okay?"

Nothing.

She stood by the kitchen phone and turned the dial a few times without picking up the receiver. She muttered at the phone for a minute then walked back to the den. "I just talked to Momma, baby. If I have to, I might just stay the night at her house."

If he heard her shut the back door neither of them knew it.

On Sunday morning, Mabel Hollinsworth's miraculously recovered mother filled her up with eggs, sausage, and half a waffle, then sent her home to check on her husband and get dressed for church. She tiptoed through their back door at eight o'clock and found him cracking eggs into a mixing bowl. He offered a tired smile. "Hi, honey. You hungry?"

He had cooked breakfast for her once, in the first week of their marriage—it was a disaster.

She made a noncommittal sound and stepped past him so that she could see into the den. The glass of whiskey was still full, and his mother's Bible was open on the coffee table. She smiled at him and hugged his arm. "I'm starved."

In prison, when a man's sleeping, he calls it "doin' fast time." The injured boy slept all day Saturday and through the night. Mose was sitting on the porch swing, reading his Bible, when the boy came out of the cabin. It was a cool Sunday morning; Eagle Nest Brake was fifty miles to the south, thirty fast hours in a deepening past. "How you feelin', son?"

"Kind of dizzy." The boy chose the chair next to the swing and took his time getting settled. He slumped there, his good hand strayed to the dog stationed at his knee, the other arm was bound in a cast from his knuckles to his upper arm. He didn't ask why he was in a strange cabin surrounded on three sides by a forest of huge trees.

"The doctor said you'd get over that soon enough. Can I get you somethin' to eat?"

The porch faced out over a slow-moving river. The man in the swing looked vaguely familiar, and not so much harmless as trustworthy. "No, sir, thank you." A too sweet smell came up from the riverbank. "I guess I'm a little sick to my stomach." He didn't need to ask about the cast on his arm; he remembered the man with the ax handle. He ran his hand over the red dog's slick coat and waited for the man to mention his mom, but the man seemed content to just swing gently and watch the river.

The boy didn't want to ask the question because he knew he didn't want to hear the answer, but when the man persisted in his silence, the boy finally spoke, hoping he was wrong. "Where's my mom?"

The swing stopped. The man looked off in the distance for a moment, then turned steadfast eyes on the boy. "The last thing she ever said was to tell you that she an' yo' daddy would be waitin' for you in Heaven."

The boy took the news calmly. "I knew she was dead, or she'd have been here when I woke up."

"Yes, nothin' else could've stopped her. She was that kind of a woman."

"Did you help her?"

"Not much, son. There was little enough we could do."

"I mean, did you help get her away from those white men?"

"I helped a little." Mose made a circling motion that took in the boy. "All of us did. They was a white man come out of the woods that done a lot to stop it."

The boy remembered the ghost. "I thought he was a ghost."

"Mm-hmm," the man nodded. "Angel is more like it."

The boy busied himself with the dog for a while before he asked, "Did you take her to the hospital?"

"I'm 'fraid not. There wasn't nothin' could be done to save her, son. She died right after the shootin'."

"The shooting? What shooting?"

That the boy might not remember the shooting had not occurred to Mose. "The two mens that hurt yo' momma, they was shot."

The boy ran his fingertips over the new cast. "That man that broke my arm. Was he one of the ones who got shot?"

Mose nodded. "He was."

The only way to know for sure was to ask. "Is he dead?"

"He is."

It was the first good thing the boy had heard. "I've never seen a man that was crazy before. He was crazy."

Mose nodded again but stayed silent; the boy might not understand about demons.

The dog nudged the boy's good hand; the boy looked down and rested his hand on the dog's head. "What's his name?"

"I jes' calls him Dawg."

"My name's Bill."

"Well, my name don't matter none 'cause we might have to change it anyways. I been thinkin' maybe you can call me Poppa till we comes up with somethin' better."

"Yes, sir." Bill didn't seem interested.

Mose got up and went into the house, he came back with a small paper sack. "These here is a few things from yo' momma's purse, an' the box has yo' daddy's watch in it. I got some of yo' clothes an' things in another sack."

Bill looked at the pictures from his mother's purse then picked up the box and opened it. "Mom gave my dad this watch for their anniversary; my dad told me it would be mine when I finished college. He took it and had something written on the back for me, but the jewelry man messed it up a little."

"Well, it looks mighty fine."

"I guess."

"What happened to yo' daddy?"

The boy ran his thumb over the watch crystal. "He died right before Christmas. He's buried at a place called Tuskegee."

"Well, if it makes you feel better, you can wear the watch till we gets ready to get back on the road."

"Maybe I'll put it on after a while." He handed the watch to Mose, and a tear ran to the tip of his nose and fell free. He turned back to the hound. "I guess I never had a dog before."

Mose didn't smile. "Every man ought to have a dog."

"Yes, sir." The boy nodded slowly, watching his good hand move over the slick red coat. He took a breath. "Did you have a funeral for her?"

"We did, son. It wasn't a big funeral, but it was special."

The boy waited a full minute before he asked, "Did you ever see an angel?"

Mose knew what was coming. "No, but I know they're here."

"How can you know if you can't see them?"

" 'Cause God tells me so in the Book."

Another tear fell. "If angels are here, why didn't God send them to help me and my mom?"

Mose let the swing stop. "Son, if you don't never remember nothin' else, you need to remember that yo' momma didn't question God 'bout what happened to her . . . or to you. She went to Heaven after gettin' my promise I'd raise you up like you was my very own. She was trustin' in the goodness of the Lord when she drawed her last breath."

The boy took another deep breath and let it out slowly. He looked out across the river at nothing for a moment, then back at the dog. He wiped the next tear with the back of his good hand. "I guess I better get back to bed. I'm getting dizzier."

The dog followed him back into the cabin.

Mose picked up the little sack. The watch looked expensive; it had a half-blue, half-red circle around the outside of the face; the writing on the front said it was a Rolex. The two color snapshots were of a black man in a flight suit; he was sitting in an airplane cockpit in one picture and standing by a different airplane in the other. The driver's license said the woman's name was Cherry Prince. Mose looked down at the handful of things from the sack and prayed for the boy; the child had precious little to show he'd once had a family.

An invisible messenger, the near-twin of the one who had watched over the doctor's shoulder, stood near and waited as Mose turned the watch over and held it up to the light while he looked at the words inscribed on the back: . . . BE A MANN. Two years earlier, the jewelry store owner in Pensacola, Florida, apologized to Major Bill Prince for the errant character in the last word; they would order a new back for the watch and redo the engraving. The confused jeweler didn't need to know his engraver had correctly etched six of the characters into the stainless steel—the seventh was put in place by the being who was now standing by the boy's bed.

The mirror finish on the surface around the letters flashed in the midmorning sun, demanding Mose's attention. Something about the words nagged at his thoughts.

The porch swing stopped, and the man left it to kneel on the porch. As he prayed, a fresh breeze moved the swing and carried the smell of the water from the river, stirring it in with the perfume from the honeysuckle that grew thick along the bank . . . just like Old Miz Parker's . . . June would be fifteen years . . . he had been kneeling on the Cat Lake bridge, watching his wife hold their son while Junior spoke his last words: "You tell . . . my daddy . . . I watched out for her . . . like a man."

Mose smiled, remembering how his friend Sam Jones ended up in Parchman with him. He bowed his head. *That's mighty fine, Lord, that You let me see Yo' hand in this! Ain't nuthin' like this can happened 'cept for You doin' it. This here's gonna work out just fine!* He raised his head and looked out where the Sunflower River bent toward the south, working its way down to Allen County, and spoke aloud, "I thank You, Lord. I think that's a powerful good name."

Just after noon Dr. Carlson's car could be seen coming along the road to the cabin. Mose met him at the foot of the path.

The doctor said, "Well, you missed a fine church service this morning."

Mose smiled. "I had me a pretty good one right here."

Carlson looked out at the slow-moving river. "This is a good place for it. How's the boy doin'?"

"He come 'round this mornin' an' come out on the porch for a minute. He's dizzy, an' he ain't had nothin' to eat."

"Mm-hmm. Just keep him watered; he'll eat when he gets hungry. Let's take a look at him."

After satisfying himself that the boy was indeed getting better, the doctor encouraged him to stay in bed and sleep as much as possible. He beckoned Mose to follow him onto the porch.

When they were settled, the doctor reached in his pocket and produced an envelope. "Belle said for me to give this to you but for you not to tell me what it says."

Mose took the envelope. "She say why not to tell?"

"Yep. The fewer people who know what you're doin', the fewer can slip an' say."

Mose nodded; Belle was a thinker. He said, "I better read it in case I needs you to tell her somethin'."

Belle's note said:

My Brother,

I talked to a friend in Chicago last night. Starting a week from tomorrow, and for the following two weeks, he will go to the Illinois Central Railroad Station located at 12th Street and Michigan at noon each day. There is a large clock in the middle of the station, and he will pass below it about every minute or two for ten minutes. He will be wearing grey work clothes, with a yellow bandana tied around his neck. He is a wise man, and you can trust him. You will need new names, and he can help you. I will pray for you and that young boy every day for the rest of my life.

In His name, Your Sister.

Below her name she had penned *Philippians 1:3*.

Mose nodded again. He had been trying to decide whether to go to Detroit or Chicago; Belle helped him decide.

The doctor looked at the clear sky. "Weatherman's promisin' more rain for in the mornin'."

Mose thought about the rain. "That's good. Will it be okay for the boy to travel by then?"

"I expect him to be doin' noticeably better by this evenin'. If he is, he can travel in the mornin' with no consequences. Either way, I think he'll be safer somewhere away from here 'cause folks in town know about this cabin."

Mose pondered that. "The rain will make things good for us on the road. The law don't want to be out in the rain no more than nobody else."

The doctor agreed.

The two had good ideas about how to disappear, and they spent a short while planning what needed to be done and how best to do it. An hour after their planning session ended, the car that had come to Mound Bayou was transformed. Ragged—though recently installed—mud flaps had apparently not kept layers of dirt and splotches of mud from covering the car; the heaviest concentrations were around the back bumper and license plate. The radio antenna was bent, two of the four hubcaps were at the bottom of the Sunflower River. One of the spark plug wires was disconnected, and a small measure of motor oil had been poured into the gas tank. Several cane fishing poles—the doctor's idea—were stretched along the car's top, tied in place with string on one end and a piece of rusty wire on the other.

On Monday morning Mose would have one stop he needed to make before he left Mound Bayou.

CHAPTER SEVEN

If a bunch of fools from over in the Great Smokey Mountains wanted to keep sending a reprobate back to Congress every two years, that was their choice. For today—and until the FBI was officially involved—Special Agent in Charge Bertrand B. Fuller Jr. would choose whether or not he would be at the whim of the Dishonorable H. Bainbridge. Just before two o'clock, when the nondescript government car pulled up in front of the Allen County courthouse, Special Agent Fuller was ninety miles away, getting ready to tee off at the Canton Country Club.

While at the FBI Academy, Agent Wagner had done well in academics and the physical disciplines but he had confounded more than one evaluator because of his relaxed attitude toward the Bureau's desired "image." His willingness to forego a false front explained why his first assignment was to Jackson, Mississippi—the only posting in the nation ranked below Bismarck, North Dakota. Agent Wagner got out of the car, carrying a thin briefcase, and gave the two lawmen waiting on the courthouse steps their first look at an FBI agent wearing a T-shirt and blue jeans.

Dr. Watson called before they got settled in the sheriff's office to let them know that the medical examiner's preliminary tests showed Whitacher's blood/alcohol content at less than .04, along with trace amounts of marijuana. "According to what they've got here, it happened just like those boys said." Watson would be coming back to Indianola when he had the paperwork on all four causes of death; they were still working on Whitacher.

When four o'clock came, the sheriff's office was a cluttered mess of paper cups, scribbled notes and doodles, a roll-around blackboard, and a slew of pictures taken at Cat Lake. The pictures of Farrell Whitacher stayed facedown in the FBI agent's briefcase. The three men—Wagner, Hollinsworth, and Dixon—had gone over the statements made by the five surviving boys and thoroughly sifted through the evidence and pictures from the scenes. Everything about the events that took place in the brake appeared to be fairly cut-and-dried—two men beat the lady, the boy shot the men, the lady died. All they needed now was an answer to the question of why Farrell Whitacher would choose to mutilate himself.

Wagner scanned the chalkboard for the thousandth time. "Okay. The woman's body was found in the cabin. That leaves a young boy—evidently her son—a mild-mannered old black man, and a real tough white man unaccounted for. After we catch the old man and the kid we'll—"

Dixon wagged his finger and shook his head; he was smiling for the first time that afternoon. "Hold your horses there, Tex. You might want to wait till you've got that mild-mannered *old* man in a cell before you start counting your prisoners." Hollinsworth was nodding his agreement.

Wagner was at home in his role as the new kid on the block. Unlike his contemporaries—who were bad about wearing their dark suits to picnics—he knew when to stop talking and start listening. "What am I missing?"

The sheriff said, "It would take all night to tell you the stories, but it comes down to this . . . Mose Washington is only mild-mannered till he's pushed. In the last ten years he's been on the good guys' side in three shootings, two out at Cat Lake and one up at Parchman. Add those to what happened last night an' you've got a mild-mannered old man who's still standing while . . .," he looked at the ceiling and counted on his fingers, "six bad boys are down and dead."

It was Dixon's turn to nod.

Wagner looked from one man to the other. "A farmer? How on God's green earth does a farmer manage to get mixed up in four shoot-outs?"

Hollinsworth shrugged.

"Let's take a break at the Dairy Freeze and get some food," Dixon suggested.

Wagner said, "Good idea. Have they got good burgers?"

"Best chiliburger in the Delta."

Wagner made a mental note that no one had answered his question regarding the old man and the shoot-outs.

What there was of Sunday afternoon in Indianola was taking place at the Dairy Freeze.

The three cops parked out back; Watson pulled in next to them before they could get out of their cars. Peavine pushed open the kitchen's screen door and yelled at the doctor to "put that see-gar back in yo' car an' roll up th' windows."

The men walked across the back parking lot with Wagner trailing the older men, thinking. Had he been paying attention to his surroundings, he would have discovered more good-looking women parked beside one little out-of-the-way hamburger joint than he had encountered in six months of touring Europe. Every car under the curb service awning was occupied by at least two beauties.

The two prettiest girls at the Freeze—or maybe in the entire Western Hemisphere—were sitting in a convertible midway down the lineup. The brunette with the dark eyes and long hair was well ahead in the local competition to see which girl could have the darkest tan when the first cotton bloom showed—it wasn't fair that she spent her life with a summer's worth of natural head start. The blonde sitting behind the wheel was medium-complected and blue-eyed, and when summer came she would pay quarts of sweat for any infinitesimal graduation in skin tone. The two beauties, normally the center of attention wherever their car slowed, were by themselves. Every white boy in Indianola—and most of the men—stood or sat in clusters, gossiping about the white boys and black woman getting killed out at Cat Lake.

The blonde was picking up drops of a coke with her straw and making splotches on a napkin; the Everly Brothers provided musical accompaniment from jukebox speakers under the awning. "What time are you going back to Jackson?"

The brunette was slouched in the seat with her knees touching the dash; she was chewing the end of a straw and watching a sparrow build a nest next to one of the speakers. "Not till in the morning. I'm gonna stay and go to church with Momma and Daddy."

"Sunday night church has got to be the most boring thing in the world."

"Not as boring as sitting here watching the world stand still. Are you going back tonight?" In a land where slow-talking people were the norm, Caroline Davis's drawl turned heads.

The blonde didn't answer because the lawmen and doctor chose that moment to move down the sidewalk between the building and the line of cars. The sheriff, Watson, and Dixon nodded at the girls. The tall, lean man in the T-shirt and jeans was watching his penny loafers follow each other along the narrow walk, frowning.

Beautiful girls can tell the difference between a man who is pretending not to see them and one who doesn't know they exist. The blonde in the convertible looked at the distracted stranger trailing the sheriff and state trooper and became interested—partly because the stranger wasn't, but mostly because he was tall, lean, and more appealing than Sunday night church.

"Who is *that*?" She spoke without moving her lips.

"FBI," said the bird watcher. "Came down here to solve those killin's out at the Parkers'. Daddy says he's a Yankee." Caroline's great-granddaddy claimed to be somehow related to President Jefferson Davis.

Some people appraise land; others appraise jewelry or maybe art. The blonde was a gifted appraiser of men. "You tell your daddy that if that boy's a Yankee, then so's your Uncle Jeffie."

"Humph." The Davis girls were nothing if not loyal to their patriarchs. "Betcha."

"How much?"

Caroline—Ceedie to everyone she knew—dug through a purse that had cost twenty-eight dollars at Goldsmith's. It took a full minute for her to find what she was looking for. "The usual." She dropped a nickel on the console between the seats.

The blonde used a red-nailed finger to poke around in the money on the curb service tray until she uncovered a matching coin. She held it over the console. "Who has to go first?"

"It's your turn, sweetiepie."

Polly Ragsdale was watching the T-shirt disappear around the corner of the cafe. "I wanna bat clean-up."

Ceedie was easily the most reserved college girl in the county, and going first wasn't a role that lent itself to a person who was more comfortable remaining in the background. She balked. "Uh-uh. You batted clean-up last time—with that tennis player from Millsaps. Every time I have to go first, I get scared and get the dadgum hiccups, and you know it."

The negotiations started, and Polly pulled the biggest gun

she had. "Good gosh, Ceedie, the man works for the FBI. A year from now he'll be livin' some place up north."

Polly might be right—smart girls didn't invest their time in a man who might want to move to someplace where everybody talked too fast. Ceedie knew she didn't want the Yankee, but Polly had just given her enough leverage to gather some future eggs. "Okay, but I wanna go second on the next four."

"No fair. You can have the next three."

"Uh-uh. Four."

Confident that Ceedie would lose count before church let out, the blonde put her nickel on the console. "It's a deal."

"Promise?"

Polly held three fingers in the swearing position. "Scout's honor."

The two beauties stepped out of the convertible in a way that beauties seem to have perfected. They, like Wagner, were dressed in jeans and T-shirts—the fashion ensemble looked better on the girls. Every male in sight forgot about the happenings out at the lake long enough to watch the two predators stroll into the Freeze.

The sparrow was working at building her nest. Sunday night church was two hours in the future. And two of the man-killers at the Dairy Freeze were plotting an ambush. The world in Indianola was no longer standing still.

Watson wrangled with Peavine, and the proprietor allowed the four men to gather in the Freeze's miniature banquet room to talk about what they knew and to speculate on what they didn't. Watson and Wagner told the waitress they wanted burgers; Dixon said he just wanted coffee. Hollinsworth glanced at the envelope in Watson's hands and took Dixon's cue. "Just coffee."

When the waitress finally left, Hollinsworth said, "What about it, Doc?"

Watson patted the manila envelope in front of him. "They finished with Whitacher."

The sheriff had to prompt him. "And?"

Watson leaned back and rubbed his chin. "Well, boys, I'll tell you right now, you're not gonna like any part of it."

Watching the doctor hesitate to express his conclusions was a new thing for Dixon and Hollinsworth. They waited.

Watson let his gaze go around the table. "The wounds on his arms are postmortem."

"That's not possible" Wagner responded for the audience. "Not if he inflicted them himself."

Watson nodded. "I hope you're right, son. The ME didn't like it either—he put the body on ice so you government boys can do your own autopsy." He patted the envelope and thought about the contents. "I sure hope you're right."

Dixon took a turn speaking for the lawmen. "Can you give us the short story on how they came up with their findings?"

"Yep. The pattern and size of the bite marks are a dead match with the measure and spread of Whitacher's teeth; he did it." Watson took a deep breath through his mouth. "The wounds were obviously postmortem . . . minimal bleeding. The detail pictures tell it all." He poked different color photos while he made his case. "No footprints in the blood on the deck, fragments of muscle tissue overlaying the brain and scalp tissue scattered on the float—the brain tissue was in place first, and he did it all. He banged his head on the deck of that old float till he beat his own brains out . . . that was the cause of death. Then, after he was dead, the rest of the damage was done by his own teeth."

The waitress came through the door with their orders. Hollinsworth and Dixon had a picture of the boy's remains forever emblazoned in their minds; they were glad they had stuck with coffee.

Wagner waited till the waitress left. "You got any idea how a man could do that, Doc?"

Watson cut his eyes at Dixon and shrugged. "I'm just a small-town sawbones, son. I think I'll drop this one in the hands of your boys up in Washington."

The window unit in the room hummed; dishes in the kitchen rattled. Watson sat under a wall-mounted Rotary Club medallion, pushing the manila envelope around in a flat circle with one hand and eating his burger with the other. Wagner stared at the table, taking bites of his burger and chewing them slowly. Hollinsworth smoked and played with his coffee cup. Dixon was watching the silent doctor.

When Watson finally made eye contact with him, Dixon said, "What else, Doc?"

Watson nodded and swallowed a mouthful of his burger before answering. "His legs were broken."

"Those boys already said he broke his leg when he fell," said Hollinsworth.

"Actually *he* broke only one leg. The femur in the other one was cut."

"Cut?"

Watson was pulling a small stack of photographs out of the envelope. "The right femur—the large bone in his upper leg—was severed with something sharper than a surgical saw." He put the top two pictures side by side in the middle of the table. "That's what his broken bone looked like—it's typical. This bone," he pointed with a toothpick, "was cut—the surfaces bordering the cut are slick as glass; no splinters or fragments, not even any saw residue. And no invasive trauma evident in the surrounding tissue."

The air conditioner hummed while Dixon, Wagner, and Hollinsworth took turns studying the pictures. Dixon was the one who asked, "What about Bainbridge and Dailey?"

Hollinsworth said, "What about 'em?"

Dixon knew something. "Their legs were broken, weren't they?"

The lawmen looked at the coroner. Watson spoke around a

mouthful of hamburger while he tapped one of the pictures. "Nope. Technically, they were cut, just like that one. Three dead men, five severed femurs. How'd you know?"

Dixon wasn't ready to answer the question. "Tell me the bones were cut in the same spot on all three men, probably at the midpoint on the bone—cut straight and square."

Watson used his free hand to separate two more pictures from the stack. "That's Bainbridge. That's Dailey." He picked up the toothpick again and touched one of the pictures. "An' that's the ME's ruler. I can only estimate without taking out the bones, but I'd say the cuts are within a quarter inch of the midpoint on all five cuts . . . engineering-school square."

Wagner and Hollinsworth queried Dixon at the same time. "How'd you know that?"

The doctor answered for Dixon. " 'Cause he's a Christian."

Dixon nodded.

Hollinsworth remained noncommittal because he had the advantage of being familiar with Dixon's theory; Wagner thought he had misunderstood the doctor. "You mean to tell me you think some kind of devil broke those boys' legs? Why would you think that?"

Dixon was shaking his head. The doctor answered, "Kenny's the Christian, an' he knows his Bible better than me, but I've been studying on this since daybreak. Now I'm not a churchgoing man, but I think an angel cut those bones some way so a demon wouldn't be able to use the dead bodies to chase down the kids that got away. If somebody's got a better explanation, I'll give mine up."

Dixon nodded in agreement. "And he—or they—did it in a way that would make it obvious that spirit beings were involved. The demons wanted us to know they'd killed Whitacher, and the angels wanted us to know they'd stepped in to protect one or more of those boys."

Hollinsworth surprised Dixon and Watson by changing sides. "I think you're both right."

FBI Agent Jeff Wagner's hamburger hung suspended between the plate and his mouth; he was staring at the other three men and thinking, *Well, Hot-Dog-J-Edgar-Hoover. I'm down here in the sovereign state of Mississippi, on my first case for the Federal Bureau of Investigation, sitting in a room with three normal-acting men who are serious about blaming part of what happened at a crime scene on black magic or voodoo or something. Unless . . .*

"I get it." Wagner was half-smiling; checking the other men's faces. "This is a joke, right? Putting on a show for the new boy."

Dixon had been looking at Hollinsworth, deep in thought. He turned to Wagner. "Sorry, Tex. If you can come up with a better explanation, I'm listening."

Wagner picked up the nearest picture. He didn't have an answer. Yet.

"Well, boys, I think that'll 'bout do it for me." Hollinsworth stood up. "I'm takin' Mabel to church. I'll be back in the office first thing tomorrow."

The sheriff was right. The talking part was pretty much finished; now they needed to find the missing men and the boy.

"Yep. I'm headed for the house." Watson gathered his pictures and followed Hollinsworth to the door.

Dixon watched the doctor until he was out of sight. When the two men and the pictures were out of the room, Dixon got hungry. He slid his chair back and looked at Wagner, "You want another burger?"

Wagner had nowhere he needed to be. "I guess."

"Let's go out front and find a booth."

Wagner's mind went back to the bite marks on Whitacher while he followed Dixon toward the front of the cafe.

* * *

Polly and Ceedie didn't have anywhere they needed to be either. When Dixon and Wagner walked out of the back room the girls were waiting.

Polly's eyes followed the men while she stood up and hissed at Ceedie, "Here he comes."

Ceedie nodded.

Dixon watched the clandestine exchange and saw Ceedie take a firm grip on a large tumbler. He smiled a greeting at the girls as he approached their table and whispered his own message. "Watch out, Tex."

"Huh?"

Wagner was abeam the table when a blur with dark hair came out of the nearest chair, whirling in his direction. At the edge of the swirl was a full glass of iced tea—extra sweet. The practiced survivor of a thousand encounters with cat-quick defensive backs got the tips of his fingers on the girl's guiding hand and kept it moving to his right while he did a smooth shift to his left. Ceedie tipped the glass at the right moment—but her arm was in the wrong place.

The tea left the glass.

Twelve years on the country club's tennis courts had imbued Polly's brain with the ability to predict the impact point of most moving objects, or—as in this case—substances; she emitted her first squeal and initiated an attempt to shield herself with her hands before the amber liquid reached the top of its arc. When the ice-cold brew drenched her, the shock took her breath long enough to give Ceedie time to join in and accompany her in a protracted chorus of more squealing. The Everly Brothers would not've been jealous of the girls' harmony.

The menfolk from outside crowded into the cafe to see what the racket was all about. They found Polly Ragsdale, blond-haired darling of the Delta, tea-soaked from her neck to her knees; she was laughing and shrieking unintelligible things at Ceedie Davis. Ceedie was doubled over by the table where they had been sitting, holding onto a chair with one hand and trying to cover her face with the other—laughing at how stupid they must look.

The crowd in the Freeze whistled and applauded the girls' performance. Dixon and Wagner both clapped a little then slid into a booth by the front windows.

By the time most of the racket died down, the male spectators had determined that the Yankee FBI man was innocent of any offense against one of their women and returned to their gossip groups. When the girls recovered, they stopped by the booth to meet their elusive target.

"Uncle," the wet girl surrendered. "Introduce us to your friend, Kenny."

The assassin with the dark hair hiccupped.

Dixon and the blonde beauty had a history. Six or eight years earlier, when she started driving, he got tired of having to stop her once a week for speeding; he finally told his friend Wheeler Ragsdale to take the car away from her or he would take it himself.

Wheeler took the easy road and told him to "Have at it, sonny boy. It'll sure save me havin' to put up with her bein' mad at me."

The next time he stopped her, Dixon sentenced that year's convertible to a week in his front yard; the time after that he made it a month and promised her twice that for a third offense. The fast driving stopped, and the friendship started.

"Ladies," Dixon said, "this is Special Agent Jeff Wagner, FBI. Agent Wagner, the Misses Polly Ragsdale and Caroline Davis of the Allen County Vaudeville Company."

Polly threw a tea-soaked napkin at Dixon and hit the window; Wagner slid out of the booth. "Evenin', ladies. Nice to meet you."

Ceedie cocked her head to one side and wrinkled a really pretty nose at the man wearing the dry T-shirt and gentle drawl. "I've got an uncle named Jeff. Where're you from, Agent Jeff Wagner?" She didn't hiccup.

"Born and raised in New York City, ma'am."

"Uh-huh. So was my Uncle Jeff."

Wagner had seen some beautiful smiles; Ceedie's was the kind movie stars try to buy. The blonde girl's image, along with the conversations in the cafe and the racket from the kitchen, faded to the edges of his awareness.

Ceedie interrupted the silence before it got awkward. The girl who had waited till she was in the fifth grade to speak a word out loud in class said, "Can we sit with y'all if Polly promises not to drip?" She pronounced it *dree-yup*.

A bedazzled Wagner separated himself from the smile and looked at Dixon. Dixon rolled his eyes.

Without waiting for an answer, Ceedie slid into the side of the booth Wagner had vacated when he stood. "How sweet."

Polly spent the first crucial moments of the exchange being mystified by a total transformation in the Ceedie she had known all her life. When her friend grabbed the seat by the FBI man, Polly stiffened her arms and stomped her foot. It was her turn to bat clean-up, and her accomplice—who normally could be depended on to be painfully shy—had just cut her off. "Dadgum you, Ceedie! I can't sit down now; you just threw a glass full of sticky tea all over me!"

"Oh, bless your heart, I sure did." Ceedie bestowed a fake version of her smile on the unintended victim of their plot. "I tell you what. You run home and change, honey. We'll be right here when you get back. Okay?"

Only the village idiot could miss how Wagner was looking at Ceedie.

Polly knew when she'd been outfoxed, she knew when to fight, and she knew when to retreat. She threw a copy of the fake smile back and said, "Fine."

In the feminine world, a mere mortal would find it impossible to look attractive with sweet tea dripping from her elbows—for Polly Ragsdale it was a downhill stroll. Polly went home; Wagner took the vacant seat next to Ceedie.

The girl who used to be timid said, "So, Agent Wagner, how long are you going to be in our fair city?"

"Probably a few days. And my friends call me Jeff."

"I'm Ceedie."

Dixon rolled his eyes again and changed his mind about the hamburger. "See you children later."

Wagner looked at Ceedie and talked to Dixon. "Can we get together tomorrow?"

Dixon stopped. "She or me?"

Wagner considered the question then pried his attention off the girl again. "You, for now. I've got a couple of things I need to ask you about."

"I'm pretty loose tomorrow. Pick a time."

Wagner pulled a scrap of paper out of his back pocket. "Fuller is picking me up at the Holiday Inn at seven in the morning to do a couple of things. I'll call you when I get loose."

"Why don't you meet me here for breakfast at six? We'll get it over with early."

"Thanks. I'll be here."

The patrolman walked out, and Wagner turned back to Ceedie. She was grinning. "I've never ridden in an FBI car before."

Wagner forgot that he had come into the dining room to get a hamburger. "Where're we going?"

"Over to our house."

Wagner was sliding out of the booth again. "Okay. For what?"

"My daddy thinks you're a Yankee. We've got to go tell him you're not before somebody in town tells him I've been sitting in a booth with you."

"Yeah, we can't have that, can we?"

"Where're you from, anyway?"

"West Texas."

"Really? I believe Momma's got some cousins in Texas."

"What about that girl you're supposed to wait on?"

"Who? Polly?" Ceedie grinned again and winked. "Oh, I'm pretty sure most of her kinfolks are from around here."

They both laughed.

Ceedie stood by while Wagner paid his bill, and the two walked outside.

Coveys of men and boys turned from their serious conversations to pay homage to Ceedie. The men tipped their hats at the girl; they inspected the FBI man while nodding and frowning. Boys spoke and blushed at Ceedie while wondering why local girls always went for the newest guy in town. Cars sprinkled with attractive females lined the curb-service walk because girls go where the boys are. All the misses waved or spoke to Ceedie; a handful smiled and called *Jay-yuff* by his first name. Wagner took it in stride.

When they got to his car, he got in and put the key in the ignition; Ceedie was waiting by the passenger door. He reached across the seat and pushed the door open. "It wasn't locked."

The girl was standing one-legged, one hand holding the leather straps of the Goldsmith's purse, the other balled into a tight fist and resting on a perfectly proportioned hip. She was looking at him from under a dark brow and chewing on the inside of her cheek, deciding something.

He smiled up at her. "Hop in."

That was all she needed to hear. "Do those Texas girls let you get away with not opening the door for them?" The bright red bottom lip was out of place by at least an eighth of an inch; the smile was somewhere else.

"Oops. Sorry."

"Mm-hmm." She snapped around and headed back where she came from.

Oh, shoot! Wagner came out of the car fast. "Hold it, Ceedie! Wait a minute!" He was having to jog to catch her.

When he called to her, the boys, men, and girls outside the Freeze looked toward them. Ceedie didn't slow down. Pockets of men parted so she could pass unhindered.

Wagner took a fast-moving second to notice that roughly half the population of Indianola was standing outside the Dairy Freeze, and they had temporarily ceased acting on the vital elements in their own lives to witness the current developments in his. As Ceedie marched in front of the parked cars, the girls in the audience noted the coordinated use of the dark hair, red lips, and Goldsmith purse; the men and boys were preoccupied with the rhythm contributed by the back pockets of her jeans.

When he caught up with her, she stopped and turned. She and her lower lip had their minds made up. She was also pretty when she was frowning. "I do not date, ride with, or make friends with boys that don't pay attention to how they treat me."

He was holding his hands up. Surrendering. "Wait! Wait! Look, I was wrong. It won't happen again. I promise. I had my mind on something else."

A man's voice near them said, "Preach it, brother."

The crowd laughed. Ceedie didn't.

Wagner was uncharacteristically flustered. He decided he didn't care what the crowd thought, because the beautiful girl looked like she just might be willing to believe him.

Ceedie hadn't decided.

"I messed up, Ceedie. Okay? How 'bout if we try this over?" He was almost begging, and he almost didn't care.

He looked cute when he was worried. At least, he looked cute when he was worried about her. The bright red lip receded slightly. "Okay—one more chance. But just one."

The rigid index finger she used to number his remaining chances was also beautiful. He allowed himself to smile. "Thanks."

Some of the spectators clapped.

He played to the crowd by touching her elbow, bowing

slightly, and making a sweeping gesture toward the car. "This way, ma'am, if you please."

"Uh-uh." She pulled her elbow free and turned. "Not today."

She was walking away again, and he had no idea what he'd done wrong. "Not today, what?"

Ceedie spoke while she made her exit, stage right. "You can call me next Saturday."

A girl in one of the nearby cars said, "You tell 'im, honey."

This cannot be happening, he thought. "But I don't have your number."

The purse, ponytail, and back pockets were almost to the front corner of the Freeze; when she whirled around the centrifugal force carried the bag and hair out in color-matched arcs. "Your social skills need a little polish, Special Agent Jeff Wagner, FBI." She drawled at him and those present, without troubling herself to smile. "Try not to let us down in the professional realm."

She and her accessories were around the corner and gone; he was standing on the shallow stage, surrounded by their audience.

Of the men and boys who interrupted their committee meetings to watch the show, eighty percent smiled, the rest laughed out loud, a few clapped—their side was bloodied and bowed but still breathing. The girls in the audience applauded and cheered because their side had scored a sweeping victory in the battle; two or three young ladies were trying to yell phone numbers at Wagner but were drowned out by the pandemonium.

Two and a half seasons of playing football in front of Saturday afternoon crowds at A&M had not prepared Wagner for five minutes of public courtship in the Delta; his face was the color of a newly painted barn. He pretended the audience's applause was for him and lifted a hand to acknowledge it, then tried to act nonchalant on his way back to the car.

He started the car and sat without putting it in gear, cursing to himself. He went back over the scene and his face got hotter. He wanted to ask himself, *Why would I care whether I get to see her again?* but the answer was obvious. The woman looked good laughing, lecturing, or walking away—and the sound of that drawl was addictive. *Well, it could've been worse—it could've been really worse.*

He was still hungry, but he wasn't going back into the Freeze.

A message telling Wagner to call Fuller was waiting when he returned to the Holiday Inn.

He called Fuller and was told that the Federal Bureau of Investigation had officially taken charge of the case; Moses Lincoln Washington, William L. Prince Jr., and an unknown white male were wanted for questioning in the deaths of Oliver W. Bainbridge, Stanson B. Dailey, and Cherry C. Prince. The bulletin gave sketchy descriptions of the three fugitives; they were considered armed and dangerous. The bulletin did not say that the bureau had no desire to become the lead law enforcement agency in the case—the action was the result of behind-the-scenes maneuvering by Congressman Halbert Bainbridge. The assistant deputy director of the FBI who acted as a liaison with Bainbridge likened him to a rabid animal "The meanest person I've ever come in contact with."

That same ADD had never come in contact with the congressman's wife.

CHAPTER EIGHT

Wagner pulled up in front of the Dairy Freeze Monday morning at six straight-up. The clatter of dishes and the smell of bacon frying met him when he stepped out of the car. Dixon was sitting in the same booth they'd been in the day before, sipping on his second cup of coffee. The sky said more rain was on the way.

Monday was Peavine's youngest daughter's day to be the breakfast waitress, and she was the only woman visible in a room of wall-to-wall men. She intercepted the agent at the booth. "You want breakfast?"

"Yep. Four eggs, over medium, extra bacon, toast, hash browns."

"No hash browns. Grits." The scale-model waitress had an apron snugged up under her arms to keep it from dragging the floor. She was all business.

"Okay. Grits."

"The biscuits are better'n th' toast."

"Okay. Biscuits."

The kid didn't come up to the men's sitting height. She had bangs, long hair, and held her tongue between her teeth while the pencil fought with the order pad. "Coffee?"

"Yep."

"Who died?" The pad-pencil battle was over.

"Huh?"

The waitress was gathering information. "Nobody wears a suit durin' the week 'cept for a funeral. You're not goin' to a funeral?"

"Nope. My boss is real mean. He's the one that makes me dress like this."

The brows under the bangs moved toward each other. "Where're you fro—"

"Scat," said the big highway patrolman with the gun.

The kid had the home-field advantage. She took a backhanded swipe at her bangs and tilted her head back so she could glare down her nose at the policeman. "Daddy told me to be nice to the customers."

"He didn't tell you to worry 'em to death. Now git."

She frowned at Dixon and pointed an accusing pencil at Wagner. "He's a Yankee, ain't he?"

Dixon made a move to slide out of the booth, and the kid took off in a flurry of apron strings, long hair, and tennis shoes.

Wagner looked outside at the darkening sky. "You think it's gonna rain?"

"What I think is, you wanted to meet me here so you could ask me some questions."

Wagner grinned. "They taught us at the Academy to spar around a little till we got a feel for the situation."

Dixon waved his coffee cup in the direction of the kitchen. "You just watched me go three rounds with an eight-year-old defender of the Confederate cause. I'm sparred out."

Wagner told him the FBI had taken over the search for the two men and the boy and shared the details of the bulletin.

"Armed and dangerous. I swear," Dixon shook his head. "It must be the tap water."

"Tap water?"

"People who spend more than a week in Washington end

up making decisions that make you think their brains are congealed."

"*That,*" said the agent with a history of nonconformity, "is a true statement."

They waited while the kid put Wagner's coffee on the table and topped off Dixon's.

When she left, Dixon said, "So, what's on your mind?"

"I'm in my midtwenties, Ken. In the eight years since I left high school, Moses Washington has been in four gunfights that resulted in the deaths of six men. Doesn't that strike you as a bit unusual?"

"He wasn't in all the fights, and it was eight men."

"Eight men?" Wagner's notebook was consulted. "The sheriff said six."

"I guess arithmetic never was Dubby's strong suit." Dixon put down his cup, so he could use his fingers to keep track. "Back in '52 a black man who'd never been anything but an easygoing boozer started acting like he had rabies; he was bragging around about what he was going to do to Washington's wife and a white girl named Missy Parker. The man showed up in Mose's front yard with a knife, and Mose was sent to prison for killing him with a shotgun.

"Five years after Mose got to Parchman there was an escape attempt, and Mose and another convict saved the life of their work gang's boss—the boss was a white man named Bill Williams. The convict who kicked off the attempt was shot and killed. Within a year of Mose's getting out of prison, a churchgoing college boy went berserk out at Cat Lake and tried to kill that same white girl—Missy Parker. There were several shots fired: the crazy boy was killed on the porch of Mose's cabin; a white seminary student took a bullet meant for the girl and died two days later at the hospital. That's four. A little over a year ago two armed white men went out there to the Parkers' woods and chased a thirteen-year-old black girl—a close friend of Missy Parker's, named Emmalee Edwards—out of her house and into the Parkers' woods; one of the men had a gun, the other had a knife. The one with the gun happened to be Oliver Bainbridge's younger brother, and there was bad blood between him and Missy Parker. Emmalee overheard enough to know they were planning to kill her and go after Missy. The two apparently got sideways with each other and had a meeting of their own knife and gun club—both died. That's six. The two Friday night make eight."

"Plus Farrell Whitacher."

Dixon picked up his cup, shaking his head. "Uh-uh. Mose was nowhere around when Whitacher bought it, but I guess you could count the woman. With those eight men, Mose was probably no more than ten feet from the victims when the shooting started. The only one he wasn't practically standing next to was the preacher boy who threw himself in front of Missy Parker; all the rest got what they asked for, and Mose either pulled the trigger or watched it happen."

Wagner was taking notes. "Who in the heck is Missy Parker? And what's the deal with Cat Lake?"

Dixon offered a rare smile. "Ask me that again when you've got a couple of days free."

The kid came back with Wagner's breakfast, and he buttered his biscuits while he asked, "Whadda you think?"

"About what?"

"You know." Wagner was stirring butter around in his grits and reaching for the sugar dispenser with his free hand. "Why has Washington been involved in more gunfights than Wyatt Earp?"

Dixon pointed at Wagner's plate. "If that Davis girl finds out you put sugar on your grits, she'll drop you like an oil-slick anvil."

The sugar made a ninety degree course change. "I just take a little in my coffee."

"Uh-huh."

He dumped five grains of sugar into his coffee. "And what would you know about me and *that Davis girl*?"

Dixon's answer was to lean to his side so he could yell past Wagner. "Pea! Who was the winner last night?"

Peavine Isabell was on the other side of the room at the cash register. He yelled back in his fake Irish accent, "Ah, t'was the lass by a TKO, but the boy dinna do too bad fah ah goov'ment fellah."

His statement was greeted by cheers and clapping. Several men nodded at Wagner and said, "You did fine, son, real fine."

Wagner's chin hit his chest. *What did I do to deserve this? If I'd played the bureau's little game at the Academy, I'd be out in Texas with the normal people.*

Dixon loved it. "So, Agent Wagner. What else do you need to know?"

The agent shook off the self-recrimination. He leaned back and took a deep breath. "Okay. You've told me all about Washington being in—or on the edge of—more gunfights than any lawman since the old west, but you haven't said why. The only way you get in that many shoot-outs is to be in a war."

"You just broke the code, Tex. It's all about a war."

Wagner picked up his coffee and blew on it. "It's that Christian stuff the doc talked about, isn't it? Good versus evil."

"It is. Now, if you'll sit there and eat your eggs, I'll tell you a story."

"Shoot."

"Do you believe in God?"

Wagner had filled his mouth with food. "Whaa?"

"Nod if you believe in God."

Wagner swallowed. "Are you going to tell me God put the man in the gunfights?"

"I'm going to answer your question if you quit interrupting, so just answer the question. Do you believe in God?"

"God?" Wagner was trying to figure out why his beliefs would matter.

"Yeah—God. As in heaven."

"Yeah, I guess I do."

"Do you believe in angels."

"Angels?" This wasn't an explanation; it was Sunday school.

"Boy, were you raised in an English-speaking family?"

Wagner took out time to blow on his coffee again then said, "Okay, I believe in angels, but I've never seen one. What has this got to do with people shooting each other?"

"If you'll take a breath, I'll explain it to you."

Wagner shrugged and drank his coffee.

When he decided Wagner was going to stay silent, Dixon said, "What I'm about to tell you is not a fairy tale; this is good supposition based on strong evidence, and it's a stand taken by people who're a whole lot smarter than me." Dixon put his elbows on the table and leaned forward. "At some time before Adam, God created what had to be billions of angels—the Bible calls them the heavenly host. Back before man sinned, the highest angel, the one God chose to stand at His right hand, led a rebellion among the angels. The most beautiful, most powerful being ever created by God wanted to take God's place, and a third of the angels followed his lead.

"The rebellion was a lost cause from the start. The Bible says God threw the rebels out of Heaven and made this world their domain—the Bible calls Satan the prince of the power of the air. Mankind can inflict ample destruction on the world without any help from the devil, but in those areas where Satan wants additional influence, he probably has billions of dark angels—the demonic realm—who answer his orders."

Oh, great. I'm working with one of those hysterical Christians. But Dixon didn't act hysterical. Wagner lifted one of the fingers he was using to hold a biscuit. "Billions?"

Dixon didn't want to squabble over numbers. "Call it dozens for our purposes—numbers aren't the issue here. My point is . . . there are fallen angels called demons—dark spirits, you name it—and there are those angels who are still part of the heavenly host—bright beings, eternally on the side of God, whose sole desire and responsibility is to do God's bidding. You and I each have a guardian angel, an eternal being who never sleeps, who allows only those things into our lives that are ordained by God. Are you with me so far?"

Wagner really hated to tell the man, but he didn't want to waste his time on Bible stories. "Look, Ken, I'm sure this is all good stuff—and I respect what you believe—but I'm trying to talk about one man being on the scene of multiple murders, and you're telling me about goblins. Bible stories will not help answer the questions that are in front of us."

Dixon was praying while Wagner was talking. *Lord, he can't see it. Would You give me the words that he needs to hear?* He told Wagner, "Okay, Tex, we'll let it lay, but let me put a couple of thoughts in your mind. Remember when you said a man had to be in a war to be involved in that much shooting? Well, Mose Washington is on the front lines of a war between the forces of evil and all that's good in the universe; that's one. The other is this: You're gonna be the guy who gets to try and figure out what happened out there at that lake. And in about two weeks, you're gonna get to explain to the tapioca team up in Washington how a man who was already dead managed to tear the flesh off his arms with his own teeth. There's a little thought that oughta curb your appetite."

Wagner knew better. "Not a chance. Fuller likes being in the spotlight—he'll be the front man on any briefings."

"Humph," Dixon snorted. "Don't bet your blue suit on it, buddy. Fuller wants to sit behind a bigger desk. By now, he's talked to the ME in Jackson, and he's drawn his own conclusions—men like him won't run the risk of getting crossways with the big boys over something that can't be explained without bringing up the subject of the spirit world."

"It'll never happen." Wagner was smiling and shaking his

head. He'd been watching Fuller for more than a month—the guy was a prima donna. "And I'd bet a hamburger on it."

A movement outside the window caught their attention, and they turned to watch a twin of Wagner's nondescript car pull up at the curb out front. The subject of the hamburger bet stepped out of the car and put on his funeral coat.

Wagner made room for Fuller, and a suspicious, pint-sized waitress met the new arrival at the booth. "You want breakfast?"

"Just coffee, thanks."

She stayed where she was, threw a glance at Dixon, then pointed her pencil at Wagner. "Are you his bo—"

Dixon grabbed at her, but she was too quick. She made a face at him and prissed off to get the coffee. Dixon laughed.

Wagner had inhaled his breakfast. "Well, what's on our agenda?"

Fuller was straightening his tie. "Mound Bayou, Mississippi is the best place to start. It's about an hour north of here."

Wagner had never heard of the place. "Your car or mine?"

"Both. I've got to be back in Jackson by midafternoon. There's nothing up here you can't handle by yourself."

Dixon saw the investigation falling into Wagner's lap and had to get out of the booth before he started laughing. He grinned at Wagner, "How long you gonna be in town?"

Fuller answered for the rookie. "Probably all week, maybe two. We're not going to find anything up here, but we've gotta cover all the bases."

Dixon grinned. "I've got some places I need to be in a few minutes. We can do this again tomorrow." He pointed at Wagner. "You can buy."

The two FBI men held a long planning session, lined out what Wagner should do for the rest of the week, and left the Freeze at eight o'clock. It started raining before they hit the city limits of Indianola.

* * *

At nine o'clock the two-car caravan turned down Mound Bayou's main street; the rain showed no signs of letting up. The street was almost empty; the few pedestrians to be seen were hustling to get out of the rain. When the federal officers passed in front of the bank, Wagner's car hit a wide puddle and nearly splashed a man who jogged across the street in front of him.

Without slowing, Wagner said, "Sorry, fellah," to the retreating back and followed Fuller until he pulled up in front of the city hall. They left Fuller's car there after getting directions to the house of the man they wanted to interview first.

The fellow Wagner almost splattered was expected in the bank. The president greeted him when he entered and asked him to step into his office. When the door was closed and locked, the bank officer said, "It's good to see you again, Mose, though I wish the circumstances were different. What can I do for you?"

The banks in Switzerland—famous around the world for their discretion—were gossip mills compared to the Mound Bayou Bank and Trust Company. The accumulated rental income from his section of cotton land was a substantial sum of money, and Mose took a short time to explain what he wanted done with it. On a handshake deal with the bank's president Mose moved half the money into an account under his new name and told the man that Spring and the doctor would come down separately to put their names on the signature card; he left the other half of the money in an account for Pearl. When their business was finished, he and the president bowed their heads in a brief prayer before Mose went on his way. At fifteen after nine, the FBI men were mounting the steps at Dr. Carlson's house; Mose and his companions were turning north on Highway 61.

* * *

Dr. Carlson told the FBI agents the old man and boy had been there, but they left soon after he set the little boy's arm. He asked what they'd done.

The FBI men said they just needed to talk to them. Might any of the doctor's neighbors know anything? The doctor cordially invited them to find out for themselves.

The FBI agents thanked Dr. Carlson and trudged back to have a powwow in their car. The initial consensus was that their job would be considerably easier had Ollie Bainbridge possessed the good grace to get himself killed in the middle of a long dry spell.

"Which side do you want?" Wagner asked. There were times when the junior agent wasn't going to like his job, and this was one of them. He didn't like having to work outside in the rain, and he didn't like looking for an old man and a boy who had apparently done the right thing.

Fuller was wearing new shoes. "You take the mud."

Wagner was looking forward to several hours of rain-soaked misery and he wanted to get it over with; he got out of the car and navigated around most of the puddles to get to the house across the street from the doctor's. The lady who came to the door, a Mrs. Bishop, hadn't seen anything on Saturday or Sunday or any other day, "Now get yo' wet self an' them muddy feet offa my clean porch."

At the end of an hour, the street had become little more than a narrow lake, and the two lily-white agents in the tan raincoats had talked to people in most of the houses along its banks. They regrouped inside the car to compare notes.

The only gracious response had come from a middle-aged lady down the block. "Mrs. Fernhold was born and raised here, and said she'd really like to help." The senior agent consulted his notebook and shook his head. "But every time she referred to the doctor's house, she pointed the wrong direction."

"What now?"

Fuller looked at his watch. "You're going to take me back to my car, and I'm going to go see if it rained in Jackson. You're going to stay up here and keep wasting time and shoe leather."

"Okay." Wagner thought he knew the answer to his next question. "Which way do you think Washington went?"

Fuller talked while he poured water from his new cordovans. "North, I expect."

"I thought so." Wagner pulled away from the doctor's house. "If he gets to Chicago or Detroit, they'll never find him."

Fuller stopped pouring to look at Wagner. "You mean *we'll* never find him."

Wagner's briefcase held the crime scene photo of Cherry Prince and the ME's account of how she had died. A recent picture of Mrs. Prince had come over the wire on the previous evening; she was the spitting image of the black lady who managed the athletic department's laundry at Texas A&M. For four years, that lady had singled him out—speaking the words that created a desire to excel in the heart of a somewhat irresponsible young football player. The football player went on to law school and from there to the FBI because he wanted to use his life to make a difference. The junior agent stayed busy with his driving. "Yeah, that's what I meant."

Wagner parked by Fuller's car at the city hall.

Fuller stepped out of the car and leaned back inside to say, "Call me every day at noon and five to let me know what's developing. Keep track of your interviews and come down to the office once or twice a week and give me a face-to-face."

Wagner said he would and went back to work the neighborhood around the doctor's office; the rain had turned to cold drizzle. Eleven thirty found him on a brick walk that led up to a house on Peach Street. He mounted the steps just as a petite black lady pushed open the screen door.

"Good morning, ma'am."

"Good mornin', yourself." She was wearing a light blue dress that set off her tan complexion and blue eyes. She held the door open with one hand and fluffed her apron at his feet with the other. "Take off those muddy shoes an' come in this house."

"I just need to ask you some questions, if you don't mind."

"I know what you need, young man." She spoke as she turned and went into the house, calling back, "Get those shoes off an' come in here where it's dry. You can hang your raincoat on that coat rack inside the door."

She was in the kitchen when he got his shoes off and coat hung. He crossed the living area in his socks, leaving wet footprints on her clean floor. When he got close he displayed his badge and ID to her back. "Good morning, I'm—"

"Agent Wagner from the FBI," she finished while turning to face him. "Young man, every person in this town knows who you are, an' by now, most of 'em know you're in my house."

Wagner looked down at his socks. Water dripped from his pant cuffs, spotting the floor around his feet. He looked up and shook his head, agitated. "Walking these streets to ask these questions has got to be the stupidest thing I've ever done."

Her glasses had bright gold rims that sparkled when they caught the light. She smiled. "Well, if the good Lord lets you live a little longer, you'll probably top it."

"I hope not."

"I'm fixin' to take a chicken out of the stove. Have you had your dinner yet?"

Breakfast was six hours in the past, and several of the houses in the neighborhood smelled of fresh-baked bread and everything that went with it. "I hate to trouble you."

"No, you don't, an' I don't want to eat by myself." She waved a pot holder at a short hallway off the living area. "Go down to that bathroom an' wash up. I'll have the food on by the time you get back."

When he returned, she was pouring sweet tea for both of them. His plate was hidden by half a baked chicken, rice covered with brown gravy, and green beans—all steaming. Hot rolls were wrapped in a clean dish towel and waiting in a basket near his right hand.

"This looks real good." He held her chair while she sat.

When he was seated, she took his hand without asking, and said, "Lord, it all comes from You. Grant that we would understand that an' appreciate it. Father, if You would, I beg You to guard an' bless the choices made by this young man. Amen."

She put her napkin in her lap then held the roll basket out to him. "Now, tell me what you think you're doin' up here huntin' for two innocent black people."

He took a roll and kept his eyes on his plate. "How do you know they're innocent?"

She didn't answer. He looked up to find her watching him, gauging him. She pointed her fork at him and said, "I expect I know it the same way you do. I heard what those white men did to that young mother. If that had been yo' momma, you'd of done what that little colored boy did, wouldn't you?"

He let his eyes go back to his plate; the hand holding the roll came to rest on the table. *If the FBI is looking for men who care more about their image than they do about the truth, they hired the wrong boy*. He said, "Yes, ma'am, I hope that's exactly what I'd've done."

"Well, then. Looks like you an' me are gonna get along just fine."

"How did you hear about the killings?"

She waved the question away. "We'll have time for all that over our coffee an' dessert. Right now, let's talk about somethin' important."

"What's important?"

"Whether or not you're going to heaven, Agent Wagner. Are you?"

"Well, I'd like to."

"Do you believe in God?"

He finished chewing and swallowed. "You're the second person to ask me that today."

"Have you stopped to wonder why that is?" The gold frames glittered. "What'd you say to the other person?"

He put down his fork. "I told him I believe in God."

"Do you believe Jesus is His Son?"

"I do."

"Have you ever prayed to receive Christ . . . to ask Him to be your personal Savior?"

He held his tea glass near his mouth while he thought then said, "I know He's God's Son; I've believed that all my life. What else is there?"

She pointed at his plate. "What we're talkin' about is more important than food, but we don't need to let any go to waste. You eat while I explain somethin' to you." She reached across the table for her Bible.

Wagner set aside most of what he had learned about the elements of interrogation by saying, "Before you start, let me ask you something. Do you believe in demons?"

She had the Bible in front of her. "Let's get the important thing out of the way first. We can come back to that." She touched her finger to her tongue and flipped a few pages until she found the passage she was looking for.

"I want you to listen to this." Her finger traced down the page. " 'But these are written, that ye might believe that Jesus is the Christ, the Son of God; an' that believin' ye might have life through His name.' That tells you what I'm tryin' to say about Him bein' your personal Savior. The only way you get to go to heaven—to have eternal life—is through Him—through His name. His name . . . it's like bein' His brother. That's why we can call ourselves God's children."

"I've already said I believe He's God's Son."

"Young man, the Book says those demons you asked about believe just like you, an' it scares them. The Lord says real clear that for you to be saved, you have to confess Him with your mouth an' believe in your heart that God raised Him from the dead. It's a thing of speakin' an' believin'."

"I haven't done that."

"Folks usually haven't because they don't understand about the atonement."

"What atonement?"

"*The* atonement. I can tell you about it if you like."

Wagner pretended to look at his watch. He had not come there to talk about atonements, hearts, or confessions. The chicken was better than anything he had tasted in a week, but he was deciding that no meal was worth getting preached at the whole time he was trying to eat. He slid his chair back. "Well, I hate to just eat and leave, but I guess I'd better be finishing my job."

If the lady was disappointed, it didn't show. "Well, I guess you won't be havin' any cake an' coffee."

"How about giving me a rain check?"

The lady made a gesture at the window. "That's what you had today, boy. Next time will be your first real visit."

He extended his hand. "Thanks—" he stopped. "I don't know your name."

She put her hand in his. "My name's Belle Hodges, son, an' I'm mighty proud to get to know you."

When she gripped his hand he looked down, surprised at the strength in the tiny hand. "Yes, ma'am. It's my pleasure."

He had his raincoat on when he remembered. "You didn't tell me what you believe about demons."

"My, my, my." She wagged her head slowly and lifted a reproving finger. "I'd of thought those FBI people taught you to listen closer than that. I told you that the demons believe just like you an' shudder; the Book says so. Knowin' that should keep you from sleepin' at night."

Belle Hodges was the only person in Mound Bayou who didn't seem inclined to lynch him, but Wagner had wasted enough time. He was out the door and bending over to pick up his shoes when he remembered something she'd said. "How'd you hear—"

She interrupted and answered his question before it was asked. "Mr. Mose Washington told me."

He was incredulous—and back in the house. "Washington? When?"

"Saturday. Before noon." It was ancient history now.

He dripped across the floor to look out her back window. Dr. Carlson's backyard started where hers ended. *That's great,* he thought. *I was getting ready to walk away from the only person in the whole town who's willing to admit that Washington exists.*

"You went over there?"

"No." She was beckoning him away from the kitchen. "If you're stayin' in this house, you get that raincoat off."

"He came over here?"

"Mr. Wagner, you're drippin' on my floor." She was speaking calmly and pushing the screen door open. "Now, get over here an' stand out on the porch or take off that coat."

He took the coat off and hung it back on the hall tree, and she said, "Good. Now, I've got a three-layer chocolate cake that's still warm. You want a slice with some coffee?"

He stayed by the hall tree. "Are you going to preach or answer my questions?"

Belle's calm demeanor became less apparent. She stepped closer to him and one fist moved to a waist as tiny as the rest of her. "You listen to me, sonny boy. I'm past gettin' old, an' I'll be lookin' to the good Lord to guide when I choose to preach, not to some young white boy who can't tell his right hand from his left. Now, do you want the cake or not?"

Wagner could hear Fuller telling him, *Most of the black people will yield to any white person that comes near them. The cooks don't always yield.*

He smiled to himself and made a guess. "How long were you a cook?"

"We can talk about that later." She turned and walked toward her kitchen. "Take a seat there on the sofa."

Belle returned with a broad wedge of warm chocolate cake and hot coffee for Wagner. She sat beside him on the sofa, contented with black coffee.

She waited till he got a bite of cake in his mouth and said, "Now, you listen close to me. What you're gettin' yourself mixed up in is something that got started before man got settled on the earth, and something that happened back in 1945 showed it up in this part of the country real good." She began by giving a brief account of the death of Washington's son and worked her way through an abbreviated chronology of the terrors that had visited the environs of Cat Lake. Like Ken Dixon, she blamed demonic activity for most of what had happened. When she talked about the recent events at Cat Lake, Wagner knew he was hearing what Mose Washington had told her. He neglected his cake to compare what she said with what was written in his notebook; her narrative was consistent with everything he already knew.

When she finished talking, he asked, "Was he driving his pickup?"

"Did you hear me tell you what you're up against?"

"What I'm up against?"

She shook her head. "Son, what your ears refuse to hear could fill a number two washtub."

Wagner put his fork on his saucer and his saucer on the coffee table. "I don't believe in demons, Mrs. Hodges. And I can't spend my time chasing fairy tales."

"Mm-mmm," she let her eyes linger on his face and grimaced. "Son, tomorrow is comin', an' so is trouble. You're right smack dab in the middle of somethin' that has cost the lives of lots of folks—bad an' good." A slender black finger tapped his arm in time with her words. "I'll be here, an' I'll be prayin'. An' you need to come an' see me when you decide to hear the truth."

Well, he hadn't gotten what he wanted, but it was more than he'd had. He tried to turn the discussion away from angels and demons. "Was Washington driving his pickup truck?"

"*Mr.* Washington. I didn't see any truck."

He glanced at her back window. "You can see most of the doctor's yard from here."

"I wasn't lookin' at his yard; I was prayin'."

"Are you sure?"

Belle Hodges was on her feet when the last word left his lips. He watched her pick up his unfinished cake and coffee. She straightened and took unhurried steps into her kitchen. "Now," she was scraping the dishes off and putting them in the sink. "I'm fixin' to give you a lesson your momma should've given you."

She came back to stand by the coffee table; Wagner sat on the sofa and waited. She clasped her hands in front of her apron and began to teach. "When you have me down at the calaboose—or wherever you take your criminals—you can say you doubt my word. But when you come in my house an' do it, you better be gettin' ready to leave. Is that clear?"

Wagner was on his feet. "I'm sorry, I didn't mean to—"

She held up one of the small, firm hands. "Yes, you did—an' I'm too old to waste my time puttin' up with it." She walked over and pushed the screen door open again. "Now, you get yourself out of this house before I cut me a pecan switch an' get in trouble with the law for givin' you somethin' else your momma should've given you."

He was passing through the door as she said, "Just a minute."

He stopped.

Mrs. Hodges held up the finger she used to enforce her orders. "Wait there a minute." She stepped into the hall and returned seconds later. "As long as I'm talkin' 'bout what I ought to give you, I better give you this."

Without thinking, he put his hand out and she put a coin in it. "A silver dollar?"

"That was my husband's. I want you to have it."

"Mrs. Hodges, FBI agents can't take money from people. And I can't take your memento."

"Let me show you something." She touched the coin. "Read those words."

He knew what the words said, but he read them. "In God we trust."

She stepped back, and the rims of her glasses flashed as she lectured. "Now, you listen to me. If the people you're workin' for think you can be bought for a dollar, you're workin' for the wrong people." She put a hand on the doorknob. "An' it's not a charm. I want that dollar in your pocket while I'm prayin' that God will use it to remind you that you need to trust in Him—an' that's what I'll be prayin'. Now, scat." She closed the door.

Things in the Mississippi Delta were not going well for Agent Wagner. He had left the FBI Academy thinking himself well-qualified to handle whatever the job brought his way. Then—in the last twenty-four hours—he'd been saddled with the responsibility for an investigation that was doomed to put a black mark on his record, he'd been ridiculed twice because he didn't believe in demons, a Southern belle had cut him off at the knees in front of the entire population of a farm community, and a black lady half his size had threatened to whip him with a tree limb. He puffed his cheeks and blew out two day's worth of frustration.

He took one silver dollar, two muddy shoes, and three fast bites of food, and walked back to his car in the drizzle. The score was Mississippi Delta and Friends—4, Agent Jeff Wagner and the FBI—0.

* * *

He stopped in Cleveland for lunch. When the waitress came to his table she said, "Hi, hon. You must be goin' to a funeral."

Wagner didn't even bother to look up. "Sure looks that way to me."

An hour later—about the time Special Agent in Charge Bertrand B. Fuller was walking into his Jackson office—an older black man, a boy with a broken arm, and a Redbone coon hound were pulling up to the gas pumps in front of a small-town grocery store thirty-some-odd miles northeast of Memphis.

Special Agent Jefferson T. Wagner called it a day at four o'clock. He was looking forward to a full week of chasing non-existent leads on Washington, the Prince kid, and a white man who had left no more trail than a puff of smoke. He took a hot shower, got into some dry clothes, and called Fuller to tell him nothing was happening. He avoided the Freeze and drove to Greenwood to eat.

His plan called for him to spend two or three days talking to people in Moores Point with a possible side trip to Jackson to check his in-box. He'd save Friday morning for his first look at Parchman State Penitentiary; maybe he could uncover something there that would give him some small indication of how to go about locating Washington.

The man, boy, and dog paused in the late afternoon and found a quiet place to spend the night. When the man started redoing the car's camouflage—mixing dirt and water then flicking the mixture on the car with a handful of long grass—the dog and boy sat in the evening shade and watched. The man was pleased when the boy asked one or two questions about what he was doing. When the boy came close and offered to help, the man put him in charge of the easier tasks.

After midnight, and miles away, a woman moved silently along the upstairs hall in her home. The sheer material that drifted through the darkness behind her was not worn for modesty's sake but against the eventuality that she might meet one of the house staff. In earlier days, when she was in the habit of moving about in the nude, a male staff member had mysteriously disappeared after misinterpreting the woman's unconventional practices. Along with the flowing material, the woman trailed an overpowering odor of rancid sweat; for the demons who controlled the woman, personal hygiene was exercised only as means of baiting their trap.

She stopped at the door on the far end of the hall, paused to listen, then eased the door open. The air in the room was thick with cannabis smoke; the only illumination came from a small lamp by the bed. The man she sought had been in the room for two days, celebrating his son's death. He was reclining on the couch, his hairy belly hanging over the waist of a pair of filthy boxer shorts. Under normal circumstances, the close proximity of what had been his wife promoted fear and dread in Halbert Bainbridge; in his drugged state, he was as far as he could get from fear and still communicate. "Yes, dearest?"

That her husband and his surroundings were a recipe for repugnance seemed not to register with the woman standing near the door.

"I want them killed—all three of them," wheezed the woman.

"I know what you want, but they can't be killed until they've been found, and I can't find them. When the FBI does its job, they'll be questioned. After the FBI finishes with them, I'll have them killed."

The glaring physical contrast between the two people grew

more pronounced with each year's passing. After their arrival in Washington, Estelle Bainbridge became even more slender, smooth, and beautiful; her face and figure were a testimony to the effectiveness of the best spas in New York and the most skilled plastic surgeons in California. Bainbridge was apparently content to become more sleazy, greasy, ugly, and obese. Many of the congressional wives who envied the woman her looks and charm whispered about her willingness to wear provocative fashions; the congressmen were foolish enough to envy her husband.

The woman spoke without emotion; her voice carried no inflection. "I will give you six months to find them."

"Then what?"

"Then you will have failed me."

"You can always call on one of your little friends."

The human was right. The budding actress Estelle met on her recent trip to the West Coast confided that she was captivated by the things of the occult. The dark angels warmed to the thought—*captive* was an excellent root word. The woman said, "I believe I have just the person." The foolish young girl from Hollywood was in line for a new role.

"Until that day then." He offered the mouthpiece of an ornate water pipe. "Join me?"

In the dark recesses of what had been the woman's mind, a feeble impulse strained to influence its captors. The flicker of thought was a longing—a desperate hunger—for anything that might serve to anesthetize it, to spare it—if only for an instant—from the unceasing torture to which it was continuously subjected. The thought screamed, *Yes! Yes!* The beautifully shaped mouth formed a word. "No."

CHAPTER NINE

Wagner was up early on Tuesday. He decided to abandon his dark suit in favor of jeans and a light jacket. When he got to the Freeze, Dixon was waiting in their regular booth. The smell of sausage and bacon tried to drown out the cigarette smoke that formed a thick haze in the room. A few of the locals spoke, others nodded.

A new version of waitress showed up with coffee. She was a grade or so taller than her predecessor; long bangs ran in the family. "Mornin'. You want breakfast?"

Wagner ordered the meal like a native. "Four over medium, four biscuits, double order of crisp bacon, grits."

The girl topped off Dixon's cup and walked back to the kitchen, yelling short-order shorthand at someone in the next county.

They made small talk until Wagner said, "You never told me about this Parker girl that keeps popping up."

"How much time you got?"

Wagner checked his watch. "I'm gonna waste my day anyway. How about letting me have the *Reader's Digest* version."

"Okay, but demons might get talked about, even in the short version."

"I can handle it."

"Fine. Tell me what you've heard so far about the war out at Cat Lake."

The waitress put Wagner's breakfast on the table, and the conversation held still while he buttered his grits and biscuits. He held half a biscuit poised near his mouth and said, "How much more Cat Lake stuff do I have to go through to hear about the Parker woman?"

"The girl and the lake are practically inseparable and end up on the edge of most of the stories you'd want to hear."

"Okay," Wagner resigned himself. "I've got what you told me about the demons. A Mrs. Hodges in Mound Bayou retold some of the stories to try to convince me of Mose Washington's innocence." He snapped off a piece of bacon and stuck it in his mouth with the biscuit.

Dixon could've read the signs while blindfolded; people were telling a pretty smart man the truth, and he wasn't hearing it. He prayed, *God, if it's Your will, would You have the man hear the truth? And would You protect him till he does.* He said, "Tell you what, let's talk about Missy when I've got more time."

Wagner picked up a forkful of eggs and another biscuit. "Suit yourself."

"How was Mound Bayou?"

Wagner slowed the feeding operation enough to grumble, "Underwater, under-hospitable, and underinformed—otherwise, the trip was a waste."

"Colored folks don't talk to white law dogs, Tex. You federal boys need to hire you a few black men."

"We've got black agents." Wagner grinned wryly. "What we *don't* have is black agents who're willing to waste their time on a wild-goose chase."

"Well, you just called it, son. Your chances will get better if you blindfold yourself and go hunting for a quiet duck."

Wagner didn't believe him. "Ken, that old man may be

good, but he's probably never been outside of the state. I don't know about that white fellow, but Washington's out of his element."

"Uh-uh." Dixon's head moved back and forth. "You're wrong there, buddy. The rules are always the same; it's just the territory that's different. All he and the boy have to do is stay quiet, sprinkle a little of the local dust on their clothes, and stay out of touch with people who know them. You can't find 'em if they're invisible."

"No one is invisible."

"You sound like you know something."

Wagner put his fork on his plate and looked into Dixon's eyes. "I know this, Ken—it may take me a while, but I intend to be the one who finds them."

Dixon saw the fixed determination. "That's bold talk for a Yankee man in the middle of cotton country."

Wagner picked up his fork and went back to the business of breakfast. "You just hide and watch, amigo."

While Wagner and Dixon talked, three of the travelers in question worked their way north along well-chosen country roads in Tennessee without attracting so much as a sidelong glance. They were just ordinary colored folks, going fishing in a shabby-looking old car that—thanks to a disconnected spark plug wire and a small measure of motor oil in the gas tank—ran poorly and trailed a thin cloud of blue-white exhaust smoke.

It was four thirty in the morning on the West Coast, and the white man who had helped Mose save the boy was standing where he could hear the ocean.

The rest of Tuesday was a write-off for Agent Wagner. He had breakfast with Dixon on Wednesday then wasted the rest of the day trying to talk to some of the black people in Moores Point. He spent part of Thursday in Jackson, checking in at the office and picking up a load of clean clothes. When the sun came up on Friday, he was on his way to Parchman Prison Farm.

The warden at Parchman welcomed him to the Farm and offered him the complete cooperation of his staff, but the staff let their boss down. The people in the warden's office would never forget that one of the prison's favorite former sergeants owed his life to Mose Washington, and they were fed up with the FBI man and his incessant questions before noon. When two o'clock came, the entire office staff was hiding or in rebellion. Two ladies had become suddenly ill and gone home; the assistant warden informed his boss that he was "cogitatin' on shootin' that carpet-baggin' so-'n'-so an' takin' my chances with a jury."

Most of what Wagner heard at Parchman was more of what he already knew—Mose Washington had spent five years there for killing a man in self-defense, and he was pardoned in 1957 for saving the life of Sergeant Bill Williams. What Wagner hadn't known—but discovered that Friday—was that a fellow named Sam Jones had joined forces with Washington to save Sgt. Williams. Sam Jones, of Pilot Hill, Texas, was one of Washington's best friends.

Dixon missed their unscheduled appointment for breakfast on Saturday. Wagner ate by himself then drove seven miles to Moores Point.

* * *

The people hanging out in Dennison's Store weren't happy to see him; conversations stopped, and men moved toward the door when he stepped inside. In a short minute, half the crowd was gone, and the ones who stayed didn't know anything or didn't have time to talk. He gave up and went back outside to plan his next failure. The only person outside the store was a large black man. He was relaxing by the front door, using a wooden drink case for a seat.

Wagner needed a little help. "You know where I might find a Mr. A. J. Mason?"

The black man rose and took off his hat. He pointed south down the muddy highway. "Mistah A. J., he gen'ly down to Mistah Scooter's fillin' station."

Wagner nodded his thanks and turned.

"Boss?"

Wagner looked back. "What?"

Doc Perriman looked down at his hat. "Boss, them Bainbridge people is bad folks."

"I don't understand."

Doc made a quick check over his shoulder before speaking. "If you catches Mose Washington, they'll kill 'im dead. They evil."

"Nobody is going to kill Mr. Washington. We just want to talk to him."

Doc stepped closer to Wagner and lowered his voice. "You listen, now, boss. They's evil here you don't know nothin' 'bout—you mind my words, now. Mistah A. J., he's a fine Christian man, an' the good Lord knows he's a tough one, an' he can tell you Mose Washington ain't done nuthin' wrong. They's evil here 'bouts what stands for killin' good mens, an' Mose an' Mistah A. J. been in the middle of it befo' now." Doc checked over his shoulder again. "You needs to be careful, 'cause you the one gittin' in the middle of it now."

"What kind of evil?"

"They ain't but one kind, boss. Just like they ain't but one kind of good. You needs to be powerful cautious, boss."

Wagner nodded. "And the one kind of good is God."

Doc nodded. "That's right, boss."

Wagner thanked the man and walked to his car.

They's evil here 'bouts. Wagner shook his head as he drove south. The Delta was thousands of square miles of superstitious fanatics.

The population at Scooter's filling station dropped from twelve to three when Wagner displayed the gold badge; none of the men actually ran, but they managed to leave expeditiously. Scooter and Wagner stood outside the front door and watched the men hurry to their pickup trucks for a Le Mans start, scattering in several directions as soon as they had their engines running.

Scooter walked back into the service station, waving a chewed match at the departing loafers. "Well, son, if you can do that with *four*-footed rats, I'd 'preciate it if you'd stop by my barn on your way outta town."

The only other person remaining in the station was an older fellow who was semi-reclining in a tall seat—fashioned from heavy lumber by an amateur carpenter, the contraption was half throne, half lawn chair. Whoever occupied it always had a full view out the front windows of the station. The man in the chair was doing a careful job of polishing his glasses on a red bandana. When his glasses were clean and back in place, he motioned at Wagner. "That must be a scary lookin' thing, boy. Lemme look at it."

Wagner handed the man the badge case. For the briefest instant something about the man looked familiar. He was wearing a long-sleeved khaki shirt buttoned at the neck and a brown felt hat.

The man frowned at the gold shield. He tilted it this way

and that in the light, running age-ravaged fingertips across its surface, tracing the outline of the eagle. When he finished his inspection, he handed it back to Wagner. "That's 'bout one of the finest things I've ever seen. You got any idea how come it scared all them men off like that?"

Wagner folded the case and turned his back on the old man. "Who knows?" *Because they're all rednecks like you, and they don't like federal agents.*

"Don't you?"

Wagner moved to the door. He was concentrating on the oil spots on the station's concrete drive, wondering what his next move should be. "Don't I what?"

The old man's voice had an austere quality to it. "Don't you know why men are scared of that badge?"

"Nope." Wagner was thinking about going out to Cat Lake. Maybe they had missed something in Washington's old cabin.

"No, sir." The old man had dismounted from the chair without making a sound and was standing at Wagner's elbow. He was shorter than Wagner, slightly built.

"What?" The old goat was getting on Wagner's nerves.

"I'm forty-somethin' years older'n you, son. You oughta say 'sir.'" A lesson in conduct from a man who had to tilt his head back to make eye contact with his student.

Wagner looked into the old man's eyes and had that flash of something familiar again. He said, "Who're you?"

"Somebody that's forty years older'n you, an' maybe fifty times smarter."

Wagner was having a hard time believing what he was hearing. The old man wasn't trying to provoke him; he was stating what he believed to be a fact. The agent looked at Scooter. Scooter was propped against the counter by the cash register, arms crossed, stirring the end of the match around in his mouth with his tongue, staying quiet and listening while his friend tried to straighten out the Yankee.

When Wagner didn't respond, the old man answered his own question. "They're scared of the badge because they're supposed to be, son."

What? Wagner turned back to the station owner to get his reaction. If Scooter Hall was surprised at what the old guy was saying, he wasn't showing it. Wagner gave his attention back to the old man. "Those people are supposed to be scared of a badge?"

"The Book says, 'For he beareth not the sword in vain: for he is the minister of God, a revenger to execute wrath upon him that doeth evil.' The Lord is talkin' 'bout any man who bears arms for a righteous gov'ment, son. I reckon that'd be you."

I should've been taking notes all this time, Wagner thought, *I could write a book about this place.*

The old man was finished with his sermon; he turned away and walked over to rummage through the drink box. Scooter moved over to lean against the pinball machine. An air compressor kicked on somewhere outside.

Wagner went back to the oil spots for a moment. The old man's words nagged at him. "I'm supposed to be a minister of God? What're you talking about?"

"You're carryin' a gun an' a badge, son—you're God's appointed man to protect innocent folks from evil ones. Them fellows probably took off 'cause they felt guilty." He smiled for the first time. "Or it just might be they think more of Mose Washington than they do white FBI folks."

"Humph."

The man pulled a Grapette out of the cold water and showed it to Wagner. "You wanna drink?"

Wagner shook his head. "Uh-uh."

The man said, "No, thank you."

Wagner ignored the lesson in etiquette. "I'm looking for a man named A. J. Mason."

Scooter's head came up, and he took the match out of his mouth. "For what?"

Wagner turned his search in Scooter's direction. "I'm told he was the man who shot some of those snakes when that thing happened out at Cat Lake. I'd like to hear the straight story."

"Mmm." Scooter nodded and went back to his match.

A bottle opener hung on a dirty string by the drink box; the old man concentrated on using it. "He comes in here a lot."

"Mason does?"

"Yep."

"Has he been here this morning?"

The man stripped the water off his Grapette and flicked it on the concrete floor. "Yep."

The man was too calm. "You're Mason, aren't you?"

"Well, now. There may be hope for you after all." Mason poked through packages of peanuts, inspecting them individually till he found one that suited him. He carried his snack back to the tall chair.

Wagner went back to stare out at the street. He had probably just managed to completely alienate the man he needed to talk to.

A bell by the door rang when a lady pulled up to the gas pumps. Scooter went out to see what she needed.

Wagner waited till Scooter was pumping gas into the lady's car and looked at Mason. "I don't suppose you'd be willing to tell me what happened out there, would you?"

Mason was engrossed in pouring the peanuts into the opening of his drink bottle. Wagner waited.

When the peanut-to-Grapette ratio was nearing perfection, Mason said, "I reckon not."

"Look . . . Mr. Mason." Wagner wiped a palm hard across his mouth. "It's been kind of a long week, and I've run into more than one wall. I fouled up everything about this conversation, and I apologize."

Mason was adding more peanuts, holding the bottle at eye

level, measuring accurately. "Tell you what. Why don't you bring that badge back by here a week from today, say 'bout noon. Me an' you'll go out there an' take a look at the lake."

Wagner said, "Yes, sir. Umm . . . thanks, Mr. Mason."

"My friends call me A. J." Mason had to talk with peanuts in his mouth. "Now why don't you mosey on outta here so them wicked fellers'll have a chance to come back here an' visit with me."

"Thanks."

"Don't mention it."

Scooter came back in, made a notation on a piece of paper, and put it behind a clip that held the lady's charge slips.

Wagner was already out the door when Mason called him. "Boy?"

Wagner thought, *Boy?* but answered, "Sir?"

"You do carry a gun, don't you?"

Wagner pointed at his foot. "It's in my ankle holster."

Scooter looked where Wagner pointed and nodded wisely. "That's in case you get in a gunfight with a midget, ain't it?"

Mason ignored his friend and spoke to Wagner. "You might want to think about puttin' it where you can get it into play quicker. The few times I ever needed a gun, I wanted it quick-like."

Wagner nodded. "I'll think about it."

Mason went back to his Grapette. Wagner went to his car.

Lessons on evil people, etiquette, and the art of gun handling—Wagner sat in his car and mentally tongue-lashed himself for not being more objective and less irritable. When he felt thoroughly chewed out, he started the car and drove away from the station. Cat Lake was five miles south of town.

The reason for the large population of pickup-driving men wasting their time in town was evident as he drove toward the lake. Water stood between rows of last year's cotton stalks, and a cool breeze blew continuously from the northwest. The farmers needed to get their cotton planted, but they were having to wait for drier ground and warmer weather.

As he approached the lake, he saw the sheriff's car. The sheriff was on the bridge near the ladder, standing motionless, one hand in his pants pocket, the other holding a cigarette. He was staring at the water near the float. Wagner parked by Hollinsworth's car and looked at the two Parker houses. He had yet to talk to any of the Parkers, and judging by the deserted look of the places, he wouldn't be seeing any of them today. He got out of the car and walked onto the bridge. The wind from the north stirred across the water and pushed at the tops of rapidly greening trees.

"Morning, Sheriff."

Hollinsworth kept his eyes on the water. "Mornin'. What're you doin' out here?"

"Who knows? Thought maybe I might get inspired. You?"

The sheriff shrugged. He took a final drag off the cigarette and flicked it at the float; Monday's rain had washed away all evidence of the previous week's horror. The wind caught the white missile and carried it out and away from the float and dropped it in the lake. "Been comin' out here every day since the killin's. Gettin' to be a habit."

Wagner didn't have a response. He was hunching his shoulders against the effects of the wind; if the sheriff was cold, he didn't show it.

The two men stood quietly until Hollinsworth said, "Well, you've been here almost a week; you findin' out anything?"

"Yeah, I'm drowning in information," Wagner scoffed. "I found out I'm impolite, I don't wear my gun right, and this is a good place to run into evil spirits."

Hollinsworth lost interest in the lake and looked at Wagner. "Somebody's been talkin' to you about evil spirits?"

Wagner didn't know the man's name at Dennison's Store.

"Yeah. Some lady over in Mound Bayou, and a black guy in town."

Hollinsworth turned to face the agent. "Who'd you talk to in town?"

Wagner wasn't sure he wanted Hollinsworth to know. "I don't know who he was—just a black man I crossed paths with while I was looking for A. J. Mason. I didn't ask his name."

When Hollinsworth didn't say anything, Wagner added, "I wish I could say he's wrong, but nothin' about what happened out here makes any sense if you try to explain it naturally."

"Well, I gotta get back to the office." The sheriff turned toward his car. "It sure would be nice if you came up with a good explanation for all this. The whole thing is 'bout to drive me nuts." He walked to his car, muttering and growling to himself.

Wagner stood on the bridge, hands jammed into the pockets of his windbreaker, and watched the sheriff's car drive away; when Hollinsworth was out of sight, he turned back to the lake. The wind had picked up, rippling and snapping the fabric of his jacket; the coffee-colored lake was sprinkled with tiny whitecaps. Water slapped at the sides of the float. He was wasting his time; if the black waters harbored any secrets they weren't inclined to share them with a Yankee government agent. In a stand of tall pecan trees on the east side of the lake, he could see the cabin where they found the woman. He considered walking over there, but he didn't want to get his shoes any muddier. This was a good time to take the rest of the day off; he'd start fresh on Monday.

When he returned to Indianola, he called the Davis home.

Ceedie and her mother were getting ready to go shopping in Greenville; they'd be back late.

How about tomorrow?

Well, she'd go to church in the morning and had a tennis

date after lunch. "Can we just meet at the Freeze sometime after three?"

Sure. Sounds great.

He hung up and sat on the side of the motel bed, thinking, remembering what Doc Perriman and Belle Hodges had told him. The information given to him by Dixon and A. J. Mason was wrapped around indirect warnings. He opened the drawer in the nightstand and took out the Bible placed there for bored travelers to read; it looked new. He held it in his hands, unopened, glad no one could know what he was contemplating. He pulled in a deep breath, exhaled, then said, "Okay, God, I'm willing to look if You're willing to show me."

He closed his eyes, opened the book near the center, and stabbed the middle of a page with his ballpoint. He opened his eyes and read the carefully selected words in Jeremiah 9:24. "But let him who glories glory in this, that he understands and knows Me, that I am the Lord who practices steadfast love, justice, and righteousness in the earth; for in these things I delight, says the Lord." No demons. No help.

He used a sheet of stationery for a bookmark and took the Bible when he left the room.

It was barely eleven in the morning, and the curb-service side of the Freeze was sparsely populated. Jagoe, the black carhop, was standing by the car before Wagner could switch off the ignition.

"Mornin', boss."

"Hi. Two burgers and a chocolate malt, please."

Jagoe took off for the kitchen.

While he waited for his lunch, Wagner picked up the Bible and started paging through it, glancing at the words. He didn't see anything about demons.

His hamburgers arrived, and he spent fifteen minutes eating and paging through the Bible. No demons.

The boy kept his first name; that helped. On the rare occasions when they had to meet people, the man introduced himself as Mose Mann. The boy called his "grandfather" Poppa.

At noon on Saturday the fugitives were still taking their time, moving north according to their needs. Having a safe place to stop was more important than hurrying to Chicago. Chicago would be cold.

The boy and dog watched the man. The boy said, "It's starting to get cold 'cause we're going north."

The man had a small fire going, getting ready to heat soup for their noon meal. "Yes, sir. Gonna get some colder in Chicago. I hear tell it comes a hard freeze up there right regular."

"You think we'll get too cold?"

"No, no. We got all we need to keep us warm." He smiled. "I recall once when that dog right yonder kept a young child from gettin' too cold. Wrapped 'em both up in this here coat, snug as a bug."

"He already keeps me warm at night."

Mose smiled wider. "Well, maybe he's good for somethin', after all."

The dog snorted.

The boy reached his arm around the dog, and the dog leaned closer. "He likes me, I guess."

"Yes, sir. He does, for a fact. Truth be told, he's the smartest dog I ever been around, an' I reckon he knows a good man when he sees one."

The boy stroked the dog. "I figure it's been a week since my mom died."

"I been waitin' on you to talk 'bout that."

"You told me she had a funeral."

"She did. You were there."

"I don't remember it."

"There's no way you could, boy." Mose left the food preparation for the moment. "You'd took a good lick on the head.

When I prayed, you was by her bed in the arms of that fine white man. I taken yo' fingertips an' touched 'em to yo' lips, an' then I touched 'em to her lips so you could kiss her goodbye."

The boy let Mose's words sink in—warming himself with the picture they painted—then said, "When I was little, I was scared of school. She told me if I'd go, she'd have a piece of chocolate cake waiting for me when I got home." The boy petted the dog and let the tears run down his face unheeded. "I bet I'm the only kid in the world that's had chocolate cake for his school snack for five straight years."

"That's a fine thing."

"She was the best mom ever."

Mose knew the boy didn't need his agreement. He went back to heating the soup. The dog scroonched closer to the boy.

Ceedie and Polly Ragsdale were already at the Freeze when he got there Sunday afternoon, and so were half the boys in Indianola. The most recent events at Cat Lake were over a week old and had been rehashed to the point of monotony; the Delta's beautiful girls were back in their roles as the centerpieces of male consideration. When Wagner pulled under the awning, Ceedie said something to Polly and got out of the convertible. He was waiting outside his car with the passenger door open when she got to him.

Jagoe brought Cokes and they made small talk while they rebroke the ice. She seemed relaxed—leaning back against the seat, talking about nothing and listening to the music from the jukebox while she tied her straw wrapper in a series of flat knots. He was going more slowly, doing more listening than talking, feeling his way.

The Coasters were *Searchin'* on the juke box. Two or three girls in the car next door were singing along.

She noticed the Bible. "You're readin' the Bible?"

He looked at the book and thought for a moment. "No, not really."

She waited.

"I've got a lot of people telling me that demons have been involved in the things that happen at Cat Lake. I don't understand how they can think that."

"Mmm." She wasn't going to rush him.

"No comment?"

Finally she asked, "Do you believe in the devil—in Satan?"

"Sure."

"Then you have to come to the conclusion that he has his own helpers—demons."

"But do I have to believe they're to blame for people getting killed at Cat Lake?"

"No."

Her answer surprised him. "I don't?"

"No. People can be mean without the help of the devil or anybody else, but I can tell you right now, what happened out at Cat Lake fifteen years ago was brought on by demons."

The Coasters were being lawmen . . . making bold promises about apprehending a good-looking woman.

"How can you say that?"

She touched her fingers while she made her points. "Because Missy Parker was Polly's best friend, an' I've known the girl all my life—we all grew up together. An' my daddy was out there the day it happened. Every person that was out there knows exactly what happened."

"Can I talk to your dad?"

"Well," she hesitated, "he was there, but he didn't see it."

"I don't understand."

"Daddy an' all the other men were at a coon-on-the-log up at the end of the lake when it started. All the shootin'—the attacks by the snakes—pretty much happened on an' around that old float an' up on the bridge. Why don't you look up Mr. A. J. Mason? He was on the bridge when it started—right in the middle of it."

"I've got an appointment with him this Saturday."

"Then you can hear about it from the horse's mouth."

It finally occurred to him that he was wasting his time talking business with a beautiful woman when he should be taking his cue from the Coasters. "How would you like to spend the rest of the afternoon?"

"Let's ride around a while then we can go to my house an' let Daddy see for himself that bein' an FBI man an' being a Yankee aren't necessarily the same thing. If we get him convinced, you might can eat supper with us."

CHAPTER TEN

The facility was separated into twenty some-odd camps, each at least a mile from its nearest neighbor—all surrounded by razor wire and men with rifles; most Delta folks called it The Farm. It bordered along US49, about twenty miles south of the intersection of highways 49 and 61—the very intersection where Robert Johnson is reputed to have traded his soul to the devil in return for fame as a blues man. Some say the blues were born on The Farm—sad stories of hard lives and the folks who lived them, moaned in plaintive words to the accompaniment of whining harmonicas and guitars like Robert Johnson's. Blues or not, the devil didn't travel far from home to conduct his exchange with Johnson. The Farm was twenty-three thousand acres of flat cotton land transformed into the third level of Hell for every prisoner in the Mississippi State Penitentiary at Parchman.

In the quiet of the night, or on those rare days when the rain kept them inside, the newer convicts would ask how it used to be, and the old-timers would tell the stories. They'd tell about the meanest guards and the smartest dogs and the famous convicts. Pepper Jack Bradley, when he was predisposed to talk, was the man they liked to listen to the most. Bradley was the one who had taken the beating from Sam Jones. Even the old white prisoners agreed that Jones was—for less than an hour—the youngest and toughest trusty-shooter that ever picked up a rifle on The Farm.

Bradley would start his story by telling how he'd been attacked by those two fools down at the Busy Bee—that tonk down there between Midnight and Belzoni. He'd recount every thrust and parry in the ensuing knife fight—and how the doctor took four hours to sew him up, and he had the scars to prove it. He'd tell about the trial, and he'd brag about how he'd sassed that white judge in Yazoo City—the one who'd sent him to Parchman for killing those boys. He'd work up to his encounter with Sam by going into detail about how much bigger he was than the young college boy—and then the listeners would hear about the first and only time Sam Jones ever raised his hand on The Farm.

Bradley would warm to his story and his hard expression would mellow. "I'd done made my brag that I's fixin' to be the first nigger what ever spent less than twenty-four hours on this here place, but it didn't work out like I 'spected. Now, shooters back then was badder than they is now—if you ran an' they kilt you, the warden sent 'em home free that very day. But what didn't nobody know was, my cousin Po' Boy Weeks was the shooter on Boss Bill Williams' gang, an' me an' him had it fixed up how to get loose.

Well, I mean to tell you, things went sho' nuff bad soon as Po' Boy pult that trigger. He got off two shots at Boss Williams, an' hit 'im both times, but that white man shucked his belt gun an' put Po' Boy dead in the dirt real quicklike. Boss Williams went down, an' the two convicts what stepped up for him was ol' Mose Washington an' a fellah name o' Sam Jones. Mose taken Boss Williams to the 'firmary, an' while they was gone, Sam Jones took it on hi'self to be the shooter. The worst thing

I believe I ever done was decidin' I could take on that college boy what was holdin' that rifle."

"Soon's ol' Mose got outta sight good, I stood up to put that Jones boy in his place. Whoo-wee! I done seen a water moccasin git a frog plenty o' times," Bradley would shake his head and chuckle deep in his chest, "but I ain't never seen no kind of a snake move like that boy could move his hands." He'd do a quick one-two with an imaginary rifle. "It was over 'fore I ever got my feet set good." He'd chuckle and shake his head again. "That college boy put me in that turn row dirt 'fore I knowed the fight had done started."

Bradley's smile would fade slowly then disappear behind a memory. "When I come to, an' got so I could set up a little, I knowed Jones had done made a powerful big mistake—he done showed he wouldn't shoot. I couldn't even stand up yet, but I was near to smilin' 'cause I knowed that soon's I got so I could see right, I was gonna try him on again. Mmm, mmm, mmm. 'Bout then that boy seen me lookin' 'round an' says, 'Will Green, you an' Pop Willie strap Mr. Bradley to that wagon wheel yonder.' "

The memory always made him wince. He'd look around the circle of younger faces and digress. "Back then things was tough. You so much as looked a white man in the face, or didn't git yo' work done, they wasn't never no discussion—they let Black Annie tell you 'bout it on the spot."

He'd hesitate again, pausing as if in prayer, remembering what happened in the dirt of that turn row. "Mmm, mmm. I mean to tell you that man tol' 'em to strip off my shirt, an' he taken that big black strap an' whupped me 'til I didn't know c'mere from sic 'em. After that, he left me tied to that wheel 'til a whole passel of guards an' such come out to see 'bout what had happened. That evenin' they taken me an' got me sewed up over to the 'firmary, an' had me back pickin' my share the next day."

At this point a note of wonder could be heard in his voice,

as if a revelation had come to him in that very moment. "That man knowed he didn't need to use no bullet to stop me; he just had to show me an' them others what happened to folks what didn't do right while he was the boss."

He'd pause again and the smile would come back, only quieter. "I'm gonna tell you fools sumpin' right now—there ain't no kind of a man nowhere can stand up to a man like that; that college boy was *mannish*."

The men listening to the story would nod their heads and be glad they hadn't known Sam—they knew they didn't want to meet Annie.

On a warming Sunday afternoon, a rowdy bunch of Parchman convicts were trying to play baseball on the drying ground. Pepper Jack Bradley, who didn't like to be disturbed during the game, sat by himself in a large, unoccupied section of the makeshift stands. When a young black man in striped pants climbed the bleachers and approached the big man, Bradley turned a serious frown on the smaller convict.

The young black man sat down without being invited and smiled confidently into the dark face. "I got somethin' for you, Mr. Bradley."

Most of the convicts in the rickety stands quit yelling at the players and turned to see who dared to draw near the big man.

"Boy, folks knows I don't like nobody to be botherin' me durin' the game."

The boy lost little of his enthusiasm when confronted by Bradley's frown; he had serious news. "Yes'r, but I kind of figured you'd want to know 'bout this."

"Well?"

"I works up at the main office, an' the FBI come in Friday afternoon an' paid us a visit." He paused.

"Boy." Coming from the big man, the single word constituted a significant threat.

"I'm gittin' there, Mr. Bradley." He took a breath to refuel his enthusiasm. "It's 'bout them white boys gittin' kilt last week down to Moores Point. A FBI man come up here an' was lookin' to find out who Mose Washington knowed when he was here on the farm."

Bradley forgot the game. "Did you hear 'em talkin'?"

"Yes'r."

"That fellow from the FBI . . . did he hear 'bout Sam Jones?"

"Yes'r."

Bradley let his eyes stray to the game while he considered the news. He turned back to the convict. "Can you git word to Sam?"

"Yes'r."

"How you gonna do it?"

"They got us tryin' out a new thing called a area code. I can dial straight to a phone anywheres in the country without talkin' to no operator. The phone company lettin' us try it out an' ain't even keepin' up with the calls yet."

Bradley let that sink in. "You can call Sam an' won't nobody know?"

"Yes'r." He looked to see if anyone was close enough to overhear. "I got his number."

"Okay. Here's what you do. You call Sam Jones an' tell him Mr. Bradley says 'Hello.'" He chuckled to himself. "You got that, now? You be sure an' let him know the word come from me. An' you tell him 'bout what's happenin' here, you understand? Them gov'ment boys will be listenin' to his phone pretty soon now."

"Yes'r. I'll take care of it first thing in the mornin'."

"You did good comin' to me."

"Yes'r. Thank you."

Bradley pointed at a spot a few feet away. "You can sit over there an' watch the game for a spell . . . but don't be talkin' none, hear me?" Bradley could use a man in the warden's office. "You wanna drink?"

"Yes'r. That'd be nice." The boy looked expectant.

"Well? Whatcha want?"

"Oh!" He hadn't known he'd have a choice. "A RC would be nice."

Bradley nodded at a man.

The Royal Crown Cola was so cold it had ice in it. And somebody had already pulled off the bottle cap, just like in a fancy cafe.

Wagner and Ceedie rode the streets of Indianola and the surrounding countryside for half the afternoon; other riders passed and waved. She showed him the high school, the country club, her church, and her daddy's furniture store. An hour before dark she said, "Let's go see what's for supper."

Ceedie led Wagner through the Davises' back door and into the domain of their cook, a certain Maddie Mae Phillips. The aroma of a cake getting ready to come out of the oven mixed itself with the thick smells of more substantial food; pot roast, the obligatory fried chicken, hot rolls, mashed potatoes, and cream gravy were all lined up, steaming, ready to be served.

The cook stood with her back to the door, last-minute-busy at the counter.

Ceedie said, "Hey, Maddie Mae, what're we havin' for supper?" She reached past the woman and stuck her finger into a mixing bowl full of fluffy white icing.

Maddie Mae patted at the girl's hand with plump fingers and kept stirring. "Better'n what you can git down at that cafe place. You got no business—" She saw Wagner out of the corner of her eye and turned her head. "Who is you?"

Ceedie's mouth was full of icing-covered finger. "Did id Jep Pwacker. Jep, did id Bahhy Bay."

Wagner acknowledged the introduction with a nod because Bahhy Bay was already talking.

"Humph. Is he stayin' for supper?" The question came from a face that was round, shiny black, and forged into a perpetual frown. The rest of the cook was five feet in height and width—roughly three hundred pounds topped off with a neatly done red bandana around a fuzz of white hair.

"I have to ask Momma."

"Ain't no Wagner folks live in the Delta. Where 'bouts you from, boy?" Her voice wasn't smiling either.

"Be nice, Maddie Mae. Jeff works for the FBI."

This was welcome news for neither Maddie Mae nor Wagner. "You's a FBI man?"

"I just said he was." Ceedie's finger was coming out of the bowl again with more of the sweet-looking white stuff on it.

Maddie Mae abandoned her stirring duties. The round body tilted from side to side as she struggled against the forces of gravity to turn and face the enemy head-on; the color, texture, and assumed flavoring of the mixture in the bowl were pointed contrasts to the countenance she showed Wagner. "He can talk for hi'self, can't he?"

Ceedie was concentrating on dipping a heretofore unused finger into the bowl. "I guess nobody's gonna find out if you don't give him a chance to open his mouth."

"Hush up." Maddie Mae picked up a butcher knife, and every word of Fuller's lecture on cooks occupied Wagner's brain at once. The cook started tapping the tip of the blade on a too-narrow table that stood between the knife and the Yankee. "If you's a gov'ment man, then you done come down here 'bout them killin's out to Cat Lake, ain't you?"

"That's right." Fuller was right for once. One of these days some overpaid scholar was going to do a study comparison measuring the exercised territorial defense of a mother grizzly in her den versus a black cook in her kitchen. The findings would prove conclusively that it would be significantly safer to don a breech cloth and attack the resident of the cave with a willow switch, rather than employ a machine gun to confront a black cook in a Delta kitchen. Ceedie was still fooling around with the mixing bowl, oblivious to the fact that the old woman was planning to use the kitchen knife to do to him what Farrell Whitacher had done to himself.

"Well, boy, I'll tell you somethin' right now." She put one fist in the neighborhood of where her waist would've been and lectured with the knife. "If Mose Washington had anything to do with them trashy white boys gettin' theyselves kilt out at that lake, then they was beggin' to be dead."

Ceedie stayed with the mixing bowl and spoke without looking over her shoulder. "Maddie Mae, don't run the man off till he's had his supper. Where's Momma?"

Maddie Mae Phillips wasn't going to be distracted while the enemy from up north was standing right there in her kitchen. The knife was longer than her arm and she was leaning over the table now, waving its tip an inch from the interloper's nose; the black frown was deeper and darker. "An' I'll tell you somethin' else, white folks. I raised this here child from the cradle jes' like her momma before her. You messes 'round with her an' I'll slice out yo' gizzard an' feed it to my pigs, you understandin' me?" She redirected the tip of the knife so that it was making tight circles in the vicinity of his gizzard.

Well, this is just peachy, thought Wagner. Nothing in the FBI's extensive training had even brushed against how to handle a situation like this. Wagner was trapped between an unyielding wall and a world of backcountry people who feasted at every meal, believed in voodoo, and fed their enemies to their livestock. He could feel his T-shirt sticking to the sweat under his arms; his ankle holster—contrary to A. J. Mason's wise counsel—was three feet from his hand.

He was trying to decide whether he would rather risk death in order to pursue the possibility of another date with the girl, or shoot the old woman, when Ceedie lost interest in the bowl. "We're gonna go find Momma." The brown-haired beauty gave the crazy lady with the long knife a peck on the bandana. "The icing is perfect, just like you."

"Humph." The cook watched the girl take the Yankee's arm and tow his gizzard out of her reach.

Ceedie walked into the dining room, leading Wagner away from danger. When they were out of earshot, Ceedie whispered, "Don't pay any attention to Maddie Mae; she likes to pretend she's mad at somebody an' then start dreamin' up all kinds of wild exaggerations."

Wagner had to smile. "She sounded believable to me."

"That's silly." She made a piffing sound. "Humans don't have gizzards, an' Maddie Mae hasn't raised any pigs for five years. Besides," she patted his hand with sticky fingers and grinned wickedly, "if you *messes* with his only daughter, my daddy will take his shotgun an' blow your insides—gizzard an' all—clean into Leflore County."

Wagner met Mrs. Davis first—she was the one who had given Ceedie her looks and drawl. Mrs. Davis invited the southern-born-and-bred FBI agent to stay for supper. Ceedie arranged it so that Jeff sat in a chair that allowed him to keep an eye on the kitchen door.

After he said the blessing, Mr. Davis told the ladies to leave Wagner alone about the killings out at the Parkers', then asked the agent ten probing questions about what the investigation had turned up so far. Mrs. Davis was interested to note that her daughter, who was normally content to spend no more than ten words on a meal, was inclined to participate actively in the conversation. She also noted that the FBI boy hung on every word her daughter spoke.

* * *

When supper was over, Wagner thanked Mrs. Davis. He followed Ceedie through the kitchen and thanked Maddie Mae for the great meal. Maddie Mae told him he was welcome; she was still frowning, but she left her knife on the table. He and Ceedie walked outside.

"What now?" They were standing on the driveway by his car. The sun was down, and the sky was barely light in the west.

She looked at her watch. "Church for me. You wanna to go?"

"Not this time. How about after church?"

"Not tonight; I have to get up early. I practice-teach at Bailey, an' I have to be there at eight o'clock."

"What about later this week?"

"Better call me. We're supposed to go to Memphis Saturday."

He told himself not to be pushy. "That sounds fine."

He was in the car when she said, "Jeff?"

He stepped out of the car to answer. "Yes, ma'am?"

She moved closer and rested her hands on the top of the driver's door. A gentle breeze teased her hair, and she moved a hand to hold it back. The brown eyes looked over his shoulder. "Let me think a minute."

He wanted to put his hand on top of hers but told himself again to take his time. He waited.

Pink showed through the tan on her cheeks. She said, "I can't remember what I was goin' to say."

She was lying. That was probably good. He smiled. "Tell me later."

"Okay. Bye."

He smiled and drove away.

Ceedie went back in the house to answer the questions.

Her mother's first comment was, "He seems like a very nice boy."

Ceedie plopped down on the couch. "I guess he does,

doesn't he? An' he chewed with his mouth closed." Ceedie was not ready to let anyone forget that she had once been forced into a blind date with the son of her mother's college roommate. It hadn't turned out well at all.

"What kind of name is Wagner, I wonder?" Mrs. Davis took a seat across from her daughter.

"I'm not sure . . . German, maybe? Kenny Dixon calls him Tex."

Mrs. Davis nodded. The girl had said more words in the last hour than she normally spoke in a week. "Tex is cute."

The girl winked at her momma. "Not as cute as J. W." Four syllables.

"Is J. W. a Christian?" Mrs. Davis was in no hurry to have a son-in-law, and she was decidedly against her daughter marrying a man who was not a Christian.

Ceedie picked up a throw pillow and put it in her lap. She fluffed the pillow then hugged it. "I don't know. He wasn't interested in going to church tonight."

"Ceedie," her momma stood and smoothed her skirt, "you need to take your time, hon."

"Don't worry, Momma. I intend to."

The day might come when Ceedie would fall in love with a descendant of William Tecumseh Sherman, marry, and raise her children in New York City. Marriage to an unbeliever wasn't going to happen.

On Monday morning, when the caller identified where he was calling from, Sam Jones could feel sweat accumulating on his forehead. For the legend who had been the youngest, bravest, toughest shooter that ever picked up a rifle on The Farm, Parchman was a nightmare where he had been trapped for two years. Dreams that he was back on the farm still came to steal his sleep.

"What can I do for you?"

The young-sounding black man on the phone was hurrying, "I'm callin' with a message from a friend of yo's, an' I needs to talk real quick."

"I got no friends on The Farm, mister."

The young convict was proud to be actually talking to the most famous man he'd ever heard of. "I reckon you got one now, Mr. Jones. Mr. Pepper Jack Bradley say for me to call you."

What could happen at Parchman that would cause Bradley to call himself Sam's friend? "What's going on?"

"Mose Washington got in some troubles down to Cat Lake, an' the FBI is lookin' for 'im. Mr. Bradley say to tell you that the gov'ment mens was in here on Friday, an' they'll be listenin' to yo' phone 'fore the week is out, tryin' to catch 'im."

"What kind of trouble?"

"I ain't got time to say, but it wasn't none o' his doin'."

Sam paused to digest what he'd heard then said, "Listen, you tell Mr. Bradley I'm obliged to him. Okay?"

"Yes'r, I'll sho' tell 'im."

"If he ever needs anything," he actually laughed, "anything legal, that is—all he needs to do is let me know."

"Yes'r."

"And you tell him this too, boy. You tell him he's a better man than he thinks he is."

The silence on the phone lasted a moment because the young man had to add an extra phrase to his speech: "I'm proud I got to talk to you, Mr. Jones, an' I reckon I'd tell him whatever you say."

"Then you tell him that God's there in that place, son."

Another short silence followed Sam's pronouncement. The man at Parchman figured that Sam Jones would know as well as anybody what life on The Farm was like. The young man was forgetting to hurry when he said, "I reckon I'll tell 'im just like you say, Mr. Jones, but sometimes it don't seem like there's nobody here but me."

Sam said, "God's there, son; He says He is. Don't you ever forget it."

The line clicked, and the caller was gone.

CHAPTER ELEVEN

At noon on Monday, a phone rang on the third floor of a state office building in downtown Jackson. The man sitting behind the desk punched a button and picked up the receiver. "Hello, Williams here."

The voice on the phone was that of a black man. "Mr. Williams, you may not remember me. I was given an opportunity to stop in and visit with you while hitchhiking to college in 1955. I stayed two years."

In that instant the man in the office could see the small puffs of dust raised by the hooves of the mules that pulled the wagon; the weather had been clear and hot, he could smell the sweat of the men on his work gang. A tall, scared black kid slid off the back of the wagon and stared at an unending world of white cotton. Bill Williams had been a sergeant, a boss, at Parchman Prison Farm in those days; the man on the phone was the kid in the wagon. His name was Sam Jones.

In 1957, two years after Jones first put his feet on the Parchman dirt, two convicts on Boss Williams's cotton-picking gang attempted an escape. Williams did what was needed to stop them. In a close-quarters gunfight, Williams shot and killed one of the convicts and was shot twice himself. Jones was one of two black men who had been willing to lay down their lives to save the life of a white boss at Parchman.

Ten seconds after the last shot was fired, Williams was unconscious and losing blood; Sam Jones and old Mose Washington were holding the guns. Washington climbed on Williams' horse and took Boss Williams to the prison infirmary; the young college boy was left in the cotton field to deal with more than a dozen tough convicts. Pepper Jack Bradley, the killer who set up the botched escape, remained unscathed during the attempt.

After Williams recovered from his wounds, his mother's brother—the sitting governor of Mississippi—rewarded him with a job in an air-conditioned office building in Jackson. Sam Jones and Mose Washington were pardoned the day of the shooting.

Williams said, "I remember you. I hope you and yours are doing well." He knew about the recent events in the Delta. "There's been some excitement here since I saw you last. A fellow from the FBI came in to talk to me."

The man on the phone understood. He asked, "Are you talking where somebody else can hear you?"

"Most folks here are at lunch."

The caller sounded hesitant. "I need to ask if you can do me a favor."

"Whatever it is, I'll do it." Williams spoke without hesitation or reservation. Had it not been for those two black prisoners, Williams would have bled to death in that cotton field turn row while Bradley and the other prisoners escaped. The past two and a half years of good life had been a precious time for a man who should rightfully be dead.

"Do you remember where I was coming from when they picked me up?"

"I do." Sam Jones' young cousin had died in Pearl County, and Jones was hitchhiking back to college from the funeral. The police arrested Jones for vagrancy, and the judge sent him to Parchman to pick cotton.

"Do you remember the person's name I had been to see?"

"As a matter of fact, I do."

"I need for that person to be in good health."

Williams digested the last statement and understood the implications immediately. It had the makings of a great plan. "I know just what to do. Consider it done by Thursday night, no later than Friday."

"My friend told me to tell you this means a lot to him."

"I understand. I like to think he's my friend too."

"Yes, sir. He'd be pleased to know that."

"Before you go . . . have you heard that my wife and I have a new son?"

"No, sir. I'm real happy for you." The caller wasn't sure why Williams would be sharing with him about his family.

"My wife was getting ready to have a baby the last time I saw you—our son will be three years old on his next birthday. His name is Samuel Washington Williams."

"Mercy, Bo—I mean . . . mercy," the caller stammered. "I'm . . . I don't know what to say. I never heard of a thing like that." The man on the phone stopped to think then said, "I'm honored, and I know our friend will be."

"It's as good a name as we know. We're praying that he grows up to be a real man, just like the men we named him after."

"That's a real fine thing, sir. I'll tell our friend, and we'll be praying for that young man."

* * *

That afternoon Bill Williams talked on the phone with seven different county clerks in the Hinds County vicinity. There was room for more efficiency at the state level, and he had heard about how well their offices were run. Could he stop by in the next day or so and take an unofficial look at how they did their record keeping and filing?

By all means, Mr. Williams, come in and help yourself. Our doors are always open to you boys from the state. Glad to be of service.

Tuesday night they were north of Indianapolis, sleeping in the car because of the cold. Mose was semireclining on the front seat; the boy and dog were on the back, wrapped up in several quilts.

"Poppa?" The boy's teeth were chattering.

"Mm-hmm?"

"How long is it going to be this cold?" The temperature outside the car was near ten degrees.

"Well, I don't rightly know. I think winter must last a long time up here."

"How long are we gonna stay up here?"

"I ain't rightly sure. I been thinkin' we'd visit with this man up at that train station, an' maybe get us some papers with our new names wrote on 'em. I 'spect, from what Miss Belle say, that he's gonna know how to do such as that."

Mose was starting the car every thirty minutes or so and getting it warm, then shutting it off because of the danger of gases from the exhaust.

Bill was having a hard time getting to sleep. "Poppa?"

"Mm-hmm?"

"Those people in Chicago—do they know what happened to my mom?"

"They do. The doctor say Miz Hodges, she gonna tell 'em."

"Is it going to be colder there?"

"I 'magine so, but spring's comin'."

"Do you think we might freeze to death?"

"Well, I reckon anything's possible, but I generally figures God'll take care of us like He's been doin' all along. But that don't mean it ain't gonna get colder."

"If He can take care of other things, can't He make it warmer?"

"Well, son, He can do anything He wants to." He hesitated. "I just don't see Him bringin' warm weather in the winter when He done give us these here covers an' this car heater."

"What happens if you pray?"

"For Him to change the weather?"

"Yes, sir."

"I guess we could do that. You want to pray?"

Things on the backseat stayed quiet.

"Boy?"

"Sir?"

"You want to pray?"

"Is it okay if I don't?"

"Well, you sho' don't have to. But how come you don't want to?"

"Well." Teeth chattered. "I hate to ask Him for anything since Mom died. I don't want to ever ask Him for anything again."

"You reckon you mad at Him?"

"Maybe." A pause. Then, "Is that bad?"

"Naw, son, it ain't rightly bad. It just means you don't know how much God loves you."

"Will you be mad at me if I don't pray?"

"Naw, son. I ain't ever gonna be mad at you for somethin' like that."

"Then I don't want to pray."

"Well, I don't figure to push you, but you might think on

this: someday, when you all by yo'self, an' you needs help that can't nobody else give, you might just speak a prayer to Him. He loves you, an' He's waitin' to hear yo' voice."

"If He loves me, why won't He just give me what I need."

"That's a hard question. He tells us He'll always give His children what we needs. But I believes He likes hearin' our voices."

When the boy didn't say anything, Mose said, "Lord, this boy don't know 'bout You yet. I ask that You send us some warm weather, so we won't be so cold. An' I ask, Lord, that you'd see fit to show Yo'self to him. Amen."

They arrived at the Illinois Central railroad station two hours early. The miracle wasn't that they were able to find their way through the streets of Chicago; the miracle was the weather. The skies in Chicago were clear and sunny. The temperature was setting a record in the high sixties.

A black man wearing a yellow bandana tied around his neck walked back and forth under the station clock while Mose looked him over. He wasn't pacing, he was ambling back and forth to keep from attracting attention; he wore a greasy snap-brim hat and dirty coveralls with obscured lettering on the back that said something about moving furniture. While Mose watched him, he pushed up his sleeve and looked at a gold wristwatch. Mose said, "C'mon."

They were camouflaged in shades of brown and a leisurely pace, coming from the trains. The boy was wearing an overlarge coat and scuffed shoes; the man was pushing a handcart that carried a wooden crate with ICRR stamped on the sides. They were within ten feet of the furniture mover before he picked them out. The waiting man looked at the plaster cast peeking out from under the coat and figured the crate contained a good-looking Redbone coonhound. He nodded at them.

The man pushing the cart said, "They don't ring no bell at noon?"

"All the bells are gone." *Pretty good,* thought the furniture mover. He smiled. "My name's Frankie Metts. Wait a couple of seconds then follow me out. My truck's just to the right of the entrance. I'll have the tailgate down."

When the travelers got to the truck, the two men loaded the crate without talking; the boy followed it into the bed of the truck when they got the tailgate latched. Metts started to comment about the boy riding in the back, but Mose was already on his way to the cab.

The truck pulled away from the curb, and Metts said, "You've been traveling quietly. Apparently no one knows where you're headed."

"That's good. I been told the FBI is lookin' for us. If they finds us, that boy back there won't live out the week."

"The Bainbridges?"

"They the most evil peoples you ever gonna hear 'bout."

"Well, unless the good Lord decides differently, they won't find you on the South Side—smart white people don't come here hunting black people. We're on the way to my place; you can plan on staying there for as long as you like. Your new history—your driver's license, birth certificates, and such—will be ready in a day or so. By this weekend you'll be able to go or stay, your choice."

"Miz Hodges say you know how to do such things."

The man's face came close to smiling again. "The Mississippi Belle. And, yes . . . I know how to do such things."

"How come you know Belle Hodges?"

"There was a time when she lived up here—singing in my father's gambling hall."

"Don't say? An' the two of you was friends?"

"I guess you could say we *came* to be friends. I thought I was tough—thirteen or fourteen years old and running with a bad crowd. She was maybe twenty. She came looking for me one Sunday morning—said she was tired of watching me make a fool of myself—said it was time I started going to church. I made the mistake of saying something that should've been left unsaid." He winced. "Belle had these long red fingernails. She took a hold of my ear and practically ran her thumbnail all the way through it." He laughed for the first time. "What a spectacle. She drug me all the way to that church, me squalling and her pulling on my ear and preaching. Old folks still stop me to talk about watching that little bitty woman dragging me into that church. Mm-mmm, that is one hard woman."

"An' now you a Christian."

"Yes, sir, and now I'm a Christian." He had to laugh. "I'm not sure I'd go around endorsing her method, but it sure worked for me. I thank God every single day for that little bitty woman."

"Tell me 'bout this here movin' business?"

"The moving business." The man looked at the sleeves of his coveralls. "My father was a big man on the South Side back in the twenties—gambling and whatnot. He used the trucks to move his gambling tables when things got too hot. He's gone now, and I'm the last of the Metts. But I guess you could say that we're still in a moving business of sorts," he smiled, "but I gamble on people."

"Like me an' that boy."

"Yes, sir. Like you and that boy."

They paused at a traffic light. Metts was looking through the windshield, not seeing the people that walked in front of the truck, thinking of what Belle had told him on the phone. "He's not very big."

Mose knew what the man was talking about. "No, he ain't. I reckon he ain't big as David was when he kilt Goliath."

The light changed, and the truck moved. "How's he doing?"

"Hard to say. I think he's naturally quiet, an' all of what's happened to him has kept him from talkin' much."

Metts said, "I can understand that."

"An' he don't know he shot those men," Mose warned.

Metts took his eyes off the traffic to look at his passenger. "He doesn't know?"

"Not yet."

Metts weighed the new information then said, "Are you going to tell him?"

"Not for now. I been thinkin' he'll find out when the time comes."

They drove a few blocks down a busy street and pulled up to a long, two-story building that stood across the alley from a vacant lot. Metts stopped at an overhead door and beeped the horn. The door slid up and they drove inside. The door came back down and they were out of sight in a storage area that took up most of the first floor.

Three black men, two middle-aged and one in his midtwenties, were waiting for Metts when he stepped down from the truck.

Metts slipped out of his coveralls, pointing at the rear of the truck. "The boy and dog are in the back."

The boy climbed down and stood by the truck while the two older men put the crate on the warehouse floor. The boy looked at the dog. He looked at Mose. "Can I let him out?"

Mose nodded.

Metts watched the boy open the crate. "We've been just about as anxious to see this hound as we have you two."

If the dog was surprised at his surroundings, he didn't show it. When he came out of the box, he nosed the boy then padded over to sniff at Mose's hand and get his ears rubbed. When he was satisfied that his charges were all present and safe, he stretched himself thoroughly and sat down next to the boy's feet.

The older helpers, both of whom could appreciate a good-looking coon hound, said more than once that Dawg was the prettiest they'd ever seen. While those two admired the dog, the third man, the younger one, stood to the side and watched.

The boy said, "Poppa?"

"Mm-hmm?"

"Is it okay if I take him outside?"

Mose looked at Metts; Metts pointed at a side door. "Stay close to that lot across the alley till people around here get used to you."

Without being told, the youngest of the three workers followed the two guests outside.

When they were outside, the young black man said, "My name's Perk, an' I'll be close by. You need anything, you just call for me."

The serious little boy stuck his hand out. "I'm Bill Mann. Pleased to meet you."

Perk knew about the kid. "How old are you?"

Mose and the boy practiced it every day. "Almost twelve. How old are you?"

"Be twenty-five on my next birthday."

"When's your birthday?"

"Next month."

"Mine too. What day?"

"Twelfth. How 'bout you?"

No hesitation. "I guess you got me beat. Mine's the fifteenth." A hint of a smile.

Perk thought, *You just might make it, boy. But it ain't gonna be easy.*

Bill looked around at the city; car horns were blaring, people were yelling.

"It's a busy place," said Perk. He motioned at the building. "Like Mr. Metts said, stay close till folks get to know who you are."

The boy nodded and followed the dog into the knee-high, garbage-cluttered weeds. Perk was content to stand near the building and smoke.

The dog and his sidekick explored the block-deep lot, working their way toward the street that ran along its south boundary. Perk stood at the north end of the building, dividing his time between watching the boy and visiting with passersby.

Fifteen minutes later, Bill was leaning against a telephone pole, watching the people and traffic; the sun was out and he was warm under the big coat. The dog sat by his boy's leg, apparently unperturbed by the clamor of the city.

Bill was brought up in a white world; his dad had been a pilot in the Air Force, his mom's friends were the wives of the pilots in their fighter squadron—all white. He had no way of knowing that there was a place like Chicago's South Side—full flowing streets and crowded sidewalks, no white faces; a place where black people lived and worked and ran their own black city inside a white city. He'd heard three sirens in the short time since he'd climbed off the truck.

The dog made a whuffing sound. Bill looked at the dog then looked where the dog was looking. He saw three boys; they were half a block away, looking at him and laughing, walking in his direction. The dog made the sound again, stood, and took a step forward.

"Easy, boy. Easy, now." Bill straightened and looked for Perk. Perk was talking to an attractive lady, smiling at something she was saying. Except for his Poppa and the dog, he was on his own; he might as well get used to it.

The approaching boys looked to be teenagers. They were identically dressed; blousey black slacks with snug cuffs, shiny black shoes with pointed toes, and bright blue satin jackets over white T-shirts. They were walking abreast on the sidewalk; other people on the walk stepped out of their way. They stopped when they got to Bill.

People detoured around the group as the one in the middle, the smallest of the three, spoke to the boy with the dog. "Who're you, shrimp? An' what're you doin' on our turf?"

Bill remembered the words of his dad: *When you're outnum-*

bered or outgunned, negotiate if you can, run if you can't, or fight if you must, but don't bother backing down. Backing down just delays the inevitable.

"My name's Bill. What's yours?"

The tallest of the gang grinned at the spunky kid. The one in the middle said, "How much money you carryin', Billy boy?"

He couldn't outrun them, and talking wasn't going to help—and his dad was always right. The shortest gangster was taller than he was, on the lean side; the flankers were bigger. Bill took the conversation where it was pointed: "I'll fight you first, or all three of you at once, but if you want anything that belongs to me, you'll have to take it." The dog growled.

The tallest one laughed out loud at what the kid said and put his hand on the leader's shoulder. "C'mon, Sash. Let's git on down the street 'fore this midget gets mad or one of us trips over that lazy lookin' dog."

Sash jerked away. The people on the street were watching a squirt of a kid stand up to him. "Boy, you messin' with the wrong man."

From the edge of the sidewalk a calm voice said, "One of you is, an' that's a fact." Perk Founder wasn't talking to the attractive lady anymore.

The three in the blue jackets turned to see who was challenging them. Bill and the dog kept their eyes on the troublemaker in the middle.

Sash tried to sound gruff. "What's it to you, Perk?"

Perk stayed where he was, standing with his arms folded across his chest—relaxed, confident. He jerked his chin at Bill. "The young gentleman is a guest of Mr. Metts."

One of the taller gang members said, "Oh." The flankers stepped back.

Sash stood his ground. "We didn't know."

"So now you know. Spread the word to your friends, if you got any."

The leader forced a laugh and decided to ally himself with Mr. Metts's young friend. The decision was wise, his method of implementation was not. "We didn't mean no—"

Content to pass themselves off as one of the more lackadaisical breeds when they're not on the job, the Redbone hound's second most-notable characteristic is ferocity. The hound watched as the man who had made the threats took a step forward, moving to put a hand on his boy.

Sash, the self-commissioned minister of peace, was in midstride when the warmonger left the ground. A coupling of the dog's understanding of humans with the fact that he was eighty pounds lighter than the man—and considerably smaller in stature—probably saved Sash's life. Instead of going for the man's throat, the dog grabbed the offending arm in his mouth, landed with his feet planted against the gangster's chest, and—using the man's body like the trunk of a tree—pushed off with a mouthful of jacket and a small piece of forearm clamped in his teeth. The instant he was firmly on the ground, the hound jerked a staggering Sash off his feet and into a rolling arc across the sidewalk—the dog's angry snarls were loud enough to be heard a block away. When the bright blue jacket's sleeve and a teaspoon-sized plug of the arm that had been in it were torn from their owner, Sash's screams went several decibel levels above the sounds being made by the dog.

Mose, Metts, and the two men in the building stepped through the side door in time to watch the dog shake the blue sleeve from his mouth. People on the sidewalk and across the street were crowding closer to watch, enjoying their first opportunity to see a dog attack a man—or rather, a two-footed animal. They were smiling and laughing—and yelling encouragement to the dog.

Mose recognized the sounds made by the dog, but his view was partially blocked by people in the crowd. He assumed the boy was somewhere in the middle of what was happening. Metts touched Mose's sleeve and pointed at Perk, who was grinning at whatever was taking place out of their sight, and the two men interpreted Perk's expression as a sign that the boy was safe. People were jogging past them, hurrying down the alley to get to the action.

The dog had done his job and was willing to quit, and the battle would've been over if Sash hadn't tried to flee from an enemy who wasn't pursuing. He was terrified, in pain, and hysterical—bleeding, screaming, and scrambling on all fours, trying to get away from the hound—and headed in a poorly chosen direction. Bill Mann was centered in the punk's intended escape path.

When he saw where his victim was trying to go, the dog launched himself again, grabbed the closest and softest part of Sash's offered anatomy, and chomped down. The men standing by the door watched Sash suddenly appear above the heads in the crowd—not unlike a jack-in-the-box—and wrap himself around the telephone pole at the six-foot mark. The terrified young man got his hands and feet on the metal climbers and moved further up the pole, alternately squealing and screaming for help. The dog put his front feet on the pole and bayed at Sash in a voice that crooned up and down the scale between bass and baritone. The crowd hooted, cheered, and clapped. The two gang members who were not under attack were doubled over, laughing and slapping their legs. Mose smiled; Metts laughed. One of the older men said, "Have mercy, that there is one fine sound."

The bright blue of the jacket wrapped around the telephone pole was visible for two blocks in both directions; Sash's white boxer shorts were prominently displayed through a rent in the black pants, and the baying of the hound echoed between the tall buildings. Vehicles of all types stopped in the street, their drivers stepping out to get a better look at the hound's work. Pedestrians were still hastening to the scene when the little boy walked up to put his hand on the red dog. "May as well let him down, Dawg. He can't hurt us."

When Sash was fully assured that the dog wasn't going to attack again, he crept down the pole. The crowd began to drift away, laughing and telling each other what had happened. Bill looked at Sash's arm and turned to Perk. "He's bleeding."

Perk didn't care. "The dog let him off easier than I would've."

Bill said, "You told me to call you if I needed anything." He pointed at Sash. "I'm calling."

Perk gave thought to what Bill said and considered the bleeding boy, then snorted. He grinned at Sash, "Well, how about it, tough guy? The gentleman wants me to clean that up if you're finished tripping over that lazy-looking dog."

Thirty minutes later, Sash was cleaned up, thoroughly chastised by Metts, and professing a future filled with the pursuit of a more prudent lifestyle.

Perk turned his attention to Bill. "You asked me to help that punk, but you didn't call for me to help you." It was an observation, not an accusation.

"No."

"Why not?"

"Because we didn't need you."

"You might've needed me if one of those boys had been carryin'."

"Carrying a gun?"

Perk nodded, patting the bulge under his arm. "Carryin'."

The boy looked at Perk, then at the dog. "When we leave here, I won't have anything but the dog, and Poppa, and me. I guess I'd better start getting used to it."

"There's God, Bill. He'll be with you when you leave. What about Him?"

"He didn't stop those men down there from killing my mom." The ten-year-old shrugged. "I can see Dawg and Poppa—and I can see you. I can't see God."

Down in Mississippi—on Tuesday, Wednesday, and Thursday—Mr. Bill Williams visited seven county courthouses in the Jackson area. He took his time and did a painstaking study of drawer after drawer of files, papers, and records in each county seat. For county clerk staffers, the only thing more boring than being stuck in a records office is watching a fellow bureaucrat carefully examine file after file in drawer after drawer of musty-smelling, out-of-date documents. By the time he made his third stop, Williams was gifted at making himself invisible to the people in the offices. On Thursday night, in something near to being a resurrection, the former boss at Parchman burned a pale green certificate he had taken from one of the many file drawers he examined; it was the only record of the death of a young black child who died in Pearl County. He washed the ashes down the drain in his kitchen sink; his wife and youngest son watched. When William Patton Mann, the cousin of Sam Jones, was killed in a car accident in August of 1955, he was three months past his seventh birthday.

CHAPTER TWELVE

Early Friday morning, Wagner walked out of the Freeze and looked at the sky. The farmers in the cafe had been talking about getting to plant their cotton pretty soon if the weather held. The ground was beginning to dry and, according to the experts in the cafe, the skies were going to stay clear and the weather warm through the weekend. He climbed in the plain-looking car and pulled onto the highway. He'd make a sweep through Moores Point, stop at Cat Lake to see if the Parkers were home yet, then make an overnight run to Jackson.

He made his first stop on the north end of Moores Point at Dennison's Store. He managed to learn that the black man who had warned him about evil was named E. C. Perriman—they called him Doc—but that was all the information he managed to pick up. A stop at Scooter Hall's service station yielded less. He gave up on Moores Point and headed south.

There are no natural lookout points in the Delta. Wagner reasoned to himself that God hadn't seen fit to waste good dirt on a high overlook in a country that was devoid of topographical attraction. The country around him was tabletop flat; where there were no trees, the land was set up to farm cotton and soybeans. Five miles south of town that all changed when he rounded the wide corner at Gilmer's Grove. Only a few hundred yards east of the corner, tinted with the once-a-year shades of late spring, the setting for the Cat Lake bridge captured the color of the Deep South.

The Parkers' houses—one white-frame, one red-brick—were on the right side of the road. Antebellum oaks dotting acres of manicured front lawns were arranged to hold the afternoon sun and cotton fields at bay; the grounds behind the homes sloped gently to the lake; moss-hung cypress trees stood in the shallows at the water's edge, marking the lake as their territory. Dixon had explained that Old Mrs. Parker lived by herself in the white house—a mansion in any state north of Tennessee. The brick home, smaller and more modern, was a short walk farther from the road; Old Mrs. Parker's son and his family lived there. A front driveway—bordered on both sides by crepe myrtles—meandered through the trees to the homes' entrances, ready for formal callers.

The Parkers' gin sat on the north side of the road—grey and weathered, wintertime quiet, gathering its energy for the coming cotton season. Two or three cotton wagons, sagging over flat tires, were hibernating under the gin sheds, resting until they were needed.

The Cat Lake bridge—two hundred yards long and a-car-and-a-half wide—was centered in the portrait.

He pulled off the gravel road onto a driveway that led up to the back porches of the homes, stopping near a late-model Cadillac. A black man was busy inside the car, sweeping it out with a whisk broom. It was the first car Wagner had seen on the property since he arrived in the Delta.

When Wagner opened his car door and stepped out, the man left his cleaning duties and took off a faded ball cap. "Mornin', boss."

Wagner walked over to the Cadillac. The man was about sixty, greying hair, pleasant. "Good morning. Is anyone home?"

"Naw, suh, boss. The ladies, they gone down the big road." He made a motion with the cap that took in half of the compass. "Pat, he here 'bouts somewhere, but I ain't for sure where."

"Who's car is this?"

"This here M'Virginia's car—Old Miz Parker. I just gettin' it swept out some."

The car's sides were covered with a thin layer of dried mud. "It looks like she's been doin' some traveling."

"Oh, you know how they is, boss," the man smiled and laughed. "Women ain't happy less'n they watchin' them white lines go by on that highway. I be gittin' it cleaned off this afternoon, if they lets it set long enough."

"My name's Wagner," he opened the wallet with his left hand and held out his right. "I'm with the FBI."

The man's eyes widened slightly. "My name Leon Daniels." He stared at the badge first, then at the extended hand. His own hand moved forward tentatively and took Wagner's. He smiled again. "That there is some fine lookin' badge."

"Thanks. Do you work for Mrs. Parker?"

Leon became the resident Parker. "Sho' do—been on this here place since I was just a tad. My momma raised Mr. Bobby Lee, an' my Sis, she raised his chillun."

"So you knew Mose Washington?"

"All my life, I reckon. He married my Sis."

Wagner had finally found someone who was willing to talk. "Can you tell me anything about what happened out here?"

"You mean 'bout them killin's—that woman an' them boys?"

"That's right."

"We wasn't here, boss. Me an' my momma, we was over in the hills, but I know 'bout what happened."

"What happened?"

"It was demons, boss. Plain an' simple."

"Demons." Profanity came close to Wagner's lips, but he kept it in his mouth.

"Boss, that Mose, he different from other folks. Why, him an' Mr. Bobby Lee bes' friends. If Mose is in on somethin', you can bet that fine badge you holdin', he standin' right where the good Lord wants him to be at. Demons been makin' trouble for Mose since '45, an' they ain't let up yet."

Wagner had all the information he wanted from Leon, and his opportunity to escape came from behind him. He heard a yell and turned to look. A man standing near the center of the Cat Lake bridge was motioning to him.

Leon said, "Well, how 'bout that. There's Pat right out yonder."

Wagner told Leon thanks, then slipped off his windbreaker and threw it in the car. The man named Pat waited near the center of the bridge. A book and an empty coffee cup were arranged on the railing beside the ladder that led down to the float. As he drew closer, Wagner took practiced note that the fellow was thirty-ish, about six-four, maybe five, not much fat.

"You were wise to shed the jacket," the man said. "It's going to get warm."

Wagner had guessed close on the height; the man outweighed him by fifteen pounds and carried most of it in his upper body.

"That's what I hear." Wagner showed him the badge. "Jeff Wagner, FBI."

"I know." The guy held out his hand without bothering to smile. "My name's Patterson."

Wagner played with the badge wallet while he mulled over something. He finally said, "Just for my own information . . . that man back there—Leon—he referred to you as Pat. Every other black man I've talked to has prefaced any white man's name with 'Mister.' Why would he call you by your first name?"

"That's easy. I worked for the Parkers one summer; Leon was one of my bosses."

"A white man working for a black man in Mississippi? What was it like?"

Patterson was giving his attention to the trees along the lake bank—remembering. "It didn't start well, but I enjoyed the finish."

"How so?"

"It's a long story."

Wagner watched Patterson look at the trees. "Stories have been scarce since I started on this case."

"That won't change. Mose Washington is revered by black people and white alike; they don't want him hurt."

"Including you?"

Patterson turned so that he could look directly into Wagner's eyes. "Especially me."

Wagner thought it wise to take a different tack before he alienated the man. He pointed back at the houses. "Do you know where Mrs. Parker is?"

"I can make an educated guess. She and my wife took our car and went shopping—that means they're probably in Greenwood, Greenville, Jackson, or Memphis."

"When do you expect them back?"

"Probably not till after dark. Knowing them, they'll leave me to fend for myself and eat dinner out." He waved at the houses. "Would you care to wait?"

Care to wait? The guy talked like a college professor. "No, thanks. Will she be here tomorrow?"

"I would imagine so."

"Do you know Mr. and Mrs. R. L. Parker?"

"Bobby Lee and Susan," the professor helped. "I do."

"Are they expected home any time soon?"

"Not to my knowledge."

"Do you know where they are?"

An I-wish-I-could-help headshake. "Sorry."

"Do you know when they'll be back?"

The professor shook his head again. "Can't help you."

"Would Mrs. Parker know?"

A third headshake. "I guess I'm not much help. You'll have to ask her."

It wasn't much, but it was more than anyone but Leon had been able—or willing—to tell him. "I'm supposed to be back out here a little after noon tomorrow. I'd like to come early, say eleven, and ask Mrs. Parker a few questions."

"Well, I haven't been appointed to speak for her, but I'd expect her to be here. And if she's here, I'd be surprised if she wasn't willing to talk to you."

Wagner's glance was repeatedly drawn to the float, requiring him to harvest memories of how much devastation had been inflicted on a young man's body. His right hand strayed to his pocket. His fingers found the silver dollar and his thumb traced across its surface. *In God we trust*, he thought. *Trust for what? Certainly not for protection in a war that's a figment of a bunch of superstitious people's overactive imaginations*. He took the coin out and stared at the words. They hadn't changed. *Demons fit in the category with goblins and ghosts, Wagner. They're the things of scary stories*.

Patterson interrupted his musing. "Lucky charm?"

"Not according to the lady who gave it to me," Wagner snorted. He was thinking, *Use your time trusting God for something constructive, son, like another date with Ceedie Davis*. He flipped the coin into the air, put out his hand, and watched himself miss the catch. The coin fell through a perfectly-sized gap between two of the bridge's thick planks. It clicked when it struck something beneath the bridge flooring, but there was no follow-on splash. Wagner cursed.

"I didn't hear it hit the water," offered Patterson.

Grumbling curse words, Wagner got on his knees and put

his eye close to the narrow slit between the planks. The area below the space looked dark; he thought he could see a glimmer of white or silver but wasn't sure. Being able to see the coin wouldn't have helped, it was irretrievable; the bridge planks were four inches thick and snugly fitted. He looked up at Patterson.

The professor was standing closer—a silhouette against the clear blue of the sky—shading his eyes and asking, "How bad is it?"

That miracle of the mind that allows a person to recall a memory in vivid detail—and take no more than a microsecond to play it back in slow-motion—took Wagner to College Station, Texas. It was the eighteenth day of September, six years earlier. The Texas A&M Aggies were playing at home; the game was midway through the first quarter. It was football weather—clear skies, mild temperatures, very little wind. He could hear the crowd. They were on their feet; apprehension laced the noise they made.

He'd been sprinting parallel to the scrimmage line, five yards deep, looking to his right, watching the quarterback release the ball. The Texas Tech outside linebacker had been sucked out of position and was sprinting in his direction, closing rapidly—trying to minimize the damage a completed pass would cost.

Wagner could hear the approaching defensive back exhaling in racehorse snorts, straining for more speed. The pass was coming in six inches off target, trailing.

He turned his upper body, compensating, and extended his arms. The ball hit him in the upper right corner of his chest—the Red Raiders linebacker took most of what was left.

The thick turf of the field was probably soft against his back, but he couldn't feel it—he was in pain. The shadow that stood over him bulged with protective padding. The jersey was black—red numbers with white outlines—54. The linebacker took off his helmet and held one hand up to shade his eyes. "How bad is it?"

The edges of his vision blurred to grey when he tried to inhale. "You . . . broke . . . my ribs."

The trainers sprinted up from the sidelines, and Number 54 faded into the gathering crowd. The Aggies gained five yards on the play and lost their best offensive end for the same number of weeks.

The Red Raiders went on to beat the Aggies 41 to 9.

Wagner got up and dusted off his knees; the silver dollar was momentarily forgotten. "You were Number Fifty-four."

"I'm afraid so." The professor offered his hand again. "I'm really sorry about the ribs."

Wagner took the hand and held it while he reevaluated the professor, then nodded. "It was a clean hit. I was busy doing something else when you got to me."

Patterson smiled for the first time. "I think I remember that you seemed preoccupied."

Wagner returned the smile, shaking his head. "You knew who I was when I drove up."

"Mm-hmm. My wife and Ceedie Davis are old friends. I picked up bits and pieces of the gossip. It all fit together."

"This is beginning to sound like you're married to Missy Parker."

Patterson smiled wider. "Not bad for a rookie."

"And she'll be here tomorrow?"

"Well, I haven't heard any differently, but you'd need to check with her to make sure."

"Would you tell her I'm coming by and that I'd like to visit with her for a few minutes?"

"I'll be glad to tell her, but I may as well warn you ahead of time—Missy makes up her own mind about who she spends her time with."

The statement offered more information than Wagner took in.

They talked football for a while, then chatted about the FBI and being a college professor while Patterson walked Wagner off the bridge and back to his car. They continued to visit when they got to Old Mrs. Parker's yard, comparing notes on half-a-dozen mutual friends from their college days. Fifteen minutes later, Leon and Patterson watched Wagner leave for Jackson.

Wagner was on the outskirts of Yazoo City when he remembered the silver dollar.

Wagner walked into the Jackson office of the FBI thirty minutes before noon, managing to carry his briefcase, two soft drink cups, and a sack that was brim-full of Krystal burgers and fries. Fuller saw him as soon as he stepped across the threshold.

"Well, I'm glad you're finally here," snapped Fuller. When the SAIC wasn't sounding senatorial, he was working on sounding efficient. "We have preparations we need to be making."

"Preparations?" Wagner looked at the receptionist, the other member of Fuller's two-person "staff."

Martha Mayerhoff was young and skilled, and knew when to keep her mouth shut. She had her back to Fuller and critiqued her boss's comment by rolling her eyes. Wagner put one of the drink cups on her desk.

"Step in here a second." Fuller was coming around his desk. "Assistant Deputy Director Dearden is coming in from Washington on Monday, and we need to make sure we're ready."

"Assistant Deputy Director Dearden?" Wagner stopped on the threshold of Fuller's office because there was barely enough space for Fuller's desk in the tiny room. "Why would he come here?"

"He's overseeing the liaison to keep Congressman Bainbridge informed on the bureau's progress. He thought it wise to see the scene firsthand. We need to get ready."

What do you do differently because your boss is coming to town? "What do you think we should be doing?" *Especially since we haven't made any progress.*

Fuller stopped at the full-length mirror mounted inside his door and talked while he fussed with his perfectly straight tie. "First of all, I want to get this office straightened up. I've got the cleaning crew coming in today and tomorrow to spruce things up."

"Today *and* tomorrow?"

The "cleaning crew" was Ames Forsythe—the building's sixty-six-year-old janitor. Forsythe, under Fuller's incessant supervision, maintained a level of cleanliness in the three-room area that would rival the most sterile operating room at University Hospital. Although easygoing and affable with most of the other tenants, the janitor had not found a place in his heart for Fuller.

Wagner walked into the other, and smaller, office in the three-room suite and began unloading himself onto a scaled-down desk. He took a seat in his chair and pulled the sack with the food close and started unpacking. "I'm on my way back to the Delta, Bert. Is there anything you want me to do before I leave?"

Fuller had hinted on numerous occasions that he would be receptive to being called Chief, but Wagner had failed to catch on. He watched Wagner preparing lunch. "What's the current status of your investigation?"

"Same old stuff—the devil did it."

The humor was wasted on Fuller. He surveyed Wagner's cubbyhole. "Make sure your office is straight—files put away, desk neat, that sort of thing. What time are you going back up north?"

Wagner pointed at the small pile in his in-box. "Soon as I finish that little stack and eat my lunch." He held out the Krystal sack. "Want some burgers?"

Fuller was looking at the grease-soaked sack, conveying distaste without changing his expression. "Thanks, no."

Wagner, because Fuller wanted him to use the intercom to talk to a woman twelve feet away, put a greasy finger on one of the buttons. "How many?"

Her real voice and the electric one spoke to him simultaneously, "This is Martha, Jeff. Three, please." Martha, unlike Wagner, could not fabricate an important errand every time Fuller pulled out a copy of the memo he'd written and started ranting about Proper Protocols For Communicating Via Intercom.

Wagner dug into the sack and made the delivery.

The Assistant Deputy Director's pending visit to the Jackson field office was not getting the consideration it warranted, and Fuller was fidgeting by the time Wagner returned to his desk. "I'm on the way to Mendenhall to speak to the Lions Club, but I should be back here by two. Will you be here?"

"Probably." *If someone seals that door shut with concrete.*

"Good. I have a list of things we should discuss before you leave." Fuller re-straightened his tie for the tenth time and left.

From the outer office, in a perfectly normal tone of voice, Martha said, "Fries, please."

Wagner was getting up to make the delivery when Fuller stormed back into the front office. "Wagner! Your car's a mess!"

Wagner had to laugh. "Bert, I've been riding on gravel roads in wet country."

"Well, get it washed before the ADD gets here . . . and get it cleaned out."

"Consider it washed and cleaned."

"And you've got a Bible on the front seat."

He was right. Wagner shrugged. "That's okay. It's stolen."

Martha choked on a bite of hamburger and Fuller's face got red. He said, "Well, get rid of it. The ADD might think you're some kind of Bible nut."

"Bert, we're standing in the buckle of the Bible Belt. Normal people read it."

"I'll remember that. In the meantime, get rid of the Bible."

"Consider it burned."

Fuller slammed the door on his way out. The FBI would hire fewer, if any, wisecracking athletes when he moved up to a position where he could help make policy.

Martha said, "Fries, please."

Wagner fetched two orders of fries and put them on her desk. Martha spoke around part of a Krystal burger, "Bring me some of that stuff in your in-box. We'll need to get you out of here before one." She added fries to the burger mix in her mouth.

"I plan to instruct my lawyers to put you in my will."

"Gmmph."

Late on Friday, with the shooting almost two weeks behind them, William Patton Mann and his grandfather, Lucas Moses Mann, officially became who they said they were. Mr. Mann kept a faded copy of his grandson's birth certificate in a tattered manila envelope containing an assortment of age-yellowed documents; his own Illinois driver's license was in his billfold. The personnel down at the Cook County Records Bureau could verify the authenticity of the birth certificate; their counterparts at the state level could do the same for Mr. Mann's driver's license.

Two beings clothed in resplendent white stood on the invisible side of the time-space continuum, overseeing those who ministered to the man and boy. The taller of the two spoke to his companion, *The three are safe for now, my leader.*

For this short while, yes.

Is nothing to be done to show the boy the futility of his decisions?

I understand your desire regarding the boy's eternal security, my friend, but I rest comfortably in my knowledge of our Father's love for all men. For now, because achieving a victory is crucial to the maintenance of the child's well-being, you and I would do well to occupy ourselves with planning for tomorrow's encounter.

CHAPTER THIRTEEN

Folks who didn't have anything better to talk about said the old place was too big for just one man. His children were grown and scattered around the Delta, and his wife had passed away in '58. The folks that said the place was too big were right, but he stayed where he was because he and the house were used to each other. He was content to live in a small few of the rooms and have someone come in every now and then to dust and vacuum the areas he kept closed off.

He started every day by throwing two large scoops of coffee into a saucepan full of water and boiling it; he drank it strong, a halfcup at a time because he liked it hot. Routinely up by four in the morning, he'd have his first cup while he read his Bible and prayed. His second cup kept him company while he shaved. To begin with, and for almost as long as he'd been drinking coffee, he'd used a straight razor. Up until four or five years ago, shaving had been almost a ritual: getting the warm lather to the right consistency, listening to the slick hiss and click of the blade on the strap, then guiding the cutting edge on clean sweeps through the white lather gave him satisfaction—but those days were gone. A. J. Mason still had a good grip, and he could shoot as well as ever, but an increasing unsteadiness in his right hand ruled out using it to manage fountain pens, straight razors, and coffee cups. Shaving became a necessary nuisance, requiring that he put up with the racket made by his electric razor—part of a seventy-year-old man's grudging concession to rapidly passing years.

Technically, it was Saturday morning, but the stars were bright in the sky. He prayed some more while he shaved—bits and pieces of thoughts and thanks—insulating himself from the electrical whirring that was almost loud enough to wake the chickens. Steam rose from his coffee cup and fogged the lower left corner of the mirror. From over his right shoulder, swathed in the electric whine from the razor, the voice spoke clearly, *Be ready*.

Mason didn't even bother to glance in the direction of the voice. He lowered the razor and flicked it off while he looked into the mirror, staring hard into his own eyes, remembering. The room's only window was directly behind him; his image in the mirror was a portrait painted on the morning's darkness. What he heard wasn't *a* voice, it was *the* voice, and it had just broken a long silence to bring him the same two-word admonition it had brought years before.

The first time he heard the voice was on a warm day in a long-ago June. He was getting into his car after church when it spoke to him. Back then, because he couldn't find the voice's origin, he worried he might be losing his mind. He heard the voice two more times that day, and he chose to prepare himself. He took two rifles and a shotgun with him when he went riding that fateful Sunday afternoon. When the War at Cat Lake was over, he'd made good use of all three. That was coming up on fifteen years ago.

He left the electric razor on the counter, picked up his coffee cup, and walked down the hall to his room. When he got there he set the cup on his nightstand, opened the drawer, and took out a .38 Colt. He put a sixth bullet in the pistol and settled it behind his belt before he lifted two guns, one at a time, off their wall-mounted rack and laid them side by side on his bed. The guns he took down were a Winchester pump shotgun and his deer rifle—a pump-action Remington .30-06 with open sights. He left a .22 automatic on the gun rack. His choice of pumps for the heavier two guns was weighted by a bred-in-the-bone desire to do things for himself. Without wasting any movements, he picked up the deer rifle and checked to make sure it was fully loaded. He pumped a round into the chamber, topped off the clip, and put the gun where it was ready at his hands. Next, he broke down the shotgun and removed the plug from the magazine so it could hold two additional shells. When the shotgun was reassembled, he loaded it with double-aught buckshot, including one round in the chamber and a handful in his pocket. While he made his preparations, he sat in his desk chair with his back to the wall, facing the bedroom door. Fifteen years earlier the voice had found it necessary to speak to him more than once to get his attention. This time, because of his experience on the Cat Lake bridge, he figured maybe one warning would be enough.

When the guns were configured the way he wanted them, he went to the kitchen, poured the ceramic mug half full of simmering coffee, and walked back to the bathroom to finish shaving.

The razor whined, making slow circles on the weathered face, while Mason prayed, "Lord, I reckon I'll try to expect the worst, an' just take whatever you send me. I'd be obliged if You'd see fit to give me strength, an' wisdom . . . an' insight . . . an' . . . whatever else I'm gonna need to do what it takes to please You." He flicked the razor off again and looked for a moment into his own eyes before bowing his head. "Father, if today is like that last time, things are gonna get terse, an'—"

He used a towel to stop a tear before it got his cheek wet and restarted his petition. "Lord, You've blessed me with a long an' fine life. If somebody's gotta die savin' somebody else . . . an' I guess I'm runnin' close to tryin' to tell you what's best . . . but I reckon it would be better if it was me, since I've already had all these good years. Amen."

After he said Amen, most things around the place picked up pretty much where they'd left off. He got the razor going and put it back to work . . . the chickens were still sleeping . . . the coffee was busy fogging up the lower left corner of the mirror . . . the world outside the walls of the big house was dark. The only exception was the addition of the shotgun. It was carefully positioned on the narrow lip of countertop between the old man and the washbasin, inches from his hands. Ready.

Mason stopped by Mr. Blair's newsstand to pick up his paper and was waiting in his customary parking spot when the Moores Point Cafe opened. Moores Point was a country town, and men came in the cafe often enough carrying one kind of gun or another—Mason's shotgun didn't even rate a glance. He was on his way to his regular seat when the phone rang. Evelyn Harris answered it, then waved the receiver at him. "It's for you. Old Miz Parker."

Mason held the shotgun in the crook of his left arm and talked with the other hand. "Mornin, Virginia. Heard you were back in town with the girl."

"Mm-hmm," said the phone, "an' Pat. That boy from the FBI is comin' out here to talk to us around eleven o'clock, an' Pat said you two had a meetin' at noon. I was wonderin' if you wanted to come out here early an' have coffee. We could all talk at once, an' you an' that Wagner boy could eat dinner here."

"Probably not, thanks. I reckon there's no sense in me gettin' tangled up in y'alls' visit; he might want to talk to y'all by yourselves. How 'bout if I get there for dinner, an' me an' him can talk later."

"Well, do whatever you want to. Dinner'll be at noon, straight up."

"Sounds good. I'd 'preciate it if you'd pass it on to that boy that I'll just meet him out at your place."

"Be glad to. Bye, now."

"Ginny?"

"Mm-hmm?"

"Is Bobby Lee around?"

"He'll be back this afternoon."

"Mmm." Mason deliberated for a moment then said, "Well, I reckon you'd want to know—I heard the voice this mornin' while I was shaving."

Silence.

"You still there?"

"I'm here. Did it say the same thing?"

"Yep."

"Are you carryin' a gun?"

"Got one right here in my hand."

"Well, I guess I better walk over an' tell the kids." She hung up and went to get the shotgun she kept by her bed.

Wagner's alarm woke him five minutes before the phone rang.

Fuller was at some country club for an early tee time, but he would be at Cat Lake that afternoon. Assistant Deputy Director Dearden had stated that he would drive down from Memphis on Monday and take a firsthand look at the crime scene. A meeting today would give them a chance to plan Wagner's briefing.

Wagner told him he would meet him at the lake.

Good. Fuller would try to get there between one and two.

Fine.

The first dust he'd seen in two weeks followed Wagner to the lake and reminded him that his car was dirty. He rounded the corner at Gilmer's Grove and debated with himself on whether to use the front driveway or the back; the back won.

The Cadillac was at home under the porte cochere. The ladies had obviously stayed off the "big road" long enough for Leon to wash and polish it.

Old Mrs. Parker met him at the door. "Well, good mornin'. Come in."

"Thank you, ma'am. I'm Special Agent Jeff Wagner."

"Of course you are. I'm Virginia Parker." She pointed to her left. "You already know Pat."

Pat Patterson was standing by a "kitchen" table that would seat ten. The kitchen itself was capable of accommodating two more of the tables and a Little League baseball diamond. The room had brick floors, tall white cabinets, and the Delta-kitchen smell of something hot and sweet.

"Does eating in the kitchen suit you?" asked the lady.

"The kitchen suits me fine."

"Have a seat with Pat, then. We'll have ham sandwiches later. What would you like in your coffee?"

"Black's fine, thanks." He and Patterson shook hands and sat down.

When she had his coffee placed, she sat at the end of the table. "Well, you met Leon and Pat yesterday, and me today. That just leaves Missy."

"Yes, ma'am." *Make small talk for a minute or so to help the interviewee relax.* "It looks like Leon managed to get your car washed."

"Leon could manage to get a lot more done than he lets on."

Wagner remembered Fuller's dictate about his car and spoke his thought. "I'd give a dollar to have him wash mine. My boss and I would both be happy."

"Well, if you're really serious, I'll call him," said Old Mrs. Parker. "He came by here ten minutes ago wantin' to know if I had anything for him to do. You offer him two dollars, an' he'll have yours clean inside an' out before we get up from the dinner table."

Wagner stood up. "Where do I find him?"

They found Leon. He didn't want to "git M'Virginia's drive all muddied up," so he took the car over by the gin to wash it.

When they were back at the table, Wagner said, "You mentioned Missy, Mrs. Parker. Is she here?"

"Call me Virginia," she said. "Missy? Heavens, no. Tryin' to keep that child inside the house is a lost cause. She said if she wasn't back by noon to start dinner without her; she'll show up eventually."

"Oh." Wagner sighed and settled into his chair.

"Was it her you needed to talk to?" asked the grandmother. She was back on her feet, using her potholder to push sweet-smelling hot things around in the oven.

"Well, to tell the truth, I'm not sure. I've been in the Delta for two weeks and haven't accomplished much, but what I have found out is . . . I can't go more than an hour without hearing something about Missy Parker. Sorry," he looked at Patterson, "make that Missy Patterson. And no one within ten miles of this lake has talked to me about Mose Washington without mentioning her. Why is that?"

Patterson and the lady looked at each other, and he nodded for her to answer.

"Well, son, tell me what you know about what happened out here in 1945."

"That's just it. Three or four people have mentioned it, but it's all sketchy. Mr. Mason is the first one to offer any details. He said we'd meet up town at noon, and he'd tell me about it."

It all made sense to the lady. "Well, I talked to A. J. this morning, an' he said for you to just wait here, an' he'd come out. The three of us can talk till he gets here—an' Missy too, if she shows up—then when A. J. comes, everybody's gonna have dinner."

"So, you think I'd be wise to wait on Missy to get her version of what happened?"

Old Mrs. Parker started to answer, and reconsidered. "Well, you better let me ask you something first. Do you believe in demons?"

Wagner couldn't contain a long sigh. *Well, here it is again, folks, in living technicolor. The gracious lady of the manor house joins forces with the little black lady in Mound Bayou, the highway patrolman, the doctor, the sheriff, and Doc Perriman, and they all want to tell me about evil spirits.*

Before he could answer, Old Mrs. Parker smiled gently and winked, "I think you better let me tell you the story of Cat Lake first. Missy's gettin' more patient in her old age, but she doesn't always—" she paused to clear her throat "—take well to people who doubt what she tells them."

She dropped the potholder on the counter and sat in her chair, leaning forward to rest her arms on the table. "Missy was seven years old that summer; her brother, Bobby, was twelve, an' Junior Washington was eleven. Junior was Missy's best friend. The Washingtons—Mose an' his family—lived in that little cabin right across the lake. Newcomers that moved into the area were usually warned the day they got here that they 'better watch out for those Parker children, 'specially that black one an' that girl.' "

She smiled as she talked, enjoying the expressed memory. "Bobby was adventurous but fairly cautious. Junior was compliant for an eleven-year-old boy but willin' to try almost anything. Missy was tough as a tractor tire an' harder to handle. I expect she still is." She shared a smile with Patterson then continued, "Back then, Junior was the only person around here, besides my husband, who held much sway with her."

She warmed to her story and told it well. Wagner listened to the modern fairy tale of two white children and their black friend—three citizens living in a world of their own making on the banks of a lake they claimed for their own.

She paused to take a pair of apple pies out of the oven and sat them in the window to cool.

"The huntin' club was havin' a coon-on-the-log contest up on the lake that day—maybe a mile north of the bridge—with a few hundred men gathered around talkin' an' watchin'. Missy an' Junior were playin' on that old wooden float out there by the bridge—climbin' up on the bridge an' jumpin' offa the railin'. Bobby was right close by in their little homemade boat."

"Around three o'clock, A. J. came across the bridge in his car right when Missy was perched on the railin'. She screamed an' fell off, an' A. J. got out to check on her. When she came up, there was a cottonmouth right in front of her nose. A. J. shot that snake, an' another one took its place; an' so it went. They weren't bitin' at her; they were just gettin' close, crowdin' her. We figured out later that they were herdin' her toward the float.

"Within seconds there were several snake bodies in the water with her. A. J. had shot every one of 'ems' heads off, but the bodies were still on the surface. They were possessed by demons, an' the demons could make them swim, but they couldn't hurt her. They were just squirmin' in the water, drivin' the child toward the float. A. J. an' Junior were the only ones close enough to help her, but A. J. had to stay where he was so he could see the water around her an' shoot the snakes."

She stopped and lifted her glasses so she could touch the corner of her apron to her eye.

Wagner misinterpreted the pause and asked the obvious, "What about Junior?"

Thoughts of Junior brought more tears, and the lady wiped them while she nodded and held up a finger for him to wait. When her glasses were back in place, she resumed.

"What about Junior?" she repeated. One or two more tears came, but she was smiling. "Junior was terrified of snakes—an' he'd gotten out of the lake an' was safe on the float. Or, at least he was till Missy called his name . . . an' Junior Washington did the most wonderful thing—he jumped back in the water an' went to get my granddaughter. When he jumped in, more snakes started coming out. One bit Junior, an' some others were tryin' to get in the boat with Bobby while he was tryin' hard to get where he could help. A. J. was shootin' snakes that mounted the sides of the boat, Junior was draggin' Missy through the water to the float. By then the men up at the north end of the lake had heard the shootin' an' were runnin' for the bridge. Only the good Lord knows how many snakes A. J. shot.

"Junior finally got Missy up on the float, an' they thought they were safe. They weren't." She shook her head. "Missy's skin and clothes were pink with bloody water. Junior was on his back—exhausted. A bunch of young boys from the coon-on-the-log had gotten to the bridge by then, an' they saw it first—a huge moccasin, probably over six feet long, had come up on the float while Junior an' Missy were tryin' to recover. When the children saw the snake, Junior put Missy up on his shoulders, tryin' to get her out of the snake's reach. Between Junior havin' her boosted up an' A. J.'s shootin', Junior got her to the ladder, an' the boys on the bridge pulled her up . . . Junior didn't make it. The big snake bit him at least twice before A. J. could get down the ladder to blow the thing's head off with his shotgun.

"Bobby finally got to the float with his little boat, an' when he stepped out, a snake that had come up to the float unseen tried to strike him from behind. Junior fell forward, got his hand between Bobby an' the snake, an' took the bite in his palm. It was over . . . Bobby and Missy were unhurt . . . Junior lived for only a few minutes after he saved their lives.

"It took a while to figure it all out, but if the demons had wanted nothing but to kill Missy, they'd've bit her while she was in the water. If they'd wanted Junior, they'd've killed him when he went for Missy, or the big one would've killed him before he ever went after the girl. The snakes were herdin' the girl to the float so the big one could kill her in front of all those people. Junior, because God allowed him to, stopped them from killin' Missy an' saved Bobby to boot. A right thinkin' person only has to understand the facts to believe the truth."

When Virginia finished, she and Patterson waited for the agent's reaction.

Wagner fixed his attention on his coffee cup, pushing the handle out in a small arc with his thumb, pulling it back with his finger. When he did speak, he was frowning, tightlipped, frustrated. "Demons."

The follow-on silence sounded strange in the huge kitchen, and when it lasted too long, Old Mrs. Parker rose from her chair and undid her apron; an air of gentility settled over her like a mantle. Both men stood.

"You'll have to forgive me, Jeff. I guess I'm more like Missy than I thought." The man was her invited guest, and the lady's words were spoken quietly and with grace. She said, "I'm afraid my attitude is gettin' as rigid as my joints, an' I expected more than I had a right to from someone who has no reason to believe as I do. Would y'all excuse me for a moment, please."

"Mrs. Parker?" The guest spoke before she could turn away.

"Mm-hmm?"

The lady's gracious behavior uncovered an innate sense of propriety in Special Agent Jeff Wagner. His words came from somewhere beneath the layers of summers spent with rough men on oil rigs and autumns with sometimes-tougher ones on the football field. "I'd appreciate it if you'd let me have the blame here, ma'am. My response was impolite and inappropriate. There's something going on here that I haven't been able to grasp yet, but I'm beginning to understand that I need to stay more open-minded. I'd be in your debt if you'd withhold your judgment of me for a few more days."

Virginia Parker did what good people do in the face of genuine penitence; she forgave the man. She said, "You've made a wise choice."

"Thank you."

She extended her left hand, and he had to step around his chair to take it. She held his hand and said, "A few seconds ago you weren't ready to hear this . . . maybe you are now, maybe you're not, but you need to be told. Back in 1945—a few hours before the demons attacked Missy and the boys—a voice spoke to A. J. Mason an' said two words: *Be ready.*" She put her right hand over Wagner's heart, patted his chest with her fingers, and spoke as if commissioning him for service, "You may not have 'a few more days,' Jeff Wagner, because that very same voice said those very same words to A. J. just before sunup this mornin'."

He looked across the table, and Patterson barely nodded. He turned to Virginia. "You believe something's going to happen today?"

"I'm hopin' an' prayin' that it doesn't." She pointed at the corner by the back door. "But I put that shotgun over there because I want to be ready. You need to be careful today."

Sounds of gravel crunching under car tires came from the backyard.

Missy Parker Patterson was home.

CHAPTER FOURTEEN

During the past two weeks—while he was concentrating on people's accounts of demonic activity in the Delta—some distracted segment of Wagner's mind was painting a vague representation of Missy Patterson. When she came through the back door, Wagner's initial thought was, *I haven't been listening.* The contrast between reality and his blurred supposition gave him a substantial jolt.

While releasing the pressure on Wagner's hand, Virginia Parker said, "Missy, this is Jeff Wagner. Jeff, this is my granddaughter, Missy Patterson."

Ceedie Davis, Polly Ragsdale, and several dozen other women he'd met in the Delta were notably attractive women, and that's probably what saved him. His time spent in their company—like a series of immunizations—served to lessen the initial impact of meeting Virginia Parker's granddaughter. The key word there was *lessen*, not *annul.* He recovered soon enough from the effect of her beauty, but the clear impression that she could see into his heart had adversely affected his brain function.

Wagner's hand was still holding the grandmother's; his brain came back on line when Virginia gave his palm a clandestine tap with her fingernail. Missy's extended hand was hanging between them, waiting patiently.

He took the hand and said, "Hi. It's my pleasure."

"Hi." The girl was unfazed by his reaction. Half the men she met had not seen Ceedie or Polly, so they paused and stared before acknowledging an introduction. A small segment of the remaining ones babbled in unknown tongues while pumping the hand of their new best friend.

Ringlets of short brown hair were sweat-plastered to her forehead. She was wearing a too-big, green North Texas State College T-shirt and white Bermuda shorts. He had expected her to be tall; she was petite.

Patterson noted Wagner's semiconscious state and cleared his throat to remind him that he hadn't released the girl's hand. The FBI man turned loose and felt his face getting hot. Patterson smiled; it was an everyday thing for the girl and her husband.

When she got her hand back, the girl said, "I saw A. J. in town, Granny. He said he'd be out here in just a little bit."

"That's fine. We can eat whenever he shows up."

"Hi." The girl stood on her tiptoes to give her husband a kiss.

"Tough game?"

"Nah." The girl pushed him into the chair and sat in his lap. "Nobody really wanted to play, so we just messed around." She had court burns on an elbow, one palm, and both knees.

Virginia opened a cabinet and took down a stack of plates. The girl said, "I'll help."

"Never mind. All we're havin' is sandwiches, an' I've got everything almost ready. Y'all get out of the way till I call you." Virginia got busy at the kitchen counter.

"We'll be outside." The girl got up and walked out the back door; the men followed.

Missy led the way to the driveway, and the three strolled toward the main road. The couple linked arms; Wagner stuffed his hands in his pockets and watched the toes of his penny loafers come and go. The sky was holding at clear and blue; an almost-breeze drifting from the east was laden with the perfume of Virginia's honeysuckle.

Missy said, "Granny said you wanted to ask some questions. She also asked me not to be mean to you." Actually, Granny had said, *He's our invited guest, Missy, an' he's not a believer. If you scare him off, I'll tan your hide.*

"Yes, ma'am, but to tell you the truth, I think I need to rethink what I want to ask." No one had mentioned that her voice was low-pitched. Lauren Bacall could probably work with a voice coach and approximate the tonal quality.

"Like what?" She hadn't smiled yet.

"I've been warned by several people that some kind of demonic activity is behind what went on out here two weeks ago. Until your grandmother told me about what happened to you and that Washington kid, I hadn't realized I was discounting what was being said—and the people saying it—because I didn't think it plausible." Wagner was thinking while he talked and lapsed into law school's formal phraseology. "While Virginia spoke, it came to me that this talk of demons was coming from people for whom I would otherwise have nothing but the utmost respect. I've been rejecting the input of sound witnesses because of what I believed, not because of what I knew to be true."

"That doesn't mean you believe it."

"No, it doesn't. But it does mean I'm learning that I need to move past my own presuppositions and start weighing the evidence. I've got a lady I need to interview again, and I need to talk to Ken Dixon."

She had both her arms wrapped around one of Patterson's, pushing at pieces of gravel with her toes while she walked. "Is it okay if I ask you a question?"

"Sure."

"What's the most important thing in the world?"

He was torn between an unexplainable loyalty to Ceedie and looking at another man's wife and thinking about how attractive she was. When he elected to look, he immediately realized that he wasn't arrested by her beauty; Ceedie was easily as beautiful, if not more so. What stopped him about Missy was her commitment to a cause—that's what he'd seen in her eyes. Intensity.

This has to be something about God. "In what category?"

"By definition, there can be only one most important thing. What would you say it is?"

"Do you know?"

"Mm-hmm."

"Is it something about God?"

"This isn't twenty questions. You have to decide for yourself."

She smiled for the first time and Wagner got a taste of what life would be like if he married Ceedie; he'd spend the rest of his life watching distracted men walk into trees or trample over old ladies while trying to carry on conversations with his wife. His follow-on thought was, *Married?* He said, "Let me think about it."

Leon had set up his operation a few feet the other side of the main road, positioned so that he could make good use of the water faucet in front of the gin and the shade of an oak. The entrepreneur had all the car doors open while he broomed it out.

When they got close, Missy said, "Leon, we're having sandwiches for dinner. You can come down there and eat, or I'll bring some to you."

Leon straightened and took off his hat. "I done already et, thank you, ma'am. I reckon I'll keep on with this here car."

"That's fine. We're gonna walk down to the bridge."

"Yes, ma'am." Leon held up a book. "Boss, I found yo' Bible up under the front seat. Where 'bouts you want me to put it at?"

Wagner didn't want them to think he was ashamed of a Bible, but he didn't want it in view when Fuller showed up.

He was trying to compose an answer when Missy stepped forward and said, "I'll take it."

Leon handed her the book and went back to work.

A piece of Holiday Inn stationery was peeking out from the middle of the book, and Missy opened it there. She saw the mark his pen had made, read for a moment, then cocked her head at Wagner. "Did you mark this place?"

Patterson watched as Wagner glanced at the verse he'd randomly selected and said, "Yeah . . . sort of. Why?"

She used her finger to keep the place and crossed her arms around the Bible. "You were reading in Jeremiah?"

Wagner hated to lie, so he didn't. "Not exactly."

"Not exactly?" The girl exchanged a glance with her husband. The couple knew something Wagner didn't know.

When they were moving again, almost to the bridge, Wagner said, "I was trying to find out about demons."

She stared at the surface of the gravel road as she walked. "I don't understand. If you don't believe in demons, why would you try to find out about them?" She wasn't accusing; she was seeking to understand.

"Let me rephrase that. People keep telling me that Mose Washington is in this war with the angels of Satan. I was trying to find out if the Bible really says anything about a war with the forces of evil."

"Pat or I can show you where it talks about demons later. I still don't understand how you ended up reading Jeremiah." She was hugging the Bible while she walked between the two men—perplexed and frowning, trying hard to make sense of what he wasn't saying.

The woman should be giving FBI interrogators lessons in tenacity. He could remember his spur-of-the-moment words. *Okay, God, I'm willing to look, if You're willing to show me.*

"Okay." He sucked in a lung full of air and blew it out. "I

don't know anything about the Bible . . . I mean *nothing.* And this even sounded stupid when I did it." He tried to laugh at himself. "I asked God to show me what He wanted me to know. I opened the book with my eyes shut and put my pen on whatever page was there. It landed between those verses about know—"

His eyes went out of focus, and he coasted to a stop. Patterson and Missy stopped and watched him, waiting. Pat smiled.

Wagner turned his back on the couple and stepped to the bridge railing. His eyes were on the south end of the lake, but he wasn't looking at it. When he finally spoke, he said, "No."

Patterson and Missy stood quietly, praying silently, letting him think. Far down on the south end of the lake, a crow cawed once, then silence settled back over the dark waters.

Wagner turned and reached for the Bible. "May I see that?"

She kept her finger in place until he got the book open then sidestepped so that her arm was touching her husband's.

Wagner read the words aloud, "Let him who glories glory in this, that he understands and knows Me."

Patterson and Missy watched him read the words again to himself. He stared hard at the words and said emphatically, "It cannot possibly be that easy."

The couple spoke in unison. "Why?"

Wagner started walking again, slowly, aimlessly, moving onto the bridge, frowning and shaking his head slowly. "It can't be that simple. He wouldn't do that."

Patterson and Missy walked beside him. Pat said, "I would say that you have evidence to the contrary."

Wagner came to a stop again. "What's the most important thing in the world?"

"You're beginning to catch on." Missy half-smiled. "It's twofold." She raised one finger while she pointed at the Bible and said, "To know God," then made a sweep with her hand that took in the world and raised a second finger, "and to make Him known."

Wagner wanted one of them to tell him that this was all a coincidence. He looked at Patterson. "Do you believe God figured some way to have me read those words?"

"That's precisely what I believe." Patterson could've been saying that he thought the world was round.

Wagner became aimless again in the same easterly direction. They got to the center of the bridge and stopped by the ladder. Wagner looked at the float. "Pat, it doesn't make sense that He'd do something that small and insignificant."

"A—He did it. And B—the things He chooses to do are neither small *nor* insignificant. Ever."

"And you believe it." It was a statement.

"Jeff, the Bible makes it abundantly clear that He's in control of all things." The linebacker-turned-philosopher who had messed up the FBI man's ribs said, "I rest firmly in the belief that God choreographs the dance of every molecule in the cosmos."

"Every molecule in the cosmos." Wagner moved to the railing and studied the south end of the lake. "It sounds like poetry."

Pat and Missy remained silent while Wagner thought about what he'd just witnessed.

While the three stood on the bridge talking, Bobby Lee Parker sat in the office of Planter's Supply Cooperative in Greenwood—when the phone rang he was five feet away. The lady in the office handed him the phone, and he asked her to give him some privacy. Within three minutes he and Mose worked out a way to stay in touch and hung up. The lady who handed Bobby Lee the phone would later tell an FBI agent that a black man had been on the line and that the operator said he was calling from Chicago.

Susan Parker was waiting for Bobby Lee in the Planter's Supply parking lot, working on a cross-stitch piece she'd picked up in a little shop in Asheville. As soon as he was back in the car, they drove downtown to eat dinner. They were taking their time, planning to get back to Cat Lake by late afternoon.

Wagner broke the long silence. "There's a lady in Mound Bayou I need to talk to. What's been happening here would make sense to her."

There weren't any white people in Mound Bayou. "A black lady?" Missy asked.

"Mm-hmm. And she said something about atonement. What's an atonement?"

"Atonement means to give satisfaction for a wrong, and that payment was made at the cross," said Pat. "By His atoning death—the payment of His blood—Jesus paved the way for our salvation. To become Christians, we have to acknowledge and accept what he did."

"Mmm." Wagner lost interest halfway through the explanation. He tapped the bridge planking with his toe. "She's the one who gave me the silver dollar."

"The silver dollar?" Missy looked at his feet.

Wagner told her about Belle giving him the dollar. "I was out here yesterday with Pat and dropped the dadgummed thing. It went right through—" he searched near his feet, then pointed "—through that little space right there. Boy, I hope she doesn't ask if I'm taking care of it." The Delta was replete with women who wanted to beat him with a tree limb, cut out his gizzard, or embarrass him in front of the multitudes.

Missy looked at the narrow space between the planks then walked to the railing and looked over the edge. "Did you hear it hit the water?"

Wagner looked at Pat.

Pat said, "As a matter of fact, I don't think we did. How'd you know that?"

She grinned and pointed at the butt end of a horizontal bridge timber sticking out just below her feet. "I bet I know right where it is. C'mon." She put the Bible down by the space in the planking and was over the railing and on the ladder before she finished speaking.

Staying on the bridge and looking over the railing seemed to satisfy the needs of both men; neither moved for the ladder.

Missy was halfway down the ladder. "C'mon, you two."

Patterson was happy where he was. "That ladder's not strong enough to hold us, kid."

Wagner didn't like the looks of the ladder either. "I weigh twice as much as you do, Missy. I'll watch from here."

"C'mon, y'all." She was standing on the float, one hand at her waist, the other shading her eyes. "Don't be such a bunch of sissies."

"He's right, cutie. That thing wasn't built for big boys."

"For gosh sakes, the farthest you can fall is ten feet. C'mon down here." Tenacity and stubborn insistence went hand in hand.

Patterson grimaced at Wagner and growled, "I swear, it's like being married to Wonder Woman." He went first.

Wagner got to the float as Missy was stepping onto one of the bridge's angled cross-braces. "Y'all wait here," she ordered.

They watched her clamber up the support structure, switching cross-braces and ending up a foot or so below the floor of the bridge. She got her feet set and turned loose with one hand to point into the shadows between the beam and the bridge floor. "We used to use this for a hiding place. I bet that dollar went through that little slit and landed right where we kept all our secret treasure. Lemme check somethin' first."

She scrunched up so that she had to tilt her head to peek over the edge of the big beam. "Uh-huh." She eased one hand into a dark recess and pulled out a rusty mousetrap, already sprung. She held it with two fingers so that the sissies could see it and grinned. "For burglars." The mousetrap made a small splash when she dropped it in the water.

The next treasure was a stick with a rotten piece of flour sack tied to the tip. She displayed it and grinned again, "For sendin' emergency signals." She waved it, and the rotten material separated and fell in the lake. She let the stick follow it.

They watched her hand go back in, explore for a bit, and come out with the silver dollar. She held up the prize for them to see, put it in her pocket, and said, "It feels like there's something else."

She sent the hand back in. The final exploration took several passes and yielded a small piece of paper. She blew dust off the paper, swiped it a couple of times on her shorts before sticking it between her teeth, and skimpered down through the wooden maze to the float.

Patterson smiled. "I will never cease to be impressed."

The superhero was enjoying herself. She dug out the silver dollar and handed it to Wagner. "There's no telling what all we hid in that place. Junior and Bobby kept their corncob pipes up there till R. D. broke 'em from smokin'." The piece of paper was a yellowed three-by-five card with horizontal lines of neatly printed block letters. She tilted it this way and that, trying to make out the words written on it.

A. J. Mason lifted a hand as he drove past the tree where Leon was running his car wash and continued down the driveway to park behind the white house. Virginia Parker came to the back door as he stepped out of his car. She pointed at the lake. "The kids are out on the bridge. Walk out there an' tell 'em dinner's ready when they are."

He lifted a hand that said "Whatever you want" and bent over to retrieve something from his car. His shotgun was good inside of fifty to seventy-five yards, but there were no potential threats within that range. In his hands, the .30-06 was lethal out to a quarter of a mile—and that's the one he selected. He wasn't the kind of man who needed reassurance, but he was methodical—he moved the gun's slide far enough to show himself the bright brass of a chambered round, pocketed two spare clips for the rifle, and walked up the drive toward the road.

"Oh! My! Gosh!" Missy read the card again then pressed it to her chest. "Y'all, I can't believe this."

Patterson held his hand in a swearing position. "We can keep a secret."

"Pat, this is one of Emmalee's memory-work cards."

"From that day?" Pat became mildly interested.

"Uh-huh."

"What day?" Wagner had no clue what they were talking about. "The day the snakes attacked?"

"No, no. Sorry." Patterson shook his head. "From summer before last. I was walking back to the gin and Emmalee Edwards was going home," he used his hands to tell the story. "When we met, she dropped a stack of Bible verse cards on the bridge, up there by the ladder. One of them must've gone through that same crack that swallowed your dollar. It's been sitting there—" he did a quick calculation "—almost two years."

Wagner's skepticism had been beaten, but it wasn't dead. "Waiting to bring another message from God, no doubt."

Missy didn't see the humor. "You're too smart to start acting like you're foolish," she admonished.

"True enough." Wagner held up both hands and surrendered. "Keep me straight."

Patterson said, "I'll remind you one day that you told her to do that." *With a little work*, he thought, *our new friend could turn out to be an okay guy.*

* * *

"Mornin', Leon."

Leon had finished sweeping out the car and was closing its doors. "Mornin', Mistah A. J. You come out for dinner?"

"Mm-hmm." Mason stood one-legged, carrying the deer rifle in the crook of his arm. "You taken to washin' gov'ment cars?"

"Yassuh," Leon smiled. "He payin' me two dollars."

The subject of warmer weather came up and the two men relaxed in the shade of the oak and speculated on when the farmers might get to start planting.

Leon looked past Mason and said, "Yonder come the high she'ff."

Mason looked over his shoulder to see Dubby Hollinsworth's car approaching the Cat Lake bridge from the other side.

"He been comin' out here right regular since that last killin'," observed Leon. "Just stands out there on the bridge an' looks at the water."

"Mm-hmm."

The crow on the south end of the lake uttered three long caws, but no one was listening to her.

The people on the float heard the car mount the east end of the bridge and looked up to see who it was. The angle wasn't good, but they could see a white car roof with a red light mounted on it. When it pulled even with the ladder, it stopped and they could see the door open; Sheriff W. W. Hollinsworth's head and shoulders came into view.

"Well, well." He saw the girl and took off his hat. "Hello, Missy. I did not know you were here." His eyes were hidden behind dark sunglasses, his hair damp with sweat.

"Got in yesterday." She reverted to the local dialect. "How you been, Dubby?"

Instead of answering he said, "It is good that you are here . . . very good."

What little Missy could see of the man's shirt was sticking to his skin; sweat seeped from his mustache and dripped from his chin.

Hollinsworth glanced furtively to his left and right. "What are you doing here?"

Missy held up the faded card. "Learnin' 'bout demons. You?"

Something in her voice alerted Patterson.

The sheriff laughed at her question then said, "I think you can safely say that I have become an expert."

Missy had seen it before, too many times. She held the card in front of her lips and whispered, "Demons."

Patterson already knew it. Wagner was catching on fast.

A drop of bright red blood leaked from Hollinsworth's nostril into his mustache, the hissing sound that came from his mouth found its origin in hell. "Clever girl."

The crow cawed again. Three times.

Mason had heard a million crow calls in his lifetime, and he couldn't remember ever noticing how many times one cawed—until that very moment. If a man needs to attract attention, he blows his car horn or shoots his gun three times. He was turning to see what was happening on the bridge when Leon said, "Have mercy, Mistah A. J., the she'ff done pult his gun."

Mason had already noted that Hollinsworth had the pistol out, holding it by his leg; the angle kept it hidden from the people on the float. Mason dropped his right foot back; the deer rifle was coming up, seemingly of its own volition.

Mason was watching it happen while Leon voiced it, "Boss, he comin' back with the hammer on that there pistol."

The rifleman thought he knew what was going on, but he

couldn't shoot a man for holding a cocked pistol. He *could* distract the man while letting the kids know what they might be up against. Mason moved his finger, and the rifle's safety ticked off.

Hollinsworth stepped closer to the railing, swung his pistol up, and hissed, "It is indeed an honor to welcome you home, young woman. You cannot know how much we have missed you." He brought the gun to bear on the girl at the precise moment that the bridge railing in front of him exploded into an angry storm of wooden shrapnel.

Wagner pushed Missy into Pat and crouched to get his revolver out of the ankle holster.

The boom of the deer rifle arrived in time to blend with the roar from the sheriff's handgun.

Missy's heart was no longer where the sheriff's first shot went. Wagner had displaced the girl, and the sheriff's bullet almost missed him because he was stooping to get his gun out. The FBI agent went down hard and rolled onto his back. He was hit behind his left shoulder.

The blow to his back knocked most of the breath out of him, but he could move his arm. He could feel his back getting wet and warm from the blood. The pain hadn't come yet; it was waiting behind the initial shock caused by the bullet. In that small slice of his lifetime, with splinters of wood raining around him, Jefferson Travis Wagner left the ranks of somewhat arrogant, sometimes intelligent, and always petulant former athletes and crossed over to become what God said he was—a revenger to execute wrath upon him that doeth evil.

He worked at scraping his pant leg up with a numb left hand, still fumbling for his gun with the other, trying to get air back into his lungs—cursing himself with every fought-for breath for keeping the gun where it was "out of his way."

On the bridge, the sheriff cost himself precious seconds by glancing toward the gin to see who had shot into the railing.

Mason! The demons in the sheriff's body committed themselves to kill the interfering old man after the girl was dead.

Mason saw where the sheriff's first bullet went. Everything he saw was evidence to the contrary, but it was remotely possible that what he was watching from over a hundred yards away had an innocent explanation he couldn't know about. Maybe the kids were moving quickly to escape from a snake. Maybe the man had been aiming at something behind the boy and missed. If that were true and Mason shot Dubby Hollinsworth, he would be killing an innocent man. He prayed while he waited to see what the sheriff was going to do next. He could see Wagner rolling around on the float, and he could see his mouth moving, but he couldn't make out what the boy was saying.

Wagner was yelling at Patterson, "Get her under the bridge! Hurry! Under the bridge!"

Missy dropped the note card. When she stooped to pick it up, Patterson wrapped one arm around her waist, scooped her up like a feed sack, and carried her to the little bit of protection offered by the bridge's overhang. Wagner watched Hollinsworth swing his gun to track Patterson and the girl. They weren't going to make it.

CHAPTER FIFTEEN

From where Mason stood, it appeared that the sheriff was bringing his gun to bear on Pat or Missy. He couldn't run the risk of letting the man fire at the kids again, so he elected an option that would minimize any damage to Hollinsworth while insuring protection for the kids; he'd like to think that any reasonable man would do the same for him. The 220-grain bullet, Mason's agent of compromise, was heavy enough to knock down a moose—it didn't just sweep the weapon out of Hollinsworth's hand; fragments of the handgun probably came back to earth east of Atlanta when Mason blew the pistol to smithereens. The effect wrenched the big man on the bridge into a tight spiral and threw him against the car. If he was wrong about Hollinsworth, Mason would buy the man a new pistol and pay the doctor bills for what was sure to be a broken wrist.

Wagner fired from the float an instant after Mason's bullet hit the gun. He missed Hollinsworth but removed all doubt about what was happening on the bridge. The sheriff was backed against the car and out of Wagner's view, and the agent didn't want to be caught in the middle of the float if he reappeared. He hurried to get to shelter. Above them, Wagner and the Pattersons could hear a raspy string of unrecognizable words.

Hollinsworth, or the thing that had been him, had enough angle to use the car to shield himself from Mason. It held both arms over its head with its fingers splayed, and something between an angry bawl and a roar came out of its mouth and echoed down the lake.

Mason nodded to himself as he pumped a fresh round into the chamber. There was a shotgun in that sheriff's car, and Mason knew what he would do if he was a demon. "This ain't over yet, Leon." He jerked his head at Wagner's car. "Go git that car started."

Leon turned as rapidly as age allowed and shuffle-sprinted the short distance to his customer's car.

From somewhere near the house, a screen door slammed. Mason didn't have to look to know that Virginia Parker was marching up her driveway with a shotgun.

Mason walked into the center of the road to wait for Leon or the sheriff, whoever got there first.

The thing that had been Hollinsworth tried to operate the car door with its broken hand, but failed. It changed hands and managed to get the door open.

When the being got into the car, Mason lost sight of it behind the reflection on the windshield.

He heard Leon start Wagner's car and motioned for him to bring it closer. Leon brought the car up and stopped with the passenger door by the shooter's left arm.

Wagner's shoulder was bleeding badly, but he didn't feel weak. He heard the sheriff's car start and did a quick head-dart to see if he could tell what was going on. He couldn't. He looked at the float and the water's surface, but the sun was directly overhead—there were no shadows to tell him what was going on above him. He shrugged. "Can't stick our heads out yet. He's got all the protection—we'd be in the open."

Missy said, "You can't hurt him with that gun unless you blow his arms off—or maybe break both of 'em." She was shivering.

Patterson was worried about her. "Are you all right?"

She nodded. "Scared."

Wagner said, "We can get in the water and make our way—"

Pat and Missy both shook their heads. "Nobody goes in the water," said Pat.

"Snakes?"

Pat was nodding. "We have to stay here or go up the ladder. If we get in the water or climb up in the bracing, we have to assume they'll trap us."

"We're safe for now," said Missy. "If he comes over the railing, A. J. will have him trapped. He has to take care of A. J. before he comes for us."

Wagner shook his head. "If he can possess any person he wants to, it doesn't make any difference whether A. J. kills him or not; he'll just get a new body."

Patterson said, "Demons can't possess a Christian."

That was one of the things Wagner didn't know. He said, "That can't be true. Hollinsworth went to church."

"That doesn't make him a Christian." Missy's teeth were chattering. She was hugging herself and looking hard at the FBI man. "And you're the only other unbeliever out here."

Wagner locked eyes with the girl. She was watching him, frightened of him.

He rubbed the back of his gun hand across his mouth while he thought. She was right.

He didn't trust his left hand to reverse the gun so he put it on the deck at Patterson's feet. "Take it."

Patterson looked at the gun then at him. "Are you sure you want to do this?"

Missy was. She scooped up the gun and handed it to Pat. "He's doin' what needs to be done."

Wagner's words were calm, thought out. "If what I've heard is right, those things could use me to kill her." He looked at Patterson and pointed at Missy. "I want to know you'll do whatever she tells you to, so I won't hurt her or you."

Pat said, "You're right."

Wagner was resolute. "Swear."

Pat said, "I promise I won't let you hurt us."

"Good." He put his good hand on the ladder. "I need to see what's going on up there."

Over their heads the car's engine went to full power.

Mason watched the patrol car slew sideways; smoke was boiling from the rear wheel wells before he heard the tires start squealing. He stepped toward the center of the road, gave the approaching car measured seconds to increase its speed, then shot out both front tires. The car swerved to its left, ricocheted off the south railing, then veered the other way and crashed through the railing on the north side. It came to rest teetering over the water—its front end suspended over the lake, the rear wheels barely touching the bridge surface.

"All right, Leon." Mason slid into the car. "Let's go finish this."

As they closed on the car, they could see that the thing had put it in reverse, trying to get it back onto the bridge. The tires squalled and smoked; the engine shrieked with every attempt to back the car. Enraged howls of the demon, mixed with the mechanical protests from the car, echoed up and down the lake. Mason braced himself against the dash and said, "All right, Leon. Put 'im in the lake—hard."

Leon was a black man in a white man's world who'd just

been told to do harm to the county's chief law enforcement official. He didn't know what "the horns of a dilemma" meant—but the phrase had nothing to do with the role that had been thrust upon him. What needed doing was not about skin color; it was about good against evil, and Leon had been handed a God-given opportunity to serve the cause of good. He pressed the accelerator to the floor and held it there—spinning the tires, slinging gravel—and the action on the bridge escalated from gunfight to war. He was still accelerating when they hit the disabled car in the center of the driver's door and knocked it off the bridge. It rolled slowly in the air and went into the lake upside down, sending up a mushroom-shaped geyser of water that drenched the bridge surface and what was left of Wagner's car.

Between the two of them, Leon and Mason suffered a few loosened teeth, a split lip, and some cuts and scrapes in the collison.

"My . . . soul!" Leon was wheezing, fighting to get his breath. "You reckon he's gone, Mistah A. J.?"

"Not hardly. We just bought us a little time." The front end of their car was crumpled, and steam was spewing from a damaged radiator. Mason forced the passenger door open with his shoulder and got out of the car. He pointed behind them. "Drive this thing over there by the house an' go stay right by Miz Virginia. I'm goin' after those kids."

"Yassuh." Leon was watching bubbles come to the surface near where the other car disappeared into the black waters.

"There's a shotgun on the front seat of my car, Leon. Use it if you need it."

"Yassuh. You reckon it ain't over yet, then?"

"Naw, it ain't over." Mason looked at the newly wrecked government vehicle. "You can bet that two dollars you'd' o' made washin' this car, we're fixin' to see that boy again."

* * *

The three on the float heard the second crash and watched the car with the lights on the roof do a slow half-roll and go into the lake upside-down.

Wagner said, "They got him," and moved to the ladder.

Patterson held up a hand. "Not if he wasn't in the car."

Seconds later Mason leaned over the railing and said, "Okay, y'all, he's in the water right now, but he won't be for long. Y'all gotta get off'a that float."

Wagner's back was bloody from his shoulder to his waist, but his was the only wound they'd suffered. Missy pointed at the ladder. "C'mon, Jeff. You first."

Wagner didn't know how demons went about possessing humans, but he knew he could be a threat to the Pattersons. "I'm vulnerable, Missy. You need to go first."

On that fifteen-years-ago June day, Junior had told her to go up the ladder first. She had argued and delayed their escape, and Junior had died. She scuttled up the ladder, and Pat followed as soon as she was on the bridge.

When Pat helped Wagner over the rail, Mason looked at the blood and asked, "How bad is it?"

Wagner was pale but steady. "I think he missed hitting any bones. Everything works, but I'm bleeding."

"You gonna pass out?" asked Mason.

"Not just yet."

Mason motioned with the rifle. "Okay, let's get back toward the driveway. If he comes out on the west bank, I don't wanna be shootin' toward the house."

Virginia and Leon were waiting for them at the mouth of the driveway.

"He's been in the water a long time, A. J. You think he's done for?" She had the shotgun ready, her finger on the trigger.

"Don't plan on it. He could be behind a cypress with his nose stuck out of the water, just waitin' till we quit—"

"Boss," Leon interrupted, "that gov'ment car is startin' to smoke."

Everyone turned to see a mixture of smoke and steam rising from under the car's crumpled hood; it grew thicker as they watched.

"Probably shorted somethin' when we tore up that front end." Mason was matter-of-fact. "Leon, git in it an' pull it away from the houses." He pointed. "Move it down by the lake in case it catches on fire."

"Yassuh." Leon got behind the wheel. He fooled around for a second and stuck his head out. "She ain't gonna start, boss. Won't even twitch."

Mason took Pat's arm and pointed. "Take my car an' push that one outta here." More smoke was coming from the wrecked car. "An' bring my car back up here."

"I got it." Wagner was getting in Mason's car. He was beginning to feel weak, but he could function. "Pat'll be better used here."

Mason turned to the rest of his troops. "Ginny, give that 16 to Pat. You an' Missy go git a pair of 12-gauges an' a handful of shells an' come back out here. Pat," he pointed, "stand over there at the corner so you can watch that side of the house."

Leon steered the wrecked car while Wagner pushed him across the deep back lawn to a spot near the lake. By the time Leon stepped out of the car, flames were showing around the edges of the engine compartment, smoke roiled from beneath the car and was picked up by the undecided breeze. Some of the black fog crept up the gentle slope of the lake bank; the rest drifted out around the thick bases of the cypress trees and over the calm waters. Wagner backed Mason's car, getting it away from the fire—the front of the other car was shrouded in dense smoke before Leon took ten steps. Wagner was anxious to get further from the burning vehicle, but he was too weak to motion at Leon to hurry.

Missy and Virginia were back on the porch in seconds. They arrived as a minor explosion in the burning car's engine compartment lifted the hood clear of the flames and folded it back over the windshield. The fire took new energy from the fresh air and generated its own wind; the heavy smoke curled around the car and into the oak trees. The lake bank near the car was hidden from view.

In Mason's car, Wagner pulled Mason's shotgun next to his leg to make room for Leon. Leon jerked the door open and jumped in. "It's already gittin' powerful hot out there, boss. We needs to git outta here."

Wagner was too tired to nod. He took his toe off the brake and pressed the accelerator.

The car hadn't rolled ten feet when Leon's legs jerked straight, pressing his back against the seat and jamming his feet against the floor while he yelled, "Stop! Stop!" He was stabbing his finger at the windshield and shouting, "There he is . . . right there! That's him! An' he got his shotgun!"

Wagner turned the wheel and angled the car so he could see where Leon was pointing. The car skidded to a halt. "I don't see him."

"He was right there, boss. The smoke's done come up all 'round 'im." Leon's hand moved for the shotgun. "I gotta git 'im."

Wagner took the gun and used his weight to push the car door open. "I'll do it. Turn the car sideways in case I need to get behind it."

The slender old black man wasn't suffering the effects of blood loss. He leaned across the seat and snatched the gun out of the white man's hand, saying, "You better let me handle this, boss. You mighty stove up."

Leon slid out of the car and dropped to his hands and knees in the soft grass. His being low to the ground presented less of a target, and the thinner smoke there afforded cleaner air and better visibility.

Wagner didn't waste his strength trying to shut the car door. He backed far enough to turn the vehicle sideways to the threat, then used handholds to get himself out of the car. He pushed away from the car and staggered toward Leon.

The watchers at the house saw Wagner pull himself out of the car and move in the direction of the fire. Leon was on his hands and knees, peering under the smoke. Wagner was walking toward him like a drunk, weaving slightly and dragging his toes.

It was obvious to those at the house that Hollinsworth, or whatever was using his body, was hiding in the smoke. They were praying when Leon pushed himself up and shouldered the shotgun. When Leon fired at the smoke, the recoil kicked him hard; he rolled twice and came to rest at Wagner's feet.

The kick from the gun hadn't knocked the black man down; he'd taken a full load of buckshot just below his shirt pocket. Wagner sank to his knees by the man's side.

Leon was dying and knew it. "I hit 'im hard, boss, but he ain't down yet. You the only one . . . what can stop 'm from hurtin' that girl." He was trying to push the shotgun toward Wagner, straining to make his whispered words heard. "I be . . . prayin' for you . . . till I dies. Tell . . . my momma . . ."

He was dead before Wagner could get his hands on the shotgun.

Wagner leaned across Leon and took the gun then swiveled toward the threat, trying to form a plan.

Blood loss and overexertion, coupled with ingested smoke, were exacting an extreme toll. Someone had told him, *You're the only one what can stop him from hurting that girl.* He was on his knees, wobbling and lurching, moving closer to the fire. *What girl? That Davis girl? What's her name?* The world's colors were fading to grey. He could feel his ability to reason becoming disjointed and forced his mind to seize the only thought that mattered: the final responsibility for stopping the thing rested on his shoulders. His knee caught an exposed cypress root; he could feel the fall coming and led with his right shoulder.

* * *

When Wagner tilted sideways and went down, Mason heard the harsh *BOOM!* and grimaced, assuming that the fall had caused the boy to accidentally discharge the gun. The people at the house watched as he recovered and pushed himself back to his knees. He held the shotgun out with one hand and fired into the smoke on the far side of the car. When his gun discharged, he sprawled forward on his face. Mason realized that the boy hadn't needed to pump the shotgun because that first shot wasn't his; Wagner hadn't fallen, he'd been shot again.

Nothing about Mason's makeup would allow him to stay where he was. He yelled at the others to "Stay here!" and ran to help Wagner.

Dried grass and leaves swathed Wagner's body from his knees up, glued to him by his own blood. He got his elbows under him, grounded the shotgun's stock, and began to climb the gun; his left arm—the one with the most blood on it—wasn't helping much. He made it to an almost-standing crouch but had to keep shifting his feet to maintain his balance. He brought the shotgun in close to his waist, holding it steady with the weak left hand and working the slide with his right. He fumbled as he changed hands, dizzy and weaving, trying to hold the gun out and discovering that it had become too heavy for him to point and shoot with one hand. He pulled it close and fired from the hip. *BOOM!* He missed, and the kick twisted his body; he staggered backward. His legs started to give up, and he sagged to his knees before he fell—working at getting another round into the chamber and almost losing control of the gun. He could see Hollinsworth's body standing by the front of the burning car. What had been the sheriff looked like any other corpse that had been brought up from a lake bottom—only this one was intent on killing people.

Wagner's blood loss had cost him his peripheral vision and

his ability to reason well. His senses told him the thing was moving zombielike through a tunnel swirling with smoke and fire—a portal that opened on hell—coming closer. Unblinking eyes were stark white spots in the soot-covered face; the body was mud-covered and streamered with decaying moss. Leon's shot had hit it high in the right shoulder—the arm was hanging useless, but it wasn't bleeding. The monster was struggling to pump its shotgun with one hand. Moving closer.

Mason was captured in a bad dream. One of his friends was already on the ground—bloody and unmoving, and he was running in slow motion with no forward movement, getting no nearer the place where he could make a difference. Whatever Wagner and Leon had shot at was hidden from him on the far side of the burning car. He wanted to yell at Wagner to pull back, but the thing had to be stopped. He remembered to pray as he ran, and got as far as, *The man needs my help, Lord . . .*

His foot came down in a shallow depression not much wider than a dinner plate. If he'd been fifty-five—maybe even sixty—he might've recovered, but he was seventy years old, and he needed to be reminded that Wagner didn't need *his* help. He tossed the rifle to free up his hands, but he was too slow to catch himself. The gun arced away from him, flashed in the noon sun, and he collided with the ground like a tightly-packed sack of potatoes. The rifle stabbed itself into the lawn like a hurled javelin, plugging the barrel and rendering itself useless.

He made it to his hands and knees, breathless and angry with himself. When he could take a breath, he restarted his prayer and straightened his glasses while he looked for Wagner. *Lord, I guess I get things messed up sometimes. I apologize.* He called on reserves he didn't know he had to get to his feet and fell when he took his first step.

Wagner was in front of him facing the fire. He too was on

his knees—his head bowed, his upper body swaying gently. He had managed to work the action and make the gun ready to shoot, but he was too weak to stand. He folded over and let himself sink to the ground on all fours. He wrapped his good hand around the Winchester's barrel and started crawling . . . dragging the shotgun . . . going to meet the enemy.

Mason's face twisted as he watched—waiting for a shot to erupt from the smoke and kill the young lawman; his mind cringed—playing a continuing picture of the boy's body being thrown back by the expected blast. The old man made it to his feet again. He lurched toward the burning car. *Lord, that should be me. He ain't a Christian, an' he ain't nothin' but a kid. Lord, let me get there in time, or save him Yourself . . . Please, Lord, just give him a chance.*

Wagner crawled to the edge of the thickest smoke and stopped again. He rocked back so that he was sitting on his feet and fumbled with the gun until he pointed it at something hidden by the smoke. He took precious seconds to turn loose of the gun with his good hand and swipe at his eyes, then took another grip and peered into the smoke that was gathering energy even as it surged out to engulf him.

Mason was trying to yell, but all he could do was croak, "I'm comin'!" His words were swallowed by the roar from the fire.

Wagner straightened so that he was on both knees and fired. The recoil knocked him onto his back, and the gun landed on top of him.

Pat, who'd sprinted from the house to the battle, got to the downed man a second behind Mason. Wagner was blood-covered from the neck down. Mason bent over him and saw that he was still breathing. The old man jacked a shell into the shotgun and tried to yell at Pat, "See 'bout Leon." He held an arm in front of his face to shield it from the heat and crawled toward the body that had been Hollinsworth. They had to be sure.

It was evident that Leon died from a grievous chest wound, but Pat checked for a pulse to be sure. He heard a sound and looked up to see Mason returning.

The old man's face was black with soot. He was crawling on his belly, pulling two guns, one with each hand; his clothes were smoldering and he smelled of singed hair. He was coughing, trying to clear the smoke from his lungs. He looked at Leon, then Patterson. Patterson shook his head. Without speaking, they each took a gun and one of Wagner's arms, alternately coughing and dragging till they were clear of the burning car.

When he could form words, Mason pointed at Wagner and gasped between fits of coughing, "He'd . . . already done it. I'll . . . be back." He got up, staggered, and fell back to his hands and knees. He pulled his jacket over his head like a hood and crawled toward his car.

He got the car started, pulled it forward, fumbled with the gearshift until he got it into reverse, and backed it into the smoke. He emerged within seconds, pulling himself across the ground with his elbows. When he got clear of the smoke he rolled onto his back, hacking and spitting out globs of black soot.

Missy was there, bending over Wagner—blood was seeping into the grass around him. "He's losing too much blood." She straightened and waved both arms at her grandmother. "Granny! Bring your car down here! Hurry!"

The Second Battle of Cat Lake was over. The casualty count was, as yet, undetermined.

CHAPTER SIXTEEN

He opened his eyes to find himself surrounded by a brightness with ill-defined edges. Two people clothed in white stood by him, one on either side. He could recall being shot, but his senses didn't seem to be picking up any pain.

"Where am I?"

One of the figures, a man with a deep voice, said, "Well, welcome back. How do you feel?"

The people were coming into focus . . . a doctor on one side, a nurse on the other. A second nurse stood at the foot of the bed.

"Probably better'n I should." He could tell he was slurring his words, but no one seemed to notice. "What'd you give me?"

"Something you wouldn't be able to pronounce—strong painkiller. We just gave you a booster that should be taking effect soon, and you'll be going back to sleep." The doctor continued to talk while he leaned over and lifted his patient's eyelids one at a time and shined a light into them. "I'm Phil Latham. I count Mr. Mason and the Parkers as my friends. If you need anything—night or day—you tell the nearest staffer to give me a call."

Keeping the doctor in focus was more than his eyes could handle. "How long've I been 'ere?"

"Little over four hours." He spoke over his shoulder. "What time did y'all get here, A. J.?"

"Before one." A. J. Mason was standing by the room's only window. The nurse moved down to make room for the old man. "It'll be five o'clock in a few minutes. I'll tell your boss you put in a full day."

Wagner could see well enough to make out the shotgun cradled in Mason's arm. It didn't make sense. "They let you bring a shotgun in here?"

Latham looked to be in his midfifties. His freckled face didn't get much sun, his thinning hair was going from light brown to grey. He answered for Mason. "Smart folks have a tendency to let Mr. Mason carry whatever he wants, wherever he pleases." The words were spoken lightly, but the doctor didn't smile.

The place smelled like a hospital. "How long am I gonna be here?"

"Not too long, I imagine. You had two clean-through penetration wounds—buckshot—in your left arm," the doctor used his own arm for show-and-tell, "one in the bicep, one in the tricep. I had to go in and do a little interior repair work on the muscles. The damage was minimal, and you'll recover to full use. In the short term, the arm is going to be fairly sore and practically useless for a week or two. You're a bleeder, my friend, and the long wound in your back was the principal cause of blood loss, but it only required cleaning and closing." He jerked his thumb at an IV stand. "We're topping you off right now, but you're still weak, and probably suffering from mild shock. You can leave tomorrow if you can walk on your own, but you'll be more comfortable here for tonight."

"Two spots?" He looked at Mason. "How many times was I shot?"

"He hit you in the back while you were on the float," said

Mason. "When you took the shotgun an' went after 'im, you fell down right when he pulled the trigger on his shotgun. Two balls of the shot hit your arm; the rest missed."

"Mmm. My arm's okay?"

"Everything's going to be fine," the doctor repeated, "but like I said, that fix-up work I had to do on your muscles is going to make them pretty tender. I've written you a prescription for some painkillers you can take with you when you check out."

Wagner looked at Mason. "Hollinsworth?"

Mason shook his head. "He's gone. Dead."

"I don't remember much." He didn't want to remember anything.

"I can imagine," Mason nodded. Wars were like that. "It was pretty rough there for a while, but you did real fine."

Wagner didn't want to hear the answer, but he asked the question. "Leon?"

Mason was comfortable with his answer. "Leon was a good man, son, an' a Christian one. An' he died protectin' his best friends. Not many folks get to go out like that."

Wagner settled further into the pillow, and his gaze went to the ceiling. "They spent a lot of time at the Academy training us on how to handle ourselves in close-quarters armed combat." The tear in the corner of his eye spilled over and dropped on the pillow. "I think I pretty much went through everything I learned 'fore I got my gun out."

Mason's own eyes were shining. "Academies can't teach what you done, son."

There was a box of tissues on the table under the window. The bedside nurse gave one to each of the combatants and took one for herself.

Latham wasn't teary. "We have a man out in the lobby who says he needs to talk to you as soon as you're conscious."

"A man?"

"Fellow named Fuller."

"Oh, yeah." Wagner's brow wrinkled. "Where're Pat an' Missy?"

"They're out there too."

"I need to see 'em first."

The doctor signaled to the nurse at the foot of the bed.

Wagner tried to raise his head but failed. The tissue nurse cranked the bed so that he was nearer to sitting up. She smiled when he thanked her.

The errand nurse held the door for Pat and Missy to come into the room. The tissue nurse moved back so the Pattersons could get to the bedside. Missy looked concerned; Pat smiled. "How're you doing, big boy?"

Wagner ignored the question. "I need for you to tell me how to be a Christian."

No one in the room seemed shocked at his words. Latham stepped into the hall, and the nurses followed.

When the door closed, Pat said, "This is a little sudden, isn't it?"

Wagner's struggles to get comfortable were unproductive. One arm was trussed up and useless; the other had an IV stuck in it. Being hemmed in by medical paraphernalia was making him irritable. "Is there a waitin' period?"

Pat saw his point. "What's your question?"

"I just told you . . . I want to be a Christian. What do I have to do?"

Pat looked at Mason. Mason was frowning. Pat said, "First, I need to ask you a couple of questions, Jeff."

"Fine. But let's do the abbreviated version."

"We'll see. Tell me why you're in such a hurry."

He thought, *Because you said what happened to Hollinsworth can only happen to a person who isn't a Christian, and I don't want that to happen to me.* He said, "Because I'm ready."

"Tell me what you believe."

"What I believe? I believe what you do—Jesus was God's Son and died on the cross for our sins."

"What about accepting Him as your Savior?"

"I don't know what that means, Patterson, but that's something I can find out later, isn't it?"

Mason and Patterson exchanged another look; Missy moved away from the bed to face the window and closed her eyes.

Pat concentrated on Wagner. "When He died, Jesus paved the way for our salvation. To become a Christian, you have to accept and acknowledge—with your heart and mind—that He died for you. You have to acknowledge Him as your Savior, and we need to pray for you to understand that."

As far as Wagner was concerned, the forces behind what happened to Farrell Whitacher and W. W. Hollinsworth were no longer fodder for academic speculation. Some of the details from the day's encounter at the lake were vague; others would never be recalled, but a pair of impressions from the past two weeks were firmly fixed in his memory. He didn't have to close his eyes to see Farrell Whitacher—or what was left of him—lying in a peaceful setting surrounded by shreds of his own flesh. The same was true of Hollinsworth's image. The man was walking in slow motion, his charred body draped with lake leavings and rotten moss for grave clothes . . . limping toward him through the smoke and fire . . . his eyes unseeing, his mouth slack . . . his good hand was jerking at the shotgun, trying to pump it with one hand. A person didn't have to go to three years of law school and the FBI Academy to know that evil beings brought a drowned man from the lake bottom with the intention of using him to kill people.

"I don't wanna pray; I wanna be a Christian. We can pray after I'm a Christian."

"You've got the cart before the horse, amigo." Patterson touched one of his hands to Wagner's bandaged arm and motioned for Missy and Mason to join them. "Let's hold hands."

The medication masked Wagner's pain, but it didn't serve to calm him. He pushed at the bed with his good hand—struggling to sit up—and peeled another layer off his frustration when he failed. "You're not doin' this right, Patterson. I don't wanna be left hangin' here. I'm gettin' sleepy again."

The three by his bed held hands. Missy held Wagner's right hand; Patterson touched his other arm, Mason stood between the Pattersons. Wagner blinked slowly and said, "Y'all, this is gonna take too long."

Missy tried to calm him. "It's gonna be okay, Jeff. You need to listen to Pat."

Bert Fuller stepped into the room as they bowed their heads. "Tell me I haven't been waiting out there so you people could have a prayer meeting." He spit the words as if they left a bad taste in his mouth.

Most of the people in the hospital had met Special Agent in Charge Fuller. He had been at the hospital three hours, and when he wasn't commandeering the hospital administrator's office to conduct important FBI business, he was alienating the people in the halls and waiting room.

Virginia Parker came through the door next and stepped around Fuller.

Pat beckoned to Fuller. "I wouldn't call it a prayer meeting, but we're going to pray. Would you like to join us? Granny?"

Old Mrs. Parker said, "That's what I came in here for."

Fuller's face was red and his voice was harsh. "Your prayer time will have to wait until after I ask this man some questions."

Wagner looked past Mason. He frowned at Fuller; a trick of the light coming from the window made it appear that someone had painted the man's head black. "What happened to your hair?"

"Nothing happened to my hair. It's combed."

It was, indeed, combed. Along with his new voice the SAIC had decided he could better portray himself as a no-nonsense leader by plastering his hair to his head and combing it straight back. The effort to appear severe and iron-willed was as effective as his new voice inflection.

Wagner watched a matched pair of his boss drift back and forth across each other. He squinted at both of them, offered an affable drunk's one-sided grin, and slurred, "Dick Tracy."

It was comic relief for the ones who were recently returned from the war. Patterson, Mason, and Virginia Parker tried not to smile. Missy covered her face and her shoulders shook.

The redder parts of Fuller's face took on a purple hue. "I fail to see the humor here, Wagner. What you've done is inexcusable. I trusted you to run this operation, and you turned it into the bureau's biggest fiasco of the century."

Wagner seemed confused by his boss's animosity. One of his toes moved under the sheet and momentarily distracted him. He took a full five seconds to blink. His attention wandered back to Fuller's face, staying there long enough for him to murmur "Demons . . ." before his train of thought coasted to a stop.

"Demons!" Fuller screamed the word. He stomped back and forth at the foot of the bed, railing at Wagner and a Delta full of rednecks. "I've got an assistant deputy director arriving here in less than forty-eight hours, Wagner." He gripped the bed rail and notched the volume up in an effort to attract the attention of his uninterested audience. "He's going to be justifiably curious about how a man who is supposed to be a well-educated, highly trained federal officer has managed to cause the destruction of a county law enforcement vehicle, incinerate two more—one of which belonged to the government—allow a civilian to get shot and killed, and barbecue a county sheriff. Can you possibly grasp how he's going to react when you try to blame it on ghosts?"

Wagner was missing the well-rehearsed speech. His eyelids drooped, then closed. He strained to force them open again and let his head loll to the side so that his face was pointed at

Mason. He mustered the strength necessary to raise one finger from the sheets, but his eyelids didn't make it. "Stay . . ."

It was just as well Wagner wasn't making the request of Fuller, because elements of the South Allen County Hospital's staff had other ideas for him.

Latham strode through the door with the head nurse an inch behind him, matching his stride; their caboose was a black orderly the size of a Volkswagen. The doctor remained calm as he spoke to Fuller. "You are in my territory, sir, and you've overstepped your bounds." Latham's hand was resting on the nurse's arm. "This lady will escort you to the front door. If you come back into this facility without my express permission, and in the unlikely event you survive the ensuing encounter with this woman, I will see to it that you spend a day in our local jail." The doctor lifted his hand from the woman's arm, and she immediately took Fuller by the elbow and—with the orderly rolling along in their wake—steered him from the room. During their hasty trek to the hospital's front door, she explained to the man from the Yankee government—without resorting to medical jargon—that he would be well-advised to get out of her hospital and take his arrogant attitude, shiny badge, and one or two other things of a private nature with him.

Mason had someone bring him a comfortable chair and settled down for a night of guard duty.

The appointed guardian was watching the sun come up when Wagner's eyes opened. "Mornin'."

"What time is it?"

Mason looked at his wrist. "Comin' up on six."

"Sunday?"

"Yep."

"I'm about to starve. Let's go over to the Freeze and get some eggs and biscuits."

"You reckon you can walk?"

Wagner was moving slowly, swinging out his legs over the side of the bed. "You bet. Where's my .38?"

"Fuller took it. Said he'd hold it till after the investigation."

"Investigation?" Wagner lost some of his color when he sat up. "Just as well. I don't think I've got what it takes to carry it and me both."

The duty nurse heard them planning the escape and came in to fuss and threaten. She was wasting energy and oxygen.

The crowd at the Freeze was Sunday-morning small.

Conversations stopped. The tinkle of dishes being washed and the cooks singing out in the kitchen were the only sounds Mason and Wagner heard when they stepped into the cafe.

Mason led the way to a table in the center of the room, passing booths and tables filled with silence and hard stares, nodding and speaking as he went. His presence in the equation slowed the formation of any snap decisions by the men, but didn't placate the crowd's animosity. A shortage of details had not hampered the rumor mill; the patrons in the cafe knew that the federal man had shot Dubby and incinerated his body.

A stone-faced waitress, the Sunday stand-in for the Isabell sisters, presented herself and took their order. Wagner wanted six eggs and all the trimmings, Mason settled for "a poached egg, dry toast, an' halfa cuppa hot coffee."

Mason and Wagner ignored the stares and made small talk, avoiding the subject of demons. The cafe crowd was multiplying their dislike for Wagner when Pat Patterson, Missy, Bobby Lee, Susan, and Virginia Parker came through the door. They spied the hospital fugitives and threaded their way through the false quiet to the table.

Anger was fast replacing reason in the room, and what had been silence fueled by contempt was becoming audible aversion. Scattered individuals were questioning the right of the Parkers to offer favor to the enemy.

Mason stood as they approached the table—it took a few seconds for Wagner to make it out of his chair. Old Mrs. Parker picked up Wagner's coffee and directed the butting together of two tables, while Bobby Lee and Susan introduced themselves to Wagner. Susan hugged the bandaged man without hurting him and made sure she got a chair next to his. The waitress got to their table and served Mason's breakfast while everyone was getting seated.

Virginia Parker gave the waitress a grandmother's smile and said, "I'll just have coffee, hon." Patterson looked at the rest of the Parkers and showed the waitress five fingers when they all nodded.

The waitress said, "Comin' up," and turned to let Wagner's fully loaded plate fall to the table from a height of three or four inches. A side dish crashed next to it, spilling the man's coffee and knocking two of his biscuits to the floor.

Wagner made an instinctive move to contain the wreckage with his left arm; he cursed and went a shade whiter when the pain stabbed him.

Too many of the cafe's patrons smiled at the exacted revenge, and the waitress drawled, "Oh, I'm so-o-o-o sorry."

Missy Patterson had a well-deserved reputation for no-nonsense responses to any mistreatment of the innocent—real or imagined; folks would say "she comes by it natural." She was coming out of her chair, trailed closely by her parents and Patterson, when Old Mrs. Parker held up her hand. "I'll handle this."

When the lady got to her feet, she held her hand out to Patterson, "Pat, steady me while I get up on this chair."

Noise in the cafe diminished as Old Mrs. Parker took her grandson-in-law's offered hand and climbed onto the chair seat with the grace expected of a lady. She stood erect in the chair, rested a hand on Patterson's shoulder as a precaution, and addressed the crowd using a tone cultivated during four years of teaching at Central Delta Junior College. "May I have your attention, please." When she spoke, men put down their cups and turned toward her.

"Thank you," she said. "I promise to be brief."

She cleared her throat. "Y'all know what happened out at our lake back in '45. Well, I'm here to tell you that we've just had another dose.

"Yesterday at noon, Dubby Hollinsworth tried to kill my granddaughter. This man," she let her free hand sweep in Wagner's direction, "pushed her out of danger an' was wounded by the bullet intended for Missy."

Without surrendering her composure, Virginia spoke to a man at the table in front of her, "Toby, hand me a napkin, please."

"Yes, ma'am."

She touched her eyes with the napkin and continued. "The fact is, callin' that killer Dubby Hollinsworth would be unfair. The killer—or killers—were demons who had possessed his body. W. W. Hollinsworth was, for all practical purposes, already dead when he drove up on the bridge.

"In a horrible fight up by my house, my good friend Leon Daniels was killed—givin' his life to protect a bunch of white folks. This man right here was shot again when he stepped in for Leon an' brought things to a halt. It's hard to know how many of us owe our lives to him."

She paused to take a breath, her voice softened, and she gestured at Wagner again. "This mornin' I followed a trail of his blood from that old float to my back porch. An' there's more of it on the lake bank between my house an' the place where he stood off those creatures—blood he spilled lookin' out for me an' mine." She lowered the napkin because it was important that she be able to see the men when she spoke her final words. "My family is now—and forever will be—in Jeff Wagner's debt. You each need to know that if you see fit to choose to be his enemy, you are most assuredly not my friend."

The speech was over, but she made use of her rostrum to address the owner of the cafe. "Peavine, this man's breakfast was served poorly an' probably got cold while I was makin' my little speech. Be kind enough to throw this food in the garbage an' see to it that his breakfast is served properly."

When Peavine signaled the waitress to make things right, A. J. rose and spoke for the first time. "Not her, Pea—you." His voice was not as soft as Old Mrs. Parker's. "That young lady don't understand 'bout respect, an' I don't want her servin' the man who stood up for my friends."

Peavine left the cash register and executed a rapid broken-field walk through the tables. "You're right, A. J. Sorry."

While Peavine worked, Mason turned his attention to the men in the cafe; Virginia's words had turned the tide of hate, but the men needed to know where he stood. He didn't stand in a chair to say his six words, and he didn't offer a challenge—he looked over the gathering and stated a fact. "What Virginia said goes for me."

Radd Fulford, from up on the north end of the county, was seconds away from destroying the hopes he'd harbored about replacing Hollinsworth as sheriff. He stood up two tables away. "That's all well an' good, Mason, but lettin' a man burn ain't right. I reckon I got as much respect for Mrs. Parker as anybody in here, but it ain't right to burn up a man's body like that after he's dead."

Mason addressed his answer to Fulford but spoke so that all could hear. "Nobody *let* Dubby's body burn up, Radd. I figure there's only one sure way to stop a demon-possessed man who's tryin' to kill folks, an' that's to fix the body so the demons can't use it. I backed my car into the fire till I felt the thing roll under the back bumper, makin' sure the gas tank was right over it. I wanted to hold it down till there wasn't anything left of it but cinders." He turned his attention to the other patrons. "It was a bad time, boys, but if you got a problem with Dubby gettin' burned up, I reckon your gripe is with me."

The men in the crowd noted the singed eyebrows and peeling skin on the old man's face and drew their own pictures of what Mason had demanded of himself to accomplish his purpose; few were surprised. They nodded their understanding and went back to their coffee, breakfasts, and anticipation of warmer weather. Radd Fulford went on to obscurity.

When they finished their coffee, the three oldest Parkers left; Missy and Pat settled in to visit.

Wagner speared the last piece of biscuit with his fork and used it to clean his plate.

"Well, bein' shot don't seem to hurt your appetite," Mason observed.

Wagner almost smiled and pushed his plate back. Missy put a brown package in its place. "We didn't have any wrapping paper, so we used a piece of grocery sack."

The parcel was barely larger than his hand. "What is it?"

Missy was having a hard time sitting still. "Well, it's not a flea circus. Here." She picked up the parcel and held one end out to him. "Open it up."

Wagner hooked an uninterested finger under a fold of paper and looked up; three pairs of eyes at the table followed his. Ceedie Davis was standing inside the front door of the Freeze.

CHAPTER SEVENTEEN

Ceedie worked her way through the cafe, smiling softly and murmuring "Mornin'."

The three men were standing when she got to the table. Missy made a move to vacate the chair next to Wagner, but Ceedie picked a place on the opposite side of the table. She sat down, and the three men followed suit.

Peavine was at her elbow with a cup and a fresh pot of coffee. "Mornin', Ceedie. Is Maddie Mae lettin' you eat breakfast down here now?"

"No, sir. An' you don't have to be blabbin' to her that I've been in here." It was an old joke. She looked at the coffeepot. "The boss got you waitin' tables?"

He put down the cup and touched her shoulder while he poured. "It's a long story, hon."

"Mornin'." She was speaking to Wagner, but the others answered. She didn't hear any of their replies because she was looking at Wagner. "I'd've been here sooner, but I didn't know."

"No problem. I was asleep till just a few minutes ago."

His arm was swathed in bandages and immobilized against

his body; his color was two shades short of parchment. "Are you okay?"

"I'm fine."

He hadn't smiled, and she didn't believe him. "They said you were shot."

"I got hurt worse in a bike wreck when I was a kid. I'll be a little sore for a while." No smile.

She wasn't sure she was satisfied, but he was sitting up and drinking coffee. She looked at the rest of their group and remembered her manners. "Mornin', y'all."

Patterson and Mason said "Good morning" again while Missy was saying, "We got Jeff a present, an' you got here just in time to watch him open it." She started to hold the package out to him again and caught herself. She handed it to Ceedie, and said, "Here, hold one end so he can get it open."

The wrapping paper rattled in Ceedie's trembling hands. She put the package on the table and held it down while Wagner pulled at the wrapping; something silver showed through the hole. Ceedie said, "It's a picture frame."

Wagner picked up the frame and turned it over.

Ceedie recognized the ornate little frame but couldn't see what was in it. She fixed unbelieving eyes on Missy. "You gave him your baby picture?"

Missy grinned and shook her head. "No, ninny. Momma gave me the frame to put the present in."

"Oh." Ceedie didn't notice that she felt a measure of relief. "What is it?"

Behind the glass was a faded note card covered with block printing and scattered reddish-brown splotches. Wagner held it in his good hand, tilting it to get the glare off the glass. He read, "Put on the whole armor of God, that you may be able to stand against the wiles of the devil. For we are not contending against flesh and blood, but against the principalities, against the powers, against the world rulers of this present darkness, against the spiritual hosts of wickedness in the heavenly places." He looked at Missy. "Darn."

Missy was loving it. "Life's just full of little coincidences, huh?"

There was more writing in the lower right-hand corner of the card, but it was obscured by one of the stains. "I can't read what it says in the corner."

Missy quoted without looking, "Ephesians six, eleven and twelve."

He looked up to find Ceedie's uncomprehending eyes fixed on his. She said, "I don't understand."

He pointed at the Pattersons. "They do." He didn't have the energy needed for a long explanation. "One of y'all tell 'er."

"Tell me, too, while you're at it," said Mason.

Missy started the story while Wagner leaned back and stared at the faded card in the silver frame. The splotches were dried blood—his blood. Remembered conversations and the faces of earnest people swirled in his mind—the words, the warnings, his own protests. *Did you hear me tell you what you're up against . . . I don't believe in demons . . . do you believe in God . . . do you believe in demons . . . the book says the demons believe just like you . . . did you hear me tell you what you're up against . . . it's all about a war . . . five severed femurs . . . I think an angel cut those bones some way . . . the demons wanted us to know they'd killed Whitacher . . . God threw the rebels out of Heaven . . . made this world their domain . . . the prince of the power of the air . . . I don't believe in demons . . . it's all about a war . . . in God we trust . . . been involved in more gunfights than Wyatt Earp . . . the only way you get in that many shootouts is to be in a war . . . in God we trust . . . it's all about a war . . . did you hear me tell you what you're up against?*

Did you hear her?

Missy touched his arm and asked him again, "Did you hear her?"

He managed to sit closer to the table. "Sorry, my mind was somewhere else. Were you talking to me?"

"Ceedie wants to know who gave you the silver dollar."

"A lady in Mound Bayou . . . a black lady."

Ceedie waited for an explanation that didn't come. Instead he tapped the frame and said, "This is the war that Mose Washington was in."

Mason and the Pattersons exchanged a look. Mason said, "*Is* in. Every Christian in the world is in that war, son," he gestured at the bandages with his coffee cup, "an' some that ain't Christians."

Wagner stared at the faded writing. "He did this . . . God did."

Missy, Pat, and Mason nodded.

Wagner said, "I've been listening, but I haven't been hearing."

If anyone answered, he didn't hear. He was distracted. Thinking. Belle Hodges had said, *An' you need to come an' see me when you decide to hear the truth.*

He reread the words in the picture frame then said, "I didn't tell her thanks for the dollar."

"What?"

"Belle Hodges—that lady in Mound Bayou—I didn't thank her."

Missy was reading ahead. "An' you're thinkin' about goin' back?"

"Yeah, I'm going back." He began the labored process of getting out of his chair. "Right now."

Patterson spoke for the first time in minutes. "Indianola's a little short on taxicabs."

Wagner's car was a pile of melted metal. He said, "I need to borrow your car."

"Humph. Are you serious? A sane man wouldn't turn you loose with a tricycle."

"But we'll take you," volunteered Missy.

Ceedie said, "I'm comin'."

The decision was made and Wagner's attendants started getting up.

"Virginia an' Evalina are gonna be plannin' a funeral," said Mason. "I'll stay here."

They took the Pattersons' car; Pat drove, and Wagner sat with him on the front seat. The girls sat in the back.

The house was still neat, the walk was still brick—all that was missing was the rain. Wagner was on the top step with his entourage when the door opened.

She was wearing light blue again because it set off her eyes; her apron top reached almost to her neck to protect her Sunday dress. "Well, well, well . . . Agent Wagner. This *is* a surprise." The tiny woman stepped back and held the door. "Y'all come on in."

Their hostess took in the bandages and pallor, and told Wagner, "Why don't you take a seat on the sofa. The rest of you make yourselves comfortable where you please." Her glasses flashed in the light; he remembered that there was something about Mason that reminded him of someone else—that was it. The glitter of polished gold eyeglass rims—such a small thing. Two separate people—a white man and a black woman—marked with identical flashes of thought—parallel wisdom rooted in the same truth.

Wagner made the introductions while they found seats. Belle Hodges expressed her pleasure at getting to meet them and offered them a choice of sugar cookies, strawberry cake, or warm biscuits.

They all said coffee would be nice, thank you. The ladies declined the food; Patterson opted for strawberry cake and two biscuits.

When everyone was served, Belle brought a ladder-back chair from the kitchen and pulled it up to the coffee table so that she was facing Wagner. She gestured at his arm. "Now then, tell me what you've gotten yourself into."

There was no need to dance around the truth. "I was wounded yesterday by a man who was demon-possessed."

She nodded, unfazed. "Out at Cat Lake?"

"That's right."

"Mm-hmm." She was sitting straight with her hands in her lap. She turned to Missy. "An' your maiden name would be Parker."

"Yes, ma'am."

"Of course," she spoke formally. "Havin' you in my home is a God-given honor."

"Thank you." Missy was the almost-daughter of the Delta's most respected—and famous—black man; special treatment from Christian black people was a way of life for her.

"I was honored to have Mr. Mose Washington here two weeks ago yesterday."

Missy reflected the lady's demeanor. "I worry about him."

"I know, child." Belle brought her palms together. "Well, you folks didn't drive all the way over here to listen to me prattle on." She addressed herself to Wagner. "Now, why don't you tell me why you came to see me?"

The others answered, taking turns telling her what had transpired at the lake. When they finished, she addressed herself to Wagner again, "An' how is it that you came to be on my doorstep?"

Wagner had been waiting. He opened his fist and showed her the silver dollar. "I'll give you a dollar to explain what an atonement is."

"*The* atonement." The sigh that followed the words defined deep contentment. "Atonement just might be the most beautiful word in our language." She leaned toward him and tapped the dollar with her fingernail. "An' I would give everything I own to have you understand its meanin'."

He didn't smile. "I don't think it's gonna cost you anything."

"Ahh, yes . . . cost." His statement made her smile—even white teeth against a smooth, tan complexion. "I want you to remember you used that word.

"Atonement means to make payment for a wrong," she said. Her eyes twinkled, and she inched forward in her chair. "Because God loves us," she touched her index finger, "He offers us an eternal relationship with Himself." She touched the next finger. "But He has made it clear that we only get to come to Him if we are perfect—His just nature demands that. That means our sins have to be forever paid for . . . an' there will never be enough sacrificial animals in the world to atone for the sins of one, single person—to make him perfect in God's sight." Another finger. "Only the life of a perfectly innocent person—the Lamb of God—is worthy to forever satisfy God's justified wrath. The Book says, 'the Lord has laid on Him the iniquity of us all.' " She moved an inch closer and tapped the forth finger. "That same Book tells us, 'For God so loved the world, that He gave His only Son, that whoever believes in Him should not perish, but have eternal life.' " She spread her hands, palms up, and stated the simple conclusion. "A perfect Man died a cruel death so that imperfect people could live a wonderful life." She leaned toward him and took the dollar and ran her finger under the four all-important words—*In God We Trust.* "The currency God used to purchase us was the precious blood of His only Son . . . that's atonement, Jeff Wagner."

For Wagner, she was the only person in the room. "What do I have to do?"

She put the dollar back in his hand. "You have to accept that what He did was for you, an' you have to tell Him you believe."

The memory came to him from the distant past. "It's a thing of speakin' an' believin'," he quoted her two-week-old words back to her.

"Well, bless your heart, you *were* listenin'," she approved. "The Book says, 'If you confess with your lips that Jesus is Lord an' believe in your heart that God raised Him from the dead, you will be saved.' "

"I'm ready."

"Of course you are."

"What do I do?"

"All you have to do is pray. Just tell Him what you know to be true."

Belle was pulling the coffee table back to give him room, and he was using his good hand to pull himself forward on the sofa. A sheen of sweat popped out on his brow and his face paled.

Ceedie put her hand on his arm. "You shouldn't try to kneel, Jeff. Just sit here to pray."

He shook his head and eased himself to the edge of the couch. "I don't want to be sitting down when I do this."

"Leave him be, child." Belle was moving from her chair to her knees. "He'll want to remember this as a special time."

When Wagner was on his knees, Patterson followed, and the two girls joined them.

Wagner closed his eyes and said, "God, I know now what You did for me, and You and I both know why. I thank You for sending Your Son here and that You let Him die so I could be forgiven of my sins. I believe in Jesus as my own Savior, and I ask that You keep reminding me to be thankful for what You did. Amen."

One or two of the others said, "Amen," and looked up to see Wagner's head still bowed. He added, "God, I ask that You'd make me as stubborn on this side of Your fence as I was on the other side."

When he looked up, Patterson winked at him. "A-*men*."

Wagner used the table as a prop to help himself to his feet. He looked at Belle. "What now?"

Belle looked to Patterson for the answer. "Do you know about God, son?"

Pat nodded. "I'm learning."

She held out both hands as if to introduce Patterson to Wagner and handed the agent boy off. "You find you a man who knows more about God than you do, an' you get him to help you start learning. An' you don't believe anythin' he tells you that he can't back up in the Book."

When they left for Indianola, Ceedie told Missy to sit up front with Pat. "J. W. can sit in the back with me."

They'd left Chicago early on Saturday and were in the middle of Ohio by Sunday noon. Old Mr. Parker's car was gone, and they were driving one the FBI couldn't trace. Their "new" car was a few years old; the color and body style blended with any background. The few people who took note of their southbound passage were mostly old men who appreciated the look of a good coon dog. They'd be on the outskirts of Nashville by late Monday.

"We got new names now, an' new lives," Mose was saying, "we bes' learn to wear 'em real good. We'll spend our summer puttin' 'em on, 'cause we ain't never gonna be takin' 'em off.

"You got to be ready for seventh grade this fall; that means we got three months to teach you everything you'd o' learned in them two grades you gonna skip. We'll do schoolin' in the cool o' the mornin's, an' other learnin's after dinner."

"Yes, sir." The boy never sounded eager, but he never balked; right now he was concentrating on the job at hand. The hound sat close to the boy, offering moral support.

"The FBI is huntin' us, an' them Bainbridge folks is bad as

they comes. They say that old man is plum' crazy, an' they still got a son left. If that last boy is like them other two, he gonna come lookin' for us, so this here's gonna be like one o' them army boot camps. It'll be hard for a while, but when we gits finished, we'll be done taught ourselves to hide out pretty good, an' we'll be ready to fight if we has to."

The three could've made the trip faster, but they chose to spend part of their time riding the back roads so they would attract less attention and Bill could learn to drive. The deserted road in front of them rose and fell, hill after hill through the countryside, taking them to the Ohio River, then Kentucky. The boy was about average height for his age, but car seats aren't designed for ten-year-olds. He sat on a wooden Coke case and used the steering wheel to pull himself up enough to see where he was going. He'd told Mose he'd never heard of a ten-year-old boy driving a car. Mose countered that he wasn't like other boys; he'd been called on at an early age to act like a man, he "might as well start learnin' to do mannish things. An' besides, you ain't ten, you twelve."

The boy was forced to choose between forming long answers and keeping the car on the road. He kept his eyes on the road while he wiped a sweaty palm on his jeans. "Yes, sir."

Bill Mann remembered a dad who had survived a boot camp of sorts.

In the evenings, while his mom tried to read, Bill's dad would entertain him with often told—and always hilarious—yarns garnered from six brutal weeks of preflight training and a year in aviation cadets. Stories of nineteen-year-old boys being rousted out on winter nights to jog barefoot around the barracks area in nothing but their skivvies, then, after they were thoroughly sweat-covered, standing at attention for hours in the freezing night air. Of getting up every morning so their cadet class could spit shine the barracks prior to reporting to the flight line before sunup. About getting thrown into a lake in January to commemorate their first solo flights and retaliating by pulling elaborate, diabolical pranks on the upperclassmen and instructors. His mom always pretended she wasn't amused at the foolishness men inflicted upon their world but inevitably ended up giggling at his dad's past antics.

His dad and the men he trained with endured the harassment and hazing, the torturous flying schedules and demanding academic work, and they earned their pilot's wings. And in so doing they became a part of the famed Tuskegee Airmen. The Big War was their next stop.

After Korea, as a result of integration in the military, most of his dad's squadron mates were white. When the pilots got together, Bill would listen for hours to the tales of how they used their rigorous training and wartime experiences to keep themselves alive in aerial battles with the nation's enemies. Real stories of real wars. Wars fought in the skies over North Africa, Europe, and Korea. Wars his dad fought and won in the P-51 Mustang and the F-86 Sabre Jet.

Bill knew his dad wouldn't see anything funny about what his son was facing, but he would expect him to be a man—he said so on the back of the watch. The boy knew he was smart; he could do two grades worth of learning in three months, and that would put him two years closer to graduation from college. The only thing that stood between him and what he wanted for his life was time. Taking only three months to make the leap from ten years of age to twelve meant he would get to the Air Force two years sooner.

Mose said, "She might be a little easier to han'l' if you was to put some more juice to 'er."

"Faster?"

"Just a wee bit. She be easier to line out if she know where she goin' to."

"Yes, sir." Bill wiped the other palm on his jeans and scooted up so he could get closer to the gas pedal. The dog tried to help by resting his chin on the boy's shoulder and moaning when they got too near the roadside ditches.

When the ringing started, it told him three things: (1) it was early Monday morning, (2) he'd made the mistake of getting in bed without moving the phone to the night stand on his "good" side, and (3) the pains from his wounds were worse.

It took five rings and a cup of sweat for him to position himself to get his hand on the receiver. "Hello?"

"Wagner? Where've you been? I've been trying to get in touch with you since yesterday." Fuller sounded like Wagner was playing hooky during a national emergency.

"I've been asleep, Bert." The pain in his arm, coupled with the effort he'd expended to get himself to the phone, had him near panting.

"Asleep!" Fuller's voice went unsenatorial. "It's seven in the morning, Wagner. I've spent the last fifteen hours telling those people up there that I needed to talk to you! You can't just—"

"I gave the lady at the desk five bucks, Bert," Wagner interrupted, "and told her not to let you or anyone else disturb me until one minute ago. Now, do you want to tell me why you woke me up?" The invasive surgery required to stitch up the muscles in his arm had not left his arm "pretty tender"—the throbbing aftereffect of the muscle repair was closely akin to being rhythmically stabbed with a sharp-pointed pine tree. He was mopping his face with the sheet, the pain side of him thinking uncharitable thoughts about that lying dog Latham while his fair side argued that Latham had offered him a bottle of painkillers, which he'd refused.

Fuller didn't like his subordinate's tone. "You can't make a whimsical choice to isolate yourself, Wagner; it doesn't work that way. You're a representative of the nation's chief law enforcement agency, and we all have superiors to whom we answer. This is a good time for me to tell you that I haven't been impressed with your work, and your apathetic attitude regarding professionalism borders on being deplorable."

Listening to Fuller practice being a leader was sucking out what little energy he had stored up. "I haven't been sitting out on the veranda sipping mint juleps, Bert. I slept fifteen hours because I couldn't stay awake."

The rookie agent's excuse didn't satisfy him, but Fuller would solve the attitude problem in a face-to-face briefing. "We'll discuss that later. Can you arrange to have someone transport you to Cat Lake before noon?"

Transport? "I can."

"Fine. The ADD is driving down from the Memphis office and expects to meet us there around one o'clock. I'll meet you at the lake at noon and get you pooped-up before the briefing. Any problems?"

Only you, thought Wagner. He said, "None."

When he got off the phone, he picked up the frame and read the note card again. *War.*

Wagner called his transport service of choice.

Ceedie would be in town all day, and she would be more than happy to drive him out to the lake.

They arrived at Susan and Bobby Lee's house thirty minutes early, thus allowing Missy's mother and Virginia Parker sufficient time to make sure the wounded man wouldn't starve between noon and supper.

CHAPTER EIGHTEEN

Patterson sat at the table with Bobby Lee, finishing his third glass of iced tea and second slice of pie. "What time is our favorite bureaucrat getting here?"

"Noon." Wagner was propped in Bobby Lee's recliner, chewing aspirin and counteracting them with black coffee.

Ceedie was sitting where she could keep an eye on him. Cringing. "How can you stand the taste of those things?"

Patterson answered for him. "It's an acquired taste. He got it from going up against the Red Raiders once too often." It was the second time he'd alluded to the damage he'd inflicted on his friend—he'd called it "ribbing" the first time.

Wagner had been trying to ignore him—it wasn't working. "Speaking from experience, I'd take getting shot over busted ribs nine out of nine times. It's passing through my mind to give you an opportunity to do your own comparative analysis."

Patterson hoisted his tea glass. "Touché."

"So. When do you start teaching me about being a Christian?"

"Pick a time. We'll be here a few more days, and we can keep it up by mail."

"Doing what?"

"Scripture memory, Bible study methods, the works. Know Him, and make Him known."

"Is there anything in there about killing your boss and telling God it was an accident? I've been thinking I could—"

Ding-dong chimes interrupted his errant theological speculations, and Patterson went to invite the potential victim into the parlor.

Those left in the kitchen could hear sounds of greetings coming from the entry hall. Seconds later, Patterson escorted Fuller and a near-visible odor of Vitalis hair tonic into the room.

Bobby Lee stood. Patterson introduced Fuller to Susan, Bobby Lee, and Ceedie.

Susan indicated a chair. "Agent Fuller, please have a seat. Can I get you some coffee or tea?"

The straight-combed hair swiveled back and forth. "No, thank you. If you'll excuse us, Agent Wagner and I need to take a walk and discuss some bureau matters." He was the sound and picture of efficient federal law enforcement.

Wagner said, "Good idea."

Pat watched his new friend working himself out of the recliner and said, "I'll tag along."

Fuller didn't think so. "I'll have to ask you to stay here. What Jeff and I have to discuss is confidential."

Patterson was patient. "He outweighs you fifty pounds. Can you keep him on his feet if he passes out?"

Fuller looked at Wagner's color and wavered. "He looks strong enough to me."

"I don't think your confidence will keep him vertical."

"I'll be okay." Wagner was feeling stronger. He moved carefully to pick up his windbreaker. "C'mon, Bert."

Ceedie stepped close and took the jacket from him. "Put your arm in here, then stand still." She got him jacketed by standing on her tiptoes. When he was dressed, she patted his good arm and momentarily set the stability of his knees back twenty-four hours when she locked eyes with him. "You stay calm, now, an' be nice to the other children."

"Yes, ma'am." The special attention caused his cheeks to use blood he couldn't spare.

He led his boss to the covered back porch, where four metal lawn chairs were lined up facing the lake. "How about here?" Without waiting for an answer, he took the chair that would put him upwind of the Vitalis.

"Fine." Fuller carefully folded his suit coat so that only the lining touched the surface and laid it on the table. He sat on the lip of his chair to avoid wrinkling his pants. "Before we get to the briefing for Assistant Deputy Director Dearden, let's talk about being out of touch for fifteen hours."

"I tried to make that clear to you this morning, Bert; I wasn't any good to you or the FBI." Either he was still in shock or the lake's peace was soaking into him. He took a deep breath of the clean air and leaned back. "I called your house, the office, and two country clubs before I gave up. I wasn't going to drive to Jackson and mount a house-to-house search to tell you I had to have some rest. I went to sleep."

"Sarcasm isn't going to help here," Fuller fumed. If he moved forward another millimeter, he was going to be sitting on his imagination. "Having a fifteen-hour hole in our duty log reflects an attitude of complacence."

"An attitude of complacence? You need to listen to yourself, Bert." A crow called from the far end of the lake; the gin's pigeons were pecking in the gravel on the western approach to the bridge; the late spring foliage on the trees across the lake was trying to hide the cabin where they'd found the body of Cherry Prince. How could a setting so overtly peaceful spawn so much violence? He was slowly shaking his head without being conscious of it. "In the past two weeks six people have died violent deaths within a few hundred yards of where we're sitting; the investigation is our responsibility—my responsibility—and you're twittering about a piece of paper." Speaking gently came easily, being nice was a challenge.

Fuller wasn't watching the pigeons, listening to the crow, or interested in what Wagner had to say. "You took an oath, Wagner. Being tired doesn't negate your responsibility to the bureau."

Negate? Wagner split Ceedie's dictate down the middle; he stayed calm, but he didn't trouble himself to be nice. "You haven't kept your impressions a secret, Bert. And this is a good time for me to tell *you* something: the price tag on that encounter out here was more than I wanted to spend." He pointed at the already-rusting skeletons of the two cars. "My car got burned up, you left me here without my gun, I'm running about a quart low on blood, and tomorrow I'm going to attend the funeral of a bona fide hero who got killed doing my job. Now—do you want to hear me recite the Pledge of Allegiance, or do you want to get on with this dadgummed briefing for our buddy Dearden?"

A hoarse voice behind the two said, "I'm willing to spot you the allegiance. Why don't we get on with the dadgummed briefing for our buddy Dearden, and let me sit in on it."

Both men turned to see a man standing by the back door. He was wearing tan slacks and a white dress shirt with a red tie, his hands stuffed in the pockets of a dark blue windbreaker. A gold FBI shield and three small letters—A.D.D.—were stenciled on the jacket's left-hand side. Assistant Deputy Director Dearden was on the scene an hour early.

Fuller vaulted to his feet before Dearden could say, "Keep your seats." Wagner was slow enough to do as he was told.

Fuller glanced at his just-out-of-reach suit coat and looked pained. It was his turn to sweat, and he was good at it. "Good afternoon, sir. We're glad you could come."

"Mm-hmm. Two biggest lies in the bureau, Bert. The

fellow from the field office says, 'We're glad you're here,' and the Washington guy always says, 'We're here to help.' "

Fuller chuckled and shook the boss's hand. "Good to see you again, sir."

Dearden walked over and gripped Wagner's hand firmly without shaking it. "I'm Hud Dearden." The ADD was two inches too short, ten pounds shy of a good weight, and as pale as the rookie agent. Dark circles under his eyes and large horn-rimmed glasses gave him the appearance of an owl that had missed too much sleep.

"Jeff Wagner, sir. My pleasure."

Dearden frowned at the empty sleeve. "What's your prog?" He sounded like he needed to clear his throat.

Fuller answered, "Pretty good, sir. The doctor says he'll be as good as new in a couple of weeks."

"Mm-hmm." Dearden turned to watch Fuller slip into his coat. "I understand Wagner is running this end of the investigation."

They say rats know instinctively when to leave a doomed ship. "That's right, sir. This has been his only assignment since day one. I was helping him sketch out his briefing when you arrived."

Dearden glanced at the burned-out hulks of the cars and back at the empty sleeve. "You feel like taking a walk?"

Wagner was tired of sitting. "That sounds good, sir."

Fuller looked at the area around the burned cars. He was thinking about what the charred grass was going to do to his shoeshine when Dearden held out his right hand. "Bert, if Wagner's the lead on this thing, I can let you get back to Jackson."

Fuller forgot about his shoes and stared at his boss. His hand met the director's and his mouth came open, but no words came out. Dearden shook the hand while taking the Special Agent in Charge by the elbow and guiding him the first few steps toward the house. "Thanks for taking the time to be here," he said warmly.

Fuller could hear the hollow thump of his own heartbeat. He managed to blurt, "Sir, I've blocked out the entire afternoon. I'll be glad to stay up here as long as you need me."

"I appreciate that, Bert, but there's no reason to use both of you to do one man's work. I'll call you later this week if I have any questions."

Ten seconds later, Fuller was climbing the back steps of the Parkers' home as if he were mounting his own gallows—he'd forgotten to button his coat, but his tie was perfect. Dearden and Wagner were walking in the direction of the burned cars. They weren't thinking about shoes.

The grass was gone, and the ground was burned black. Tree limbs overhead were charred. The stench of burned rubber and old fire was everywhere. Wagner's car, because the tires were burned off, sat flat on the ground; the windows were broken and melted; wire framing and springs were left where upholstery had been. Mason's car had been rolled onto its side to allow access to what little remained of Hollinsworth's body.

Neither man spoke. Wagner took a position near the water. He leaned against a tree with his good thumb hooked in his belt while his eyes reminded him of what he'd been through. Dearden took his time, walking with his hands in the pockets of his windbreaker, lingering here and there to examine small details, covering every foot of the scene. Halfway through his boss's inspection, Wagner turned his back and gave his attention to the lake.

When Dearden finished, he came to stand by Wagner. "You thinking about quitting?" he asked.

Wagner made himself turn and look at the devastation beneath the trees. A hard sigh puffed out his cheeks. "The thought comes and goes."

Dearden understood. "No sane man would blame you." He took off his glasses and rubbed his forehead. When the glasses were back in place he beckoned and said, "Come over here and walk me through what happened."

Wagner surprised himself with what he remembered. When he finished his account, his boss indicated a spot several yards from the burned-out area and said, "Daniels died there."

"No, sir." He pointed. "Leon Daniels died over there closer to the cars." He took a breath. "He was doing what needed to be done."

Dearden walked to the indicated spot and studied it. Without looking up, he said, "Not many men get to die doing what needs to be done."

He moved from where Leon was killed to the place he'd pointed to initially. A wide patch of the springtime-green grass was rust-coated with dried blood. The hands came out of the pockets, and he squatted by the stain. He pulled a tuft of the grass and inspected it. After he finished with the grass he took a pinch of the dirt and let it trickle through his fingers. He satisfied his curiosity, brushed off his hands, and spoke without looking up. "You?"

"Yes, sir."

"Mmm. You up to taking a walk on the bridge?"

"Yes, sir. I've been on my backside for two days; being outside feels good."

The grass under their feet was soft; the oaks offered noonday shade. Wagner took his time, watching his step and listening to the sounds of the lake. Dearden ambled slowly and talked about nothing. He'd been raised on a ranch in the Nevada mountains; they had pretty lakes there, but this was different.

When the sheriff's car went out of control on the bridge it

damaged part of the railing on the south side and tore forty feet off on the north; Mason's .30-06 had taken out a good part of the top rail near the ladder. The county crews had been out to clean off the debris; they'd start repairs "come Wednesday."

When they got to the middle of the bridge, Dearden swept some gravel out of the way with his foot and asked, "You mind sitting in the dirt?"

"The dirt's fine."

They sat in the dust—two men leaning back on a bridge railing and resting their arms—or arm—on their knees, enjoying the springtime sun and the glade-like surroundings.

When the quiet had soaked into them, Dearden asked, "Where'd you park the first time you came out here?"

Wagner pointed. "Right off the end of the bridge, across the road from the gin."

"Okay. Start there and tell me all of it."

Wagner started over and told it as it happened. The ADD listened, picking up a stray piece of gravel now and then and rolling it around between his fingers before flicking it at the ladder. When Wagner mentioned the demons, Dearden seemed to take it pretty well.

Inside the Parkers' house, Dearden's driver stood at the back window, drinking coffee and watching his boss. He looked at his watch—they'd been out there thirty minutes. The man was more than Hud Dearden's driver. Dearden probably didn't need a bodyguard, but a driver who was qualified to fill both roles on one salary saved the taxpayers money.

Bobby Lee tried playing host to the quiet man, but the driver was only interested in one thing.

"It's a nice day outside. You wanna move out on the back porch?" asked the host.

"Thanks," the man smiled.

"Think we oughta get a coffee refill first?"

"That'd be nice. Thanks."

The air was still, and the sun was doing its job; the men on the bridge shed their windbreakers and draped them over the railing. The pigeons from the gin made infrequent sweeps over the lake; two or three cars crossed the bridge and gave the men a wide berth. The crow carried on her one-sided conversation down on the south end of the lake. Wagner fished his sunglasses out of the windbreaker and kept talking.

The people at the house trickled onto the back porch one at a time, bringing more coffee one time, cookies another. Pat brought out more chairs. It got warm, and Susan offered iced tea; everyone made the switch.

An hour passed. The men on the bridge talked while the spectators visited and watched.

After Wagner finished talking, Dearden had eight or ten questions for him. When the questions were answered, Dearden took his glasses off again and let them fall into his lap. He rubbed his face with both hands. He said, "It's a good thing you were here."

He put his glasses back on and stood. Wagner got to his knees first and used the railing to make it to his feet.

Dearden was frowning at an empty spot on Wagner's belt. "Where's your piece?"

Wagner looked down and touched his side. "My gun?"

"Yeah. Where is it?"

"Bert took it till after the investigation."

"What investigation?"

The question struck Wagner as funny, and he had to grin. "I don't know, sir." Fuller was a certified twit.

Dearden let it go. "Do you know what your primary responsibility is as an agent, Jeff?"

"Yes, sir." He took a deep breath and laid his cards faceup on the table. "The Bible says something about me being a minister of God against evil. A. J. Mason showed it to me in the Bible. I read it, but I don't remember where it was."

Dearden rubbed his chin. "And now you believe you're a minister of God?"

"That's right . . . against evil."

"Okay," Dearden absorbed the declaration. He motioned for Wagner to follow and started for the house. "When are you going to make your decision about staying with the bureau?"

Wagner gestured at the lake. "I want to get a few weeks between me and what happened out here. I need to get my feet under me before I make any big decisions."

"Good move. I've got a proposition for you—a job offer."

Right. Put the religious guy where he won't embarrass us. "I'm not interested in being a clerk, sir."

"Don't start swinging till the other guy climbs in the ring, Jeff." Dearden didn't smile. "I want you to take on a special project for me."

"What project?"

"I want you to find those three people who were here when Bainbridge and the others were killed. I'll set up a special section when I get back to the office; you'll be the only agent in it. You'll work for me, but you'll make most of your own decisions. I want to find out where Washington and those other two are before one of them gets hurt. I intend to arrange for them to be protected."

It didn't make sense. "Why choose me? I'm the new kid on the block."

"That's one of the reasons. You're new. You went through the Academy caring less about filling squares than you did about getting the job done, and you probably won't lie to protect yourself." He went on to describe the job. "You can work out of the field office of your choice or out of your house. I don't expect you to need a secretary, but you can make that decision for yourself."

Wagner held up a restraining hand. "This is coming kind of fast."

"Don't let it throw you. I've been thinking about this for a week, I just didn't know who I was going to get to fill the slot. Take a few weeks to get over that beating you took, then call me. If you want the job—and you will—we can hash out details as we go."

They were almost to the burned-out cars. Wagner wondered, "What about the Jackson field office?"

Dearden stopped and faced him. "You can worry about Jackson when they make you an ADD." He unclipped the holster on his belt and handed his gun over. "Take this till you get yours back."

"Thanks."

"And give that ankle holster to someone you don't like."

"I plan to burn it." He clipped the revolver over his right hip.

"Move it back and tilt the butt forward."

Wagner made the adjustment.

The teacher said, "Back just a little more . . . right about there . . . comes out smoother. Taking second place in a gunfight can get expensive."

"Winning ain't always cheap either." He pulled the gun, flipped the cylinder open to check the loads, relatched it, and put it back on his hip. "Thanks for the loan. It fits good."

"Well, don't get attached to it. I've got a thirteen-year-old kid who thinks it's already hers."

* * *

They got back to the porch, and Dearden mixed with the Pattersons and Parkers while Wagner introduced himself to Dearden's driver.

"Jeff Wagner."

"Reed Kirksey." He was sizing Wagner up. "You doing okay?"

"Just sore."

"Good." Sun winked on bright metal at Wagner's belt.

Kirksey got interested and leaned close. He straightened and gave the rookie more study. "He let you have his gun?"

"Yeah. Just till I get mine back."

"Hmm. He doesn't loan it out every day."

"Yeah. He said his kid already had her name on it."

"Uh-huh . . . speaking of names." He beckoned with his fingers. "Lemme see it."

Wagner handed him the .38 and Kirksey turned it over. On the butt, between the walnut grips, was a strip of engraved silver—one word followed by three initials: *Thanks JEH*.

Wagner took the gun and looked at the letters. "Hoover?"

"Yep."

"Thanks for what?"

Kirksey checked to make sure his boss was busy. "Scuttlebutt says it was something like what went on out here . . . big shootout . . . happened out in Las Vegas or Reno. They say he took a round in the chest . . . that's why he looks like a TB patient."

Dearden had fulfilled his social obligations. He motioned for Wagner and Kirksey to follow and started for his car. He let them catch up and asked Wagner, "You still at the Holiday Inn in Indianola?"

"Yes, sir."

"You'll have a car there in the morning when you wake up—the keys'll be at the desk. See if you can make it last you a month." He opened the car door, got in, and rolled down the window. "You work for me now. Call me in two or three weeks and let me know when you want to start earning your pay."

"Yes, sir."

The boss reached to roll up his window and stopped. Hezekiah Uriah Dearden, the only child of two committed Christians, said, "That verse is in the book of Romans, chapter thirteen. Look it up. Remember it."

"Yes, sir."

"All right, Reed."

Kirksey winked at Wagner and took his boss back to Memphis.

Wagner went looking for his own driver to take him to Indianola.

He stayed quiet all the way to Indianola. The tractors were busy in the drier parts of the fields, getting the land ready, hurrying.

She left him to himself and listened to the radio all the way to the edge of town. "You want to make any stops 'fore I drop you off?"

"What about a quick hamburger?"

She checked her watch. "Okay. A quick one."

"You must have a hot date."

"No." Two dime-sized spots near the points of her cheek bones turned pink; they highlighted her eyes. "I'm goin' back to Jackson this afternoon."

"Back to Jackson?"

"I practice-teach at Bailey Junior High. I thought I told you that."

"Hmm." *You can office wherever you like.* He made the calculations. "You'll be down there another four or five weeks."

"Mm-hmm."

"In that case, I think I'll do my recuperating in Jackson."

"Wouldn't that be convenient." She got busy pulling into a space at the Dairy Freeze. Something about parking the car added fifteen cents worth of pink to her cheeks.

Jagoe came out of the kitchen door on the run when Ceedie tooted the horn—when he saw Wagner in Miss Ceedie's car, he faltered and slowed. The closer he came, the slower he got. He was a step from Ceedie's door when he changed his mind and went to Wagner's side. "Afternoon, boss."

"Jagoe." Fatigue made Wagner hoarse. "How about three chiliburgers, a Coke, and a chocolate malt—extra thick."

"Yassuh, boss, comin' right up."

"Thanks."

Jagoe stayed at the window. "Mistah Jeff?"

"Mm-hmm?" The long afternoon was catching up with him fast.

"That thing what happened in here Sunday mornin'," he frowned, "that weren't right."

"Thanks, Jagoe. It's okay now." He was tired, and he had something he wanted to talk to Ceedie about.

"The cooks tol' me to tell you, next time them white folks gits spiteful, you welcome to come out an' eat in the kitchen with us."

Wagner looked at the man. He was holding his white chef's hat in both hands, standing erect—serious, dignified.

God's minister against evil got his door open and worked his way out of the car. Jagoe took the white man's extended hand, and Wagner said, "I guess that just might be the highest honor a man could have, Jagoe. We better walk in here and tell the cooks how much I appreciate it."

When he got back to the car, Ceedie said, "I'm impressed."

He brushed it off. "Public relations."

She knew better. "Mm-hmm."

Jagoe was ten seconds behind him with the hamburgers and drinks. The burgers were floating in chili, and the malt was so thick he had to hold it between his knees and eat it with a spoon.

Fifteen minutes later, Bobby Darin was splishing and splashing in the jukebox. The song started Wagner planning a one-day jump on the doctor-ordained schedule; he was going to take a shower as soon as he got to the hotel. Ceedie was tying neat, flat knots in the wrapper from her drink straw. They had the Freeze curb to themselves.

"How 'bout if we stop by the house an' show Momma you're okay?" she wondered.

Well, there it is. He wanted to date her, but she needed to know that the next time she got mad and walked off, he wasn't going to chase her. *May as well tell her before you go see Momma, ol' buddy. She might just invite you to walk yourself home, and the motel's closer from here.* The speech was composed and ready in his mind since Sunday afternoon—but amazingly enough, Jefferson Davis's descendants could read minds.

From out of nowhere, she said, "My momma gave me a little bit of a talkin' to."

"Your momma?" He said his first prayer since becoming a Christian. *God, please don't let this be about the birds and the bees.*

"She said I let myself get too carried away about the car-door thing." She worked with the paper wrapper a moment, having trouble getting one of the knots to lie flat. "She was right."

"Sounds like a wise woman." His second prayer was, *Thank You, Lord.*

"Oh, she is." She stopped playing with the straw wrapper and looked at him. "I apologize."

"I accept."

"That quick?"

"That quick."

"Thank you." She looked down and smoothed the wrapper against her jeans. "That's sweet."

It wasn't easy, but he got turned so he was facing her and took her hand. "You make being sweet real easy."

She said "Thank you" again, but didn't smile. "You don't do too bad yourself."

He thought pink cheeks looked nice on a girl with a good tan.

Mr. Davis shook his hand too enthusiastically and got lightly chastised by Mrs. Davis—"Call me Dot."

Thanks to Ceedie, the visit was mercifully brief. They were making their exit through the kitchen when Maddie Mae stopped him. "I didn't know did you like ham sandwiches or roast beef better, so I made you two of both." She handed him a paper sack. "An' I put you some of my lemon cake on the top so it don't git skushed."

Mose rented a little house out in a remote clearing northeast of Goodlettsville, about twenty miles from downtown Nashville—far enough from the city to be unaffected by it, close enough to get there quickly if the need arose.

The Manns' nearest neighbor lived a mile down the road, and, except for church on Sunday, the two kept to themselves. They attended almost every black church within twenty miles, never going to the same one twice in any one month.

The hill folks were no less curious than flatlanders, but they upheld their reputation for honoring another person's need for privacy; vague answers to polite queries were accepted without comment. The old man's name was Mose Mann; he called his grandson Bill. They came from somewhere up north. Boys normally hit a growth spurt when they turned twelve, but Bill Mann looked like he was going to be a late bloomer. Fact is, he probably didn't weigh much more than the Redbone hound that rarely left his side.

That summer, on weekday mornings, the three stayed close to the house. Bill would teach himself; Mose would help where he could. Time inside the small house went slow for the boy and dog.

In the afternoons, when the sun was high and hot, they'd load a ramshackle old pickup with yard tools and the like and drive off in one direction or another, usually east. The few folks who would bother to note the comings and goings of a man, boy, and dog failed to observe that there was little out east of town to attract folks, only deep woods and scattered lakes and streams.

In the woods, Mose—with the dog's help—taught the boy how to hunt and fish and how to become someone else. For the boy, the afternoons were too short.

Two or three times a month, they'd take the car and go to the library in Nashville. Mose liked books on religion, history, and politics. Bill chose the kinds of books boys choose—books about espionage, fighting, and flying.

The boy, sparked by what he learned from the dog, warmed to the old man. The man learned to phrase his questions in a way that required more than one syllable to answer. The boy learned that there was no way he could squander words on Mose; he always got a good return on his investment. Mose thought the boy the most polite child he'd ever seen, and it made him uneasy; boys who were awake needed to be up to some kind of mischief, on the verge of it, or planning it.

At night they would sit and read. Mose would sometimes share what he learned with the boy and dog; the boy was the only one who commented. The boy would share on occasion, but mostly he wanted to hear what Mose thought. When it came time for evening prayers, the boy consented to kneel with Mose, but he never spoke a word.

By the end of June, their routine was established—by August, the routine was a way of life. The fall of 1960 was bearing down on them, and the boy was making himself ready. When school started, a twelve-year-old Bill Mann would be facing the seventh grade.

CHAPTER NINETEEN

Two years later.

If a man wanted to occupy a political office in Clear Creek County, he had to have the vote of the ranchers and dairy farmers, and those folks drank their coffee early. On Mondays and Thursdays, Sheriff Collier worked the south end of the long narrow county, the dairy part; Tuesdays and Fridays were given over to the ranchers on the north end. On Wednesdays and Saturdays, the sheriff would park at the courthouse and walk across to the Lakeside Cafe where Nadine would have a cup of coffee waiting in his booth at five thirty on the dot; he'd be talking to the businessmen and the courthouse crowd and taking his first sip of the scalding brew while the whip antenna on his car was coasting to a stop. The fact that the Lakeside Cafe was four-and-a-half miles from the nearest body of water never seemed to attract the interest of its patrons.

Six mornings a week he'd leave the day's cafe of choice in order to arrive at his office just before seven forty-five. He'd say a couple of words to the folks in the reception area and withdraw to his office with a thermos of coffee and the Fort Worth paper for his "quiet time."

*　*　*

When Collier was elected, he inherited Diane Bell as the senior receptionist and secretary at the sheriff's office.

Three things were unalterable regarding his relationship with Diane.

The first thing had to do with politics; he couldn't fire her and keep the sheriff's job. She was kin to most of the people in the county and no small number of the rest of the folks in north Texas.

Some time back, the sitting governor had crossed swords with Diane over how he had been "received" at the sheriff's office. In his second run for the governorship, he got less than fifteen percent of the vote in Clear Creek and the surrounding seven counties and ended up back in his law office. So much for tangling with Miss Diane.

The upshot of the political situation was, barring her commission of an immoral act with a Protestant minister on the courthouse grounds at high noon, Miss Diane would be keeping her job with the county for as long as she wanted it.

Second. She had a tongue as sharp as broken glass. To her credit, she didn't use it unless she was provoked; however, her "provoked" threshold sometimes resided close to the surface.

Lastly. Although she might offer an unsolicited opinion in shard-shaped words, she did what her boss told her to do, pretty much when he told her to do it.

Collier had decided he'd keep her.

The only real altercation between the two came during his second day on the job. She interrupted his "quiet time," and he informed her—in no uncertain terms—that his time with his coffee and newspaper was more important to him than her life—or his getting re-elected. She responded by making a thirty-second speech that included something to the effect that she "would rather be buried in mud up to my neck and get stomped to death by a rabid duck than have to live with the knowledge that I caused you to miss getting to read the sports section of the *Fort Worth Star-Telegram* in coffee-soaked tranquility." After she made her speech, she walked out to her desk and assumed the guardianship of his door.

Not many people tried to cross the woman because not many could handle the aftermath. Diane and her protection of the sheriff's "quiet time" gained legend status the morning Carl Willingham shot himself.

Some years back, on a quiet Wednesday morning, a stranger near the Clear Creek County sheriff's office might've been led to believe that there was something unorthodox about how the folks around the courthouse were supposed to be notified that it was eight o'clock.

A handsome seventy-three-year-old schoolhouse wall clock hung on the wall in the reception area of the sheriff's office. On the day that would anchor the legend, the clock's pendulum was moving in grooved arcs while the secondhand took measured steps around its small track. Immediately below the clock, Deputy Carl Willingham was demonstrating his quick-draw technique to the department's newest rookie. Carl's fingers curled themselves snugly around the gun's checkered grips, and his elbow moved straight back as it bent. His thumb eared the hammer back as the weapon moved upward. He was dropping into his crouch—his left hand held out waist high, palm down, like in the movies—when the gun's front sight snagged the holster's stitching. The weapon's upward movement stopped. Carl's elbow kept moving straight back, his knees kept bending, and his snugly curled fingers kept pulling, but the pistol stayed right where it was. The only part of the gun that moved was the trigger.

Deputy Carl Willingham sent a bullet down the outside of his right calf at precisely three seconds before eight o'clock.

Nobody had ever thought the reception area particularly small until they heard its meager attempt to accommodate the sound of a deputy with six months' experience screwing up a quick-draw demonstration. The burned gases escaping from the formidable cartridge blew a decade's worth of accumulated dust off file folders stacked twelve feet away. It took Deputy Willingham an entire second to get over the shock from the sound, and, because he was familiar with the destructive power of the .357 Magnum, it was another second before he could muster the courage to look down at his blood-soaked trousers. Carl took in the long rent in his pants leg and the blood that was sprayed on the floor and thought he had blown his own leg off. The scream that followed the explosion from the gun resounded down the the hall leading to the sheriff's private office just as the second hand on the clock ticked across the top of its arc.

Chief Deputy Jon Bob Clover, moving as if launched by the blast, was in the hall to the sheriff's private office before the clock's second hand got five clicks from the top. He was making straight for the glass door that separated the *Star-Telegram*, scalding coffee, silence, and sheriff from the outer-world's pandemonium. He was three steps from the special door when he found himself confronted by the formidable barrier that separated the sheriff from mere mortals and their chaotic existence.

Diane looked up from her typewriter. "Where do you think you're going?" She satisfied herself that it was just Jon Bob and went back to her typing chores.

"Gotta see the sheriff; C. W. just shot himself in the leg." The smell of antique dust and burned cordite accompanied the white fog curling in Jon Bob's wake.

"It's eight o'clock." Diane didn't bother to look up this time. "No one sees the sheriff unless I say so. Go on about your business or take a seat."

Jon Bob had been standing fewer than six feet from the gun's muzzle and his ears were still ringing, but he heard her. His pulse was slowing to just barely over a hundred and ten, but adrenaline was pumping through his system for the same reason that his ears were ringing. The fight-or-flight stimulant circulating in his bloodstream, because it had never had an altercation with Diane, told him that going on the offensive was always a good idea—and Jon Bob made a tactical error.

The senior deputy took two authoritative steps toward the woman's desk and spoke to her as if she didn't understand English well. "The man is shot, Diane. I suppose you *did* hear the gun go off." He turned and reached for the door handle. "Seein' the sheriff *is* my business."

"Just a minute, Jon Bob." She wasn't using her razor strap tone.

He stopped.

Diane turned her chair away from her typing to face him. She stayed seated, took off her granny glasses, and held them while she crossed her wrists in her lap—she somehow looked taller that way. "Who is the officer in charge in the absence of the sheriff?"

"You know wh—"

"Can you see that man in there?" The hand holding the glasses motioned at the glass door to the office.

She waited while Clover pondered. The sheriff was tilted back in his chair, hidden behind the morning paper, his boots crossed on the desk; a steaming mug of coffee sat ready at his right hand.

Diane Bell let him look at the scene for a moment then said, "As you can see, Chief Deputy, the sheriff is busy reading his paper. He does not want to be bothered. He is, in effect, absent—and you are in charge. And if you open that door, what he will probably do to you will make any bullet hole in Willingham's leg seem like a paper cut." She put the little reading glasses back on her nose and returned to what she was doing before he was propelled into her presence. "Get away from that door and go do your job." She adjusted the glasses while she found her place in the document and went back to her typing; the conversation was over.

Jon Bob looked at her fingers moving on the keys, then at the man behind the glass enclosure. He chewed the corner of his mouth for a second then snapped around and started back through the white fog. "Frank! Pull my car around to the front," he yelled. "An' put some towels on the seat so it don't get blood all over it!"

That incident had happened back in the mid-fifties. Collier waited until no one was paying attention and gave Diane a raise. And the people in the sheriff's department made sure nobody interrupted their boss's quiet time.

The man leading the assault was wearing a dark suit, short haircut, and condescension when he sauntered down Diane's hallway. It was five after eight when he and his partner paused at her desk. "Good morning, ma'am. I'm George Hughes, Special Agent in Charge of the FBI field office in Dallas. This is Special Agent Wagner. We need to see Sheriff Collins."

"It's Collier." Diane favored the men with a glance at the little unfolded wallets and indicated the chairs lined up against the wall. "Have a seat, gentlemen. The sheriff's busy right now. He'll be with you in ten minutes."

Gene Collier took that moment to turn a page of his newspaper; otherwise, all was still in the office.

Wagner sat down. Hughes, the serious, shorter, and more ravenous of the two hounds of justice, looked at the glass door, coffee, and *Fort Worth Star-Telegram* and moved a step closer to Diane's desk. "From the looks of things, I would say that the sheriff is less than busy."

Diane pressed a button on her desk, said, "Clark," and gave her attention back to Hughes. "Special Agent Hughes," she nodded at the young man who materialized at Hughes's elbow, "this is Deputy Clark Roberts. Clark, this is Special Agent in Charge George Hughes; the smart one over there is

Wagner. They're here to see the sheriff. Would you buy them a cup of our coffee while they wait?"

Clark Roberts was lean, above average height, and easy-going. He smiled. "Be glad to, Miss Diane. Gentlemen, if you'll—"

Special Agent Hughes and the Federal Bureau of Investigation didn't have time to wait for Aunt Bea and Barney to make their way into the twentieth century. "Look, lady, we don't—"

"Coffee might be nice, George." Wagner stood up. He rarely interrupted the head of a field office, but he had watched Diane slide the drawer of her desk open and rest her fingertips on its edge. He smiled at Aunt Bea and said, "Which way do we go?"

Hughes was confounded. Wagner put his arm around his partner's shoulders like they were old friends and encouraged him to follow Roberts back down the hall.

When they got to the coffeepot, the deputy was smiling at something.

Hughes turned on Wagner. "Am I missing something here?"

Wagner said, "You were in way over your head, George. That woman was protecting her boss, and you were on your way to getting a demonstration of her willingness to sacrifice you on the altar of impatience."

"We don't have time to—"

Diplomacy was not Hughes's strong suit, and Wagner interrupted for the second time in as many minutes. "George, that guy back there was elected by the people of this county to run this office. Instead of stopping some place when we leave here and paying good money for a cup of mediocre coffee, why not drink a cup of their free coffee while we let the sheriff run this opertion the way he wants to?"

Roberts was nodding his agreement and holding out a red

mug with CCCSD VISITOR printed on it in block letters. Hughes took the proffered cup.

Wagner turned to Roberts. "You're the deputy that got in that fire fight with those three bad boys from California, aren't you?"

"Word gets around, I guess." Roberts flushed slightly.

"How's the arm?"

Roberts opened and closed his left hand. "Just like new. Thanks."

Hughes gave Roberts a long look, and a test. "The report said two of them were carrying Browning High Powers."

Roberts quit blushing. "Technically, that's correct. Two of them had High Powers, and so did the third one."

Wagner looked at Roberts's sidearm. "I see you're packing a Browning yourself."

"Yep." The young deputy was smiling again. "Won it in a contest."

"I'll bet you did," Wagner grinned.

Roberts glimpsed a bright strip of metal on Wagner's sidearm. "They let you decorate your pistol?"

"Not normally." Wagner pulled the gun and turned it over. "But my boss seemed to think it was okay."

Hughes, who had never had occasion to see Wagner's sidearm up close, looked over the deputy's shoulder at the strip of engraved silver riveted to the gun's butt. *GOOD JOB. HUD.*

"Man, man." Hughes was mesmerized. "What in the heck does a guy have to do to get a presentation gun from an assistant deputy director?"

Wagner settled the gun back in its holster. "Lemme put it this way—you don't want one." He turned their attention to Roberts. "The Dallas paper said you're in law school."

"Mm-hmm. I go some at night."

Hughes was the only one in the group who hadn't been in a gunfight. He said, "I went to Harvard."

Roberts saluted Hughes with his coffee cup. "That figures."

Wagner struggled to keep from spewing out a mouthful of coffee, and Hughes relaxed for the first time; he had genuinely been trying to be friendly. "Okay, okay. Have you considered coming to the bureau after you pass the bar?"

"That used to be the plan." The county man's smile reached to his back teeth. "Would I have to work for you?"

Hughes actually smiled then laughed out loud.

Wagner was feeling the relaxed atmosphere soak into his mind and wishing he'd become a sheriff. He asked, "What was that lady going to bring out of that drawer?"

"Miss Diane? Oh, it must've been her ruler."

"Ruler? Like you measure with?"

"Yeah. Except Diane's is two feet long and weighs about forty-five pounds."

Hughes glanced in the direction of the hall. "What could she do with a ruler?"

Now it was the deputy's turn to chuckle. "If you'd touched that door, she'd've sent your hand home in a sack."

All three men were laughing when they came back down the hall. Hughes managed to maneuver so the deputy stayed between him and Miss Diane's ruler.

Hughes and Wagner sat in front of the sheriff's desk; Roberts propped himself against the wall. Wagner took twenty minutes to give the county lawmen the high points of Mose Washington's life.

When Wagner finished, Collier stayed quiet for a long minute, looking at a picture of the woman. "And this was two years ago?"

Hughes nodded. "Just over . . . spring of '60."

He tapped the photo. "When was this taken?"

"The sheriff's office in Mississippi found her the next day;

coroner said she'd been dead twelve hours. Her body was on the bed in Washington's cabin, dressed and wrapped in that sheet. That's it."

Collier used a magnifying glass to examine the eight-by-ten photograph. Two of the cuts on her face were open to the bone but no blood was present; whoever had wrapped the woman in the sheet had cleaned her up after she died. She was wearing a dress that looked as if it was fresh out of her closet. Someone had taken the time to give her a funeral.

"Autopsy report?"

Hughes pointed at the folder on the desk. "It's all in there, Sheriff, and all bad. She was beaten to death."

"And the people with her?"

Hughes referred him to the folder again. "She had a son, ten years old at the time. The Washington fellow was there, and there was a third man, apparently white, who helped them. No one has seen or heard from any of the three since April of '60—they vanished . . . utterly. A local fisherman accidentally discovered her car the next morning; nothing much was in it. They ran the numbers—she was the widow of an Air Force pilot, fellow named Prince, no next of kin. There were several dozen fresh holes in the ground under the cabin and dirt-covered coffee cans stacked in a shed behind the house. Speculation is that Washington had some money buried. He'd been taking in a substantial amount of money but spending little."

Collier pulled the folder over and slipped the picture into it. "So. What do you want from us?"

"It's been two years and there hasn't been so much as a whisper of evidence that Sam Jones has heard from Mose Washington. We've lifted the phone taps. What we'd like to do is have your office do an informal takeover and stop by Pilot Hill every few months and see if he's heard anything."

Collier looked at Roberts.

Roberts shrugged. *Sure.*

The Feds had left. Roberts was slouched in one of the chairs across from the sheriff. "I'm surprised you took it."

"Why?"

"What the heck are we gonna do?"

The sheriff looked down the empty hallway. "Shut that door."

Roberts did as he was told and sat back down. "Okay. Tell me."

"Why do you think the Feds would include us?"

"Because they want out."

"Why?"

"Because they know decency when they see it."

"And more," said Collier, "that old reprobate in Congress has been breathing down the FBI's neck long enough. He may not live out the year, so he's off their case," he tapped the folder, "and they're off of this one. And this civil rights stuff that's coming down the pike is pulling the teeth of people who would prosecute a kid for defending his mother. The Feds feel just like you and me—they'd give that kid a medal if they could find him."

"So, what do we do?"

Collier decided to tell Roberts that Mose Washington had another friend nearby.

"I've known about this since the day after it happened. More than fifteen years ago, Mose Washington's only son died saving the life of a little white girl. That girl is married to my wife's brother and lives here in Denton."

"Are you serious?" Roberts sat up. "You mean right here in town?"

"Yep. You put Sam Jones with my brother-in-law's wife and you've got two of Washington's best friends within fifteen miles of this office." He tapped the desk. "If I was that old man, I'd bring that boy out here. And if they show up here, you and I will do what we can to make sure nobody finds them."

Clear Creek County was the closest thing to a home the fugitives had left in the world. They'd come home.

Collier pulled the folder close and flipped it open to take another look at the picture of Cherry Prince. He studied the badly disfigured face, contrasting it with the carefully pressed dress. *What kind of animals would do that to a lady?*

Roberts watched his boss's face. "You'd've killed 'em all, wouldn't you?"

Collier took his time answering, continuing to study the face of the young mother. Finally, he shook his head. "Nope." He let the cover close on the folder. "I'd've done just what that kid did. I'd've killed the ones that touched her."

CHAPTER TWENTY

In Texas, all small towns are pretty much the same. The local folks are friendly to each other and to most strangers, they know a lot about each others' personal lives, they help one another out in hard times, and they like high school football. Pilot Hill, Texas, was no exception.

All in all, Pilot Hill's was a small school district without much in the way of industry. Because there was no industry in the area, Pilot Hill depended on the surrounding cropland and ranches for its tax revenue. However, the relatively small size of the district and its limited resources were indirectly proportional to the devotion the folks in the area bestowed on high school sports. On game nights during basketball season, the hometown gym was filled to overflowing. It was the same for the stands at the baseball park during the spring. But in Pilot Hill, as in every small town in Texas, the fixation was on football, and that's where the citizens—young and old, men and women—spent most of their collective energy. The football season lasted for three months out of the year . . . and was replayed in Nettie's Café, down at the feed store, on the loafers' benches, and in the beauty shops and churches for the other nine months.

Travelers passing through Pilot Hill could tell what town they were entering because of the signs out on the highway. At each end of town, north and south, a conspicuously placed, full-size billboard proclaimed to all who passed that they were entering "Bearcat Country." The signs also listed the numerous years the Bearcats had won their conference title, the years they had won their district, and the respectable number of times they had participated in—or won—the Texas Class 2A High School Football Championship. No high school in Texas of Pilot Hill's size, or any other size for that matter, had come near their record for football success. Fresh orange paint on the bottom line of the list declared to the travelers that the Pilot Hill Bearcats were the previous year's Class 2A Texas State Champions.

The high school's newest freshman class squirmed and shifted while the home room teacher worked her way through the first day's roll call. "William P. Mann."

"Here. It's Bill."

The teacher looked up. "Well, Bill, we're glad you're here. Where'd you move from?"

Mose and the young boy had been hiding for more than two years, developing their 'history.' Fiction had become near-reality. "My grandfather and I have been living in Chicago. We moved here to be near my cousin—Sam Jones." The accent was crisp, authentic.

A high percentage of the people in Pilot Hill were kin to each other; most of those who weren't kin were close friends. "I've known Sam for years." She didn't offer the fake smile that he got from a lot of white people. "We heard you were coming, and I imagine you'll like it here."

"Thank you, ma'am." She'd be okay.

"I doubt you'll have any trouble keeping up, but if you have a problem, come see me."

"Yes, ma'am. Thank you."

Keeping up academically didn't worry the newcomer, but there might be some barriers physically. He was wearing the name of Sam's cousin who had died seven years earlier; a boy who would be fourteen years old had he lived. Bill anticipated being one of the smaller kids, but Pilot Hill seemed bent on upholding the state's reputation for size; every one of the boys in the school, and all but a few of the girls, were bigger than he was. The most well-documented fiction in the world couldn't change the fact that he was a twelve-year-old swimming in a sea of teenagers.

Back in the middle of August, young Bill Mann, Mose, and Sam had gathered around the kitchen table and plotted their strategy.

Sam told Bill, "The sheriff says the hunt's off for y'all. You can just go down there to that school and blend in—be invisible. It might take you a year or so to fit in, but kids are more accepting than most adults. Just be patient."

The new academic year was an hour old when his first problem was served up.

The second-period class was freshman English. Mann trickled into the room with a couple of other kids and looked for a place where he could be invisible; he took a seat in the middle of the regimented desks. An attractive girl offered Mann a noncommittal nod and sat down in the desk next to his. Mann returned the nod.

"Hey! You don't need to be speaking to her."

Mann looked up at a boy who outweighed him by forty pounds, looked three feet taller, and had shaved that morning. Apparently, not all of the kids were going to be as accepting as others.

"Well?" The boy stepped closer.

Tell me this is not happening. Mann didn't want to fight this boy or anybody else, but the first day of school is no time to back down, even in word choice. "Well, what?" His voice, another facet of preteen reality, chose that moment to do a two-octave modulation.

The white boy laughed. "Well, Squeaky, you're gonna be a smart one, aren't you?"

Mann, squeak and all, was sliding out of his desk. "Hey, man. If you think it's—"

"Gentlemen. Take your seats, please." The English teacher came through the door and brought order with her.

"I'll see you after class, smart boy."

Mann shrugged. The boys in Tennessee were tough too—and some of them were pretty big.

Metal trays, plastic dishes, laughing girls, and yelling boys contended in a noise contest that the printed schedule called lunch break. Mann came off the line with three cartons of milk to go with his hamburger, fries, and something that claimed to be pudding. He found an empty table and was chewing a mouthful of hamburger when the girl from the English class passed.

She slowed, then stopped and looked back. "Sorry about what happened."

Mann nodded and took two gulps to swallow the hamburger. "You didn't do anything."

She was looking at the floor. "The guy that was being a jerk was Will Pierce; he's my boyfriend when he's behaving. Well . . . anyway . . . welcome to Pilot Hill. Good luck."

"In school—or with him?"

She looked up. The new kid who should be nervous was smiling. "Aren't you scared?"

"No." *That's not entirely true.* "Well . . . a little, I guess . . . kind of . . . maybe?" He was smiling again.

She looked at the faces around her. There were three black kids in the whole school. The question just spilled out. "Don't you get lonesome?"

The smile didn't completely leave. "I don't know. It's always been this way."

He watched as a hand beckoned to her from the bedlam. She looked at the hand and back at him and became the first white person in his life to say, "Can I sit with you?"

"Uh . . . sure . . . I guess . . . if you want to."

She did. "My name's Ella Claire Stinson."

"I'm Bill Mann."

"I know. Do you want me to sit with you every day so you won't be by yourself?"

Was he hearing right? An attractive white girl offering friendship? Or pity?

The girl was looking straight at him, waiting for an answer. She didn't look like the compassionate type.

"Since this is my first day, and I don't know how things work . . . do we have to be engaged or anything?"

"Nope." She grinned and took a seat.

Both of them were laughing when Will Pierce emerged from the crowd. He put his hands on the table and loomed over them. "Well, Squeaky Boy, you are definitely begging for it, aren't you?"

Mann shared his smile with the boy. "Look, man, I can't keep you from beating me up, but there's something you better know. Me being black and little attracts people like you." The smiling face relaxed to neutral. "I've been in more fights than anybody in this room because I'm not going to let you or anybody else tell me how to act, who to talk to, or where to sit. I'll fight you every day for the whole year," he patted the table, "but I sit where I please."

"And so do I," Ella Claire snapped.

Pierce ignored the girl. "You think I'm scared because you've been in a fight?"

Mann shook his head. "I think you aren't thinking, man. I'm the littlest kid in the school . . . you've got fifty pounds on me . . . I just told you I'd fight you. Why don't you wonder why I'm not scared of you?"

Pierce jerked his hands away and stood back. "You've got a knife, don't you?"

Mann had to laugh. Did all white people think all black people carried knives? "Good gosh, man, if I came in this school carrying a knife, my grandfather would whip me till I couldn't sit down for a week." This time the relaxed smile stayed; the voice didn't squeak. "Now. We can let this go, or we can get it on right here, right now."

Pierce was more curious than he was angry. "How come you ain't scared?"

Any boy who can learn to read can learn how to fight; it's almost a science. And if skill and knowledge fuse themselves inside a boy who is willing to stand up for what he believes, the components of a formidable opponent begin to merge in his person. The negotiator at the table was suddenly tired of trying to explain it; he became a freshman again. "I guess it's because who wins doesn't make any difference. I'm not scared of you. That's it."

Pierce was formulating a reply when belligerence showed up in a bass voice. "Git up, Ella Claire. You're not sittin' here." The new boy was a bigger version of Pierce; tight jeans, tight T-shirt over muscles, long sideburns, short fuse.

The girl almost ignored the latest arrival, and it wasn't easy. Pierce stepped back.

"I said git up."

Ella Claire wasn't bothered. "You don't tell me where to sit, Buddy." She glared at Pierce. "And neither does anybody else."

Buddy was thinking only one thought. "I told you to go sit somewhere else, and I meant it."

Students were crowding close to hear and see.

That day's faculty guard saw the heat beginning to rise off the exchange and started threading his way toward their table. He wasn't going to get there in time.

"Bill, this is my brother. Buddy, this is Bill Mann."

Buddy wasn't looking for new friends. "I told you to get up."

Having a big brother could be a nuisance. "And I told you that I don't take orders from you. Now go be tough somewhere else."

Things were probably going to get out of hand anyway, but the girl's next words guaranteed it. She giggled and said, "And by the way, Bill and I are engaged."

And the heat became fire.

Buddy was reaching for his sister's arm, growling, "I'm not tellin' you again—"

Teenage sisters rarely go quietly. Ella Claire tried to snatch her arm away and managed to tilt her chair.

Pierce stepped closer to the table. "Hey!"

Mann was coming out of his chair, watching for an opening.

Smart boys who are outweighed by a hundred pounds, and at the extreme end of a height disadvantage, don't always warn their adversaries before they strike.

Ella Claire's weight took Buddy forward. Mann moved a step to his left to improve his angle of attack and started the swing from his knees.

Almost any book on boxing will tell you that a hard blow to the chin is the quickest way to end a fistfight. If you hit the chin, you move the skull; if you move the skull abruptly enough, the brain will bump against it; if the brain collides with the skull hard enough, the person will be rendered unconscious. The best way to jar the skull is to aim at a point past the target, thus giving yourself more power in your follow-through.

Mann's fist was passing Buddy's belt buckle when Ella Claire's face bumped the table. When the fist hit Buddy's chin, he released his sister and tottered backward.

Buddy was momentarily stunned, but not down.

Mann didn't hesitate. He turned completely away from the boy, rotating his upper body to put his weight behind a roundhouse swing that was gaining momentum when it impacted just below the point where Buddy's ribs joined his sternum. The air left the boy's lungs, his hands went to his stomach, and his knees sagged.

In the follow-on moments Mann and the spectators were treated to an out-of-classroom demonstration of the physics involved in a lemon-sized fist, backed by a hundred and ten pounds of slim and bone, colliding with two hundred and eight pounds of football-focused muscle. Buddy was dazed, but he wasn't going down.

Buddy was stooping over to get his breath when Mann landed between his shoulder blades and grabbed him around the neck. The big boy stayed fixed for a second, then Mann felt him bunch his muscles to straighten. In that moment someone landed hard on Mann's back, and—under the added weight—the two-man pile collapsed forward. Buddy's chin hit the tabletop, his brain hit his skull, and he hit the floor. Ella Claire Stinson's brother, High School All-American candidate and co-captain of the title-contention Pilot Hill Bearcats, was down—and out.

Mann rolled off the guy, looking around and getting his feet under him. *Maybe someone will remember that I didn't start this.*

* * *

Every kid in the lunchroom was standing, trying to see what had happened. The ones close to the action were wide-eyed and silent; the ones who couldn't see what had happened were making more noise than ever. The faculty guard finally managed to push through the tight circle around Buddy, but the fire was already out.

Will Pierce moved closer and stared down at Buddy. "Is he dead?"

Ella Claire looked at the boy on the floor and sniffed, "If he's not, he will be when I tell my daddy about his latest stunt."

The guard knelt by Buddy and rolled him over. The player's eyes opened slowly but didn't focus; by that time Pierce couldn't take his eyes off Mann. The little kid with the squeaky voice hadn't been just talking tough; he had just knocked out a potential High School All-American football player. He asked, "Is that what you'd've done to me?"

Mann was brushing off his knees. He looked at Will. "Did you jump on my back?"

"Huh? When?"

"Just now. Somebody jumped on my back."

"No way, man. Nobody came near y'all."

"I felt it." A split second after he jumped on Buddy, somebody big had landed on his back.

"Nobody was behind you. You jumped on him. He went into the table. Y'all went to the floor. You got up." He looked at Buddy. "He didn't."

Mann had felt the weight. He'd jumped on Buddy and known immediately that he wasn't heavy enough to bring the boy down. In that moment of realization, when the muscles in Buddy's back tensed, someone heavy had landed hard on his back and taken them both to the floor.

Pierce repeated his question. "Would you have done that to me?"

Mann didn't answer. Words of wisdom from Perk Founder came to him. *When the fight's over, win or lose, put it behind you. An' it don't hurt to be cool.* He reached for one of the milk cartons and finished it off. "Well, I guess you'll have to excuse me. I think I'm going to be wanted in the principal's office."

Ella Claire looked down at Buddy then at Mann. "I'm going with you. When my daddy finds out what happened, he'll give you a medal."

Pierce nodded emphatic agreement.

Mr. Robert Gilbert, the high school principal, needed to arrange for Buddy to be taken to the doctor. He told Mann and his fiancée to have a seat in front of the empty receptionist's desk and left the office.

The couch the two sat on was dark brown, as were the floor and drapes, but Mann didn't think the camouflage would help him be invisible. Ella Claire had her purse open and was doing something to the mark on her lip—putting black-looking makeup over some kind of red stuff.

"What's that black stuff for?"

She winked. "Girl stuff. I mix the mascara with a little rouge and this'll look bigger and worse. Daddy'll kill him." The tiny mark became an ugly bruise.

Mann was impressed. "Looks like girls don't fight fair."

"Not goin' to either." Ella Claire continued to fabricate her injury.

She finished her machinating and was putting away her tools when a man wearing an orange Pilot Hill sweatshirt, a color-matched ball cap, and a dark frown walked into the reception area; he was followed by the principal. Ella Claire stood, and Mann followed suit.

The man came to a halt with his hands on his hips and addressed Ella Claire. "Well, I saw Buddy off to the doctor's office. He'll be all right as soon as he knows what day it is." He pointed at the Hollywood-enhanced injury to her lip. "Did he do that?"

"Yep."

The face under the ball cap grew darker. "I'm gonna kill 'im."

His pronouncement was sweet music. "I know."

The man doing the talking was the head football coach of the Pilot Hill Bearcats. He'd already gotten an account of the fight in the cafeteria. Some black kid named Bill Mann had sent the toughest man on his team to the doctor's office. The eyes under the ball cap came to rest on Mann. When he saw the boy, the coach quit thinking about Buddy and gave the rest of the office a quick glance. When his search didn't yield what he was looking for, his feet took over and turned him slowly in a full circle. There were only four people in the room, and the only black kid in sight was shorter than Ella Claire. He walked over and looked into the principal's private office. Empty.

This wasn't happening. The man winced and started shaking his head slowly back and forth; he mumbled something to himself that sounded like a prayer. When he finished conversing with himself, he forced himself to approach Mann and rested a heavy hand on the boy's shoulder. He was close to pleading when he said, "I will give you one hundred American dollars if you will tell me that you are not Bill Mann."

The only black kid in the room locked eyes with the coach for a long second. Without smiling he said, "How long do I get to keep it?"

The principal got his hand over his mouth too late to cover the guffaw.

The coach's whole body wilted, and he started shaking his head again. "Until you become Bill Mann."

Ella Claire, who was trying not to grin, stepped in and did the honors. "Coach, this is Bill Mann. He saved my life."

The coach couldn't hear her. He backed a step and let the brown couch catch his sagging body. He lowered his head and closed his eyes. *God, You cannot be letting this happen to me. Chihuahuas do not beat up Rottweilers.*

Ella Claire was loving it. She started to tell their little group about the engagement, but wisdom took over; the joke could wait.

The coach pushed himself off the couch and turned on the principal. "What happened, Gil?"

Bob Gilbert never liked the long version of anything. "There was an argument in the lunchroom. Apparently Buddy got a little carried away and grabbed Ella Claire's arm. She got a busted lip. Bill stepped in. Buddy got knocked out."

The coach was frowning at Mann. "And this is really the kid that did it?"

The principal nodded. Mann waited. Ella Claire winked at Mann. She was grinning again.

The man in the orange shirt took the time to examine Mann. The kid didn't weigh twenty pounds over a hundred; something was wrong here. He looked at the principal, the girl, and back at the little black kid. Back to Ella Claire, who was grinning in spite of a painfully bruised lip. It had to be some kind of practical joke. Back to the black kid. "This is a joke, right? How much do you weigh, boy?"

Like Barney Fife says, you gotta nip it in the bud. Mann looked into the eyes that were roughly a foot above his and said, "My friends call me Bill, Coach—and I weigh enough."

The coach was stymied—and not happy about it. He was used to having people give way to him, and Bill Mann wasn't a giver. And the kid wasn't joking about being called *boy;* he had used Buddy to demonstrate that he had an inflexible attitude about standing up for what was right.

Will Pierce chose that moment to come into the office without being invited.

Will, Bill, an' Gil, thought Mann. *We could have our own band.*

The coach focused his exasperation on Pierce. "I thought you were supposed to be her boyfriend, Will. Where were you when all this started?"

Will slowed, but kept coming. "I was right there, Coach, but I was too late . . . or too scared of Buddy." He looked at Mann. "But he sure wasn't."

The coach turned back to what had to be the littlest kid in the history of Pilot Hill High School. "Well, son . . . Bill . . . looks to me like you do good work." He smiled for the first time. "But I'd appreciate it if you'd take it easy on my son next time; we're gonna need him this year."

"Your son?"

Ella Claire, in spite of her severe injury, was having the world's best first day of school. "Yeah. My brother—his son."

"This is your dad?"

"Yeah." She couldn't hold it any longer. "If you want to marry me, you have to ask him first."

The coach and Will blurted—"Marry you?"—at the same time. Bob Gilbert had a coughing fit.

"Bill and I are engaged." More brave grinning.

The coach could keep up with her. He looked at Mann. "If you think Buddy's tough, just wait."

Mann needed to say something before they started ringing wedding bells. "Coach, I didn't want anything like this to happen."

"You did the right thing, Bill." The coach stuck out his hand. "If you ever decide you want to play football for Pilot Hill, you come see me."

The encounter was over so suddenly that Mann thought he had missed something. A grown white man that he had already written off as a jerk was offering friendship. Mann took the hand that weighed more than his arm and went along for the ride while it shook him up and down. "Thank you, sir."

"Don't mention it. You're the one who did the man's work here." He turned and stuck a no-nonsense finger under Will's nose. "Girlfriend or not, don't wait so long next time. Some guy bigger'n you manhandles a woman, you git a two-by-four an' bring it to a halt." He turned back to Mann. "We do a Bible study at our house twice a month. You're invited if you don't eat too much." He stopped at the office door and winked at his favorite—and only—daughter. "Get that mess offah your mouth before your momma sees you."

Sam stood in the front yard with Mose and watched the school bus stop at the foot of the gravel driveway; the dog met his boy at the bus door. As the bus drove off, kids were leaning out of every window, yelling and waving at Mann. The boy grinned and lifted a sheepish hand.

Sam had to smile. "Well, cousin, I see you managed to keep a pretty low profile on your first day at school."

"I guess . . . not exactly . . . maybe." Mann was watching the bus drive off, kneeling by the dog and rubbing his ears. One more day like this one and they'd be watching him on TV.

"How much 'not exactly,' do you guess?"

The boy gave the dog a hug and stood up. "They elected me president of the freshman class." He was respectful but not apologetic.

Mose watched Sam's eyes widen slightly. "President?"

"Yes'r."

"Just 'cause you're black?" Something didn't make sense.

People who didn't know him could make an erroneous assumption about the boy's demeanor. An apparent shyness on his part was, in actuality, a patient willingness to make sure he chose his words well. "I guess that's the 'not exactly' part. A girl named Ella Claire Stinson did it."

Sam was still in the dark on the popularity issue. " 'Cause you're black?"

Mann wasn't deliberately being evasive. The circumstances in the cafeteria had forced him into a situation that called for action on his part; telling about it sounded like bragging. "Well . . . it was like . . . I kind of stood up for her in the lunchroom."

The knuckles on Mann's right hand showed signs of hard use.

Mose stayed quiet but moved so that he and the dog were bracketing the boy.

Sam filtered the boy's testimony through the grid of his own remembered youth and erred in his conclusion. He put his hands in his pockets; his shoulders fell and he started shaking his head in disbelief. "Lemme see if I got this right. You went to school to be invisible and got in a fistfight in the lunchroom?"

The afternoon sun was behind Sam's shoulder, and Mann had to squint to look into his face. "Yes'r, I reckon you could say it like that."

"And that's why all those white children elected a black kid they'd never met president of their class?"

This wasn't about being elected class president; it was about doing what was right. Bill moved almost imperceptibly toward Sam and stated a hard fact. "It was something that needed doing, and I did it. Both of y'all would've done the same."

Mose rested his hand on the boy's shoulder to let him know everything was as it should be.

Sam saw the move and knew in that instant that he was letting a perceived need for secrecy outweigh a call to be fair with the boy. "Okay, let me back up a little here. Who'd you fight?"

"Wasn't much of a fight, I guess. Ella Claire and I were talking, her brother didn't like it and grabbed her arm too hard, and I knocked him out."

Those brief facts seemed to satisfy Mose and the dog, but Sam was looking at the ground and rubbing his chin. He understood about doing what was right, and he understood about being tough, but he knew the Stinsons and there was one thing that he didn't understand yet. Still studying the ground, he wondered aloud, "That girl doesn't have more than one brother, does she?"

"Not that I know of."

"My, my, my." Sam smiled and said, "Let's go up here in the shade, an' you can tell us all about it."

They moved to the porch, and Mose listened with a half-smile while Bill Mann amazed Sam with an expanded just-the-facts version of his first day at school. The hero stayed away from the part about being engaged.

When Mann finished his story, Sam leaned back and chuckled. He smiled at Mose. "The part that got left out is that the Stinson boy is about the size of that truck out yonder and twice as strong."

Mose nodded as if what Sam said was old news, and told Bill, "I been prayin' for this day for a couple o' months. An' I figure that was a angel what was on yo' shoulders when that boy went down."

Bill nodded. "I figured you'd say that."

The men looked at each other then at the boy. Sam said, "You don't believe that, do you."

"Maybe. Maybe not." Bill shugged. "There might've been an angel there, but if I could choose between me and her, I'd rather they'd've spent their time helping my mom."

Mose put his hand on the boy's shoulder. "God don't always do it the way we want, son." He looked at the boy's hand and changed the subject. "Why'd you hit him with your fist?"

Mann smiled for the first time and winked at the man who had told him the stories of life out at Cat Lake. " 'Cause they don't keep a sawed-off hoe handle in the lunchroom."

All three men chuckled.

At noon the following Monday, Will, Ella Claire, and Bill were sitting at their regular table in the cafeteria.

Will asked, "How come you drink so much milk?"

" 'Cause I don't weigh but seventy-two pounds with my shoes on, and I want to go out for football in the spring."

The PA system clicked and came on. "Uh . . . this is Buddy Stinson. Can I have your attention, please?" The noise in the lunchroom dwindled enough for the speaker to be heard. The two boys looked at Ella Claire; she offered a "Who knows?" shrug.

Buddy continued. "I did something wrong in public last week, and Mrs. Willis told me I could use this PA so I could apologize in public. First of all, I apologize to Ella Claire . . . she puts up with a lot from me, and she deserves a better brother."

Ella Claire raised her right hand and said, "I do so swear," loudly enough to be heard three tables away. Kids laughed.

"And I apologize to all you students, 'cause I'm supposed to be a leader, not a troublemaker." He stopped to clear his throat then said, "And I apologize mostly to a new kid in our school. I've been thinking all weekend about him and about what I did. For me, this new kid's last name says it all—he's a man. Bill, I just want you to know I'm sorry for what I did."

The PA clicked off.

Any image consultant in the world would trade a piece of his face for the opportunity to take advantage of the next moments, but most of those folks would come up short of what transpired.

Stillness became the room's overwhelming attribute.

The kid who wanted nothing but to be invisible looked around at the silence; every eye in the school was on him. Seeing. Waiting. He looked at the biggest, most influential people in the room—the football players. They were looking back. Expectant. Waiting to judge.

Hundreds of people. Not one, single, solitary smile.

Buddy Stinson chose that moment to step through the cafeteria door into the silence.

Mann pushed his chair back. While he stood up, he prayed to Someone he didn't really want to rely on: *Well, God, here goes nothing.*

A ripple passed through the room when the serious-looking little black kid stood up.

Buddy stopped.

Mann looked across the waiting crowd at Buddy.

The middle-of-midnight silence bolted when the black kid brought his hands together. Clap! Pause. Clap! Pause.

The third time his hands met, Will stood up and joined him; Ella Claire and two football players were on their feet for the next beat, then everybody else. The noise became unified and launched an immediate invasion on the rest of the school building. At two-second intervals, the paired hands in the cafeteria met. Clap! Pause. Clap! Pause. Buddy ducked his head. One of the football players boosted a cheerleader onto a table and she started a chant on the off beat. "Buddy!" Clap! "Buddy!" Clap! The other cheerleaders swept lunch trays aside and scrambled onto tables to do their job. "Buddy!" Boom! "Buddy!" Boom! The walls shook. More kids mounted tables. Aluminum trays became tambourines and cymbals.

A six-year-old station wagon eased to a stop in front of the high school's main entrance. Bob Gilbert opened the passenger door and leaned over to kiss his wife. Definitive thunder came from somewhere in the school; a booming echo followed. He looked away from his wife's puckered lips and through the glass front doors to see people running in the hall. Running in the halls was strictly forbidden.

Thunder!

He bolted from the car without shutting the door.

Echo!

"Gil?"

Thunder!

He was jogging for the front doors.

Echo!

"Gotta go!"

Thunder!

What now?

Echo!

He got the front door open.

Thunder! The walls shook.

The halls were twisting river rapids of wide-eyed people and reverberations.

When the principal sprinted into the cafeteria, there was a girl on every table, swaying, chanting, stomping, clapping; food and aluminum trays littered the floor. Kids stood in metal chairs—stomping, clapping, yelling; the orchestration of a riot was in progress in his school. He didn't ask what was going on, because he couldn't hear his own voice.

"Buddy!" Thunder! "Buddy!" Thunder!

Most of the teachers were holding their fingers in their ears and looking at him. Waiting.

Gilbert watched for short seconds. He was the principal; he knew immediately what had to be done, and he knew who had to do it. He vaulted onto the faculty table and motioned for the Bearcats' head football coach to follow his lead.

Slide! Clap! Stomp! "Buddy!"

Bob Gilbert—former All SWC defensive back for the Texas Tech Red Raiders—was born to be a cheerleader.

Slide! Clap! Stomp! "Buddy!"

Synthesized bedlam with choreography; if they could figure a way to harness it, they were a shoo-in for another state title.

Slide! Clap! Stomp! "Buddy!"

The teachers who had their fingers in their ears decided they'd rather be deaf than miss out on the fun.

Slide! Clap! Stomp! "Buddy!"

Buddy Stinson was standing by the table that held his sister. She was yelling something at him, motioning and pointing at the shortest boy in school.

Buddy grinned and gave her a thumbs-up.

The little black kid's slide and sway were straight out of Motown. When Buddy reached for him, Mann thought the bigger boy was going to hug him. Instead, the young giant scooped him up and put him on the table with Ella Claire. The girl grabbed Mann's skinny black arm with both hands and raised it over his head. And things in the Bearcats' cafeteria got loud.

When the phone rang she rolled over to see which line it was. Washington. "What is it?"

Whitier Priest, her husband's chief of staff, said, "You said to call you the moment we knew something, Mrs. Bainbridge."

"Well?"

"The congressman passed away, ma'am. About two minutes ago."

"It's about time. Call the governor's office in the morning and tell him to appoint me to finish out the current term."

"Yes, ma'am."

"We'll have the funeral in Washington—we can get better network exposure."

"Yes, ma'am. I've already got someone on it."

"And get Hal Junior cleaned up. I want my only surviving son straight and sober and in uniform when he's standing by his grieving mother's side. Understand?"

"Yes, ma'am."

"Have you got anything on my son's killers?"

His hesitation told her the man had been dreading the question. "We've got some promising leads, Mrs. Bainbridge, but we—"

She cursed and slammed down the receiver to show him she didn't want promises.

The distinguished-looking grey-haired man was watching her. "So, he's dead."

"Finally." The widow had not yet started to grieve. "They'll call you tomorrow."

He smiled and raised an eyebrow. "And if I appoint you, what do I get?"

"First of all, it's not *if* you appoint me . . . it's *when*. And what you get is my people behind your run for the Senate."

Political life had taught him how to time the presentation of his warmest, vote-winning smile; he chose that moment to bestow it on his companion. "What about you and me . . . us?"

She had all she needed from him. "There isn't an *us*; there never has been." She pointed at the bedroom door. "Get out of here. I've got work to do."

The startled man, one of the most handsome and eligible politicians in the nation, tried to feign dignity as he made his exit—not an easy task when carrying an armload of carefully folded clothing. Minutes later, she stood at her window and watched impatiently as his car passed through the guarded gate. When the gate closed, she picked up her phone and dialed a number from memory. A woman answered and Estelle Bainbridge said, "My husband just died."

She listened then said, "Can you be in town on Friday?" She told the person on the phone when and where.

They became acquainted at one of those high-glitz, but very boring, social functions that were designed to allow politicians and power brokers to tell one another how clever they were while sucking down cocktails paid for by tax dollars. He had been a window-dressing bureaucrat—a reluctant stand-in for his boss—she, the token representative from Hollywood. A gentle collision between the quiet man and the vivacious—and premeditatedly careless—woman resulted in a small coffee stain on an expensive fashion statement.

His profuse apology was followed by a quiet conversation—all according to her plan.

A week later, the bureaucrat met her "accidentally" in, of all places, a sporting goods store. He didn't notice her because she was hidden behind large sunglasses and a floppy-brimmed hat; she smiled when she confided that living life on magazine covers had its drawbacks. She flattered him when she asked his opinion on a fly rod and kidded him because his hair was cut too short. One thing led to another and they ended up having a quick dinner in her favorite little mom-and-pop restaurant. She liked fishing, farming, and old cars. He was restoring a '32 Ford coupe. She was in her late twenties . . . he was nearing fifty . . . she liked to laugh out loud . . . he rarely smiled. She lived on the West Coast but was frequently in Washington. Could they have dinner again in a few weeks and pretend she was a normal person?

Two months—and a handful of quiet lunches—later she asked him to teach her to fly fish. And so it went.

They were an intelligent couple and—by Washington standards—studiously discreet; no whiff of their relationship would ever reach the nostrils of the capitol's whisperers.

Having affection poured on him by one of the world's most beautiful creatures was only slightly less addicting than her assurance that he was the first person to bring genuine happiness to her life.

He put his fishing gear in the trunk of his car on Saturday morning and told his family he would return late the next day.

His wife firmly believed that an occasional day or so to himself was a reasonable request from a man who had to function in the Washington pressure cooker; more than one good man had self-destructed while fighting the battle to protect their nation from her enemies.

She walked him to his car and kissed him good-bye.

* * *

His fishing buddy was waiting for him at a secluded cabin in the mountains of Virginia.

Late that afternoon they relaxed on a covered deck that overlooked a small lake, holding hands and watching the sunset. Ducks came by pairs and groups, gliding in to spend the night on the quiet waters.

He squeezed her hand. "Tell me what you want."

"I want to spend every minute of my life listening to you say my name."

He didn't smile. "I can arrange that."

"And you would leave her for me?"

He'd already decided that he would. "All you have to do is say the word."

She shook her head sadly. A single tear left a bright line on her cheek. "We can't. Not yet. It's too soon."

He took a sip of wine. The sun was touching the treetops on the far side of the lake.

"I have to tell you something." Her next words were whispered. "Will you think me a monster if I tell you the desires of my dark side?"

"You can't have a dark side."

"You've told me everything there is to know about what you do." She left her chair to curl up in his lap, resting her head on his shoulder. "I want to know something about you that no one else knows."

"I don't have any secrets from you."

"You told me that you're looking for someone who killed some people in Mississippi years ago. If they're innocent, why do you have to find them?"

"They need the protection that I can arrange for them."

"Will you tell me when you find them? Will that be a secret?"

"You mean I need to tell you to prove that I love you?"

She giggled first, then laughed. "No, silly. It's a thing of your heart, and I want to make the day special. The two of us can celebrate." She pushed herself up and spoofed a seductress's expression. "Maybe I can arrange zumzing special for you."

Solemn vows and oaths called out for him to steadfastly refuse her. "As soon as I'm told where they are, I'll tell you." He nuzzled the curve of her neck. "And we will most certainly celebrate."

CHAPTER TWENTY-ONE

1966.

Barfield stood at the office's front window. He was nursing a hot cup of coffee, watching a group of trainees go through a tortuous workout on the Grinder—the multipurpose area dedicated to the sole use of the SEAL Training Detachment. A fatigue-clad seaman stood motionless and alone at the edge of the asphalt. Fresh sunlight touched the fuzz of hair around the edges of the seaman's cap and turned it a gleaming orange.

Barfield inhaled the steam from the coffee. "What's with the kid?"

Fox joined him at the window. "He's throwing in the towel."

"How come?"

Fox stared at the seaman. "Won't say. He says he just wants out. Won't budge."

Barfield watched Fox watch the kid. "Do we care?"

"Yeah, we care." Fox's answer said it all. The kid was good.

"Where's the skipper?"

"He an' the XO had to go over to Admin. They've already talked to him."

"I swear, I leave you guys by yourselves for a couple of

days and the whole op goes in the can." Barfield was disgusted. He turned his back on the window, took time for a test sip of coffee, then mumbled, "We've got ourselves a banana out there who's gonna do a cut'n'run because he's found out he's too good for this outfit."

"Huh?"

"You heard what I said. That kid and I are probably the only men left on this side of a base infested with broad-beamed women wearing men's uniforms." He snorted with contempt. "I got a good mind to go with him. The two of us could probably come back here in a week and wipe out whatever's left of this Girl Scout troop."

"Just the two of you, huh?"

"Humph. He could probably do it by himself."

Lt. Cmdr. Len Fox rubbed his face while he divided his attention between his boss and the lone young sailor. A grin crept across the face behind the hand. "So what's the bet?"

Lt. Cmdr. James F. Barfield draped deep and abiding wisdom over his features. "A born leader could get him back." He hummed and nodded to himself in cadence while he touched his fingers to the desk, counting. "Two statements—ten words max."

Fox's lungs emptied. It was only April, and in this year alone, in spite of extended absences, Barfield was into him for almost a hundred dollars. The two found something to bet on every time they conversed . . . and Barfield almost always won. "Barf, you gotta be on drugs. You've come up with some wild ones before, but th—"

"Hey, if you don't want the bet, you can—"

"Want it?" An almost somber man under most circumstances, Fox slapped his hands together like a trained seal. "Man, I'm gonna break even for the year on this one."

"Really?" Barfield's expression reflected nothing but mild confusion. "Why would a real leader, *moi* for example, need more than a small handful of words to inspire a man to follow him?"

Fox and Barfield had joined the SEAL teams ten years earlier. They had served together in Vietnam, and after their tours they were assigned to the SEAL Training Detachment at Coronado.

Lt. Cmdr. James F. Barfield had been seen on Coronado Island fewer than ten times in the last six months, and no one knew where he'd been spending his time, not even his friend. He was back.

Fox was focusing his full attention on Barfield, afraid to move lest he disturb the spell that had fallen upon the small office. He was thinking Thomas Edison must have felt the same way when his lightbulb came on for the first time. "Brother, you have signed your soul away. How much can I put down?"

Barfield sat down at his desk. "I was thinking along the lines of the usual ten bucks."

"Ten bucks! Are you kidding? You're into me for almost a hundred this year, and it's not even summer yet."

"Ten seems more than fair to me." The confident officer tilted his chair back, propped his feet on the desk, and held his coffee cup with both hands, smiling contentedly.

"That's just great!" Fox snarled. His chance to get even drifted out of reach.

"I was thinking that some odds are in order," the Southern Californian reverted to his Beach Boy lingo, "because I'm thinking this may be, like, you know, a sure thing."

Fox was getting exasperated. If odds were going to be involved, he wasn't as interested. "A hundred to one, I suppose?"

"Well, man, to tell the honest truth, I was thinking, like maybe, more along the lines of ten to one."

That wasn't great, but it was still free money. "Fine. I'm in for your whole dime." The enthusiasm was gone. Barfield was probably just trying to energize his homecoming.

Barfield was doing exactly that. When he walked through the door fifteen minutes earlier, he had been greeted by too much peace. The men in this outfit were responsible for training carnivores, and Barfield was more at home when he was surrounded by the snarls of man-eating animals—hungry ones.

The animal trainer rubbed his thumb and fingers together. "Well, show me some money."

"I ain't carrying that kind of cash."

"I'll take your marker. Here's my hundred." Barfield went into his pocket, came out with a wad of bills, and stacked part of them on the desk.

"What hundred? I said I was in for ten."

Innocent confusion resurfaced. "And I'm covering you."

"What is the matter with your brain, man? At ten-to-one all you gotta put up is a buck. I'd like to take your money, but I guess your embarrassment will count for something."

"You have misunderstood, ol' buddy. I'm giving the odds."

"Givin'?"

"Yep." He took a distracted sip of coffee while he patted the stack of money.

Only a fool runs to the rainbow's end without looking for potholes. "*You're* giving *me* the odds? Something ain't right."

"Okeydokey." Barfield's fingers gathered themselves around the green pile.

"Wait!" Fox stood next to the desk and divided his attention between the stack of bills and his boss. His boss sipped coffee and hummed a Beach Boys song.

Fox swore softly but earnestly and said, "I'm gonna be sorry I did this . . . I want a hundred."

"Nope." A knuckle tapped the money in time with his music. "An' we'll have fun, fun, fun, till her dad—"

"You're chicken."

"Nope. Did you know the intro for that song came from Chuck—"

"So gimme a hundred's worth."

"Nope. Because if I do, Betty Anne will kill you and drape your ladylike carcass over the front gate as a warning to the other SEALs. If that happens, it'll scare the other girls in this outfit, they'll all become nuns, and I'll be reduced to buying those cheap cigars like the common folk smoke."

"You must be on drugs."

Barfield was immediately aloof. "Personally, I find that sort of thing immensely boring. There are no mind-altering chemicals that can bring me to a higher consciousness . . . I already exist on a higher plane. As a matter of—"

"Okay, okay, stow it. I'm in for the ten. Yeesh!"

Barfield hoisted his coffee cup. "It's always a pleasure."

The bet was already made when it occurred to Fox that he'd better cover the legal bases. "Okay. Just so you don't try to wiggle . . . the padre and the shrink and the skipper have already hit this guy up to stay. He's good at the job . . . showing real promise, and they hit on him hard." He walked to the window and looked out at the Grinder. His voice took back the somber tone. "Everybody but the pope has had a shot at that kid, and he ain't budging. He's got less than a month left till graduation—a month—and it's like his brain locked." His thoughts went to what was really important, and he shook his head. "We could use him, but his heart's gone. He stayed out in front in BUD/S . . . an eye-catcher, you know? Doing everything right . . . tough . . . leading . . . people watching him. And he's young. Then it was like his spirit left . . ." His hands spread apart, a man releasing a bird. "It did an adios thing yesterday. There ain't nobody can get to him."

The man with his feet on the desk wasn't humming. He didn't smile. "I can."

Fox looked at the immobile kid standing at the edge of the asphalt. He tapped the corner of a folded ten spot against his front teeth. "Man, I sure hope so."

Barfield hoped so too.

"Okay. Here's the deal." Barfield sat up and slid forward in his chair. "You introduce me to the tadpole before I say anything. But after you tell him my name, you give him the whole 'gee whiz' spiel."

Fox turned from the window. "For what?" Trusting Barfield when money was at stake could get expensive.

"It seems appropriate to set the stage, does it not?" The beach boy resumed his academician persona.

Fox was suspicious of the introduction bit, but he'd done it for dozens of new BUD/S (Basic Underwater Demolition/SEAL) classes and couldn't come up with a reasonable objection.

When Fox stayed silent, Barfield said, "Well then, I think that should do it." They shook hands, and Fox dropped his money on the desk.

"What's the bet?" Cecil Alexander was propped against the doorway—a hatch in Navy lingo. Alexander was the self-appointed information center, or rumormonger, for the training unit. Credible whispers carried the preamble "Cecil says . . ." Like every man in the unit, he carried a steaming cup of coffee wherever he went. Anything Alexander leaned against was in jeopardy.

Fox briefed the big man on Barfield's appraisal of the training group's qualifications.

Alexander started computing *Ten words? There's no way.* The bitter memory of uncountable cigars he had bought for Barfield normally made him cautious, but the desire for revenge flashed past his decision-making process without so much as a by-your-leave. "I want some of that."

The smell of fresh blood permeated nearby offices at the speed of greed. The other men in the training detachment didn't get to bet with Barfield as often as Fox, but when they did, they invariably lost—this time they had him cornered. Every man in the unit knew the story of the tadpole standing out by the Grinder; six of the best men in the profession, including the Skipper and the XO, had tried to sway the trainee and were stonewalled. Barfield was loitering in the kill zone, on a fast track to being dead meat.

The word spread faster, and the high probability of a kill brought ravenous animals out of every office along the building's corridor; two dozen men were yelling for entry into the wager. Mr. Cigar couldn't win; they were going to blow him out of the water and nail parts of his body to the bulkheads for souvenirs.

The newly returned provocateur stood amidst a gale of money and celebration, the picture of decorum. He held up a hand and addressed the throngs. "You gentlemen may certainly participate, but only at those odds available on the street."

Half-a-dozen voices asked, "Whaddazat mean?"

"It will be even money for those gentlemen with whom I seldom have an opportunity to experience an adventurous wager . . . with a ten-dollar cap."

It still wasn't clear to all. "How come he can't just speak English? What's he talkin' about?"

"We don't get odds."

The clamor that greeted this announcement could be heard on the second floor of the concrete building, and four more coffee cups sauntered downstairs to see what the hubbub was all about. When they came on the scene, there was a mob in the passageway—every man in sight was waving money. Barfield was attracting more attention than a bleeding man in a shark tank. After finding out what was going on, the new arrivals reached for their wallets; when the officer ran out of cash, they took his marker.

One man wasn't participating—a chief petty officer who'd transferred in that morning from the East Coast Teams. He stood on the periphery of the horde, watching the officer who occupied the center of the money storm. The CPO didn't know any of the men who had tried to talk the kid into staying, but he had been in one or two tough spots in his career, and he thought he knew what a winner looked like. When Barfield closed his books, the CPO pulled out a clip full of leftover traveling money and offered three-to-two on Barfield; he was swamped. More SEALs spilled down the stairs. The skipper and XO made it back to the building just in time to welcome the new CPO to the unit and split his last forty bucks—they were shameless.

When the feeding frenzy subsided, over two thousand bucks was riding on the trainee's response.

Barfield let the herd in the narrow corridor outside his office sweat while he made a production of finishing his coffee. He placed the cup in its designated spot on his desk, straightened his shirt, and brushed at an imaginary particle of lint on his chest. He walked to the full-length mirror by the office door and gave himself an unnecessary inspection.

"I must confess that I'm at a loss here," he used his grey-flannel-suit voice at the image in the mirror. "It's a simple matter really—a real leader has but to offer a few words of encouragement to those whom he leads. That *is* why wise and responsible individuals choose men of my caliber to lead, is it not?" He looked at his fingernails as if inspecting a recent manicure and shook his head to express either mild contempt for his fellow instructors or wonder at his inability to identify with their inadequacies. "It somehow seems ignominious that you would allow this rudimentary situation to decline to a point where you are forced to enlist the aid of a person such as myself." He stepped through the office door and proceeded through a gauntlet of instructors who lined the hall.

Catcalls followed him to the door. One of the men said, "I'll need to have you tell me where I should start buying my cigars." Men laughed.

When Barfield turned and looked at his detractors, a belatedly-wise handful started wishing they had passed on the wager. Except for a nasty scar at the edge of one eye, Barfield looked like a cross between a movie star and a military recruiting poster. His record in combat made for a high benchmark, even among warriors.

At the end of the hall he pretended to adjust his shirt again, pushed the door's metal latch bar, and stepped into the bright morning. He paused on the top step of the small landing and settled his garrison cap in place while he surveyed a typical Southern California day. Next, he took the government-issue sunglasses that had been hanging by an ear stem from his breast pocket, tilted them to the sun, and inspected the lenses carefully. Another imaginary speck of dust caught his attention; he blew at it, rechecked the glasses against the sun, and slipped them on. When everything about him was perfect, he strolled down the steps and across the hard-packed sand. Twenty-some-odd SEAL instructors followed in his wake like baby ducks, gathering in the building's shade to watch every move he made.

Fox stepped past Barfield and stopped in front of the seaman; Barfield stood on the kid's right. The youngster came to attention, arms at his side, eyes looking straight ahead but not at anything in California—insiders called it the thousand-mile stare. Five months of unrelenting California sun had broiled the kid's fair skin. Every square inch of flesh between his collar and cap was the color of ripe strawberries; thick scabs covered his nose, lower lip, and the tops of his ears.

The toughest part of the training was over for the seaman. No words could capture what he had endured to get this close to finishing the course; months of torturous physical and mental strain, all designed to teach the men who stayed the course that they could go beyond what they thought humanly possible.

"Aaron?"

"Sir. Yes, sir." The right words; not even an echo of the right sound.

"I've got an officer here who wants to have a word with you before you sign the DOR papers." Fox's tone was calm, not threatening. He thought to himself that he would rather lose the bet than lose this man. He looked at Barfield; Barfield winked at him from behind the glasses and moved to a point where the young sailor's peripheral vision could pick him up.

Fox turned back to the boy. "This officer is Lt. Cmdr. James F. Barfield. He is a summa cum laude graduate of UCLA. He holds a master's degree from USC and is currently pursuing his doctorate in psychology from that same institution. He's a two-time winner of the Navy Small Arms Championship, shoots trap from the hip, and he's been 'wet' in more countries than you've learned to pronounce. He holds a seventh degree black belt in karate, and has spent three months as an invited guest of the most respected martial arts instructors in Japan. He has been seriously wounded on five occasions and holds the Navy Cross with oak-leaf cluster. He is what every man who knows him, including me, would have their sons become. And he's a SEAL." Fox moved off to his right and spoke in Barfield's direction. "Commander."

Barfield centered himself in front of the unseeing gaze. He didn't speak initially, but let the kid get used to the change in people. He could feel quiet resolve emanating from the relaxed youngster.

He looked at the boy's face and saw the hardness, but it wasn't the right kind; the eyes always gave them away. The kid's eyes were deliberately unfocused; they looked straight ahead—at nothing. For whatever reason, this youngster had made up his mind; he had already quit. Barfield could see it—just like the skipper and the shrink and the padre had seen it. Sometimes something in a good trainee's head just misfires, and he quits. Washing out of BUD/S or any other tough course was no disgrace, but choosing to withdraw from training in an advanced program is hard on a man—choosing to leave SEAL training is worse. Most men never recover.

Barfield spoke his first word: "Rest."

Someone in the group watching from near the porch started counting, "That's one."

The young man automatically moved his left foot out slightly and relaxed his posture. He put his hands together behind his back. His shoulders sagged slightly; the jawline stayed where it was. The eyes remained fixed on that point out in eternity.

An ocean breeze came from behind the officer and brought the strong smell of cigarette smoke and coffee. The young seaman's memory carried him back to a thousand weekday mornings at his parents' breakfast table. They would all sit together while his dad and mother had a last cup of coffee, and his dad would smoke a cigarette before leaving for work. His mom would smile at the two of them while they kidded each other. Before they went about their day, his mom would insist that the three of them hold hands and pray. He could still remember the smell of the coffee and cigarette smoke of those mornings, and the prayers. It occurred to him that a cup of his mother's coffee would taste good right now. *But that's never going to happen again, is it?*

The officer in front of him reached up and pulled off his

sunglasses. The seaman's eyes came back from eternity to watch the unhurried movement as the man folded the glasses and stowed an ear stem in his breast pocket. There was nothing about the movement that was unusual, and the man's hands looked the same as a million others. When the man's hands fell out of sight, the student's gaze moved upward slightly. There was no sameness in the man's eyes.

Until that moment the young enlisted man had not thought much about the officer in front of him. His first startled thought was, *I've been drugged*. His mind sped. *They can do that. We've studied it. They spiked my coffee, and this guy is going to hypnotize me*. He thought these thoughts for a brief instant while he studied the eyes. In the next instant he realized that it wasn't drugs or the eyes, it was just something in the man. *But I can tell this one the same thing I told all the others*. He took a breath and let it out slowly.

The officer's eyes were on his, but he wasn't staring or challenging. It was as if the man could communicate without speaking. Both men stood and looked at each other, silent . . . appraising . . . comfortable. In that moment, a vague impression, like an almost remembered dream, penetrated the trainee's mental armor and tugged at the fringe of his thoughts. He allowed himself to survey the man's face and took in the scar, but saw nothing that sparked his memory. His eyes drifted down to study an impressive display of ribbons . . . then back to the eyes. The seaman became mildly interested as the officer shifted his feet in order to stand closer to him. He could smell the man—coffee and cigarette smoke.

The biggest money of the year was riding on the events of the near future. Over by the steps the audience kept their eyes glued to the scene, oblivious to the soft winds that stirred nearby palm trees. Men stood at the windows on the second floor. Cars and trucks and seagulls, barely seen or heard, moved about their business, providing a backdrop for the two-man drama. The muted whine of a commercial jet descending into

San Diego came and went overhead; no one noticed. Seconds ticked by with no sign of an exchange.

Thirty seconds took its toll, and two of the watchers took their eyes off the scene long enough to miss Barfield's move. They saw in their companions' postures a heightened awareness and snapped their heads up to see what they had missed. The commander had moved another half step closer to the man in the fatigues and leaned forward slightly.

Every man on the small porch could clearly hear James Barfield speak the remainder of his ten-word allotment. "Son, this is not a crossroads; it's a threshold."

Anyone within fifty yards could've seen the effect of the words. The firm jawline didn't relax; it collapsed.

The stunned young man pulled away slightly then leaned toward the older man and scanned Barfield's face as if examining a map. The younger man's search uncovered what he sought. It wasn't a grin; it was just a turning up of the corners of the officer's mouth . . . a gentle, we-know-each-other-well greeting from one warrior to another. The boy pulled back and nodded slowly, knowingly. And then he smiled.

A prophet standing in the group by the porch whispered a long, profane phrase.

Over the next few seconds, while Fox and the group on the porch stood mesmerized, the trainee's left heel made its way through the sand to find its mate and his arms moved in slow motion to hang by his sides. He cupped his hands, positioning them so that his thumbs touched the seams of his trousers, his back straightened. There was only a vestige of a smile left when the trainee tucked his chin and came to attention.

They all caught the transitions. They all stared at what was happening. And they all wondered at the same thing. *How does he do that?*

The trainee had just heard Lt. Cmdr. Barfield deliberately quote the exact words that the mud-covered stranger had spoken to him on the worst night of his life. The man who growled that prophetic maxim six years earlier—a stranger who stepped into a dark Mississippi night to oppose eight white men on behalf of a helpless black woman—was standing here in sunlit California. Not only that, he was offering him an opportunity to become the kind of person who made it his business to make a difference against evil people. Forest Aaron Sherman, III, known to his friends as "Tripper," took one step back. Stainless steel could not have approximated the rigidity of the arm that snapped his fingertips into their place near his right eyebrow. He became a SEAL for the rest of his life when he yelled, "Sir! Request permission to join my outfit! Sir!" The sound was back where it belonged.

The man who had been the mud-covered apparition in the woods of Eagle Nest Brake raised his hand and gave a casual return salute. "Go."

"Aye! Aye! Sir!"

Tripper Sherman faced right and jogged off.

It was over.

Someone in the group started cursing. Someone else joined in and did a better job.

One of the chiefs was so flabbergasted that he broke a cardinal rule; he asked a question for which he didn't have the answer: "What in the Sam Hill was *that*?"

The only reply was a discordant chorus of men helping the first two someones curse.

One lieutenant, who had already lost twenty dollars,

earned an opportunity to contribute an extra ten bucks to the unit's party fund when the skipper saw him throw his hat on the ground hard enough to disturb nearby seagulls. Alexander shook his head and said, "Barfield is unbelievable. Half of the SEALs in the Navy would charge hell with a damp bar towel on his say-so, and he hangs out around here so he can get rich on us poor slobs."

All of the listeners agreed with him, but most of them directed their cursing at him for saying it. The ones who were married could already hear their wives questioning the competence of the Navy's trained killers when it came to crossing streets by themselves.

Saturday morning, four weeks later. SEAL graduation.

Barfield stood near the fringe of the assemblage, taking advantage of a palm tree's shade while he looked out over a collage of Sunday clothes. Proud people—moms and dads, sisters and brothers, girlfriends and wives—hugging men wearing white uniforms. Flashbulbs popped, stopping time, recording a special moment for people to display on their walls or store in forgotten boxes. He watched one of the white uniforms detach itself from the gathering and walk across the Grinder toward him. By unspoken mutual agreement, they had not approached each other since the day Sherman had decided to remain in SEAL training.

Barfield dropped his cigarette and went to meet him.

The kid came to a halt and saluted. "Afternoon, Commander."

He returned the salute. "Take a break, Trip. You earned it."

Sherman had rehearsed his carefully chosen words. "I'm glad you showed up when you did, sir. Both times."

"Yeah, worked out okay, didn't it?" Barfield wandered into the crowd; Tripper fell in step.

"You pulled my fat out of the fire twice, sir."

"Nah. I just kept you in the game till you could pull it out for yourself." A table holding a punch bowl was in front of them.

Tripper took two cups and handed one to Barfield. "How can I pay you back, sir?"

Barfield winked at the kid. "I picked up a little change on the second one; the first one was on the house." It was an offhand remark. They were separated by years, rank, and experience, but they respected each other because they both knew what they had paid to become what they were—SEALs—members of the most elite group of fighting men in the world.

"You picked an interesting time to go with the SEALs, Trip."

"You mean 'cause of the way things are shaping up in Vietnam?"

"Yeah."

"Maybe. Why're you here, sir?"

"Good point. Tryin' to make a difference, I guess."

"That's the way I see it, sir." He looked to see if anyone could hear him. "I'll never cross paths with that kid again, but I just might get a chance to do the right thing for someone else—like you did; kind of like making it up to him."

"Mm-hmm. You aren't saddling yourself with an unrealistic expectation, are you?"

"Could be, but I was bendin' over him right there by that truck, sir . . . he was watchin' me . . . countin' on me to help him. I could see it in his eyes. I let him down. I let both of 'em down . . . not to mention myself and my folks. I play that scenario back every now and then, and I still come up short."

"Don't waste today's fuel on yesterday's journey, Trip."

"Good idea, sir. I'll work on that."

"Good. Maybe you'll get to pay the kid back personally."

Sherman would live his life seeing the truck's headlights

shining on that little black kid's bloody face. "Finding that kid won't happen, sir. The world's too big."

"Don't rule it out, Trip. The world gets real small when a war starts."

"Not that small, sir."

Barfield was firing up another cigarette. He snapped his lighter shut and grinned. "You found me."

While Sherman was talking to Barfield, the young man Sherman wanted to settle accounts with was attending to his own problems half a continent away.

On Sunday evening Mose showed little interest in his supper and was in bed before the sun went down. During the night the dog waked Bill about once an hour, and the young man would check to see how Mose was feeling. When the sun came up, Bill helped Mose into the truck and took him to the hospital. The doctors at the hospital said he'd had a "heart episode" and sent him home the following Friday with instructions to get more rest and avoid exerting himself.

Bill and the dog stayed in the room with Mose almost every minute of that weekend; the dog slept on the bed with Mose and Bill brought his mattress in and slept on the floor. When Mose was awake, Bill read to him from the Bible. Mose took time to pray some; the boy didn't.

On Sunday afternoon Mose pointed at his dresser. "Look over there an' bring me that box."

Bill put the box on the bed. Mose said, "This here's yo' high school graduation present." He nudged the box. "It's a tad early, but you best open it now, I reckon."

Bill pulled the box close and lifted the lid; the dog leaned close to sniff. The contents were wrapped in white butcher paper . . . something heavy, too many angles to be a book. He pulled off the paper to find an Army Colt .45 with mother-of-pearl grips.

Bill held it in both hands, stunned. “Golly, Poppa,” he whispered. “It’s just like my dad’s.”

“Well, it’s close. You been talkin’ ’bout goin’ over there and fightin’ in that war. I figured you’d need to take a good gun along.”

Bill stood up and held the pistol at arm’s length, sighting at his reflection in the bedroom mirror. “Wow! Poppa, how’d you ever—” He stopped and stared at what he saw in the mirror. He let gravity move the pistol to his side.

Mose watched the suddenly silent young man and asked, “Boy? You all right?”

Bill looked down at the gun then turned to Mose. “I shot those two men.”

Mose pushed himself to a sitting position and patted the bed. “Better c’mere an’ sit down, son.”

Bill slumped on the edge of the bed and stared at the .45. “I did it . . . me . . . I’m the one that shot those men . . . me.”

The old man nodded. “You was the only one what could do it, son. They had me an’ that white man blocked off.”

He looked at Mose. “You didn’t tell me.” It wasn’t an accusation.

“Nope, never did. Thought on it some, but never come up with a good reason to have you know. Didn’t make no difference who shot ’em, boy; they wasn’t gonna leave there alive no way.”

“They weren’t?”

“Me or that other man woulda kilt ’em. Simple as that.”

“But why me?”

“ ’Cause God sees fit to step in every now an’ again an’ fix things on the spot.”

“By having me kill those men?”

Mose shook his head. “I was there an’ watchin’, son. When yo’ pistol went off the first time, you was lookin’ down with yo’ chin on yo' chest, an' you shot that man dead-center in the forehead; same for the second one. You never even looked up from the mud in that road; you wasn't hardly even conscious."

"Then how did I manage to shoot them?"

"That ain't for me to say, son, but I figure yo' guardian angel taken care of it for you."

Bill stared at the gun in his lap while he thought. Finally, he said, "I don't think I'm sorry."

"You got no call to be. We can be sorry 'bout where them two had to go, 'cause they for sho'nuff in hell . . . we ain't called to weigh ourselfs down 'cause of how they chose to git there. Like I said, me or that white man was gonna kill 'em if you hadn't of. You understandin' me? Them men was dead 'fore you ever throwed down on 'em."

"Yes, sir. I understand." He hadn't taken his eyes off the weapon. "Poppa?"

"Mmm?"

"You've told me lots of times about what happened when Junior died. You've never told me about the night those men killed my mom."

Mose understood. "An' you wantin' to hear 'bout it."

"Yes, sir. I think I better."

So Mose told him about the night his mother died. "Well, truth be told, them white folks wasn't rightly men, they was just overgrowed boys . . ."

When he finished the account, Mose reached over and touched the automatic. "This gun can't do what God can, son—you needs to remember that. Anytime you in a place where you needs a gun, then you needs to be prayin' hard—just like I was doin' the night we lost yo' momma. You make sure you remember that."

"I'll remember, Poppa."

* * *

Mose slept most of Saturday but seemed to lose strength on Sunday. "Boy, I tol' yo' momma I'd raise you like you was my own . . . I don't reckon I done too good a job."

"Don't say something like that, Poppa."

"Time might be gettin' close for me, an' all I got is words. You needs to remember that God give me you to raise up—just like you was my own. You special, son, or God wouldn't've done all He done to get you to where you at. If you forgets everything else, you remember what I'm tellin' you. You special."

"Yes, sir."

Mose rested his hand on the dog and looked troubled. "Heaven's gonna be a fine place, but the good Lord sho' knows I'm dreadin' tellin' yo' momma 'bout lettin' her down."

Bill sat on the edge of his chair and held the old man's free hand. "You didn't let her down, Poppa. The Bible says it's my choice—I just haven't chosen yet."

Mose couldn't hear him. His eyes closed and he seemed to sleep.

"Poppa?"

Mose's chest rose slightly, hovered for a moment, and fell.

The boy who never prayed slid to the floor and knelt by the bed. "God, I'm old enough to take care of myself, and I hate asking for this because I don't want to be a hypocrite . . . and I don't deserve to have You do anything to help me . . . but would You make him well? He's the finest man I've ever seen, and he's been good to me. If You're there, would You let him live? Please, God."

He looked up to see if Mose was breathing, and the old man spoke without opening his eyes. "Move some of these here pillows for me, boy, so I can stretch out."

On the following Saturday, the convergence of a pair of shopping trips, along with a small handful of insignificant choices, worked together to change the course of more than one life.

Bill needed a suit for graduation, and Farnsworth's in Denton was having a sale. Mose was up and around some that week, but he wasn't interested in a car ride. Ella Claire volunteered herself and Will to take Bill to the sale. The couple sat on the front seat and talked in hushed tones. Bill and the dog leaned on each other in the backseat and watched the windshield wipers fight a losing battle against a warm rain.

In Denton, the dog invited himself to accompany the shoppers, but the clerk who greeted them wasn't sure that having a dog in Farnsworth's was a good idea. Bill was deciding he could wear Wranglers to graduation when Coach Stinson's daughter intervened and asked to speak to Mr. Farnsworth.

Ella Claire told the owner about the boy-dog relationship and explained about the recent illness of Mr. Mose Mann, and Mr. Farnsworth promptly gave his clerk a short course on how to run a successful men's store in Texas. The girl's daddy was a shoo-in for the Texas High School Football Hall of Fame, and the black kid was the most destructive defensive back the Pilot Hill dynasty had fielded in a generation. The owner took a moment to apologize for the misunderstanding; the dog would always be welcome in his store. Would the young man accept the suit of his choice as a gift from Farnsworth's Men's Store?

Bill thanked the man, telling him his grandfather would want him to pay his own way.

The only other customer in the store had come in out of the rain hoping to find a suit or two in his size. The discussion at the front of the store caught his attention, and he abandoned the suit search to admire the hound. The young black man who'd almost lost his grandfather murmured a distracted "thank you" to the stranger's comments about the dog. Thoughts of how close he had come to a future without Poppa crowded themselves into those areas of his consciousness normally reserved for vigilance. He failed to notice that the dog would have nothing to do with the stranger's offered hand.

The friendly stranger gave up on finding a suit, thanked

the owner, and went on his way. He was set up with a telephoto lens when the kids came out of Farnsworth's and took ten pictures as Bill Mann carried his new suit to the car.

The rain made following the teenagers easy. They made a couple of stops on the way back to Pilot Hill, including a drive-in where all four had cheeseburgers. He parked down the road from the house where the couple dropped the black kid off. Light drizzle and a stand of live oaks across the road provided all the cover the stranger needed. He only had to wait an hour to get a picture of the boy's grandfather.

Sometime soon, probably before June, he'd be telling his boss where Mose Washington and the Prince kid had surfaced. Hud Dearden would then step in and assume responsibility for the youngster's protection.

The man who took the pictures of Bill Mann stood under the dripping trees with his hands in the pockets of his raincoat, shoulders hunched, staring down the road at the house. *Lord, why should I feel such a sense of loss for doing my job?*

His only answer was the almost invisible sound of rain falling on his shoulders.

CHAPTER TWENTY-TWO

The two had been loading trucks since early morning; the last Saturday in May was winding down at Wooten's Feed Store. The world's hardest working high school graduates were sprawled on stacks of feed sacks, enjoying a lull and discussing their plans for the evening. The graduation parties were behind them, the summer and college out front.

"C'mon, Bill. We can go see *The Professionals*."

Bill was frowning and shaking his head. "Not me, son. That show's got a naked woman in it. Poppa'd hang my hide—" His own thoughts interrupted him, and he smiled. Poppa had never hung his hide anywhere, and he never would; he was going to be a perfect grandfather for as long as he lived. *But he doesn't want me looking at any naked women.*

Will continued trying to plan their lives. "Then we can eat at the Burg an' cruise the strip."

"That'd be really cool," Mann snorted. "Me, and you, and your girl . . . doing the town in Denton."

"If that bothers you, Ella Claire said she'd fix you up with a friend of hers from North Texas."

"No way, Willie Boy." Mann didn't date often. His success on the football field had offered to lower the color barrier, but he steadfastly refused to date white girls, and dateable black girls were scarce. His instincts told him that any college girl who would date a high school boy she'd never seen would probably frighten Dracula.

Will had his orders. "C'mon, man. We can roam around the square after the show or go play Gooney Golf and eyeball the chicks."

"Humph. First of all, if Ella Claire sees you so much as look sideways at another woman, you won't *have* any more eyeballs. And secondly, little colored boys that ogle white girls while they play Gooney Golf can end up wearing their putter for a necklace."

Will wasn't scared of having anyone wrap a putter around Bill's neck. The "little colored boy" wasn't little anymore—and any trouble that came to one of them came to both.

Will was insistent. "Ella Claire told me to tell you that you had to come."

"Uh-uh. Y'all been babying over me for a month. Poppa's getting back in shape, and it's time for y'all to let me off the apron strings."

"She ain't gonna like it." Ella Claire had spent the last few weeks watching over Mann like she would a blind colt.

"She'll love it. This way she'll have you all to herself."

"What're you gonna do?"

Will could be worse than Ella Claire about trying to take care of him. "I'm thinkin' about minding my own business."

Mose had accepted an appointment for Bill to meet a fellow from North Texas about getting a part-time job at the college. Mose told him the fellow on the phone had said seven o'clock, to please come alone, and to keep the meeting strictly confidential. Mann snorted to himself. The guy probably would've said it was top secret if he'd been in the military.

The days were showing off their summer lengths, and sundown was over an hour away when Mann drove into the golf-course community. He found the address he was looking for and walked up to the porch at two minutes till seven. Mose's pickup wasn't air-conditioned, and sweat was creeping down his back when he rang the doorbell.

The man who answered the door was thirtyish and big. "Bill Mann? Come in." He put out his hand. "Thanks for coming."

Mann stepped through the door into a wide foyer. The home's air conditioner was doing a good job, and someone had just baked bread.

The man led the way down a short hall and through a den, saying, "Let's pass through the kitchen and get some tea and work our way back up here."

The smell of bread got stronger as they passed through an archway; the four loaves making their presence known were cooling on the kitchen counter.

The big man waved a hand at the bread. "My wife's the cook in the family. I can do the obligatory spaghetti, chili, and stuff on the grill; after that I'm lost."

"Smells good."

"Have you eaten?"

"Yes, sir. I stopped at the Malt 'n' Burger with a couple of friends." It had been the only way to pacify Ella Claire.

"Best hamburgers in this part of the state. How about some tea?"

"Yes, sir. That'd be nice."

"Sweet or unsweet?"

"Sweet, please."

"How about a slice of hot bread?"

"I'd like that. I've never had homemade bread before."

The man smiled easily, maybe too easily. "Great. My wife'll be right back. We'll see if she'll share." He poured the tea, and they moved back to the front room.

"I appreciate your coming on short notice." The guy smiled the easy smile again.

Mann nodded. Something about the man was nagging at him.

"By the way, congratulations on your graduation. It's a big step."

"Thanks." Bill was distracted by his surroundings. Everything in the room looked expensive. "I haven't figured out why I'm here . . . at your house."

"I understand you're considering North Texas, and I wanted to talk to you about working for me."

Mann was still taking in the richness of his surroundings when it dawned on him that this man might know too much about him. "Doing what?"

"Mostly gofer stuff—you'd be the office assistant in the philosophy department. I'm the junior man there—I hire the office help, and you'd answer to me. The job usually goes to a grad student, but we don't have any candidates that'll take the job, so I picked you."

Yellow flags were starting to pop up. Maybe Mose was forgetting to be cautious. "How did you know about me? I mean, that I'd be going to North Texas."

The man hesitated too long. "Well, we—"

A door in the kitchen opened and closed, and someone called, "I'm back."

The man looked relieved. "That's my wife. Excuse me for a second."

As soon as the man was out of the room, Mann started wishing he were somewhere else. His host and the other person were talking in hushed tones in the kitchen, animated conversation blended with unloading sounds. Something wasn't right. Why wouldn't the guy interview him at his office? And why keep it such a big secret? He had come over here knowing nothing but the address of the house; Poppa hadn't even told him the guy's name.

That was what had been bothering him! He knew nothing about this man, not even his name, and the man knew too much about him. *This ain't good, buddy boy.*

Every day he and Mose stayed hidden bettered their odds of remaining undiscovered, and they'd gotten careless. He chastised himself for agreeing to meet someone he didn't know in a place no one else knew about. *If Poppa had been thinking straight, this wouldn't be happening.* He looked around the room and considered walking out the front door; that was the safe thing to do. He countered that thought by arguing that he was letting his imagination run away with him. The big man might be hiding something, but he probably wasn't some kind of evil agent.

When the word *probably* passed through his thoughts, Mann made his decision—Poppa always said assume the worst. He left his tea glass on the coffee table and walked away from the kitchen door, feigning an interest in a collection of old photographs spread along the room's far wall . . . working his way nearer the front door. He threw a quick glance over his shoulder then looked back at the wall . . . *just keep moving toward the door.* The first picture was of a young man and woman in front of a 1940s car . . . *that's right, you're doing fine, keep moving, just slide right on across to the door.* The next photo was of an older couple; she was smiling, he was tolerant . . . *just a little farther.* Next came a serious young man in a uniform, then a dog standing on a bridge . . . *the door's right there. Good job.* He checked again to make sure he was alone and looked back at the pictures. Centered in the display was a snapshot of three kids. When Mann's eyes came to the picture they stopped—the images in the picture moved closer. The snapshot was an old picture, slightly faded, taken on the banks of a lake . . . a ramshackle boat supported by two sawhorses and three barefoot children who had arranged themselves near it. Two boys stood at one end of the boat. The white boy—an earlier version of the young man from the uniform picture—stood at attention in overalls and a boy's body—straight, saluting, serious. Next to him stood a black boy, almost as tall—with a minstrel's hands gloved in white paint—one arm draped on the white boy's shoulder and one waving at the camera. Propped against the other end of the boat was a short-haired girl—a small thing—bare feet crossed at the ankles, one hand jammed behind the bib of her overalls, the other shading her frown at the camera. Trees behind the boat tried to hide a stretch of cotton field.

Mann leaned forward, his fingertip traced its way along the side of the boat; thin lines of white paint dribbled from crooked block letters that spelled out GENRALROB. Mose kept an identical picture in an old cigar box. His finger moved unbidden to the tiny thing in the overalls, and he whispered, "Amanda Allen Parker."

A hand materialized near his elbow; a small finger joined his at the picture—and he recognized a voice he'd never heard. "They still call me Missy."

He turned to the grown-woman version of the girl—past and present fused themselves when she put her hand in his. She didn't smile, nor did he. It was a solemn time.

"Those were special days." She spoke in that throaty voice Mose was never able to describe. "I'm practically Mose's daughter, Bill, that makes me almost your big sister. I've never had a chance to tell you how sorry I am about your momma."

Mann could only hold her hand and stare.

After a long minute she smiled that legendary, time-freezing smile, but he couldn't offer a response . . . Missy Parker was holding his hand.

Mose had told him all the stories. How tough she was . . . how stubborn . . . how pretty . . . how fiercely loyal. So many stories . . . in the evenings after supper, on long trips, and on a thousand mornings when they went fishing, Mose told the stories of Cat Lake, and Parchman, and Moores Point . . . and of this girl who was now a woman. Mann knew all the people, and this lady who held his hand was special. If she was as tough as she was beautiful, she was formidable.

"Mose told me all about you. Why didn't he tell me you lived out here?"

"We thought it best for you not to know until now. There are still so many risks. We decided that if any of us died—regardless of circumstances—we were to assume that it might be a deliberate killin'. When Mose got sick, we thought we'd better tell you what's been goin' on behind the scenes—which people know about you, that sort of thing—just in case you need help."

"How long have you been here?"

"Years. We've lived here ever since Pat finished grad school."

"But I've been here four years." He had missed knowing her for too long.

"I'm sorry. It wasn't safe for us to see each other—too many pryin' eyes. A white woman, an' an old black man? We'd be too conspicuous. Mose an' I got to see each other two or three times a year, usually in some remote part of Fort Worth or Dallas, a couple of times in Oklahoma City." She smiled. "Pat an' I sneaked up to see most of the Pilot Hill football games."

"You said, 'any of us.' Who else knows about me?" He realized he was still holding her hand, but it seemed natural.

"My daddy, Momma, Granny, Pat, Sam an' his wife, Sheriff Collier an' his wife."

"The sheriff?"

"His wife is Pat's sister. He lets us know about what comes through his office. Oh . . . and one of his deputies knows."

Bill made the connection. "It's Clark Roberts, isn't it? That's why we live right down the road from him."

"That's the one. He picked y'all's house himself."

Pat came back into the room and stood apart; puzzle pieces were trying to click into place for Mann.

Mann said, "So this is a planning session. Things are going to change."

Pat was impressed. "Something like that, but with no more change than necessary. We know you can play football at North Texas if you want to, but we also know you'd get more exposure. If you do well, the reporters will start asking questions."

Mann had already reasoned to the same conclusion. "So . . . I can work in your office and help pay my way through college and keep a low profile?"

Missy smiled. "An' we'll have a legitimate reason to see each other every now an' then. Bobby's a million miles away, so you're the only brother I've got."

"Bobby doesn't know?"

"Daddy an' I fixed it so he didn't have to. He's doin' well in the service, an' what he doesn't know, he doesn't have to hide."

Mann was absorbing what he could, but there was almost too much. He turned to look at the picture again. There were so many questions, so much to talk about. Pat and Missy waited.

Mose's old stories tumbled through his mind. "It's like I've known you all my life. Poppa's told me everything . . . all the stories, over and over and over . . . all the people. I grew up with you."

He pointed at the pictures. "That's Mr. Bobby Lee and Miss Susan. Mr. R. D. and Old Mrs. Parker. That's Bobby, and so's that." His finger stopped. The black boy was happy; his hand was slightly blurred because he was waving. Paint was splattered all the way to his elbows. After a long moment, Bill said, "And that's him."

"Yeah. That's Junior."

He couldn't take his eyes off the boy.

She said, "You're like him."

That didn't take long, Mann thought. *I might as well stop it be-*

fore it starts. "Nope. Poppa's already told me what he was like. I'm not like him—and I won't be. I'm not interested."

She waited.

"He was going to tell everybody all about God and Jesus—and he was brave. I'm not planning on telling anyone anything—especially about God, and brave people just end up getting killed."

She didn't smile. "Decidin' what you want from life an' stickin' to your guns could take courage. It sounds to me like you might have that capacity."

"What about the God thing?"

"What about it?"

"Poppa can't convince me that his God cares, and neither can you. If He cared, He wouldn't have let those men kill my mom."

She rested her hand on his arm. "God didn't make me responsible for convincin' you, He made me your next of kin. God gave you to me . . . an' to that man who took you to be his own . . . to love."

"What if I don't want to hear about God?"

"Well, Pat an' I aren't going to waltz around the subject just to suit you, but I'll tell you what—we'll make a deal. Anytime you feel like you're bein' forced to listen, you squeal, an' we'll back off. Fair?"

"Are you going to try to change me, or do I make my own decisions?"

Her smile was fading. "I just answered that. Are you scared to hear it discussed?"

Good question. "How?"

"Well, God is a special part of our lives, an' Pat ties Him to his thoughts for his classes . . . if you're near us, you're gonna hear the language an' the dialogue. But no one's going to force-feed you . . . any decisions you make will be no one's but yours. Can you handle that?"

Mann looked at Pat. "How about on the job?"

Pat said, "You'll be working with philosophers, Bill. They're going to say whatever it takes to make their point. But that would be true wherever you work."

Mann accepted that and turned back to Missy. "As long as I get to make my own decisions."

The smile left and took the tenderness with it. The girl in the picture squared herself in front of him; twenty-one years had transformed the little girl into an attractive woman—but the frown was a dead ringer. "When you make me repeat myself, you'd better be ready to hear me tell you that I don't like it. You an' I are goin' to be good friends—close friends—for life. One of the attributes of our friendship will be the absence of the need for lawyers in our communications. Capeesh?"

He smiled for the first time since he'd entered the house. "Have you formed any firm opinions on the subject?"

The legendary smile came back. "If any crop up, I'll write you a terse letter."

Mann turned to Pat. "If you decide to hire me, when can I start?"

Pat winked at Missy. "I enjoy sleeping in my own bed, so I've already decided to hire you."

"Can I make enough to put me through school? Or do I need two jobs?"

Pat and Missy exchanged a look. Mann saw it. "What?"

"Bill, has Mose told you about the land? The cotton land?"

He nodded.

Missy said, "Pat has been managin' the money, and Mose hasn't taken much out for y'all to live on."

Mann never saw it coming.

She continued, "Mose an' Pat sat down this week an' divided up y'alls' holdin's. For a young man, you're the next thing to being wealthy."

"Our holdings?"

Pat said, "Mose kept back enough to live on and put the

rest in your name. That way, when he dies, there won't be as much attention given to the transfer of his estate."

"Do I have enough to go to school on?"

Missy smiled at her husband. "Pat's a wise investor, an' more importantly, God's been good. If you work your way through school an' manage your money well, Pat thinks you'll be worth quite a bit when you finish college."

Mann was almost scared to ask. "How much is quite a bit?"

"In excess of a hundred thousand dollars."

Mann sat down on the couch. He didn't know if he knew anyone with that much money. He voiced his next thought. "What happens if Poppa needs money?"

"We can work together to see that he has all he needs or wants."

That suited him, but he wasn't the only person Mose was a father to. "What about Pearl?"

The couple exchanged another look. It was going to be bad news.

Mann said, "She's dead, isn't she?"

Pat said, "She died in a car wreck last year."

Mann's gaze was on the previous year. "In June?"

"That's right. How'd you know?"

"Mose got quieter, but he didn't say anything about Pearl. Why wouldn't he tell me?"

"He thought the circumstances surrounding her death were too suspicious. Mose didn't want to scare you."

Mann had never met Mose's daughter, and Mose rarely spoke of her. He said, "I'm sorry."

Missy nodded.

He picked up his glass and stopped with it midway to his lips. "Would it be okay if you kept investing this money? Is that okay?"

Pat looked at his wife. "Missy's here because Mose's other son died for her. I'll do whatever you ask."

"Thanks." He was distracted, his mind on the future. Not

having to worry about money would change some things. "That means I don't have to work in the summers to earn extra money. Can I start working in your office this summer if I'm in school?"

"You want to start to work now?"

"Except for Saturdays. I've already taken a Saturday job at the feed store."

"You don't mess around much, amigo. What's the rush?"

"I've got somewhere I need to be."

"Where?" Pat was becoming accustomed to Mann's tendency to look ahead.

Mose was the only person to whom he had told his plans. "My dad was a Tuskegee Airman—a fighter pilot. I've never wanted to be anything else, but I can't get into pilot training without college."

Missy knew where fighter planes would take him. "Bill, there's a war on."

"I know." His anticipation was forged into word forms. Bill had seen the grainy news footage of young pilots returning from their missions over Vietnam. Men who were confident, smiling, and relaxed because they were who they were intended to be—men who strapped themselves into the machines that carried them out to their war. His dad had fought his air wars in Africa and Italy and Korea. If he could get there in time, Bill was going to fight his first one in Southeast Asia.

Missy didn't like it, but she understood. Her older brother was a pilot, and Mose had been doing his part to make her younger brother a man.

Jeff Wagner felt like a weasel. He had followed the kid and watched him enter the home on the golf course. He didn't have to do any research to find out whose house it was; he and Ceedie visited there often—after all, that's what best friends do. When he broke the news, Ceedie would forgive him, Missy might not.

He made the call late that evening.

"Mrs. Dearden, this is Jeff Wagner. May I speak to Hud, please?"

He listened to the lady say her husband was fishing somewhere in Virginia and couldn't be reached. Would he like her to take a message?

"No, ma'am. Thank you. When do you expect him back?"

"He'll be here tomorrow night. Can I have him call you?"

"No, ma'am. I'll catch him at the office on Monday. Thanks again."

That night Missy snuggled next to Pat in the dark, using his arm for a pillow. "He's so . . . so hard."

"That's the word, all right. Are you disappointed?"

"Disappointed . . ." She tried the word out. "I don't think so. I'm just amazed that he could spend all those years with Mose an' still be . . . like that." She paused. "So distant . . . with all those walls around him."

"But Mose's other good traits are rubbing off on him. He's fast becoming the kind of man other men follow."

"That's not enough."

"Are you worried?"

"I don't think so. We'll have him close to us for four years. My job is to make sure he knows I love him—that's what Mose an' Pip did with me. After that, the ball is in his court. How about you? Are you worried?"

"I don't think so either. He's a bright kid, and I think he trusts us. If we love him, he'll soften. Like you said, our job is to be ready to give a clear answer when he asks a question."

"What if he doesn't ask?"

"You *are* worried."

"Mose an' Pip were God's gift to me . . . to our whole family . . . but mostly to me. It was a special time. I've told Mose I'd tell that kid about Jesus. I *owe* that man . . . an' I owe Bill."

"Mose knows the boy has to want to hear it. God didn't tell us to stuff the truth down people's throats."

"What if he doesn't ask?"

"That's God's decision, sweetheart, not ours. We pray—He answers."

"What about the war?"

She could hear him smile. "I think that's a little out of our hands too."

"Then all we can do is pray."

"When have we ever been able to do anything else? You wanna go first?"

She did. "Father, we are dependent on You for everything. We ask, Lord, for Your protection of this special young man—that You would hide him from his enemies while drawing him to the knowledge of Yourself. For us, Lord, that You would keep us reminded that his life is in Your strong hands."

When she walked onto the deck, he was watching the sun come up. She was carrying his .38 in one hand, the other was out of sight behind her.

He smiled. "You don't have to shoot. I'll come peacefully."

She showed him an expressionless face. The voice that came out of her mouth was from a time before time. "You have been a disappointment to us."

The immediate certainty of what he'd done crackled through him like a static discharge. Before the last syllable came out of the woman's mouth, he knew that he had exchanged the entirety of who and what he was for something that had existed only in his mind—a facade. After twenty-five years as a loyal husband and good lawman, he'd destroyed his marriage and career by allowing himself to be ensnared by a demon-possessed husk with a beautiful face. His was a deliberate choice that was destined to ruin his life and the lives of those he loved. As he thought these thoughts, resolve flowed through him, overlaying the self-recrimination. He would have to handle the shame, anger, and shreds of his life later—if he survived. He made his first move. "You wanted the three people involved in the killings at Cat Lake."

"We still do."

"I can help you find them."

"We know, but we have no more time for patience." Doors slammed on his thoughts of escape when her other hand came from behind her back. It was holding several lengths of rope and a claw hammer. "Come inside."

The details of the effort to find the three people who fled the scene at Cat Lake were known only to himself and Jeff Wagner, and there was only one way he could stop the dark beings who inhabited the young woman's body from finding out about Jeff. He looked out at the lake, a scene that he once thought spoke of contentment—self-loathing and disgust tasted sour to him. He took a deep breath and stood up to do what needed to be done.

CHAPTER TWENTY-THREE

In the middle of a Friday afternoon, six days after Bill Mann's visit to the home on the golf course, Wagner rang the doorbell of the same house. He could hear a lawn mower running behind the house; Pat was a fanatic about the yard.

Missy opened the door, wearing tennis togs and a smile. "What're you doin' here? I just left your wife at y'all's house."

It struck him that he might never see her smile at him again. "Hi. I need to talk to you two."

"Well, come on in. Ceedie said you were in Washington."

"Yeah. I just got in."

"An' you came here first?"

"Yeah, well, it's a long story."

"You look tired, Jeff."

"Mmm. It's been a long week."

"I'm sorry about your boss. He was a believer, right?"

"Yeah."

"I hope that makes it easier for his family. You want tea or coffee, or maybe a sandwich?"

"I'd better wait. Where's Pat?"

"Mowin' the backyard. It grew almost a quarter of an inch

this week." She stepped onto the patio and whistled shrilly. The mower noise stopped.

After he greeted Pat, Wagner said, "I don't have any right to do this, but when I finish this story, I'm going to ask you to forgive me." He shrugged. "But you don't have to if you don't want to."

Missy took in the grave expression and glanced at Pat.

Pat said, "We're your friends, Jeff."

Wagner grimaced. "I won't hold you to that."

Pat said, "Sit down here and tell us what happened in Washington."

When they were seated, three guardian angels drew close to the small circle.

Wagner said, "Let me start at the beginning."

He told it all. Mundane, smokescreen assignments from Washington filled his calendar for six years. No one had time to notice that he spent his time crisscrossing the country, chasing empty leads. His assignment to a cover-job in the Dallas Field Office was arranged during the turbulent aftermath of the presidential assassination. When he told the Pattersons how he found the boy and how he'd followed him to their house, Missy frowned. He said, "Try to keep in mind that I couldn't tell you what I was doing because I didn't know how much you knew. I wanted that kid protected."

Pat was ahead of the story. "Dearden wasn't killed in a botched burglary attempt."

Wagner shook his head. "Not hardly. He was shot at close range—five shots, all in the chest, all with his own gun."

"Why would your people not tell the press?"

"Good question. They're uncovering evidence of bad choices on his part—strange, out-of-character activity. They're trying to clean up as much dirt as they can before they release the story."

"That's not good."

"It gets worse." He tried to smooth his forehead with his

fingertips. "You think I could change my mind about that coffee?"

When Missy stood, she touched him on the arm. "When you're in this house, you can have all the coffee you can drink."

He smiled for the first time in six days. "That's a relief, Missy."

She motioned at him with impatient fingers. "Keep talkin'."

"The body was found at a secluded lake house in the Virginia mountains. He was outside on a deck." He took a brief coffee break. "Mmm. Thanks."

"And?"

"Remember what happened to Farrell Whitacher on the float in the lake?"

Pat remembered too well. "I do."

Missy shuddered.

"It was more of the same. The wounds were all postmortem, but, in this case, none were self-inflicted."

Missy was glad she was seated. She bowed her head and prayed silently.

Pat understood immediately. "He was a Christian, so they couldn't possess him."

"That's it. They found precut ropes and a hammer near the back door of the lodge. The hammer was bloody, the ropes clean. The forensic guys say he was killed before he could be tortured." He paused to breathe. "They're convinced that whoever bludgeoned the corpse with the hammer had to be demented."

"What do you think?"

Wagner remembered Hud's requiem for Leon Daniels. "He died doing what needed to be done. He made the demons shoot him so he couldn't tell them about me or any details of what was being done . . . the search and all."

Pat got up to pour himself a fresh cup of coffee and topped off the others while he thought. He sat back down and said,

"Okay. You've had a few days to digest all this. What are your conclusions?"

Wagner sat back and massaged the back of his neck, taking his time, then leaned forward and rested his elbows on the table. He kept track of his points with his fingers. "One. I think that, for now, the boy is safely hidden where he is. Two. I feel confident that God is protecting Mose and Bill by putting a hedge of angelic protection around them and those of us who know where they are. I don't think any person, or any demon, knows about my role and what I know. Three. This all points to a strong probability that God chose Mose—a man whom God has allowed to live an uncommonly special life—to protect Bill Mann because Bill has a future part in some significant plan." Fatigue etched his features as he raised the last finger and let out a deeply drawn breath. "And four." He tapped his little finger for emphasis. "I could be wrong, but I cannot escape the firm conviction that it is incumbent upon me to protect that kid to the degree that God allows me." He folded the little finger into his palm with its brothers and lowered his fist to the table.

"What about me?" Missy asked.

Wagner didn't look up. "What about you?"

"I'm special." She wasn't kidding.

Wagner was silent. He knew Missy Patterson's ties to Mann's life were stronger than his own, but he didn't feel called upon to be a recruiter.

Pat looked at his wife. "You think you're supposed to protect him?"

"You know I do," she said. "I made a promise to Junior. It makes all the sense in the world that Bill Mann is standin' in the focal point of that promise."

Pat said, "I have to agree."

Missy said, "An' his."

Wagner didn't understand. "His?"

Pat said, "This could all be for his child, or his child's child."

Wagner didn't want to go where God wasn't taking him. "Is there any way to be sure we're doing the right thing?"

"Actually, we aren't doing anything," said Pat. "We'll continue to live our lives as well as we can, and we'll bathe that kid in prayer. What we're talking about may be as simple as confronting him about a bad choice. However, if I ever have to choose between Bill Mann's well-being and my own, if it's within my power, I'll choose for the kid."

Wagner nodded; Pat hit it right. He closed his eyes and bowed his head. "Use me as You would, Lord. I ask for Your guidance and Your wisdom, for keen insight and multiplied skill, so that—if it be Your will—I may act effectively on behalf of that young man."

Patterson covered Wagner's fist with his own big hand. "I would have You choose for me to forever honor You, Lord. If it's by protecting Bill Mann or his descendants, I ask that You'd let me do it in a way that glorifies Your name."

Missy's small hands came last. She used them to cover her husband's. "What about Mose?"

The men looked at each other, and Pat said, "No less for Mose."

The girl closed her eyes. "I ask for Your blessin's on our efforts, Father. Guide my heart, Lord. For him an' his."

All three said, "Amen."

When the three raised their heads, Wagner asked, "What do we do now?"

Missy was already out of her chair. "We better go tell Mose."

Mose was sitting on his front porch when the Pattersons' car pulled into the driveway. Missy and Pat stepped from the car, and the dog left the porch to welcome his seldom-seen friends to his new home.

The couple waved at Mose then took a moment to greet the dog. Wagner stood near the Pattersons and watched Mose come down the steps; he moved pretty well for an old man with a bad heart.

Missy left the dog with Pat and walked past Wagner to hug Mose. "Hi. We came to see if we could visit for a minute."

"You always gonna know the answer to that, baby. Come in the house."

"Is Bill here?"

"Mm-hmm. He'll be out here directly."

Missy said, "Mose, this is Jeff Wagner."

Mose had heard of Wagner. He offered the man his hand. "Pleased to meet you, Mr. Wagner."

Bill stepped through the screen door in time to hear Wagner say, "Mr. Mann. It's an honor to meet you, sir."

Missy turned. "Bill, this is Jeff Wagner."

When they shook hands, Bill saw the .38 on Wagner's belt and went on alert. Without being conspicuous, he glanced at Mose.

Mose had his left thumb hooked in his belt. *Just act normally,* it said. Mose had seen the gun but apparently wasn't concerned.

When they were seated in the living room, Missy said, "Mose, I told you about Jeff. He's the one who was wounded at the lake right after y'all left."

Bill was astounded. Missy was talking about secret things in front of a stranger.

He was more astounded when Mose said, "I 'member 'bout that. You the FBI man."

Mose looked at Bill, took off his glasses, and touched an eye with his left index finger; their signal that the next words he chose were his own. He said, "This here will be okay."

Missy said, "Bill, this man an' his boss have been lookin'

for you an' Mose for six years. He's on y'all's side, an' he's here to discuss how to help protect y'all."

Bill looked from her to Mose.

Mose nodded.

Pat said, "Bill, something significant has happened since you were at the house—things that affect you and Mose. We came out here to let you know what's happened. Okay?"

People that were supposed to be worthy of his trust had chosen to let Wagner into the inner circle. Bill nodded.

Pat said, "Okay, Jeff."

Wagner looked at Bill. "Has anyone told you what happened at Cat Lake after you and Mose left?"

"They have."

"About the fight up by the Parkers' houses?"

Bill glanced at Mose. When Mose nodded, he said, "We know all about it."

Wagner said, "Good. Now let me tell the two of you what you haven't heard."

It took him an hour to lay it all out. When he talked about Dearden's death, the dog moved over to rest his head on the agent's knee. Wagner closed by saying, "Bill, given what's been going on for the past twenty or so years, Pat, Missy, and I are convinced that God has chosen you for some extremely significant role. Because of that, the three of us have committed ourselves to your watchful care. You and I know that your only sure protection is in God's hands, but—"

"I don't need it," Bill interrupted.

The comment confused Wagner. "You don't need what?"

Bill spoke without emotion. "I don't need God—I don't need His protection, and I don't need yours. I can take care of myself."

Wagner checked the reaction of the other people in the room then turned back to Bill. "You can't be serious."

Missy said, "I'm sorry, Jeff. I assumed you knew—Bill's not a Christian."

That the kid might not be a Christian had never occurred to Wagner. "You've lived with this great Christian man for the last six years, and you don't believe in God?"

"I believe in God. I also believe He left my mom in a muddy road by herself while two men beat her to death. I don't need a God like that."

Wagner leaned back in the chair and seemed to notice the dog for the first time. Mose, Missy, and Pat were silent, praying. Bill was toying with his shoelace.

Wagner rested his hand on the dog. He had not heard anything that would cause him to rethink his commitment to the kid, but he knew better than to force the issue; there was no more he could do here. He rubbed the dog's head before he stood up and said, "Well, folks, it's been a long week. I'm ready to go to the house."

The others rose and followed him to the door, saying their good-byes as they went.

Friday night was upon them; the moon was showing above the live oaks across the road. Mose walked Pat and Missy to the car; the dog stopped on the porch with Wagner and Mann.

Missy put her hand on Mose's arm. "Today's June third."

Mose nodded and smiled. "Mm-hmm. Junior's been dead twenty-one years today. He'd be thirty-two years old now, an' they ain't a hour goes by what I don't wonder 'bout what he'd of been like."

Missy said, "An' there's not a day goes by that I don't miss him."

"Mm-hmm."

They thought their own thoughts until she asked, "Do you think Bill was sent here to take his place?"

"No, child, I ain't never thought that." He looked back toward the house. "I reckon God give us Junior to make our hearts ready for that'n yonder."

"You reckon Bill's gonna ever figure that out?"

"His heart's mighty hard, but he can't hold off God. The

Book say the eyes of the Lord is searchin' to and fro throughout the world, so He can strongly support a man whose heart is completely His. I'm prayin' He's plannin' on findin' Bill Mann."

The three on the porch watched the rising moon in silence until Wagner offered Bill his hand. "Good night."

"Night."

Wagner started down the steps. "Sorry that didn't go well in there."

"I think I understand."

Against his better judgment, Wagner stopped and said, "Not hardly. I guess I'm tired, but I need to tell you—I lost a good friend this week—a guy that probably died protecting you." He looked at the people near the car. "Every person in this group, including you, has seen spiritual warfare up close . . . we've all lost friends . . . some of us, loved ones."

Bill moved to the bottom of the steps. "None of that means I have to care about God."

"Then try this on. There is no doubt in my mind that the Creator of the universe has seen fit to insert you into a pivot point in history for His good purposes. Now, I don't presume to know God's plans, Bill, but if events in your life stay on this same track, things are going to get worse before they get better."

"So what?"

The tired agent hoped he'd heard wrong. "Pardon me?"

"I said, so what?" Mann was outlined against the light spilling from the front door; his hands were spread, palms up—a blend of frustration and supplication. "What in the heck do you people want from me?"

Wagner stirred the inside of his cheek with his tongue while he looked at Mann, giving long consideration to a thought, and arrived at a decision. When he smiled the tiredness seemed to lift itself from his shoulders. He walked back to the steps while fishing something out of his pocket.

When he got close, he took one of Mann's hands and placed an object securely in his palm.

Mann held his hand so that the dim light illumined a large coin. "A silver dollar?"

"Yep."

"For what?"

Wagner rested his hand on the younger man's shoulder. "For you to hang onto—call it part prepayment and part reminder. People have been getting hurt and killed bringing you to this point in your life, friend, and I just might be next." He pointed at the coin. "That'll be a reminder that I'd give a dollar to hear you say you're going to be worth it."

THE END?

Acknowledgments

Words cannot communicate the appreciation I owe to dozens of people who have given of themselves to make this book a success, but you would want to know . . .

Gary Terashita, my editor and friend, is peerless. Gary's wife, Kim, pulled my first proposal out of a stack, read it, and became its champion. No one knew it then, but that proposal was the seed for what Gary would ultimately envision as *The Black or White Chronicles*. Gary and Kim are deserving of more credit than they will ever receive on this side of eternity.

I'm confident the job descriptions outside the editorial department include nothing of encouraging authors, but FaithWords and Hachette Book Group USA are replete with people who frequently offer strong encouragement to me and lend support to my efforts. Cara Highsmith, Gary's editorial assistant, excels at nurturing my work. Thanks also to Rolf Zettersten, Chris Murphy, Bob Nealeigh, Harry Helm, Linda Jamison, Lori Quinn, Jennette Munger, Preston Cannon, Norm Kraus, Kaye Wright, Renee Supriano, Jana Burson, Brynn Thomas, Kathie Johnson, and Jody Waldrup. And from Glass Road Public Relations, Rebeca Seitz and Kathleen Y'Barbo.

Durene White worked tirelessly to help me edit my work.

Deanna Campbell and Paul Polk helped critique, offered encouragement, and composed the questions for the Readers' Group Guide.

In the Old Testament, a young prince tells his armor bearer that he is planning for the two of them to confront a hostile force of garrison proportions. The young armor bearer tells the prince, "Do all that is in your heart; turn yourself, and here I am with you according to your desire."

My wife, Nan, has personified that young man's words of devotion, commitment, and resolve throughout every moment of our marriage. She is special beyond belief.

Above all . . . because He is exceeding abundantly gracious beyond all I could ask or think . . . God has put me in a position to express my deep appreciation to those named herein, to those of you who have taken the time to read this book, and to the many who prayed. Thank you.

Readers' Group Guide Questions

1) In Chapter One, Junior is described as an eleven-year-old boy who almost single-handedly built a bridge between two families. Describe a person, perhaps a child, who has done that in a family you know . . . perhaps your own.
2) In Chapter One, on a night when the "clouds were overpowering the moon" the Parkers were awakened to pray for their friend Mose. Describe a time you have been awakened in the dark of night to pray for someone.
3) In Chapter Two, Tripper deeply regretted his involvement in the attack. Share a time when you have made a poor decision you later regretted.
4) What memories do you have of a bully like Bainbridge in your life?
5) How often can it be said of a person like Tripper, "that one is more afraid of being a coward than of taking a beating"?
6) What is your definition of bravery? Who is the bravest person in the story? Why?
7) In Chapter Two, young Bill Prince reflected, "every angel he had ever imagined had been black." Describe the appearance of angels you have imagined.

8) In Chapter Three, Jerry Nations "spent the remainder of his life still trying to escape the effect of a single bad choice." If you know someone of whom this is true, share it.
9) In Chapter Four, it was said of Bainbridge, "Whether or not he eventually got killed mattered less to him than getting to kill the woman and the kid." Does this kind of an evil mind actually exist? In what way?
10) Have you ever had to explain death to a young child as Mose was commissioned to do? What was the result?
11) In Chapter Four, Bobby Lee said to Susan, "If we don't know, we won't have to lie." Explain the profound wisdom in that statement.
12) In Chapter Five, Mose said: ". . . the good Lord sometimes sees fit to let what seems right come up short against what is." What does this statement mean to you?
13) Throughout the book we see Bill Mann express his difficulty and reluctance to trust in God because of the pain he suffered as a result of losing his father and mother. Why is it so difficult for Bill to trust and believe but not for Mose who has experienced just as much pain in the loss of his son and his wife?
14) In Chapter Six, "the boy" said that he, ". . . didn't want to ask the question because he knew he didn't want to hear the answer . . ." Tell of a time when you've shared that same feeling.
15) In Chapter Five, Tripper Sherman and Frank McClellan were walking back to town after a night when they'd seen an innocent woman beaten to death for no reason, and Frank told Tripper, "You did all you could." Tripper responded, "Not if I ain't dead, I didn't." What do you think of that statement? What do you think about Tripper's convictions regarding personal responsibility in life? Are there things in life worth dying for? If so, what are they?
16) In Chapter Seven, it was said of Mose: "Mose Washington

is only mild-mannered till he's pushed." Who do you know of whom this could be said?

17) Aside from personality and external appearances, what are the foundational differences between SAIC Bert Fuller and Jeff Wagner? Which of these two men would you say reminds you more of yourself? Why?
18) In Chapter Eleven, Sam Jones received an unexpected message: "His name is Samuel Washington Williams." Have you ever had anyone named after you? Why? How did it make you feel?
19) In Chapter Eleven Mose prayed *very* specifically that the Lord would "show Yo'self to him" (the boy). Share a time when you asked God for something specific and tell us His answer.
20) In Chapter Fourteen, Missy was described as impressive because she was "committed to a cause." Describe someone you know like that who has impressed you!
21) In Chapter Seventeen, Wagner said, "I've been listening, but I haven't been hearing." If you could say this about yourself, explain.
22) Describe Jeff Wagner before he changes his beliefs regarding religion, God, Jesus, etc., and describe him after he has changed his beliefs. Which description would you say is a description of who you are? Why?
23) Why do you think Jeff Wagner changed his beliefs?
24) Bill Mann's dad told "yarns" to him of pre-flight training. Share a "yarn" that entertained you, told to you by one of your parents when you were a child.
25) In Chapter Twenty-two, Bill found himself in a difficult spot. Share a time like Bill's, when you found yourself in a situation from which you wanted to escape.
26) In Chapter Twenty-three, we see Bill struggling to know what to believe. Who in your life has been as resistant to God as Bill Mann?

27) How are Bill Mann and Jeff Wagner alike? How are they different?
28) Is this an inspiring story or a depressing story? Why?
29) Many of the characters in the story are Christians. Would you say they are good examples of what a Christian should be, or bad examples? Why? Have your experiences with Christians in real life been positive or negative? How have your experiences shaped your views of Christianity? Should the way one person lives out the beliefs of Christianity affect the way another person views the philosophical principles of Christianity? Why?

Summers were mostly reliable.

They always followed spring. They always got hot.

And they always promised twelve weeks of pleasure

to the three children at Cat Lake.

The summer of '45 lied . . .

Discover the battle that started it all in

Book One of the BLACK OR WHITE CHRONICLES:

ABIDING DARKNESS.

NORTH
TO MOORES POINT
5 MI.
COTTON FIELDS
GILMER'S GROVE
PARKER GIN
OLD PARKERS
YOUNG PARKERS
COTTON FIELDS
CAT LAKE